Whippoorwill

Whippoorwill

R.L. Bartram

Matador
9 Priory Business Park,
Wistow Road, Kibworth Beauchamp,
Leicestershire. LE8 0RX
Tel: 0116 279 2299
Email: books@troubador.co.uk
Web: www.troubador.co.uk/matador
Twitter: @matadorbooks

ISBN 978 1788035 781

British Library Cataloguing in Publication Data.
A catalogue record for this book is available from the British Library.

Front cover illustration by Dave Hill, Dave Hill Arts

Printed and bound in the UK by 4edge limited
Typeset in 11pt Aldine401 BT by Troubador Publishing Ltd, Leicester, UK

Matador is an imprint of Troubador Publishing Ltd

For my sisters, Linda & Julia.

About the Author

With Historical Romance as his preferred genre, Robert has continued to write for several years. Many of his short stories have appeared in various national periodicals and magazines.

His debut novel '*Dance the Moon Down*', a story of love against adversity during the First World War, gained him considerable critical praise, being voted book of the month by 'Wall to Wall Books'.

His second novel '*Whippoorwill*' tells of a passionate affair between a young southern woman and a northern man at the beginning of the American Civil War.

He is single and lives and works in Hertfordshire.

Also by this author

Dance the Moon Down

Author's Note

During the American Civil War both sides had women spies, all engaged in various forms of espionage. By doing so they risked exile, often to Canada, long terms of imprisonment and even, in some cases, execution. These women were fearless, tough and resourceful. I am reminded of Rose O'Neal Greenhow, C S A, who having acquired a vital piece of information took a horse and rode twenty miles through enemy lines to deliver it herself.

It is a matter of historical fact that over a thousand women, from both northern and southern states, disguised as men, enlisted in the army to fight and die beside the regular troops. It is their courage and fortitude that inspired me to write this book.

There are two surnames that appear in this novel, which may cause some difficulty in pronunciation. To avoid that I offer the phonetic versions here.

Cecile Prejean Prejean (Pray-Shon)
Simon Robicheaux Robicheaux (Robo-Shol)

R.L. Bartram.

Acknowledgement

My sincere thanks to Claire Bradley for all her hard work in editing and proofreading this manuscript. Thanks also to Dave Hill for the cover illustration.

Chapter One

"Cecile Huguette Prejean," her father's face had turned a delicate shade of purple, whilst the vein in his brow throbbed visibly.

Ceci cringed. All three names at once. It was a bad sign. All she could do was stand there, head down, hands clasped behind her back attempting to conceal her grazed knuckles. She had never seen him this angry before and there had been a few times.

"You broke that boy's nose," he informed her stonily. "Do you understand? You broke his nose."

"He started it," Ceci interrupted, attempting to justify her actions.

"Enough," he roared, making her flinch, "not another word." He paused, his temper appearing to ebb a little. "You're almost fourteen," he reminded her. "You should be a young lady by now. Instead you dress like a field hand and brawl with the local boys. What would your poor dear Mother say, God rest her soul, if she could see you now. Just look at yourself," he commanded. "Look at yourself."

Ceci chewed her lip and glanced down obediently, staring dejectedly at the grubby threadbare shirt, the tattered breeches and her bare toes that squirmed in the thick pile of the carpet.

Her father let out a long sigh of exasperation. "I have been patient with you for far too long," he told her ominously, gesturing towards the open door.

An attractive creole woman of about thirty, entered the

1

room. She wore the plain black dress and white lace apron of a household servant, her long glossy black hair neatly restrained in a crocheted snood. She glided forward, dipped into a graceful curtsey, rose and paused.

It was Hecubah. Ceci wasn't sure exactly what position she occupied, but she understood her reputation for honesty and fairness had made her a well-respected figure, not only in the slave quarters, but also among the entire Prejean household.

"Hecubah is going to take charge of you, Cecile," her father informed her. "From now on you will obey her in all things. All things mind, or you will answer to me. She's going to turn you into a lady." He paused to study her, his brow creasing, as if the immensity of the task staggered him. "I don't envy you," he addressed himself to Hecubah. "Are you sure you can handle this?"

"She's just a little girl," Hecubah nodded confidently.

"All right then," he conceded, "but just in case you can't." He reached behind his desk and produced a yard of hickory. "You may need this." He handed her the rod. "Use it whenever you see fit."

"Daddy," Ceci began to protest, but one glance from him silenced her.

"Is there anything else I can do?" he asked Hecubah.

She looked at Ceci, regarding her with large dark eyes, her soft, honey coloured features impassive. "No sir," she replied.

"Very well then," with a final, withering, glance at his errant daughter, he turned and left the room.

Ceci sniffed hard, choking back the huge lump that was rising in her throat. "It weren't my fault," she insisted, pressing a hand to the hot tears that had begun to sting her eyes.

Instinctively, Hecubah stepped forwards, raising a hand to comfort her.

Ceci stiffened, facing her defiantly. "You'd best get a dozen more of those," she said pointing at the hickory switch. "If you think it'll make any difference."

Hecubah glanced absently at the switch, as if she'd forgotten she was still holding it. Then, in one swift action, she grasped the rod in both hands, raised it to the level of her face and brought it down sharply across her raised knee, with such suddenness it made Ceci jump, before finally casting the broken pieces into the corner of the room. "I seen too many folks whipped for sport," she told her earnestly, "to believe it does any good for anyone."

Ceci's mouth fell open. She tried to speak, but words eluded her.

"I think we'd best make ourselves scarce," Hecubah suggested. "Stay outa your daddy's way for a while. Let him cool down."

"I guess," Ceci conceded with a shrug.

She allowed Hecubah to take her by the hand and lead her through the great house, up the main staircase and on through the maze of corridors, to her room. She slumped down on the edge of her bed and let out a huge sigh. "I don't wanna be a lady," she confided despondently.

"Well, child," Hecubah responded with a sympathetic smile. "The Lord, in his wisdom, has provided you with all the parts, so I guess you'd best settle on the job."

Ceci's face creased at the awful inevitability of it all. "Do I have to start now?"

"I guess it can wait until tomorrow," Hecubah granted her a reprieve.

"Can we eat then?" Ceci asked hopefully.

"Soon," Hecubah assured her. "But first there's some things I gotta show you."

"Oh," Ceci rolled her eyes, as Hecubah pulled her off the bed and pushed and prodded her towards the full-length mirror at the back of her room.

Once Ceci stood in front of it, she stepped back and asked. "Now, who is that?"

Ceci shot her a puzzled glance, wondering if she might

be a little simple, but the woman was adamant, insisting on her question. Heaving another great sigh, she looked back into the mirror. She saw the filthy tattered clothes that adorned her slight boyish figure. The freckles on her cheeks and nose and the mass of golden hair, matted and tangled, tied in two uneven braids, that fell over her narrow shoulders. There was only one conclusion to be reached. "It's me," she shrugged.

"Ah huh," Hecubah mused softly, as if she'd expected nothing else. "Now c'mon, I wants you to meet Tilly."

Before Ceci could object, Hecubah grabbed her by the hand and whisked her out of the room, down the back stairs and on through the kitchen. The clatter of pots and pans was unremitting, as the kitchen staff scurried to and fro preparing the evening meal. Hecubah didn't pause for a moment. Ceci slouched along behind her, her nose twitching at the tantalising aromas that permeated the room making her stomach rumble.

"Can we eat now?"

"Soon."

They continued out through the back of the house, across the lawn and down through a wide avenue of old cypress trees, their branches festooned with long pendulous swaths of Spanish moss that swayed gently in the warm breeze. Suddenly, Ceci dug her heels in, bringing them both to an abrupt halt.

"That's the slave quarters," she warned, pointing to the long rows of wooden shacks in the field beyond. "I ain't supposed to go there."

"Never stopped you before," Hecubah replied knowingly. "Besides, that's where Tilly lives."

As they entered the compound, Ceci noticed an elderly black man, with greying temples and weather-beaten features, sitting on the steps of a shack, mending a shovel. When he saw them approaching he rose, pulling a tattered straw hat from his head.

"Evening, Ms Hecubah," he smiled.

4

"And a fine evening it is too, Joshua," Hecubah returned the greeting. "We're paying a visit to Tilly. Is she home?"

"Yes 'm," Joshua confirmed, using the shovel as a pointer. "She's right over there in the woman's quarters."

They entered a long wooden building with windows down each side. For every window, there was a rough wooden bed jutting out into the room, leaving only a narrow corridor in the middle. It was full of coloured women, of all ages, washing themselves, their clothes, their hair, gossiping, busy with all manner of minor tasks. The din of chatter ebbed a little, as each of them paused to acknowledge Hecubah's arrival, before going on about their business.

She directed Ceci to a bed at the far end of the building, where a young black girl stood, viewing their approach with obvious apprehension.

"Hush, child," Hecubah crooned. "You ain't in no bother. I brought Miss Ceci to see you."

The two girls regarded each other suspiciously.

"Now, Tilly, why don't you tell Miss Ceci what you bin doing today," Hecubah suggested.

The girl looked a little bemused, but, nevertheless, complied. "Just the usual," she shrugged. "I was up at five this morning, working in the fields. Then at eight I had breakfast." She paused and grinned. "It was a good breakfast. Anyway, after that I did my chores in the house. Then at four I went back into the fields, and now I'm home. I hopes I haven't made a poor account of myself," she finished self-consciously.

"That's just fine, honey," Hecubah applauded. "Now, I wants you to be brave and do one more thing for me." She took Tilly by the shoulders and gently turned her around, lifting her thin chemise.

Ceci gasped, the colour draining from her face. Dozens of long knotted scars criss-crossed the girl's narrow back. Ugly pale puckered lines on the once smooth ebony skin. Tilly began to fidget with embarrassment.

5

"There, child," Hecubah soothed allowing the garment to fall back. "Don't you fret none. See, I got this for you." She produced a cookie, the size of a saucer, from her apron pocket and offered it to the girl.

Tilly's look of distress faded instantly, to be replaced by a huge grin of appreciation.

"That's right, honey," Hecubah assured her. "It's all for you." She rose, motioning to Ceci to follow. "Goodbye now Tilly and don't forget to say your prayers before you go to sleep."

As they moved away, Ceci felt the urge to look back. Tilly sat on her bed happily munching the cookie. Judging by her expression, it was all the world to her.

"Let's go down to the bayou," Hecubah suggested, as they emerged from the shack. "We'll set awhile and enjoy this fine evening."

They carried on to the edge of the river, to an open stretch of bank where two dead sapodilla trees had been felled. Hecubah sat on one stump and Ceci sat on the other. It was the beginning of a long silence. Ceci gazed listlessly out across the Atchafalaya, across the expanse of still green water, speckled with clusters of lily pads and hyacinth flowers. She watched an egret take flight from an overhanging branch and glide effortlessly on snowy angel wings, up and over the islands of oak and cottonwood.

"Did my daddy do that?" she suddenly blurted out.

"No, child," Hecubah was quick to reassure her, as if she'd been waiting for precisely that question. "That happened to Tilly long before she came here. Your daddy's a rare good man, very rare."

Ceci fell silent again. She noticed a heron hunting, knee deep in water, along the opposite bank. Suddenly its head darted down and came up with a little silver fish wriggling in its beak. With a practised flick, it swallowed the fish whole. Ceci watched the bird's throat contract and fancied she knew how that fish felt. "Why'd you do it?" she asked eventually. "Why'd you show me them things?"

"Tilly's about your age," Hecubah responded casually. "But she was born a slave. She's bin working in the fields since she was five years old and like as not, she'll grow old and die working in the fields." She paused, fixing Ceci with a penetrating stare. "Then, there's you. Your daddy's a wealthy man. You got a good life in front of you, but you is throwing it all away. Why is that?"

Ceci felt her mouth move. A few sounds came out, but, for the second time that day, words eluded her.

"It's late," Hecubah observed, relieving Ceci of any further obligation to answer. "We'd best be getting back. It's supper time."

The thought of something to eat, cheered Ceci up. She matched Hecubah step for step on the way back.

As they came around by the side of the house, they heard voices.

"Mercy," Hecubah exclaimed, grabbing Ceci by the arm and shoving her towards the cover of a huge magnolia bush growing against the wall of the house. "This is more than I'd hoped for. Quit your struggling girl, get in there and hide."

Ceci squinted aimlessly through the thick screen of glossy leaves, convinced that Hecubah had lost her mind.

The voices grew louder and eventually a beautiful Louisiana belle, dressed in a flowing white crinoline, her delicate features framed in clusters of auburn ringlets, appeared, surrounded by a host of young men, all eagerly vying for her attention. She carried a lace parasol and a silk fan, which she made great use of.

As they passed the magnolia bush, the young woman's handkerchief, the merest sliver of lace, slipped from her fingers and floated out on the slight breeze, like gossamer. The young men were instantly galvanised into action and a brief pandemonium ensued as they bumped and barged each other, all trying to retrieve the item before it touched the ground. Finally, one of them emerged triumphant.

The young woman covered her face with her fan, fluttering her eyelashes over the rim. "Why, thank you sir," she breathed seductively. "You are so gallant."

His face split into a wide grin, whilst the others eyed him venomously.

All at once, the circus was off again, like a gaggle of geese, down the path and out of sight. The hum of male voices, punctuated by feminine laughter, gradually fading away.

"Who was that?" Hecubah asked, as they emerged from behind the magnolia.

"You know as well as I do," Ceci scowled. "That was my stupid sister Celeste. She's my daddy's favourite," she added sullenly.

"Oh, and is you hankering to be just like her?" Hecubah observed.

"Heck no," Ceci spat.

"No? Then why you wearing them green eyes?"

"My eyes are grey," Ceci remarked sulkily, turning her face away.

"What happened," Hecubah continued, allowing her to deliberately miss the point. "When she dropped her handkerchief?"

"She did that on purpose," Ceci howled. "That was plain to see. Those fools nearly knocked heads trying to pick it up."

"What if I told you," Hecubah advised her, "that if she'd tied a rock in it and pitched it half way down the lawn, they'd have gone for it like hounds after a possum."

Ceci rolled her eyes. "Boys are stupid," she sneered, "I hate them. The only ones I know make fun of me."

"Maybe that's 'cos you looks like a scarecrow and smell like a polecat," Hecubah suggested bluntly.

Ceci's jaw dropped, her cheeks beginning to burn. "I don't smell anything," she retorted indignantly.

"Girl, you has to be standing where I am," Hecubah was unrelenting. "Look," she continued quickly, taking Ceci's hands in hers and raising them up. "This thing don't take a whole lot of learning to figure out. You skin your knuckles and land in a whole mess of trouble, just to break one boy's nose. All Miss Celeste has to do is bat her eyelids and she breaks a dozen boy's hearts."

Ceci thought about it. "That does sound better," she began to agree. "No, wait," she checked herself, "a broken heart ain't near so painful as a broken nose."

"Dear God almighty," Hecubah reeled back dramatically. One hand on her bosom, the other on her brow, eyes closed, as if she were about to swoon. "Child, you has got so much to learn."

Ceci clicked her tongue in annoyance. "Oh, now you're making fun of me."

"I think we're done here," Hecubah concluded.

"I'm hot, I'm tired and I'm hungry," Ceci complained, as they returned to her room. "Can we eat now?"

"Soon," Hecubah prevaricated, "there's one last thing I has to show you."

Ceci slumped, but after a minute of prodding and poking and Hecubah's hand pushing against her behind, she found herself back in front of the mirror.

"Now, who is that?" Hecubah asked for a second time.

Ceci stared wearily into the glass, but try as she might, all she could see was her father, Tilly, her sister Celeste and those men, the heron; and that fish. Her mouth opened and closed, her lips bobbing uselessly together, but, for the third time that day, words eluded her.

"Ah huh," Hecubah observed with satisfaction. "Ain't so sure now, are you?"

Chapter Two

"I can't stand this," Ceci wailed, as Hecubah entered the room.

"What's vexing you this time, child?" She enquired patiently.

Ceci faced her stiff with indignation. "You make me bathe every day," she fumed. "I have this stupid ribbon in my hair. I can't climb trees no more. I ain't allowed to swim in the bayou. These shoes hurt my feet and this dress is too hot," she ended her litany of complaints with a petulant toss of her head. "Then, there's these stupid drawers," she added disdainfully, grabbing two handfuls of material of the plain brown garment she was wearing and raising the skirt. "Covered in frills and bows. What's that all about?"

"They're called pantalettes," Hecubah informed her with restraint. "They're designed especially for young ladies, so that they can feel feminine and pretty right down to their skin."

"I wear drawers just to cover my behind," Ceci sniffed, clearly unimpressed.

"We all do, honey," Hecubah replied nonchalantly. "Just don't go showing them to all and sundry, like you done just now. It attracts the wrong kind of man."

Ceci slumped, exhausted by her tantrum. "Oh, what's it all for?" She implored.

"What's it all for?" Hecubah pondered for a moment. "I think you needs some fresh air."

Ceci sighed, rolling her eyes. "It has to be ninety degrees outside."

"Then, we'll sit in the shade," she countered.

The first lesson Ceci had learned during her brief association with Hecubah was that it was pointless to argue with her. She always had an answer for everything, even the questions she hadn't asked yet. Entirely against her nature, she had reached the conclusion that, as far as Hecubah was concerned, it was easier to give in.

"We're going the wrong way," Ceci noticed, as they left the main staircase.

"This is a new way," Hecubah told her simply.

The new way took them past her Father's day room. The door was open. He sat at his desk, working on some papers. Noticing a movement in the hall, he glanced up. "Ah, good morning, Hecubah," he greeted her, rising, as any southern gentleman would. "Good morning," he repeated, to include the young woman standing beside her. He paused and looked again, a quizzical frown creasing his brow. "Cecile?"

"Morning Daddy," she answered self-consciously.

"Good God almighty," he muttered, leaving his desk and crossing the room. "It is Cecile," he stared incredulously.

Ceci blushed under his scrutiny.

"Why, child, you look beautiful," he beamed. "Just beautiful." He bent down, cupping her cheek in his hand, dropping a kiss lightly on the other, before rising to face Hecubah. "Excellent," he told her. "I would never have believed it possible. Excellent," he reaffirmed appreciatively, before returning to his desk.

Hecubah glanced down at Ceci. "You still feel hot?"

"No," Ceci admitted. "I feel much better now."

"Ah huh," Hecubah mused quietly. "That's what it's all for."

★ ★ ★

"No, like this," Hecubah demonstrated, impaling a tiny morsel of food on her fork and placing it delicately into her mouth, before returning the fork to her plate. "It's called etiquette," she explained. "Which is, the use of fine manners and polite behaviour in company."

"But I'm hungry," Ceci complained.

"That don't give you no call to shovel in your victuals as if the house was on fire," Hecubah advised her.

Ceci stared sullenly at her plate.

"Child, is you expecting to die in the next half hour?" Hecubah asked suddenly.

"No," Ceci stared, taken aback.

"Then you got time to eat it slow."

"It'll be cold by then."

Hecubah's eyebrows rose. She took a long hard look at the meal and then a long hard look at Ceci. "It's salad," she pointed out. "It's already cold."

★ ★ ★

"I've asked Miss Celeste to help us today," Hecubah told her.

"Oh, not my stupid sister," Ceci's face creased, her shoes scuffing at the polished surface of the ballroom floor.

"Enough of that," Hecubah wagged a finger at her. "Miss Celeste is taking time outa her busy schedule just to help you. So, you be sweet."

Ceci wasn't sure she knew how, especially when it came to Celeste. Her busy schedule usually involved some stupid man or other. She didn't think it was costing her stupid sister much to be here. She glanced up, glowering as Celeste entered the room. The two girls exchanged prickly glances, until Hecubah intervened.

"Thank you for joining us, Miss Celeste. Would you please show us what you can do."

Smiling pleasantly at Hecubah, she moved gracefully into

the centre of the room and completed an effortless curtsey.

"Now, what did you see?" Hecubah asked Ceci.

"Looked like she was going to faint, then changed her mind," Ceci remarked churlishly.

"Don't you sass mouth me, girl," Hecubah snapped. "You know what you saw."

Ceci sighed heavily. "It was a curtsey."

"And why do we curtsey?" Hecubah pressed on, intending to teach her a lesson.

"It's etiquette."

"And what is that?" Hecubah was unrelenting.

"The use of fine manners and polite behaviour, in company," Ceci droned.

"All right then," Hecubah seemed satisfied at last. "Now, let's see some."

Being admonished in front of her stupid sister was galling, but Ceci had little choice in the matter. She heaved another great sigh. "Thank you for helping me, Celeste," she managed tonelessly.

Celeste performed another perfect curtsey, on purpose. "It is my pleasure," she responded stonily.

"That's more like it," Hecubah approved, choosing to ignore the atmosphere. "Now you try it," she told Ceci. "Remember what I showed you. Take the edges of your dress in each hand, right foot behind the left and bend your knees."

Ceci did as she was told and promptly fell flat on her back. Celeste began to snigger. Hecubah silenced her with a glance.

"No shame, child," she told Ceci. "Try again."

This time she fell on her face.

"I knows you can do this, honey," Hecubah was certain. "You just ain't putting your mind to it."

"It goes like this, Ceci," Celeste took the opportunity to rub salt into her sister's wounds, by demonstrating another flawless curtsey.

Ceci stared daggers at her, her grey eyes flashing green.

13

"Thank you so much, Miss Celeste," Hecubah decided to put an end to the unequal contest. "I think we can manage from now on."

Celeste inclined her head graciously towards her, sparing only a frosty glance for Ceci as she left.

Ceci watched her departure, through narrowed eyes, seething like a basketful of copperheads.

Taking advantage of the situation, Hecubah sidled up to her, bent down and whispered in her ear. "If she can do it, why can't you?"

Ceci stiffened, the muscles in her jaw twitching. Exhaling sharply through her teeth, she marched into the centre of the ballroom, grasped her skirts and produced a breathtakingly faultless curtsey. She dipped so low her forehead almost touched the floor.

"Ah huh," Hecubah observed with satisfaction. "Just like a red rag to a bull."

★ ★ ★

"What's that?" Ceci stared at the panels of fabric, laced together with ribbon, that Hecubah held.

"It's a corset," she told her.

"What's it for?" Ceci frowned.

"You wears it under your dress, like this," Hecubah demonstrated, holding it against herself. "To make your figure look nice."

"Are you wearing one?" Ceci enquired tonelessly.

"Yes, I am," she assured her.

"Would you be fat without it?"

"Why didn't I see that one coming?" Hecubah asked herself. "It ain't about being fat," she explained. "It's about looking pretty." She held her arms out. "Don't you think I got a good figure?" she risked the question. "Don't you think I look pretty?"

Ceci looked her up and down. "You always look pretty," she told her honestly.

Hecubah's face softened. "Won't you just try it?" she coaxed. "You is almost fifteen, child. You is gonna need to wear one sooner or later."

"Why do I have to wear one?" Ceci sighed.

"There are three reasons why we wear corsets," Hecubah told her. "To keep our waists in, our bosoms up and because we drew the short straw in life and was born girls." She put her hands in her lap and bent forwards. "I'll make a deal with you," she offered. "You try this on and this afternoon we'll go down to the bayou and you can swim for as long as you want."

"I don't care to," Ceci responded listlessly.

"Why not?" Hecubah stared in surprise.

"The water's dirty," she shrugged. "And full of gators and moccasins."

"Never bothered you before," Hecubah declared in amazement.

"It's all right," Ceci assured her, still listless. "I don't mind. I'll try the corset."

Hecubah studied her for a moment. "My my," she murmured at length. "Things is moving faster than I realised."

She helped Ceci into the corset, lacing it up until her adolescent shape more closely resembled that of a woman. "Now, will you look at that," she hooted encouragingly, as Ceci turned this way and that, admiring her reflection. "What a beautiful young woman. Where's that skinny little girl I used to know?" She came up behind her, putting her hands on her shoulders. "What's the matter, honey?" She asked softly. "Don't you like the way you look?"

"I like it fine," Ceci managed a wan smile.

"Then what's wrong?" Hecubah began to stroke her hair. "You bin quiet all day. You feeling poorly?"

"No," Ceci shook her head, "I'd just like to be by myself for a while."

"Sure, honey," Hecubah agreed. "You take some time. It's bin a long day."

Hecubah gave her an hour then returned, to find her where she'd left her, sitting on the bed, staring out of the window. As she sat down beside her, Ceci turned, burying her head in her breast, beginning to sob.

"I know, I know, honey," she comforted. "It's hard, so very hard. You is at that crossroads now. It's all very bewildering, but it'll pass," she bent forwards kissing her head. "You'll get over it," she promised. "Then you'll get used to it. Then you'll get good at it."

★ ★ ★

"Oh please, please," Ceci begged, "please let me try some."

Hecubah looked undecided.

"Celeste was wearing lip colour when she was sixteen," Ceci pointed out, hoping to add weight to her argument. "Look, she let me have these," she indicated an array of jars and tubs on her dressing table.

Hecubah shook her head. "I declare, you two are as thick as thieves these days. What happened to them two alley cats, always trying to scratch each other's eyes out? Since you two became best friends, I swear there ain't bin a moment's peace in this house."

"Oh, please," Ceci implored, her eyes large and appealing, which always tended to work on Hecubah these days.

"All right," she conceded, sitting down beside her. "Beats me why you wants to cover up that pretty face with all this paint."

Ceci had already scooped up a brush full of colour, aiming it at her mouth.

"No, not like that," Hecubah took the brush from her and scraped half its contents back into the jar. "The idea is to enhance," she told her, gently applying the colour to Ceci's

16

lips. "Not to obliterate. You can't just pile it on, like some ol' Mississippi, Madam."

"What's a Mississippi, Madam?" Ceci asked, ever curious.

"I must remember who I'm talking to, before I speak." Hecubah rebuked herself. "It's a woman without a reputation," she explained discreetly, "shunned by society."

"Why?"

"Dear Lord," Hecubah sighed, "questions, questions. These days, it's nothing but questions."

"How else will I learn?" Ceci asked.

"That's another question," Hecubah pointed out.

"Why is she shunned?" Ceci persisted.

"Because she consorts with men for money," Hecubah continued to be discreet, knowing if she didn't answer, Ceci would never stop pestering her.

Ceci's eyes widened. "You mean she pays them?"

"No, no," Hecubah clicked her tongue in exasperation. "The other way around. Now, quit your wriggling, or you is gonna end up with this lip colour in your ear."

"Can I try some rouge now?" Ceci asked hopefully.

"You don't need that," Hecubah objected. "There's a trick I learned as a girl. I'll show you." She gently pinched her cheek between her finger and thumb. "Now you try it."

Ceci copied her, wincing a little.

"See," Hecubah pointed into the mirror, "that puts natural colour into your cheeks."

The two of them sat there, gazing into the glass, until Hecubah nudged Ceci playfully. "Who is that?" she asked.

Ceci glanced at her smiling, then looked back into the mirror, taking a long look at herself. "It's me, ain't it?"

"Sure is, honey," Hecubah laughed. "I think you has arrived at last."

Chapter Three

"Lord, I don't think I shall ever be ready in time," Ceci fretted, adjusting the ornaments in her hair. "Perhaps I shouldn't have spent the whole morning gossiping with Celeste, but you know I ain't seen her in eight months, not since she moved to New Orleans. Don't she look happy?"

"Sure does," Hecubah agreed. "Married life seems to suit her."

"Oh, I can hardly believe it," Ceci breathed, flushed with excitement. "A ball in my honour."

"You turned eighteen in the Fall," Hecubah reminded her. "Now, your daddy wants to introduce you to Louisiana society."

"Why, I heard folks are coming from all over," Ceci informed her. "I believe we will have people here from every state in the Union."

"Could be," Hecubah nodded, "your daddy's a very influential man. Knows a lot of people. He got friends all over this country. Most of them with sons about your age," she added quietly to herself.

"Oh, look, Hecubah," Ceci implored happily. "Just look at my beautiful dress." She twirled, allowing the skirt to flare out. "My daddy sent all the way to Paris, France, for this."

"So you bin telling me for the last three hours," Hecubah remarked tonelessly.

"D' you think I'm showing too much bosom?" Ceci fussed, preening herself in the mirror.

"Depends what kind of an impression you wanna make," Hecubah advised, adjusting the top of her dress for her. "And who you wanna impress. For tonight, that's plenty."

"Good Lord," Ceci continued to fuss. "Look at the time. Will I ever be ready?"

Hecubah rolled her eyes, heaving a long sigh. "Make my daughter a lady," she muttered to herself. "That's what the man said, and what did I do? I created a monster of vanity." She shrugged philosophically. "Ain't got no one but myself to blame."

"What 'd you say?" Ceci asked, still preoccupied with her appearance.

"I said," Hecubah addressed her directly. "Why don't you let that mirror be, before you wears it out?"

Ceci turned slowly, smiling sheepishly. "Am I awful?" she asked.

Hecubah's face creased in a broad smile." No, child," she reassured her with a hug. "You is beautiful. You is the most beautiful girl in the world."

"I owe it all to you," Ceci acknowledged sincerely.

"Some," Hecubah agreed. "But you done well, honey. You come very far."

All at once, Ceci's smile faded, her face clouding with doubt. She sat down heavily on the bed.

"What ails you, child?" Hecubah asked softly, as if she'd already guessed the reason.

Ceci clasped her hands in her lap, chewing her lip. "I'm scared," she admitted.

"Oh, child," Hecubah sat down beside her, putting a comforting arm around her shoulders. "You ain't got nothing to be scared of."

"There's a whole banquet to get through," Ceci agonised. "And a ball later. How am I going to manage it all?"

"Just remember your etiquette," Hecubah advised. "And you dance as well as anyone I know."

"I guess," Ceci didn't sound so sure.

"Do you recollect that day we hid in the magnolia bush?" Hecubah reminded her. "And watched your sister Celeste with all them boys?"

"I remember," Ceci began to brighten a little. "She let go of her handkerchief and they all went wild."

"That's what I'm trying to tell you," Hecubah insisted, seizing the initiative. "If she'd bin chewing tobacca and spitting it into her hand, they'd still have found it charming. In their eyes, she couldn't do no wrong. What you gotta understand," she urged. "This affair ain't about eating and dancing. It's all about you." She cupped Ceci's chin in her hand and looked into her eyes. "Presently, I'm gonna take you down that main staircase. Those doors will open and you're gonna own that room. All you gotta remember is to be yourself and you'll do just fine."

Ceci's eyes began to shine again, the colour flooding back into her cheeks.

Hecubah squeezed her hand and winked. "Now it's your turn to break some hearts."

Ceci stood at the head of the great staircase. It swept down before her, the thick pile of the blue wool carpet cascading down it's steps, like a winter torrent. In the vast empty hall below, the massive oak doors of the ballroom stood shut. Beyond them she could hear the clamour of mingled voices. Two coloured footmen, dressed in full livery, awaited her approach. She tightened her hold on Hecubah's arm, reaching down with her free hand, grasping the folds of her gown, in preparation for her first step.

"I feel as if I have a sledge hammer in my chest," she whispered, "and catfish in my stomach."

"You ain't the only one," Hecubah confided.

Ceci took her first step, then hesitated. "What if I trip on my dress and fall head over heels down these stairs?" she remarked anxiously.

Hecubah raised an eyebrow. "Just remember to stand up smiling."

Descending without incident, they stood before the doors of the ballroom, as the footmen reached forward, each grasping an ornate bronze handle in anticipation of her entrance. Hecubah gave her one last hug of encouragement, her eyes conveying emotions that words could not. Then she stepped back, nodding to the footmen.

The great doors swept back, flooding the hall with the light of a thousand candles. With a final glance towards Hecubah, Ceci drew herself up, took a deep breath, picked up her skirts and stepped forwards.

Hecubah watched nervously from the shadows as Ceci glided across the room, paused and dipped, bowing her head in a long graceful curtsey and rose again. She listened as Mr Prejean announced, his voice full of admiration. "Ladies and gentlemen, friends. May I present my youngest daughter, Cecile?" She heard a soft ripple of applause spread out across the room, that welcomed Ceci into Louisiana society. Then the doors closed. For a moment, she just stood there, staring at the blank wood, before reaching for her handkerchief and pressing it to her eyes.

"Are you all right Ms Hecubah?" one of the footmen asked.

"Yes, thank you," she sniffed, "I believe I have a smut in my eye. I'll be fine directly."

With a final glance at Hecubah, Ceci drew herself up, took a deep breath, lifted her skirts and stepped forwards. Her heart was in her mouth as she moved across the floor. She paused and curtsied. Silently praying. "Please Lord, don't let me fall on my behind." As she rose, the first face she saw was her father's. For a moment, their eyes locked. Then, he smiled, in a way she'd never seen him do before.

She saw his chest swell with pride as he announced her to the gathering. "May I present my youngest daughter, Cecile."

She heard the soft ripple of applause that welcomed her

into Louisiana society. Then the doors closed behind her.

Ceci's cheeks began to burn under the unrelenting scrutiny of her guests. She opened her fan and began to waft it in front of her face, which helped disguise her trembling hand.

Celeste was first to greet her, followed closely by her new husband, Clay. "Oh, darling, you look just lovely," she smiled softly. "I am sure you will become the toast of Louisiana."

"I could never hold a candle to you," Ceci responded truthfully.

"My flirting days are over," Celeste placed an affectionate hand on Clay's arm. "But you be careful now. I can already see the young men prowling around."

Celeste passed Ceci on to her waiting father. It was customary to greet the guests before dinner. Accordingly, they had arranged themselves into an irregular column, so that she might have the opportunity to meet them all. They proceeded down the line, her father making the introductions, allowing her a bare minute to respond, before moving on.

There were congressmen and senators, businessmen and plantation owners, as well as their wives, sons and daughters. They all, very rapidly, became a blur of names and faces, which Ceci forgot almost as soon as she heard them. There were, however, a few exceptions.

"Senator Jefferson Davis, of Mississippi. Senator Davis is a hero of the Mexican war," her father saw fit to add.

"Hardly," the gaunt, hollow faced man, intervened modestly. His beard, bereft of a moustache, was mostly a tussock of hair beneath his chin. "I merely played my part."

"Mr Henry Doucet."

Ceci searched the faces of the half dozen men in her eyeline, wondering which one it was her father had indicated. Suddenly, he seemed to materialise, right out of thin air, directly in front of her. Tall and sallow complexioned, she couldn't help thinking that he was quite the most anonymous creature she'd ever encountered. "Did you fight in the Mexican war?" she enquired feebly. Under the circumstances, it was all she could think of to say.

Her question appeared to amuse him. "I did," he replied. "Although my contribution to that campaign was not nearly so grand as my illustrious colleague. I merely gathered intelligence." Suddenly, he gestured to the man beside him. "May I present my associate, Mr John Wilkes Booth, who, for his sins, is an actor."

"Oh, I adore the theatre," Ceci enthused, glad of the distraction.

"In that case, Miss Prejean," he inclined his head courteously, "I sincerely hope that, one day, I may have the privilege of performing for you."

Ceci was relieved to see that there was only one more family waiting to meet her.

"Colonel and Mrs John Sinclaire," her father informed her. "And their son, Trent. Colonel Sinclaire exports cotton from this and many other plantations, to Britain and Europe. Trent is presently attending West Point military academy."

The Colonel was a stout man with a ruddy complexion, greying hair and the biggest moustache she'd ever seen. Mrs Sinclaire cut a similar figure, except for the moustache. As for Trent. He regarded her with such blatant familiarity, it made her spine tingle. The sensation began to infuse her whole body. She wasn't sure if she liked it or not. She couldn't recall the boyish good looks, or the mass of wavy brown hair, but those pale blue eyes seemed vaguely familiar. "Have we met before?" she asked.

A broad smile lit up his face, making her tingle again. "If we had, I know I'd remember," he responded enigmatically.

The sound of the gong and the butler announcing that dinner was served prevented her from pursuing the point. She followed her father into the banquet hall, which was dominated by an immense table that stretched the entire length of the room. It was lavishly decorated with ornate silver candelabra, vast flower arrangements and glittering towers of candid fruit. Once Ceci had been seated, her father went to the head of the table.

As the first course was served, a low hum of conversation began to pass around the table. Everything from the price of cotton to the abolition of slavery. Ceci picked nervously at her food, as any number of tempting dishes passed before her, the knot in her stomach preventing her from enjoying even a morsel.

Overwhelmed by the proceedings, she endeavoured to keep up, nodding and smiling in what she hoped were the right pauses, as snippets of conversation drifted, unheeded past her ears.

"If the price of tobacca drops any lower, it will not be worth the effort of planting a crop." – "Whilst I am opposed to abolition, I feel that slavery should be confined to those states that already own them and not allowed to continue further." – "Senator Lincoln, that black republican. His policies will cripple the economy of the South." – "Miss Prejean—"

Ceci glanced up with a start, only just realising that someone had spoken to her.

Colonel Sinclaire was looking in her direction. "Miss Prejean," he repeated. "What are your views on Mr Lincoln?"

Ceci felt the ground open up beneath her. "I'm sorry," she faltered. "I'm not acquainted with the gentleman." She blushed, as a murmur of amusement crossed the table.

Noticing her discomfort, Colonel Sinclaire rose. "Miss Prejean, I hope you will accept my sincere apologies," he offered chivalrously. "It was quite remiss of me to burden an innocent young woman with vulgar politics. In deference to the ladies," he continued, addressing the entire gathering. "I suggest we choose some lighter topics of conversation."

Having survived her first blunder, Ceci was able to relax a little and enjoy the remainder of the occasion, but by the time the dessert dishes were being cleared away, she felt physically drained. When the table was completely clear, her father rose, tapping his glass with a coffee spoon.

"Ladies and gentlemen," he announced, "I give you a toast." The entire company surged to their feet, glasses upraised. "My daughter Cecile," he concluded with a flourish. They toasted her loudly and with vigour, as Ceci cringed behind her fan, her heart making her whole body shake.

Recognising her cue, she cleared her throat and responded. "Ladies and gentlemen. It has been a great privilege to meet you all and I hope to see you all again later this evening, but for now, with your permission, I shall withdraw."

"I think all we ladies should withdraw," Celeste added in support. "And leave the gentlemen to their brandy and cigars."

A round of applause adopted the motion and the guests began to disperse.

Ceci had barely risen from her chair, before she found herself surrounded by a crowd of young men, all anxiously wanting to escort her from the room. She stared in confusion, she'd never experienced so much male attention before.

"Please, allow me," Trent Sinclaire stepped in, slipped his hand under her arm, extracting her effortlessly from the midst of the melee.

For a moment, Ceci was tongue tied, then she remembered something she'd heard Celeste say, years ago, "Why, thank you, sir," she fluttered her eyelashes over the edge of her fan. "You are so gallant." She felt she'd acted scandalously, but it worked like a charm, as another broad smile lit up his face.

"I hope you're not too fatigued to enjoy the dancing this evening," he enquired solicitously, his strong northern accent in sharp contrast to her southern drawl.

"I will recover," she assured him.

"Did you enjoy the banquet?" he continued pleasantly.

Ceci thought about it for a moment. "It was so exciting and," she paused. "Quite exhausting."

"I understand," he nodded. "The first time is always the

hardest."

"The first time?" she shot him a quizzical glance.

"Certainly," he reaffirmed. "I'm convinced that you will be at the top of everyone's guest list from now on."

"Do you believe I made that much of an impression?" she asked, flattered by his remarks.

"You have on me," he informed her unreservedly.

"You are very bold, sir," she admonished him, blushing furiously.

Her criticism only served to encourage him. "In that case," he replied, unabashed. "May I press you for the first dance this evening?"

"I'm sorry," she told him truthfully. "I've already promised that to my daddy, but you may have the second."

They arrived at the open door, where Hecubah waited to receive her. Trent leaned forward, and taking Ceci's hand, brushed his lips against it. "I live in anticipation," he informed her, as they parted.

Again, she experienced the sensation of having met him before, but the reason for it still eluded her.

Chapter Four

"I'm so glad that's over," Ceci dashed into her room, leaned against the wall, one hand on her breast, fanning herself wildly. "Good Lord," she panted, "I'm sure I made a complete fool of myself."

"Why? What happened?" Hecubah frowned.

Ceci folded her fan and stood up. "Well, first I couldn't eat a bite. I blushed every time someone looked at me and I had no opinion on anything. I spent most of my time hiding behind my fan."

"Don't sound like you done anything wrong to me," Hecubah shrugged.

Ceci stared in surprise.

"In my experience," Hecubah explained. "Gentlemen don't much care for a woman who eats like a hog and contradicts them when they's talking nonsense."

"What's more," Ceci chattered on. "Every time I looked up, one or other of them boys was staring right at me."

"You don't say?"

"Yes ma'am," she replied earnestly, missing the sarcasm. "There was this one boy in particular, Trent Sinclaire, he was so sure of himself. Why, he acted just like he knew me." She paused in recollection. "He has the palest blue eyes I've ever seen," she sighed wistfully. "And soft silky brown hair. I swear, his shoulders must be as broad as a bench."

"Don't sound like he made much of an impression on

you," Hecubah observed drily. "Was he the boy you came out with?"

"The very one," Ceci confirmed.

"Ah huh," Hecubah acknowledged. "Trent Sinclaire, sounds like a rascal. I'd better keep an eye on him."

Ceci slumped, exhausted, onto the bed. "Why, I'm so nervous and excited. I don't think I could close my eyes for a minute."

"You've only got an hour before the ball," Hecubah reminded her. "Try and get your head down, honey. You'll need all your strength for this evening."

Safe in her Father's arms, Ceci began to enjoy the ball at once, but no sooner had the music stopped than Trent Sinclaire was standing beside her, waiting to claim the dance she'd promised him.

Silently, he took her in his arms. She caught her breath, thrilling to his touch, her whole body beginning to tingle again. The music played and they began to turn. She let him lead her on and on, submitting to his every move. He pressed her closer to him. She allowed it. Her head said no, but her heart said yes. She gazed up into his eyes and suddenly she couldn't see the room or hear the music. There were only his eyes, like two pools of pale blue water. She plunged in sinking deeper and deeper, drowning in the fathomless depths. When the dance ended, she suddenly found herself back on dry land, gasping for breath.

Instantly they were surrounded by a host of young men, all eagerly awaiting their chance with her. She would have shunned them all, but protocol demanded she oblige them.

She must have danced with every man in the room, but all she could think of, all she could see was him. He returned often, lesser men yielding their chance to him. He took command, dominating the floor. Casting protocol aside, she found herself living for those moments

At midnight, an interval was called, as servants began

to move amongst the guests, bearing silver trays laden with glasses of champagne and iced lemonade.

"May I offer you some lemonade?" Trent asked, taking two glasses from the proffered tray.

"That would be delightful," Ceci smiled, making use of her fan. "The room has become quite warm."

"Then may I suggest we retire to the veranda and take advantage of the night air?" With a glass in each hand, he presented his arm to her.

They slipped through a gap in the draperies and out onto the veranda. The sky was velvet black, shot full of brilliant stars. Cicadas chirruped from the silhouettes of cypress trees, as soft nocturnal breezes, laden with the scent of jasmine and lilac, sighed through their branches.

Trent placed one glass on the balustrade and offered Ceci the other. She began to remove her gloves to accept it, but in doing so, dropped one. Trent placed the second glass on the balustrade and stooped to pick it up. Ceci held out her hand in expectation, but he merely folded the garment and slipped it into his breast pocket.

She gasped, taken aback, her arm falling to her side. "Why, Mr Sinclaire," she began to bluster. "You forget yourself."

Indifferent to her protest, he reached out. Taking her by the nape of her neck, he slipped a hand about her waist and drew her towards him, lowering his lips onto hers.

Ceci was transfixed. The touch of his lips kindled a fire within her. She embraced it, surrendering to it completely, entirely at his mercy, until he chose to release her.

"Please, call me Trent," he invited.

She trembled from head to toe, her heart racing, her breast heaving, the fire unabating. "Very well," she breathed compliantly, reaching up to return his kiss. "Trent."

"Ceci."

Startled, she jumped back. Celeste was standing on the veranda, eyeing them both suspiciously.

"I hope it ain't your intention to monopolise my sister, Mr Sinclaire," she enquired stiffly.

"My apologies," he inclined his head, moving aside.

"You're neglecting your other guests," she told her, catching Ceci by the hand and leading her from the veranda.

Ceci followed, managing a desperate glance across her shoulder. Trent remained on the veranda, framed against the stars, watching her watching him.

"You didn't have to pull so hard," she complained. "I was merely enjoying a glass of lemonade on the veranda."

"So, I saw," Celeste replied knowingly. She glanced down. "Where's your other glove?"

Ceci averted her eyes, raising her fan to cover her blushes. "I must have lost it," she mumbled.

The ball continued well into the small hours, but by now there was little about it that Ceci could appreciate. Under the constant scrutiny of her sister, all she could do was go through the motions. She danced with other, anonymous men, gliding aimlessly across the floor, sometimes catching a glimpse of Trent. Every time she did, she sighed and her partner would smile, believing it was for him.

"You didn't have to stand over me for the rest of the night," Ceci whispered peevishly, as her guests filed past, making their farewells.

"I just wanted to make sure, you didn't drink more lemonade than was good for you," Celeste retorted scathingly.

In Louisiana, it was customary for a gentleman to take a lady's hand and touch his lips against the back of it, before leaving her company. Bringing up the rear, Trent appeared determined to flout convention. Grasping Ceci by the wrist, he turned her hand over, dropping a kiss into her palm.

"Thank you for an unforgettable evening," he smiled confidently, his eyes teasing her senses.

Ceci drew back her hand, speechless.

"I declare," Celeste glowered, hands on hips. "That boy's

the very devil." She glanced at Ceci, gazing longingly after him. "Then again," she recalled with a sigh. "So was my husband, when I first met him."

"Sun's coming up and you still ain't tired," Hecubah groaned. "Not even after all them men bin dragging you around the floor, like a sack of taters."

"I don't think I'll ever sleep again," Ceci responded airily.

"I'll remind you of that when you got bags under your eyes," Hecubah warned. "It's that boy, ain't it?" she realised. "Trent Sinclaire." It wasn't much of a guess. "And what about the others?"

"Why, I doubt if they'll be wanting to call," Ceci remarked dismissively. "I made no good impression on any of them."

"Oh, honey," Hecubah snorted, "they'll be wanting to call. You can rely on that."

"I'm quite sure you're wrong," Ceci insisted.

"Child, when bees find pollen," Hecubah advised her. "They don't leave until they get it all."

"All right, maybe one or two then," Ceci conceded grudgingly. "But I bet you a dollar they don't all come back."

★★★

"I can't believe it," Ceci stared at the pile of calling cards littering her bed like confetti. "They all come back." Her eyebrows rose, as she looked down at the large silver coin resting in her palm. "As well as some that weren't even invited to the ball."

"Ah huh," Hecubah acknowledged, "word gets around when there's a good thing going." She darted forward, snatching the dollar from Ceci's open hand.

"I was saving that for candy," she pouted.

"Candy's no good for your teeth," Hecubah cautioned, admiring the coin. "Your figure neither," she added absently,

31

breathing on the dollar and polishing it on her sleeve. "Which, by the way, is the reason they all come back."

"Just to look at my figure?" Ceci eyed her doubtfully.

"Looking's only the first part," Hecubah replied, still preoccupied with her prize. "Then comes the touching and the kissing, but from what Miss Celeste tells me, I guess you already knows that."

Ceci's eyes went wide, her face reddening. "Hecubah, please," she squirmed.

Hecubah pressed the coin to the centre of her chest. "I think I'll have Joshua drill a hole in this," she mused to herself. "So I can wear it like a medal." She glanced back at Ceci. "Mr Trent's card among all them?"

Ceci looked away. "No," she shrugged.

"You disappointed?"

Ceci's shoulders barely twitched. "I think I've been foolish."

"Not necessarily," Hecubah contradicted. "You see, some boys don't bother with calling cards. They just turns up unannounced."

It took Ceci a moment to realise what she was saying. "What?" she shrieked. "Are you telling me he's here now?"

"Bin pacing the morning room this last half hour," Hecubah remarked casually.

Ceci leapt off the bed. "Oh, Hecubah, I could swat you," she fumed, dashing to the mirror, desperately trying to make herself look presentable.

"Girl, it don't hurt to keep a man waiting," Hecubah informed her calmly. "And this boy's so full of himself, he deserves to be taken down a peg or two."

Ceci wasn't listening. Satisfied with her appearance, she grabbed her shawl and flew out of the door.

Hecubah looked back at the coin. "Yes sir," she nodded, "just like a medal. Lord knows, I've earned it."

Ceci paused from her headlong dash, catching her breath

in an effort to regain her composure, before sauntering into the morning room. Despite her feelings for him, she didn't wish to appear too anxious.

Nevertheless, the very sight of him made her heart flutter. "Why, Mr Sinclaire," she acknowledged, trying to sound nonchalant. "This is so very unexpected."

Trent was immediately sceptical. The colour in her cheeks contradicted her cool exterior, suggesting to him that she fostered emotions she had elected to conceal. He was more than happy to play her game. "Forgive my intrusion," he responded, the hint of a smile tugging at the corner of his mouth. "But I felt compelled to come."

"Compelled?" Ceci's eyes widened.

"And apologise," he completed his sentence.

"Apologise," she faltered.

"Yes," he continued earnestly. "For my conduct. For taking advantage of you at the ball."

"Oh, I see," she turned away, her lips taut. "You regret your actions then?"

He came up behind her and laid his hands lightly on her shoulders. "Should I?" he enquired tentatively.

She turned to find herself caught in the hypnotic gaze of those pale blue eyes. Like a moth before a flame, she was drawn to the heat and the danger. "Why, Mr Sinclaire," she breathed. "I believe you are trying to take advantage of me again." It wasn't as if she didn't want him to.

"And if I am?" he challenged softly.

Her breath quickened, the colour rising in her cheeks again. "Then I think I shall walk out of this room and never agree to see you again," her voice lacked conviction.

"Is that what you're going to do?" he persisted.

Once more she found herself trapped in the blue of his eyes. They drew her in, draining what little resistance she had. He seemed so self-assured, so certain of her. She could feel that fire beginning to burn within her again. She knew she should be angry with him, but it merely added spice to the mixture. She lowered her eyes, wringing her hands in agitation. "No," she admitted.

As far as Trent was concerned, the game was over. "Ceci, there's something I have to tell you," he began, just as Hecubah appeared in the doorway, carrying a tray of china.

"I thought you and Mr Sinclaire might like some tea," she smiled pleasantly, placing the tray on the table.

Tea was the last thing on Ceci's mind. She prayed that Hecubah would just leave the tray and go, but it wasn't to be.

"Shall I pour?" Clearly Hecubah intended to stay.

The mood had vanished, evaporating like morning mist under the summer sun. There then followed an hour of the most tedious conversation Ceci had ever endured. All she and Trent could do was glance at one another across the table, as Hecubah chattered incessantly about one trivial topic after another. At one point, she considered strangling her, or rendering her unconscious with the tea tray, but before she could put any of these plans into action, Hecubah suddenly changed the subject.

"I hear you are attending West Point military academy," she remarked to Trent.

"That is correct," he confirmed politely.

"You hope for a career in the army?" She continued innocuously.

"Yes, I do," he responded, flattered by her interest.

"Doubtless, you have a very fine uniform," she drew him in.

"I have a uniform," he agreed, a little perplexed.

"I'm sure Ceci would love to see you in it," she presumed without asking.

Before Ceci could intervene to the contrary, the heel of Hecubah's shoe caught her sharply across the shin, making her gasp. "All right," she winced, fearful of another assault. "Yes, I would."

"There," Hecubah declared, "you see. I'm sure you're not the kind of man to disappoint a lady."

"Certainly not," he assured her. "But I would have to send to New York for that."

"That's what I thought," she continued divisively. "I hope you're not going to keep a lady waiting," she concluded, leaving him little choice.

"In that case, I shall see to it at once," he complied.

Hecubah's smile broadened. "You is so very gracious, sir." She rose, forcing him to do likewise, much to Ceci's dismay.

"Oh, no, Trent," she moaned, "you don't have to go now."

"I think it's best I should," he told her, glancing at Hecubah. "But if I may, I'll come back when I have my uniform."

"Of course," Hecubah agreed, before Ceci could answer. "We'll arrange a picnic in your honour. Allow me to show you to the door."

"What' d you do that for?" Ceci stormed, when Hecubah returned. "You almost crippled me, and why' d you make him send all the way to New York for his uniform? That'll take ages to arrive."

"Exactly," Hecubah agreed unreservedly. "It'll give you both time to think, cool your heels for a spell. I told you before," she reminded her, "that boy's too full of himself. Needed taking down a peg or two. I could see you weren't gonna do it. Honey, you has got to make a man work for your attention. That way he'll appreciate you, instead of taking you for granted. If he loves you as much as you think he does, he'll be glad of a chance to prove himself."

"He was just about to do that, before you barged in," Ceci pouted.

"No," Hecubah was adamant. "You were about to fall into his hand, like a ripe plum. Mercy, child. Where's your self-respect? You got your reputation to think about."

All Ceci could think about was Trent. "I don't care about

my reputation," she snapped.

"Well, I do," Hecubah snapped back. "You can't go throwing yourself at the first man who comes along."

"He ain't the first man," Ceci objected. "What about all them other boys who called?"

"They weren't trying to jump on top of you as soon as they arrived," Hecubah pointed out.

"It weren't like that," Ceci sulked. "He ain't the same as them others. There's something about him. I feel as if I've known him all my life."

"That's just your imagination playing tricks on you," she warned. "Your heart ruling your head. Don't deceive yourself."

"I aint deceiving myself," Ceci remarked wilfully. "And I don't need a chaperone."

"Ah huh," Hecubah narrowed her eyes at her. "I knows what you need," she threatened, "and you is liable to get it, if you don't start acting like the lady I taught you to be."

Suitably admonished, Ceci thought it wiser not to provoke her any further. "You mentioned a picnic."

"What about it?"

"Are you going to be there?"

"That depends."

"On what?"

"Whether you can faithfully promise me to behave yourself in that boy's company."

Ceci thought about it. It was a tough condition to meet. "All right," she eventually agreed, "I'll behave." She crossed her heart with one hand and crossed her fingers on the other.

Chapter Five

"Is he here?" Ceci asked eagerly as Hecubah entered the day room.

"Oh yeah," she nodded.

"Well, it's about time," Ceci chaffed. "It's been almost two weeks. How long does it take to ship a uniform from New York? How does he look?"

"Like that Christmas tree we set up in the hall last year," Hecubah grinned. "I don't think that uniform was designed with the Louisiana climate in mind. He must feel like a boiled tater by now."

"You're cruel," Ceci scolded, "he don't deserve this."

"Yes, he does," Hecubah was unrepentant. "At least he asked for permission to call this time," she pointed out. "He's learning already."

"Give me a moment to get out on the veranda," Ceci told her. "Then bring him out."

"This way, General," Hecubah ushered Trent onto the veranda.

Ceci's heart gave a lurch when she saw him standing there in his uniform. He looked so tall and handsome. She was almost glad that Hecubah had played this trick on him. "Why, Mr Sinclaire," she cried, laying a hand on her breast. "You look so dashing."

He nodded, flashing her a self-conscious smile.

"Is you hot, Mr Trent?" Hecubah began to snigger.

Ceci couldn't help herself, the woman's laughter was infectious. She pressed her hand to her mouth, attempting to stifle her mirth.

Trent bore their derision in silence, clinging valiantly to the remnants of his dignity.

"I'm so sorry," Ceci gasped, catching her breath. "You must be so uncomfortable."

"I draw solace from your amusement," he responded wryly.

Ceci took a moment to compose herself. "I have prepared a picnic for us yonder," she pointed across the lawn. "I can offer you iced tea and fancies, which we may enjoy in the shade of that willow tree."

Trent relaxed visibly. He advanced, offering his arm to her. "It would be my pleasure," he smiled.

She guided him down the garden and across the lawn, to an old willow tree, its broad ancient bole casting a wide shadow across the grass, where she had laid out the picnic.

"It looks delightful," he complimented her, unconsciously tugging at the collar of his tunic.

"It weren't my idea," Ceci indicated the uniform.

"I know," he shrugged philosophically. "It's my own fault for under-estimating Hecubah."

"She won't be joining us," she told him. "So please feel free to remove your jacket, if it would make you feel more comfortable."

He inclined his head in appreciation, took off his tunic and laid it aside.

Ceci watched discreetly, her eyes devouring him, her pulse beginning to quicken. "Let's take advantage of the shade," she invited him to sit down. "It seems to be getting warmer."

She sat opposite him on the blanket, arranging her skirt in a wide circle around her. She knew he was watching her, his eyes dancing over her body. Her heart began to pound. She felt herself wilting under his gaze, barely able to admit to herself that she liked it. She reached down, grasping the jug of iced tea. The chill of it, against her hand, made her gasp, returning her to her senses. "How'd you manage to travel so quickly between here and Boston?" she asked, offering him a glass of tea.

"I didn't return to Boston," he explained. "I'm staying with my uncle. He has a house nearby, on the edge of your plantation. I used to spend my summers there when I was a boy."

"Why, I think I know that house," she recalled vaguely. "How is it that West Point can spare you for so long?"

"I requested an extended leave of absence," he told her. "So, that I might attend the ball."

"I'm so very glad you did," Ceci heard herself say.

"So am I," he confided with a smile.

His eyes engulfed her, penetrated her, laid her soul bare. She felt naked in front of him. It both terrified and excited her. She'd entered unknown territory, full of danger and wonders. A part of her wanted to stop, to retreat, but she felt compelled to go on.

She gazed at him, until the ice in her glass melted. It was as though she stood outside herself, watching this man and this woman make polite conversation, conscious only of a desperate burning need. Her soul ached, wanting him. Wanting him to want her.

The cicadas began to rasp their evening song, as the sun yielded to the soft Louisiana twilight. Ceci looked up with a start, as if waking from a dream. "My goodness," she blinked, "where'd all that time go?"

Trent rose to his knees, drawing her up with him. "Ceci, there's something I've been wanting to say all afternoon," he told her urgently, as if his opportunity to do so dwindled with the fading light.

"You don't have to keep apologising for taking advantage of me," she interrupted. "When Hecubah sent you away, do

39

you have any idea how hard it was for me to watch you go?"

"I only know how hard it was to leave," he confessed.

"I think about you all the time," she opened her heart to him. "Your beautiful eyes, your silky hair, your handsome face."

His chest swelled. "So, you think I'm handsome?"

"First thing I noticed about you," she flirted.

"You can't find any fault at all," he pressed her.

"No – Well," she paused, her curiosity getting the better of her. "There's just that little kink on the bridge of your nose. Is that natural?"

"No," he seemed to choose his words carefully. "It was broken when I was a boy."

Her eyes softened in sympathy, then suddenly widened in realisation. "God almighty," she yelped, "it's you." She fell backwards, sitting heavily on the grass, one hand clasped against her breast, the other clamped over her mouth.

"There it is at last," he exclaimed, as if he'd finally reached the destination he'd always been searching for.

"I knew I recognised them blue eyes," she stared aghast. Then a thought occurred to her. "When 'd you know it was me?"

"The night of the ball," he admitted."

"All that time and you never said," Ceci was incensed.

"I tried to tell you before," he protested.

Ceci wasn't listening. "That's despicable," she knelt up, thrusting her hands onto her hips. "You are so mean. Why, I think I'll go back into the house right now and never speak to you again."

Ignoring her tirade, he caught her round the waist, dragging her into his arms. "Am I to have no compensation for my injury?" he demanded.

She pressed her hands against his chest, looking up at him, her eyes smouldering. "What kind of compensation d' you have in mind?" she asked, her voice like warm honey.

"You are of French extraction?"

"You know that I am."

"Then kiss me in the French manner," he told her.

She gasped, the blood throbbing in her veins. "Oh, you are wicked, sir," she barely breathed.

"Are you?" he persisted, tightening his hold on her.

She hesitated, her breath quickening, the desperate burning need driving her on. She surged up, cupped his face in her hands and pressed her open mouth against his, caressing his eager tongue with hers.

His hand slipped up her waist, stroking her breast, then moved on, his fingers plucking feverishly at the buttons of her dress.

Suddenly, there was a loud cough.

"Good Lord, Hecubah," Ceci sprang away. "You move softer than a cottonmouth." She scrambled to her feet, hurriedly fastening her buttons.

"That looks like ample compensation for any man," Hecubah observed drily. "Unless that man wants his nose broke twice in one lifetime. Or," she added pointedly, "he wants to ruin the girl he loves."

"You're right, of course," Trent responded soberly, rising to his feet. "It's late Ceci," he told her, bending to retrieve his jacket. "I should go."

"Oh, no, Trent. Don't leave," she implored, reaching out to him.

He pressed his fingers to his lips and waved a kiss towards her. "I'll come back in the morning," he promised. "You can invite me to breakfast."

"Oh," Ceci groaned, as she watched him fade into the twilight. "I hate you," she snapped, rounding on Hecubah.

"Cool down, girl," she warned, "or I'll throw you in the bayou."

"We weren't doing nothing," Ceci sulked.

"Sure didn't look like nothing," Hecubah objected, reaching up and fastening a button Ceci had missed. "Now quit your pouting and help me clear up this mess."

They gathered up the picnic and started back to the house, still bickering.

"What happened to your promise? Didn't I tell you to save yourself for marriage?"

"I'll be an old maid by then."

"Kissing in the French manner. Where'd you learn that?"

"I don't recall."

"Have you bin taking any of them books your daddy keeps on the top shelf in the library?"

"No."

"Are you sure?"

"Yes ma'am,"

"I'm gonna count them, you know."

★★★

As good as his word, Trent returned in the morning. They ate breakfast together on the veranda, enjoying casual, if somewhat subdued, conversation, under the ever-watchful eye of Hecubah.

"I has some things to do in the house," she told Ceci, placing a tray of lemonade on the table. "I'll be just out back if you need me. For anything," she added emphatically, casting a stony glance at Trent.

"Hecubah is very protective of you," he observed, after she'd left.

"She raised me from a girl," Ceci told him. "She's like the mother I never knew."

He cast a wary glance back into the house.

"Are you afraid of her?" she asked, amused by his behaviour.

"Hell, yes," he admitted. "She looks at me like I'm the devil incarnate."

Ceci leaned closer. "She thinks you're a rascal," she whispered.

"And what do you think?" he asked seriously.

Ceci drew a breath to speak, then paused. "I think you were, as a boy," she remarked eventually.

"Ah, yes," he agreed guiltily, aware of what she was referring to.

Ceci sat back in her chair, her head on one side, regarding him earnestly. "You and them other boys was horrible to me," she recalled. "Always teasing, picking on me. You especially. You was always bothering me."

He looked down, running his hand across his chin, deep in thought, before looking up again. "As I told you, I live in Boston, but I used to spend my summers at my uncle's house." He smiled in recollection. "I ran wild with those other boys all summer long. Whenever the catfish wouldn't bite, or we couldn't find a dog with a tail long enough to tie a tin can to, I'd say, let's go find Ceci Prejean. She's always good for some mischief." He paused to sip his lemonade. "At first, I thought you were a boy, despite that long yellow hair and those freckles. The way you ran. The way you climbed trees. You were better than any of us with a slingshot." He paused again, running his tongue over his lips and sighed. "When I realised you were a girl, I always wanted to be around you, whether the catfish were biting or not. I looked for you all the time. I'd have done anything to make you notice me."

"Oh, my Lord," Ceci put her hand on her breast. "You were in love with me."

Trent shrugged self-consciously. "I didn't understand what it was at the time. How could I? I was only fifteen, but I guess that's what it was." He looked straight at her. "One day, I decided to do something about it."

Ceci raised her hand to her mouth, stifling a gasp. "Now I remember," she cried, eyes widening. "I remember what happened that day. You sneaked up on me. You grabbed me and you kissed me. Why, I was so surprised, I lashed out."

"And broke my nose," Trent finished for her.

"Oh, I'm so sorry," she put her hand gently on his arm.

He covered it with his. "I deserved it," he admitted. Then his face clouded a little. "My father was furious. He said my uncle didn't look out for me properly. Didn't protect me from the wild girl. He never let me come back." He clicked his tongue. "I missed those summers, but most of all, I missed that wild girl. I missed Ceci Prejean."

"I never realised," Ceci shook her head. "If only I'd known how you felt. I wonder what would have happened?"

"I guess we'll never know," Trent gestured vaguely. He took another sip of lemonade. "When my parents received the invitation to the ball," he continued. "I just had to come. I had to know if it was the same Ceci. At first I wasn't sure if it was you," he admitted. "You were all grown up, wearing a dress, ribbons in your hair, but when you stood in front of me, I knew you were that wild girl I tried to kiss all those summers ago."

"You haven't changed a bit," she smiled softly. "Still stealing kisses."

"For a moment, I thought you'd recognised me," he told her. "I had to act quickly. I was afraid all you'd remember was that foolish boy and reject me out of hand. I couldn't bear to lose you for a second time."

"I could have slapped your face on that veranda," she pointed out.

"I know," he agreed, "but by then I felt you probably wouldn't. I saw the way you looked at me as we danced. When you returned my kiss, I knew I was right."

"In that case, why didn't you tell me, when you came to the house?" she stated the obvious.

"That's exactly what I was going to do," he assured her. "Until Hecubah came in. Then again, yesterday at the picnic. I was waiting for the right moment. Then you went and remembered all by yourself."

"Yes, and when I did, you made me kiss you in the French manner," she reminded him flirtatiously.

He allowed himself a broad smile. "I didn't hear you complaining," he countered.

Ceci leaned closer, taking both his hands in hers, her eyes large and sultry. "That's because I wanted you to know," she purred, her voice as soft as thistledown. "That I'm still good for some mischief."

Chapter Six

"Quit mooning around, girl," Hecubah told her. "He ain't bin gone more than a month."

"Only a month," Ceci sighed. "It feels like forever."

"He got to do his soldiering," Hecubah reminded her. "He'll be back in the fall."

"That's even longer," Ceci would not be appeased.

Hecubah picked up a thick wad of envelopes, tied with blue ribbon, from the dresser. "He writes near every day."

Ceci sighed again. "It ain't like having him with me."

"Is that so?" Hecubah eyed her doubtfully. "Then why am I hearing all them gasps and moans coming outa your room most nights?"

"Hecubah," Ceci shrieked, mortified, her cheeks flaming crimson. "Are you listening at my door?"

"I don't have to stand at your door," she replied bluntly. "I can hear it clear down the hall."

Ceci's cheeks turned an even deeper shade of crimson. She lunged forward, snatching the pack of envelopes from Hecubah's hand. "Have you been reading Trent's letters?" she demanded suspiciously.

"I wouldn't dare," Hecubah retorted, eyes wide. "I don't want nightmares." She fixed Ceci with a cool stare, eyebrows raised. "I don't know what that boy's writing to you, but I sure hope they don't see it at West Point. They's liable to close the place down."

"Can we please change the subject?" Ceci begged, pressing

the back of her hand against her hot cheek and fanning herself furiously.

"You need a distraction," Hecubah advised. "Something to take your mind off things. What if I went downstairs and persuaded your daddy to let us go into town? You can spend some of his money. How'd that make you feel?"

Ceci's face lit up instantly.

"Ah huh," Hecubah observed, "I thought that'd be your answer."

"Oh, Hecubah, ain't these just the prettiest things you've ever seen?" Ceci sighed, drawing the delicate lingerie over the back of her hand.

"I can see your hand right through them," Hecubah stared.

"They'll be wonderfully cool to wear," Ceci pointed out, trying to sound entirely practical.

"Is that all there is of them?" Hecubah frowned.

Ceci cast her a pained look. "They're the latest fashion, from Paris."

Hecubah was unimpressed. "Girl," she snorted. "They does a lot of things in Paris, we don't do in Louisiana."

"Oh, Hecubah, sometimes you sound so old," she chided.

"All right, all right," Hecubah threw up her hands. "I'll let you buy a few pair, just so long as you promise me, that the only chance Trent Sinclaire will ever get to see them, is if he spots them hanging on the washing line, not hanging on your behind," she finished pointedly.

Ceci paused, running her eyes over the underwear, then glanced back at Hecubah. "I'll know I'm wearing them," she remarked brazenly.

"That's what I'm saying," Hecubah reaffirmed. "Just so long as he don't."

They spent another hour in the store. Hecubah wondered if Ceci intended to bankrupt her father.

"Hecubah, just look at this," Ceci ran over to her, holding a long garment of white satin.

"Ain't you got enough nightgowns?" Hecubah asked wearily.

"It's not for me, silly," Ceci told her excitedly, holding it up to her. "It's for you. There," she exclaimed triumphantly. "I knew I was right. It's just your size." She took Hecubah's hand and placed it gently on the material. "Here, feel. Ain't it just so soft and silky?"

Hecubah began to run her hand across the fabric. "Girl, what is it with you and transparent clothing?" she asked absently.

"Sheer," Ceci corrected her, offering a tenuous distinction. "You ain't going to wear it in public," she pointed out, her voice soft and persuasive. "You put it on in your room, stand in front of the mirror, look at yourself naked under it. Lay on your bed, feeling wicked."

"Honey, you is wicked enough for both of us," Hecubah commented vaguely, still preoccupied with the nightgown. "Mind, it is pretty though."

Ceci allowed herself a smile of satisfaction. "We'll take this as well," she told the store clerk.

Hecubah looked up with a start. "Girl, you is making my blood boil," she told her, wafting her hand in front of her face. "Let's go and find ourselves a cool glass of sarsaparilla."

They left the store laden with bags and packages and continued down the busy street, until a woman's scream brought them to an abrupt halt. They found themselves standing at the mouth of a long alleyway. At the far end two carts were placed back to back. A black man, manacled and chained, stood in one of them. In the other was a black woman, similarly chained, her face a wreck of tears and grief.

"Must have been an auction," Hecubah muttered darkly.

The black woman clung to the man, her hands clawing

at his arms. It took the strength of two men to drag her off him.

"Come away, child," Hecubah tugged at Ceci's arm. "You don't need to see this."

Ceci followed, too shocked to resist. They pressed on in silence, until they came to a public bench, in the shade of an ebony tree.

"My feet are hurting," Hecubah complained. "Let's set awhile."

"Was she that man's wife?" Ceci asked, as soon as they'd sat down.

"Probably," Hecubah shrugged.

"Then why'd they split them up?" Ceci frowned.

"The man that bought her, didn't want him. Simple as that," Hecubah replied dismissively.

"Will she ever see him again?"

"I doubt it."

Ceci chewed her lip, haunted by the anguished face of the coloured woman. "I've spent my whole life around slaves" she realised, "and I never questioned it once."

"You were born to it, child," Hecubah patted her knee. "You know no other way."

"Now, I see it for what it is." Ceci glowered. "It's a vile practise and we should be rid of it."

Hecubah's hand darted out, touching a finger to Ceci's lips. "I admire your sentiments, honey," she told her, in a hushed voice. "But, it's best not to go shouting them around. Leastwise, not in this town."

"I can't even begin to imagine what it's like to be a slave," Ceci voiced her thoughts. "Can you?"

Hecubah remained silent, her expression answering for her.

Ceci's mouth fell open, she clamped her hand over it, the colour draining from her face. "Oh, God, no," she cried. "Hecubah, please tell me it aint so."

"On the plantation, I lives like a free woman, even gets a wage," Hecubah told her. "I think and behave, like a free woman and everyone accepts and believes it, but the fact is, I'm a bought slave."

"Why, on earth, did you never tell me?" Ceci sobbed.

"Didn't find no reason to," Hecubah replied flatly. "You aint even nineteen, you didn't need to know. I wouldn't have told you now, if I weren't afraid you'd stumble on the truth."

Ceci pressed her handkerchief to her eyes, sobbing quietly. "We'll go home, right now," she told her resolutely. "I'll speak to my daddy."

"No," Hecubah gripped her arm, making her wince. It was the first time she'd ever seen fear in the woman's eyes. "Don't do that, child. If you loves me. I mean really loves me, you'll let it be."

"But why?" Ceci implored.

Hecubah sighed heavily, as she recalled an unwelcome memory. "I weren't no older than you when I stood on that auction block," she began to explain. "A whole lot of men wanted to buy me, for a lot of ugly reasons, but there was this one man. He out bid all the rest. Spent a small fortune and saved me from Lord knows what."

"Then why didn't he free you?" Ceci wanted to know.

"He couldn't," Hecubah sighed again. "The money he used to buy me weren't his. He smuggled me onto the plantation. Signed my name into the books and I became the property of the estate."

"Then my daddy does own you," Ceci concluded. "He will free you for the asking."

"I have no doubt of that," Hecubah agreed, "but if the truth came out, it would destroy that other man and I owe him so much."

"Don't you want to be free?" Ceci asked.

"Freedom's just a word, honey," Hecubah spared her a humourless smile. "It's what you feel inside that counts. I like my life the way it is. So, you see, child, if you go charging in with all your good intentions, trying to fix things that ain't broke, all you'll do is stir up a whole mess of trouble and hurt a lot of good people, me most of all." She reached over, lifting Ceci's chin up. "So, you keep quiet about it, child. Swear to me you won't tell a soul about what you learned today."

"I swear," Ceci agreed, fresh tears spilling down her cheeks. "But, you won't be a slave forever, not if Mr Lincoln has his way. Then you'll all be free."

"Oh, sure," Hecubah gestured casually, "that's what abolition is supposed to be all about. I told you before, freedom's just a word. Them men and women, working in the fields, don't even own the clothes they wear, the homes they live in, or the food they eat. All freedom's gonna mean to them is dispossession and starvation. If folks hereabouts has to pay for help, they'll hire a white man, not a black man."

"Surely, something has to be done?" Ceci insisted.

"That's for sure," Hecubah agreed. "I just hope it's a wise decision that prevails, or everyone, both slave and freeman is gonna suffer." Hecubah's mood suddenly brightened. "All that talking's made me dry," she exclaimed. "Let's go find ourselves that glass of sarsaparilla."

"Did you never want a husband?" Ceci asked, drying her eyes. "And a family of your own?"

"I've had my share of men," Hecubah told her, uncharacteristically forthright. Black and white. Don't you look at me that way, girl. What? Did you think you'd invented it?" She wiped away the last of Ceci's tears, before they evaporated on her hot cheeks. "As for family," she told her softly, "you has always bin my little girl. C'mon," she urged. "Buck up now. Look at me. It's still your Hecubah and that ain't never gonna change."

They gathered up their parcels, linked arms and set off in search of sarsaparilla.

"Those men you mentioned," Ceci asked, after a while,

eaten up with lurid curiosity. "Do they live on the plantation? Do I know any of them?"

"Mind your own business."

"I was just asking."

★★★

"Lace is too expensive to throw away," Hecubah explained. "So when you finds a snag, you has to repair it," she demonstrated, hunched in a chair, working deftly with a fine needle, as Ceci sat on the floor beside her, watching intently.

"Oh darn," Hecubah sighed in frustration. "I've run outa white thread." She glanced down at Ceci. "There's another spool in the store cupboard downstairs. Be a dear and save these old legs."

Ceci rolled her eyes. "You're only thirty-four, Hecubah. Your legs ain't old."

"Save them anyway," Hecubah patted her cheek.

"Of course," Ceci smiled, jumping up. "I'll be right back."

She'd just reached the foot of the stairs, when she heard a commotion at the front door. She peeked around the corner. Several men had arrived, friends of her father, other plantation owners. They all appeared to be in a state of considerable agitation. Her father quickly ushered them into the morning room, where a heated discussion quickly got under way.

Ever curious, Ceci tip-toed up to the door, wondering what all the fuss was about.

"It looks like Lincoln's going to be elected," one of them was saying. "If that happens, we'll have a president whose only interests are the North and abolition."

"We will be controlled by a federal government that has no concept of how the South lives," said another. "It is our constitutional right to oppose such an injustice."

"If South Carolina secedes, the rest will follow," her father's voice was easily recognisable among the others. "And that means war."

"Any state has the right to leave the Union, that's in the Constitution," he was answered. "But Lincoln would deny all that. The South relies on cotton and the slaves to pick it. Slavery has been abolished in every state north of the Mason-Dixon line. Neither is it legal in the New Territories. If Lincoln comes to power, he will try and enforce the same thing on the South, crippling our economy."

"As sane men, we should strive to find a better solution," her father insisted.

"The solution, as I see it," yet another voice entered the debate. "Is to create a confederation of southern states, form our own government and elect our own president. Jeff Davis would be a good man. Let's see ol' Abe try and stop that."

"Our society is based on a one crop economy." her father told them. "All the manufacturing and heavy industry is in the north. If we go to war, we'll have to import everything we need to fight it. That's where they'll hit us first, by cutting our supply lines. We'll be facing attrition. If we lose the war, we'll lose everything, for all time."

The men's anxiety was infectious. Even though she'd failed to understand much of what she'd heard, the little she had grasped terrified her.

"Where you bin all this time? I was about to send out a search party."

"What's secession?" Ceci asked anxiously.

Hecubah sighed. "You bin eavesdropping again?"

"How can there be a war? It's the same country." Ceci remarked naively.

"Child, I seen one man kill another for a crust of stale bread," Hecubah told her. "I seen two dogs tear each other apart over a dry bone. There can be a war."

Ceci crossed the room and knelt beside her. "What'll happen?"

Hecubah sighed, shaking her head. "Country turns in on itself, splits, fights. Whoever comes out on top, that's what the country will become."

"All because of slavery?"

"That's what they say. South wants to keep them. North wants to set them free. There's the war."

"Then why don't the South free the slaves and leave the war?" Ceci suggested innocently.

Hecubah sighed again. "It ain't that simple, honey. I only wish it was."

"Dear Lord," Ceci realised suddenly. "Trent's in the north. I'm in the south."

"Hush now," Hecubah comforted. "Don't you fret none. There's a ways to go yet. Hopefully cooler heads will prevail before then." She paused, squeezing Ceci's hand. "I done told you before. No good ever comes of eavesdropping. You wanna know anything else about what's going on. You come and ask me first. No more listening at doors. You'll just upset yourself." She smiled down at Ceci. "You'll be seeing Trent again soon, long before any war. If there ever is one."

Chapter Seven

"Ain't it just wonderful," Ceci danced around the room, hugging herself, giddy with excitement. "Trent's arriving tomorrow and my daddy's letting him stay here."

"Don't seem like he had a whole lot of choice, after you told him you'd kill yourself if he didn't," Hecubah pointed out.

Ceci stopped prancing and thrust her hands onto her hips, regarding her earnestly. "Why, I'm sure he didn't believe that," she remarked dismissively.

"Your poor daddy," Hecubah sighed. "I used to think Miss Celeste had him wrapped around her little finger, but these days you puts her in the shade."

Ceci wasn't listening. "Oh, just think of it," she began to dance again. "A whole month with him."

"I'll be grey by then," Hecubah muttered to herself.

"What 'd you say?"

"I said, he'll stay then."

"Why, I just said that, silly."

"I'm putting him in the east wing," Hecubah told her.

Ceci came to an abrupt halt. "All the way down there?" She put her hands on her hips again, frowning. "You don't have to worry about Trent. He's a gentleman."

"It's not him that concerns me," Hecubah informed her bluntly. "It's you."

Ceci was outraged. "That ain't fair."

"You think so?" Hecubah raised her eyebrows at her. "I done counted those books on the top shelf in the library. There were five missing."

Ceci glanced away, chewing her lip. "I put them back since."

"That's mighty big of you," Hecubah would not be appeased. "Next I suppose you'll be telling me, you've forgotten everything you've read. I looked at one chapter. Near went blind."

"They ain't that bad," Ceci pouted.

"Really? and what'd base that opinion on? Other books you read?"

"I was just curious," Ceci remarked, staring at the floor. "Nothing wrong with being curious."

"I dare say," Hecubah conceded. "But you're one cat I'm determined it aint gonna kill. That reminds me," she added, as an afterthought. "After what I read in that chapter, I locked away all your French underwear. Just for safe keeping."

Ceci was momentarily confounded by this effrontery. "Then I shall wear none at all," she retorted stubbornly.

"There's a hickory tree, right out there, in the garden," Hecubah pointed. "I can cut a switch any time I want. A bare bottom will make an easy target."

Ceci wouldn't put it past her. "All right," she capitulated, the brief battle of wills drawing to a close. "I'll behave."

"See that you do."

"Don't you trust me, Hecubah?" she asked, in her most innocent voice.

"Hell, no," Hecubah was having none of it. "Not for a minute. You forget, I was your age once."

After one of the most restless nights Ceci had ever experienced, she awoke, almost beside herself with excitement. Consequently, she spent the best part of the morning driving Hecubah to distraction.

"No. You ain't waiting at the end of the drive," she refused to permit it. "Let him come to you. Good Lord, girl. Show a little style."

Ceci finally persuaded Hecubah to let her stand on the front steps, where she waited impatiently, hopping from one foot to the other.

"Try not to wet your drawers, honey," Hecubah advised tonelessly. "It's a real passion killer."

Eventually, Trent appeared at the gate, riding a great black horse he'd rented in the town. He waved briefly, then galloped full tilt down the drive, rearing his horse in front of them, pulling off his hat in a wide, sweeping salute.

"That boy sure knows how to make an entrance," Hecubah had to admit.

Ceci was completely captivated by the gesture, clapping her hands and squealing with delight. As the horse settled down, she ran up to him. He leaned down, lifting her effortlessly onto the saddle, in front of him, where they shared a long passionate kiss.

Hecubah just stared, her mouth hanging open. "Good Lord," she murmured dismally. "This is gonna be harder than I thought."

"Did you see, Hecubah? Did you see?" Ceci asked, flushed and breathless, once Trent had set her back on the ground and dismounted himself.

"I saw," Hecubah grunted. "Looked like something off the cover of a dime novel."

"Oh, Hecubah," Ceci scolded. "What will it take to impress you?"

"Next time, he can lift me onto his saddle. That'd impress me."

"Good to see you again, Hecubah," Trent planted a particularly large, wet kiss on her cheek.

"I knew it," she muttered, pulling the back of her hand across her face. "I just knew it. That boy's a rascal." She watched as the pair entered the house, allowing herself a long lingering glance at Trent. "Mind, if I was ten years younger," she considered briefly. "Enough," she rebuked herself. "We already got one woman on heat in the house, and that's plenty."

Ceci's father welcomed Trent to their home. Whatever views he or the young northerner held on the current political situation, they were never mentioned. As for Ceci herself, all her thoughts were centred on Trent, while the threat of war gradually faded to the back of her mind.

"God almighty," Hecubah jumped. "Every time I turn a corner, there's you two smooching. You bin at it for days. Ain't you tired yet? Ain't your lips sore? You, Trent Sinclaire," she wagged her finger at him. "You hold her any closer and you gonna be standing inside her dress. I hope you can manage to keep your hands off her tonight at the theatre. There's laws against that sort of thing in public."

"Yes Ma'am," Trent acknowledged politely.

Hecubah glared at him, then marched off.

Ceci began to giggle.

"I think she enjoys scolding me," he decided.

"I think so to," Ceci laughed outright.

"Are your lips sore?" he asked, pulling her even closer.

She draped her arms around his neck. "No," she breathed softly. "Want to help me get them that way?"

★★★

"Go to sleep or I'm gonna have to knock you out," Hecubah warned. "Come on honey, you bin going at it all day, dashing around on the lawn with him, shrieking at the top of your lungs. What were you doing?"

"It was just a game," Ceci told her, her eyelids getting heavier.

"Just a game," Hecubah nodded. "You run off and if he can catch you, he kisses you."

"Something like that," Ceci responded drowsily.

58

"From what I saw, he caught you an awful lot of times. Girl, I knows you can run faster than that."

"Then he wouldn't have caught me so often."

"I figured that out. I suppose I should be grateful he contented himself with holding your hand at the theatre, last week, instead of chasing you up and down the aisle."

"I wouldn't have minded," Ceci mumbled, her eyes beginning to close.

"You get some sleep," Hecubah insisted. "He ain't gonna want to chase you, if you turn up bleary eyed and haggard."

Ceci was already asleep.

Hecubah leaned forwards and kissed her on the forehead. "That's right, honey. You dream about him. "It's safer that way."

★★★

"Trent's driving me into town in the buggy," Ceci announced. "We're going to have ice cream at the drug store."

"Ice cream," Hecubah repeated sceptically.

"You're very welcome to join us," Trent offered chivalrously, ignoring Ceci's sideways glance.

"I guess that would be as popular as a bullfrog swimming in a bowl of punch," Hecubah concluded. "You two go on ahead, but mind you keep your hands to yourself."

"Yes Ma'am," Trent assured her.

"I wasn't talking to you, son. I meant her," she corrected him.

"Hecubah," Ceci cried indignantly, "it's just ice cream."

"Ah huh."

★★★

"What's going on?" Ceci wondered, as they drove through the main street of town.

A large crowd had gathered on the sidewalk. A group of

men were addressing them. As they drew nearer they could hear them opposing abolition and inciting secession.

Trent slapped the reins, urging the horse into a trot, taking them swiftly past. When he'd put some distance between them and the crowd, he pulled the buggy into the side of the road and stopped.

"What's wrong?" Ceci asked, noticing the look of concern on his face.

"In a few months, I'll graduate from West Point," he told her. "My whole class will graduate. In that class are men from all over the Union. I've lived with them, worked with them, they're my friends, brother officers. If there's a war between the states," he frowned, "half of them will be on the other side."

"What will you do?" Ceci asked, wide eyed.

"The only thing I can do," he replied gravely. "My duty, as will they."

"Will that make me your enemy to?" she wondered naively.

He glanced down at her, a broad smile banishing his dark mood. "That's right, it will," he slipped a playful arm about her waist. "I'll have to take you prisoner."

"That will not be necessary, sir," she admonished him, easing herself from his grasp. "I believe, I have already surrendered."

"I guess that's the first victory to the North," he suggested.

She laid her hand gently against his cheek. "I think the South's won something to."

He pressed his hand over hers, serious again. "Whatever happens in this country, Ceci. Let's you and I rise above it. We mustn't let anything come between us."

"It won't," Ceci responded fiercely. "I'd die first."

He lifted her hand from his cheek and kissed her palm, then picked up the reins. "I recall I promised you ice cream."

They sat outside with their ice cream, selecting one of a small group of tables, each with a large sunshade over it, that had been set out on the sidewalk.

"This is delicious," Ceci began to say, then she stopped short, as a wagon load of slaves passed by, wretched creatures, all shackled together. "Why 'd they have to treat them so badly," she sighed. "Nothing like that ever happens on the plantation."

"The rest of the world isn't like the plantation," Trent told her. "That's why we're facing a war. A lot of men are prepared to fight to free these people."

Ceci's eyes began to mist over. She put her hand over her mouth, letting her spoon fall back into the glass.

"I'm sorry, Ceci," Trent tried desperately to console her. "I didn't mean to upset you."

"It ain't that," she wiped her eyes, struggling with a decision to break her sacred oath. "Oh, Trent. Hecubah's a slave," she blurted out.

"That's kind of hard to believe," he grimaced.

"I got it from her own lips," she assured him. "Made me swear not to tell anyone. Said it would cause all kinds of trouble."

"She's a shrewd woman," he acknowledged. "Knows her own mind. She must have her reasons."

Ceci clutched at his hands. "I want to do something."

"Do you love her?" Trent asked.

"As much as I love you."

"Then, if you want to do something," he advised. "Do as she asked."

Ceci looked away, her hopes for Hecubah's freedom apparently thwarted. As she thought about it, she began to realise that Trent was right. Hecubah had begged her not to take any action, and no matter how hard that was to do, she should honour her wishes.

"Let's get out of this town," Trent suggested. "We'll buy ourselves a picnic and drive into the country. Put all the woes of the world behind us and just enjoy each other's company."

Ceci brightened at once. "That, sir," she smiled, "is an invitation I could not possibly refuse."

They drove a mile or two from the town, found a pleasant spot on the bank of a bayou and while Trent unhitched the horse and let it graze, Ceci laid out the picnic. They took off their shoes and stockings, dipping their bare toes into the cool water as they ate the food. Then they lay down on the soft grass, letting the hot Louisiana sun lull them into a drowsy frame of mind.

Ceci lay, supporting herself on her elbow, idly picking the seeds off a grass stalk. "Did you always want to be a soldier?" she asked.

"Not at first," he admitted, as he lay on his back, staring up at the sky. "I was only fifteen. I 'd just found the love of my life and lost her. All I really wanted to do was get back to Louisiana."

Ceci glanced up, smiling. "That's sweet."

"After what happened, that year," he continued, "my father told me I should find myself a useful occupation. He said soldiering was an honourable career. I had my doubts then, but now I wouldn't do anything else." He turned his face towards her. "You never said what happened to you that year."

Ceci rolled her eyes. "Oh, Lord," she recalled, with a shudder. "My daddy pitched a fit. I've never seen him so angry. Scared the life out of me." She threw the bare stalk away. "Then he brought Hecubah in," she went on. "I didn't know what to make of her at first, but after a while, she was the only one I felt safe with." She plucked another grass stalk and began to pick at the seeds. "My daddy told her to make me a lady. She sure had her work cut out. She made me wear dresses and ribbons and frilly drawers, when all I wanted to do was climb trees and swim in the bayou. I hated it. I hated it for a long time. Then, one morning I woke up, and just like that, I was glad I was a girl."

"I'm glad you are to," Trent winked, making her blush.

"Trent," Ceci asked, still preoccupied with her grass stalk. "What' d you think of Hecubah? As a woman, I mean."

"She's very attractive," he had no difficulty in saying.

His comment made her lose her train of thought for a moment. "Prettier than me, you mean?"

"I didn't say that," he salvaged the situation in a second. "I was merely answering your question."

"Well, all right then," she continued, apparently satisfied with his explanation. "She told me she's had lots of lovers, but there's this one man, a mystery man. He saved her years ago, from a fate worse than death. I think he lives on the plantation. I think she still sees him."

"Why'd you think that?" he asked.

"Sometimes she comes in and I can smell a man's cologne on her clothes. The kind they use when they've finished shaving."

"There's nothing wrong with that," Trent responded, with a casual wave of his hand. "She's still young and available."

"I know," Ceci was just getting into her stride. "But I think she's seeing another man at the same time."

Trent rose to his knees. "What makes you say that?"

"Now and then, it's a different cologne," she raised her eyebrows at him.

"Maybe it's just one man, who changes his cologne," he suggested.

"Have you ever changed your cologne?" she asked pointedly.

He thought about it for a moment. "No," he shrugged, "I guess I've always used the same one."

"Exactly," she cried, feeling her suspicions were justified. "I've asked her who it is, but she won't tell me, and I'm just dying to know."

Trent shook his head, amused by all this feminine intrigue. "Ceci, you're incorrigible."

She sat up, putting her hands on her hips. "Oh, really?" she retorted. "Then why is it when I recall all the big trouble in my life, you're always there, stealing kisses?"

He smiled that very particular smile, the one that always

made her wilt. "Would you have it any other way?" he asked.

She lowered her eyes, mildly irritated by the way he always managed to get the better of her. "No," she admitted eventually.

"That's what I thought." He pounced on her, making her shriek, pushing her onto her back, grabbing her wrists and pinning her arms to the ground. "I've been thinking about that surrender you mentioned," he told her. "Is that unconditional?"

She looked up at him, her eyes full of devilment. "I guess you'll just have to find out for yourself."

Ceci had hoped to sneak back into the house and change before Hecubah noticed she'd returned. However, she'd reckoned without the sixth sense the woman had developed concerning her movements and found herself cornered in the morning room.

"How'd you manage to get grass stains on the back of your dress, eating ice cream at the drug store?" she demanded.

"We went on a picnic afterwards," Ceci saw no reason to lie.

"Ah huh, another picnic," Hecubah nodded. "Looks as though it ended like the last one."

"We just kissed, is all. I swear," Ceci insisted.

Hecubah shook her head, sighing. "Child, I bin where you is now," she told her patiently. "You meet a man, fall in love with him. Pretty soon, the time comes when there ain't nothing you won't do in the name of that love."

"I don't know what you mean," Ceci blustered defensively.

"Oh, I thinks we understands each other," Hecubah countered intuitively. "I seen the way you two have been looking at each other lately. Got that itch you're dying to scratch."

Ceci turned her face away, cheeks burning, unable to respond.

"Kissing and touching is passable," Hecubah continued soberly. "But if you goes beyond that, there's no coming back.

64

So, you'd best be mighty careful about which direction you take."

"Trent will be leaving soon," Ceci struggled to keep the desperation she felt out of her voice. "I love him so much. What am I going to do?"

"I got a feeling you'll think of something," Hecubah muttered to herself. "And that's what bothers me."

Chapter Eight

The day began, like any other, full of laughter and kisses, but as time passed, an uneasy restlessness began to steal into Ceci's mind. A mounting tension, straining for release, a brooding stillness, like the calm before the storm.

The desperation she had endured over Trent's imminent departure changed, transmuted, until it became something else. A fever, that began to consume her. Something she could only feel, without understanding what it was.

She could see by the way he behaved that Trent was afflicted by the same malady. Neither of them spoke of it. It went beyond words. It was the language of the heart. As the day wore on, the laughter and kisses fell away. They sat in silence for hours, just looking at each other, a palpable energy, a potent concoction of love and lust, surging between them. As twilight approached, the tension had become unbearable.

"It's just a walk in the garden," Ceci insisted, anxious to be gone.

"Whose idea is this?" Hecubah enquired, noting her agitation.

Ceci looked away. "Mine, and don't say 'Ah huh', like you always do."

"Ah huh."

"There, you said it again," Ceci's shoulders arched in frustration.

"I ain't your jailor," Hecubah informed her calmly. "You is

all grown up now. Knows your own mind. All I'm saying is, just be careful."

"In the garden," Ceci frowned. "Of what?"

"Ol' Magic," Hecubah remarked ominously.

"Ol' Magic," Ceci laughed drily. "Who's that?"

"Oh," Hecubah shook her head solemnly. "He clever, mighty powerful. He bin prowling around all day."

"Hecubah, you ain't making any sense," Ceci complained irritably.

"That's because you ain't listening," Hecubah warned her. "He comes when you least expect him. Creeps right up on you. Wears all kinds of disguises. Sometimes it's a big ol' moon, hot night, full of stars, crickets humming. Oh, you'll trys to remember what I'm telling you now, but you won't, he'll see to that. Pretty soon you'll begin to glance at the boy, he glances back, atmosphere gets charged." Suddenly, she snapped her fingers, making Ceci jump. "Honey, you is lost, he got you in his power. Trapped a lot of girls that way."

"I think you've been out in the sun too long," Ceci made light of it. "It's a beautiful night, be a shame to waste it." She made to leave, lingering by the open door. "It's just a walk in the garden," she repeated unnecessarily, taking her deceit one step further. "That's all." Now she wasn't only lying to Hecubah, she was lying to herself.

It was a relief to escape the stifling confines of the house and get out into the open. Ceci instantly felt a sense of freedom and a hint of adventure that began to excite her. It was obvious that Trent felt it to.

"Hecubah has some odd notions sometimes," she told him, as they began to stroll arm in arm across the lawn.

He looked at her. "What notions?"

Ceci caught her breath, as the familiar burst of energy surged between them, but this time, it was so intense, it took her completely by surprise.

"You were saying?" Trent prompted. "Notions."

Another charge dissipated through her. She frowned, struggling to recall what she'd intended to say. "I really can't remember," she admitted at last. "Probably nothing. Just one of Hecubah's tales."

They walked on, Ceci preoccupied with what had just happened. She began to feel more restless than ever, barely able to contain herself. She glanced at Trent, clearly, he was experiencing the same emotions.

The further they walked, the stronger the sensations became. She tried to block the confusing thoughts from her mind, but they just kept coming back, stronger than ever. Iniquitous little devils she had conjured up, that plagued and coerced her relentlessly, gradually wearing her down. She found herself defenceless against the onslaught, until finally, she yielded and abandoned herself to them.

There was something about this night. Something strange, yet vaguely familiar, that began to seep into Ceci's soul. The air was sultry, almost oppressive, drenched in the heady perfume of night flowering blossoms. She inhaled it, drank it in. It was overwhelming, intoxicating. It flowed over her, caressing her skin, beguiling and seducing her, enflaming her senses. She licked her dry lips, breathing harder, beginning to perspire. She gripped Trent's arm more tightly, pressing herself closer to him.

Cicadas serenaded the thin sliver of a crescent moon, as it rose slowly behind the dark shapes of the cypress trees in the bayou. They began to exchange glances, brief, furtive, often, that flared more incandescently each time they looked at each other. The tension was excruciating. A dreadful, urgent, bittersweet yearning, that plucked at the centre of Ceci's soul, throbbing inside her, sapping her will, tearing away the last shreds of her resistance.

She looked at Trent again. Suddenly, he seemed taller, stronger, more handsome. Her heart thudded in her chest, as the dregs of her will drained away, succumbing to the primal urges rising within her, leaving her thrall to her senses, until she no longer questioned, but only obeyed.

She gripped his arm and stopped, forcing him to halt. He turned. She could feel his hot breath on her face, the warmth of his body radiating over her. She looked up, her eyes soft and submissive, unconsciously signalling her readiness to him.

He moved closer, then paused, glancing cautiously around.

"I know a secret place," she whispered. "Where I used to hide as a girl. Hecubah won't find us there."

She shrank back as he bore down on her. Then, sweeping her into his arms, he carried her into the shadows.

When they reached the place, he laid her gently on the cool grass, then lay down beside her, leaning over her. There was only the sound of the breeze rustling the leaves of the cypress trees, the trickle of the bayou, the song of the cicadas and their laboured breathing, as two hearts beat as one.

She raised her hand, stroking his cheek, guiding his head down, until their lips met for that first exquisite, tender kiss and then a second and a third. She draped her arms about his neck, her kisses growing ever more fervent, ever more demanding.

His hand wandered, exploring the curves of her body, slipping beneath her skirt, until his fingers brushed her bare thigh, her moans stifled by his questing tongue. Suddenly, he pulled away, looking down at her, as she lay there breathless with anticipation.

Ceci gazed up at him, speaking with her eyes. She had chosen him, above all other men, to initiate her into the world. He would be the one to share the most intensely intimate moment of her life. She was his willing accomplice, giving herself to him completely. She was his, to do with as he pleased.

Trent proved to be a gentle and considerate lover, putting her needs before his own, his caresses arousing her to heights of ecstasy she'd never known before. Nothing she'd read, nothing she'd ever imagined, could possibly have prepared her for this. He began to undress her, his fingers working with feverish dexterity, kissing every part of her body he exposed, his hands kneading her soft, yielding flesh, until she lay there naked beneath him,

She tore at his clothes, her curiosity bubbling over, pulling off his shirt, as he hurriedly unfastened his belt. As she stripped the last garment from him, she caught her breath, staring in awe at the strength of his masculinity. She had never seen a naked man before. The spectacle both excited and alarmed her. He had touched her, she felt compelled to touch him. He moaned, she gasped, feeling his power pulse through her fingers, wondering how she would ever accommodate him.

He bent his head, pressing his mouth against her breast. She cried out, the blood racing in her veins, her heart beating so fast she thought she would die. Her body thrilled to his every touch, as he transported her, again and again, to the brink of release, only to leave her begging for more.

He had imbued her with the fire of his own heart. Kindled the flame. Now he poised himself above her, ready to consummate their love. In that last moment of innocence, she could feel the heat of his body, the contours of his muscles, smell his musk, her sweat mingling with his, as he lowered himself onto her. She surrendered to him, a long sobbing moan exploding from her lips, every nerve screaming, feeling truly alive for the first time in her life.

She gripped his shoulders, her body arching beneath him, her nails gouging his moist skin. She groaned and shuddered as waves of ecstasy surged through her, teetering on the brink of oblivion. Digging her heels into the bare earth, she forced herself up against him, at one with him, in rhythm with him, in a single frenzied convulsing spasm, until they both collapsed to the ground, spent and exhausted.

It was an act of beautiful violence, suffused with pain and delight. An explosive union of their bodies and souls, the final poignant kiss, before they parted, sealing the bond between them.

Ceci hardly knew where she was. She lay there, panting wildly, her mind reeling, her body tingling, tiny bolts of lightning darting up and down her spine. It was some time before she could bring herself to speak.

The crescent moon was high in the sky. They lay side by side, hand in hand, gazing up at it.

"I never imagined anything could be like that," she confided breathlessly.

"Neither did I," he admitted, his chest heaving.

She turned her face towards him. "Am I the only woman you've ever loved?" she asked him.

"Yes," he smiled. "From the very first day I saw you, I've never thought of anyone else since. You're the only woman I'll ever love."

Rested, they went down to the bayou and bathed each other, then stretched out on the bank, allowing the warm night breezes to dry them.

"It's late," Trent noticed. "We should be getting back. Folks up at the house will be wondering where we are."

"You mean, Hecubah." She moved closer. "I never want this moment to end," she sighed.

"It never will," he told her, brushing a damp curl from her brow. "This is only the beginning."

Reluctantly, she rose. He helped her dress, then dressed himself. Then, arm in arm, they strolled back to the house.

"What will you tell Hecubah?" he asked, as they moved out of the shadows.

Ceci stopped and thought about it. "I won't tell her anything," she declared defiantly. "It's none of her business, that's what she told me once. Besides," she shrugged dismissively. "She'll never guess."

★★★

"You went and done it, didn't you?" Hecubah stormed. "After everything I told you, you let him have his way. Or was it the other way around?"

"I've no idea what you're talking about," Ceci lied shamelessly, unaware that the colour in her cheeks, the lightness of her step and the airiness of her disposition had instantly betrayed her secret to a woman of Hecubah's experience.

"Don't you lie to me," Hecubah snapped, thrusting a glass into her hand. "Drink this."

Ceci chugged it back without thinking. "God almighty, that's awful," she scowled. "What is it?"

"Something that will guarantee your flow next month, instead of morning sickness," Hecubah told her.

Ceci lowered her eyes, chewing her lip.

"Ah huh. I guess you didn't think about that part, when he was crawling all over you." Hecubah noticed her reaction. "What would you have said to your daddy, in nine months' time, when you is as fat as a Holstein cow?"

"Oh, please. Don't tell him," Ceci implored.

"As if I would," Hecubah snorted. "He's liable to go after that boy with a gelding knife."

"Oh God, no," Ceci clutched at her hands. "Please don't give us away," she begged, unable to decide if she was exaggerating or not.

Hecubah shook her head, sighing. "Girl, if you is gonna go on thinking with your body, instead of your mind, you'd best marry that boy right sharply."

"He ain't asked me to marry him yet." Ceci had meant it as a simple statement of fact, but Hecubah took a very different view.

"Why not? You done had the honeymoon already. He'd better make his mind up soon, or I'm gonna be the one with the knife."

"Please," Ceci entreated, "don't say that. You've been in love. You must know how we feel."

Hecubah softened a little. "All this time I was trying to make you a lady. I guess I hadn't noticed you'd grown into a woman," she confessed. "Ain't your fault. Just Ol' Magic, doing what he does best." She glanced at the empty glass. "I guess I better go and mix a whole barrel of this."

"Did Ol' Magic ever catch you?" Ceci asked.

"Oh," Hecubah shivered, "we go way back. And before you ask who, don't, because I still ain't telling you."

★★★

Ceci's eyes were red from hours of crying. "It's Trent's last night," she sighed dismally.

"You'll have plenty of time to say goodbye," Hecubah told her, placing a glass on her night table. She went to the closet and selected a long silk nightgown, laying it on the bed beside her.

Ceci glanced down, eyes wide. "Where'd you find that?" she demanded abruptly.

"At the back of your closet," Hecubah responded casually. "Right where you hid it. It's just like the one you bought for me," she observed. "Only thinner, if that's possible. You know, I tried that on," she continued nonchalantly. "Stood in front of my mirror, looked at my brown body through it. It was just like wearing a spider's web. I could hardly bring myself to take it off. Seemed only right a man should do it."

"Hecubah, please," Ceci pleaded.

Hecubah wasn't about to pass up a chance to tease her. "Didn't say I found one. I guess that'll have to be another night."

"Hecubah, you ain't helping," Ceci sighed patiently.

"Yes, I am," she insisted. "Now you climb outa your clothes and put that thing on, before it floats away."

73

"It ain't for sleeping in," Ceci informed her, with just a hint of embarrassment.

"You don't say," Hecubah continued to torment her. "Now ain't that a revelation. Drink this." She offered Ceci the glass from her night table.

Ceci's eyes widened in surprise. "Is that what I think it is?"

"Ah huh," Hecubah confirmed. "Works just as well before as after."

"Hecubah," Ceci frowned. "What are you doing?"

"You're a grown woman now," she replied. "It's time I stood back and let you live your life in your own way and enjoy the happiness you've found. Besides I knows, no matter what I do, you're always gonna find a way to be with him. At least this way, I can protect you from yourself. I said you'd have plenty of time to say goodbye. Now you'll have all night."

Ceci threw her arms around her and kissed her. "What 'd I ever do to deserve you?" she cried happily.

"As I recall," Hecubah mused. "You drove your father to his wits end. That's where I came in."

Ceci drained the bitter liquid from the glass, stripped and put on the nightgown.

"This is gonna be one farewell that boy ain't never gonna forget," Hecubah remarked approvingly. "Now slip this robe on, we got a ways to go."

They made their way cautiously to the east wing, ever fearful of a chance encounter with one of the servants. It wasn't until they'd reached Trent's room, that Ceci hesitated.

"Lord, what am I going to say?"

Hecubah stared at her, as if she were simple minded. "Girl, ain't you learned nothing yet?" She asked bluntly. "You don't have to say anything. He'll get the message right off." She rapped lightly on the door. "I'll be back with your clothes, before the house is awake," she whispered, then hurried away.

After a moment, the door opened. Trent looked out. His

jaw dropped, as Ceci let the robe slip from her shoulders. He offered her his hand. She took it. He drew her gently into the room and closed the door behind her.

Chapter Nine

Trent certainly knew how to make a spectacular entrance, but he was about to prove that he could also make a truly memorable exit. Hecubah and Ceci's father had come to see him off. The four of them stood in front of the plantation house. Beyond a short flight of stone steps, Trent's horse was saddled and waiting.

After making his farewells to Mr Prejean, he came over to Hecubah. The pair regarded each other cautiously for a moment.

"If it wasn't for Ceci," he began to tease her.

"You stop that now," she wagged her finger at him.

Smiling, he stepped forwards, catching her in a big hug, dropping a kiss lightly on her cheek. "Do you still think I'm a rascal?" he asked.

She brushed an imaginary speck of lint from the shoulder of his coat. "All men are rascals," she told him. "What would we ladies do, if they weren't?"

"Thanks for everything," he told her sincerely.

"You just make sure that little girl never gets her heart broke," she replied earnestly. "That'll be thanks enough for me."

He nodded, then turned to Ceci.

Her heart skipped a beat, her mind in turmoil, a whirlwind of emotion. She couldn't decide if she wanted to laugh or cry. She opened her arms, expecting to embrace him. Instead, he took her by the hand and lead her to the foot of the steps.

"I spoke to your father, this morning," he told her, suddenly dropping down on one knee. "He's given me his permission to marry you. If you'll have me, that is."

With uncommon strength, Ceci dragged him to his feet, threw her arms around his neck, pressing her mouth against his, in a kiss that seemed to last forever.

"I guess that's a yes, then," Hecubah observed drily. She glanced back at Ceci's father. "You reckon they'll suffocate each other?" she wondered.

He merely shrugged, apparently unconcerned.

Suddenly, they broke apart with a huge gasp. Trent swept her off her feet. Throwing her up onto his horse, he leapt up behind her and raced off down the drive, Ceci shrieking all the way.

"I hope he stops, when he reaches Boston," Hecubah remarked, gazing after the receding couple. She looked at Ceci's father again. "She's gonna be insufferable after this, you know," she predicted. "Ain't gonna be no living with her now."

He spared her a broad smile, before turning away and sauntering back into the house.

"Oh yeah." Hecubah stared after him. "That's right, you make yourself scarce. Comes down to me, don't it?" she grumbled to herself. "I'm the one whose gonna have to put up with all the sleepless nights, the hysteria, the tears," she broke off, peering down the drive again. "Where's he taking that girl?"

Trent reined the horse in. It skidded to a halt in front of the plantation gates. Putting an arm around Ceci's waist, he lowered her to the ground and jumped down beside her.

She found herself gazing up into those pale blue eyes again. The thought of his leaving chilled her, as if her soul was trapped in a glacier, a thing of beauty and terror. He drew her gently to him, bent and kissed her, until she thought she would melt. "Let's not wait," she urged. "Let's get married now."

He smiled, touched by her impetuousness. "I think my

parents would like to be invited to the wedding," he advised her, with a more practical turn of mind. "And your sister and many others. Besides, I've been recalled to West Point. There's my graduation to consider. I'll need an occupation, if I'm to support you in the manner to which you have become accustomed." He nodded back to the plantation.

"I'd live with you, in rags," she declared desperately.

"It's up to me to see that you don't," he took his obligations seriously. "I will return in April and then we can begin our lives together."

"That seems so far away," she began to sob.

"It's barely six months," he reminded her. "I'll write every day." On impulse, he unfastened the long white ribbon, she was wearing in her hair and knotted it in his horse's bridle. "I shall tie this in the bridle of every horse I ride," he pledged. "Until the day we're married."

"I'm counting them already," she sighed, glancing down the road that would take him from her. She reached up, put her arms around his neck and drew his head down, kissing him softly, long and slow, committing every second to memory, so that it might console her in his absence. Then she let him go.

Their eyes locked for a moment, before he thrust his boot into the stirrup and mounted the horse. He reached out, their fingertips touched briefly, then he spurred the horse and galloped away.

Ceci stood in the middle of the road, tears streaming down her cheeks, watching him go, until there was only a thin cloud of dust and the empty road. She heard a foot scrap the ground and turned. Hecubah came up to her and put a comforting arm around her shoulders.

"I have the strangest feeling," Ceci confided, "that I'll never see him again."

Hecubah clicked her tongue. "It's starting already," she sighed.

"What is?" Ceci asked.

"Wedding jitters," Hecubah told her. "He ain't coming back. He's changed his mind. He's found another woman. If the mail is late by an hour, he don't love you no more. Child, I guarantee, you is gonna imagine all these things while he's away."

"No, I won't," Ceci objected hotly. She glanced back along the empty road. "You don't really think he'll change his mind, do you?"

"God almighty," Hecubah cried, throwing her head back. "All you gotta concentrate on, is April 1861. Then you'll be Mrs Trent Sinclaire, and I hope your first child is a little girl who drives you crazy, like you done to me."

"You don't mean that," Ceci pouted.

"Ah huh," Hecubah responded, non-committally. "Well, unless you wants to stand in the middle of this road for six months, which, now, I'm sure you do, you'd best come with me." She took Ceci by the hand and began to lead her back towards the house. "We got a wedding to plan."

★★★

"I ain't moody and irritable," Ceci snapped, pacing the hall. "I'm merely waiting for the mail, and it's late."

"No, it ain't," Hecubah contradicted. "You is early. You is always early. The mail'll come same time as it always does."

Ceci stopped pacing, face like a thunder cloud. "I didn't get a letter from Trent yesterday," she remarked peevishly. "There has to be one today." She stamped her foot. "Oh, why do we have to send Joshua into town, for the mail. He's old and slow."

"Maybe," Hecubah conceded wearily. "But the horse and buggy ain't. He'll be by directly."

"I bet he's in town right now," Ceci planted her hands on her hips. "Gossiping with his friends."

"I doubt it," Hecubah shook her head. "Not after last time. You near took his hand off."

Ceci began to pace again. "I've a mind to write to Congress, about the state of the postal system in this country."

Just then, Joshua came in. He took one look at Ceci, threw the whole bundle of mail on the hall table and jumped back. Ignoring him, she rushed forwards, tearing at the package, scattering envelopes right and left, like confetti.

"No, no." She glanced feverishly at each envelope, before discarding it. "No. Yes," she cried, holding up the prize. "It's a letter from Trent." She pressed her lips against it. "I can't wait to read it," she sighed breathlessly, dashing off to her room.

"That's right, honey, you go on ahead," Hecubah called after her. "I'll stay and help Joshua pick up all this mail, you done thrown on the floor. What's the penalty for murder in this state?" she asked Joshua, as she knelt down.

"I think they hangs you," he guessed.

"D'you die slow?" she wondered.

"I hear it's mighty quick," he told her.

"Ah huh, might be worth it at that," Hecubah considered. "What you grinning at?"

"You ain't fooling no one," Joshua smiled. "Everyone knows you loves that child."

"Ah huh," Hecubah sighed, as they stood up. "Would you consider holding her down, while I beat her?" she asked, handing over the letters she'd collected.

"I ain't got time to do that every day," Joshua reminded her.

"Have I asked you that already?" she frowned.

"Yes 'm," he nodded. "And the day before."

"Ah huh," Hecubah mused, "gotta get that girl in line somehow."

"Does my heart good to see the young folks so happy," Joshua told her. "Ain't bin this much excitement in the house, since Miss Celeste got married."

"Oh, don't remind me," Hecubah exhaled sharply. "That girl lost ten pounds in weight before the wedding. So did I."

"You'll think of something, Ms Hecubah," he assured her. "You always do."

"Ah huh."

★★★

"Hecubah." Ceci sat on the edge of her bed, clutching Trent's letter in her hands, reading avidly. "Trent's just graduated top of his class, as First Lieutenant. Ain't that wonderful? He said he's sent me a picture…" She broke off, noticing the expression on Hecubah's face. "What?" she asked doubtfully.

"How long you gonna go on like this?" Hecubah demanded.

"Like what?" Ceci shrugged.

"You don't sleep nights, hardly eat a thing. You read his letters, until they fall apart, and you're driving everyone in the house crazy," she scolded her. "What have I gotta do? Tie you to your bed, till you come to your senses?"

"Wouldn't make no difference," Ceci remarked stubbornly.

"I reckon it wouldn't at that," Hecubah narrowed her eyes at her.

"What you going to do?" Ceci persisted recklessly. "Threaten me with a whipping?"

"Oh, child," Hecubah leaned closer, making Ceci shrink back. "You is tempting me worse than the devil. What you aiming to do?" she asked, selecting a new weapon from her arsenal of coercion. "Give me a heart attack?"

"Don't say that." Ceci was appalled.

"That's it, ain't it," Hecubah pressed her advantage. "You won't be happy 'til I drops down dead."

"Stop it," Ceci squirmed, "you know that ain't so."

"Then, what you gonna do about it?" Hecubah insisted.

Ceci hung her head. "What'd you want me to do about it?"

"There's a big breakfast, waiting down stairs," she pointed.

"I want you to eat it all, then get some proper rest. After that, you can take hold of yourself and start behaving, like the lady I taught you to be."

There was something about the way Ceci looked that made Hecubah stop, sit down on the bed beside her and hold her hand. "What's the matter, child?" she asked. "I ain't seen you act this way, since I made you wear dresses."

"I can't help it," Ceci shook her head dismally. "I can't shake this feeling, that Trent's never coming back."

"That's plain foolish," Hecubah chided. "This is Trent Sinclaire we're talking about. If the trains stop running. If the river boats sank and all the horses died, he'd walk here. If he broke his legs, why, then he'd crawl. There ain't nothing gonna stop that boy coming back."

Clearly, Ceci remained unconvinced. "If I could only see his face again," she sighed heavily.

"Maybe I can help," Hecubah suggested, producing a small package from her apron pocket. "You missed this during your rampage downstairs."

"It's the picture," Ceci gasped, tearing at the wrapping. She pulled off the paper, opened the case and there was Trent, resplendent in his new uniform, looking back at her. She caught her breath, feeling her heart begin to glow. "Oh my, ain't he handsome," she sighed again, her eyes growing misty.

"Sure is a good looking boy," Hecubah agreed. "Still think he ain't coming back?"

Ceci managed to smile for the first time in days. "I guess I've been very foolish," she admitted, wiping her eyes on the back of her hand.

"When it comes to men, we all are, honey," Hecubah advised her. "You put all them dark thoughts behind you and, in a few days, we'll go into town and have a picture made of you to send to him. What'd say to that?"

"I'm hungry," Ceci realised. "I'm so hungry, I could eat a horse."

"I think they done served bacon," Hecubah told her. "But we can always stop by the stables."

★★★

"This is so exciting," Ceci enthused, as they made their way to the photographer's studio. "I never had my picture made before, except for that painting my daddy had done when me and Celeste was children."

"Gonna put the painters outa business." Hecubah predicted. "I guess they can photograph just about anything these days."

"Why, I heard some of them are making pictures of naked girls," Ceci informed her enthusiastically. "I don't mind. I could lay on a couch, wearing nothing but a pair of black stockings. Wouldn't that be something to send to Trent?"

"You'd wear stockings for that?" Hecubah stared. "I'd no idea you was so modest."

Ceci faltered in the face of this effrontery. "There ain't no call for that," she pouted, "it was just a thought."

"Trent is gonna get a beautiful picture of his future wife," Hecubah told her firmly. "Something he can be proud of. Something he can show his parents," she emphasised. "If he wants any more than that, he'll have to rely on his memory, which, as I recall," she raised her eyebrows at Ceci. "Is quite extensive."

"Like I said," Ceci blushed. "It was just a thought."

"Try thinking of something else for a change," Hecubah suggested.

The photographer's studio was full of strange paraphernalia, the walls crammed with examples of his work.

"It's truly amazing," Ceci stared in wonder. "They're so lifelike, just as if all these people were frozen in time."

"That's exactly right," the photographer greeted them. "They may age and die," he waved his hand at the portraits. "But these pictures are eternal. That's the miracle of modern science. A.D. Lytle, at your service."

They had come with the express purpose of having Ceci's picture made, but now they were there, she insisted that she and Hecubah have one taken together first.

"We can look at it, when we're old and grey," she told her, as Lytle set up his equipment. "And remember how we used to be."

"Don't reckon I need any reminding," Hecubah doubted. "Past few months' bin burned into my soul."

"Hush now," Ceci chided, taking her position in front of a canvas backdrop, painted with an idyllic country scene. "You come over here and put your arm around me."

"Stand perfectly still," Lytle instructed, one hand poised on the lens cap, flash pan raised in the other.

Suddenly there was a tremendous burst of light, as a great ball of white smoke rolled up to the ceiling.

"God almighty." Hecubah flinched. "Is that supposed to happen?"

"Of course, silly," Ceci assured her. "That's what makes the picture."

"Who is this portrait for?" Lytle enquired, as Hecubah stood down, leaving Ceci alone.

"My Fiancé," she replied.

"Then, may I suggest," he began, indicating how she should pose. "That you stand with your back towards the camera, looking over your shoulder. It makes a most appealing study, favoured by many of my clients."

Ceci did as he asked. He changed the backdrop to a Grecian temple, making it appear as if she were about to enter.

"She seems a little tense," he confided to Hecubah. "I feel her expression could be…" he thought about it, "well, more alluring," he suggested. "Considering who it's for."

"Ceci, honey. Turn a little more and look directly at me," Hecubah told her. "That's right. Now, remember, it's not me you're looking at. It's Trent."

"That's much better," Lytle smiled appreciatively, noticing

the instant change in Ceci's expression. "My word, she's a pretty girl. That pose would melt the heart of a stone."

"Just keep thinking of you and Trent in the garden," Hecubah coaxed, until the flash powder ignited once more, capturing the image for posterity.

"I can have these pictures ready in four hours," Lytle told them. "Two large and two pocket sized, framed and mounted."

"Good, that gives us time to eat lunch," Hecubah concluded.

They left the photographer's studio and continued down the main street.

"Well, would you look at that." Hecubah paused outside the newspaper office, studying the broad sheet that had been tacked to the bulletin board. "Abraham Lincoln has just bin elected President of the United States."

Chapter Ten

"A little more to the left," Hecubah directed, tightening her hold on Ceci's waist.

Ceci stood on her toes, feeling the stool wobble a little, as she stretched up to place a painted wooden star on top of the tree. "There?" she grunted with the effort.

"That's fine," Hecubah agreed, helping her down.

"My daddy made that star for my mama, the first Christmas they spent together," she told Hecubah, as they stood back to admire their handiwork. "When we was small, Celeste and me used to wish on it for the thing we wanted most."

"That's one tradition you'll be able to revive, after tomorrow," Hecubah pointed out. "Miss Celeste and her husband are arriving in the morning. Though why she wanted to travel in her condition, is beyond me."

"She's expecting a baby, is all," Ceci made light of it. "I guess she's already got the thing she wanted most."

"Wanting and having, are two different things," Hecubah warned. "Babies are a lot of work."

"You're sounding old again," Ceci cautioned. "I know for a fact you don't mean that." She looked back at the tree they had just decorated with strips of coloured paper, little bags of sugar sweets, gingerbread angels and tiny wax candles. "All the family back together again," she sighed happily. "This is going to be the best Christmas ever."

"I reckon you could be right at that," Hecubah agreed.

"Can we put the presents under the tree now?" Ceci asked eagerly.

"No," Hecubah replied firmly, "I told you before. Not until Christmas Eve."

"Oh, why' d we have to wait so long?" Ceci complained impatiently.

"Because you always come in here, feeling them all, trying to find out what's inside," Hecubah reminded her.

"No I don't," Ceci attempted to refute the allegation.

"You do to," Hecubah wouldn't be swayed. "You've done it every year since you was a little girl. It's the one thing about you, that ain't never changed."

"Has my daddy bought me that dress, I asked for?" she tried a different approach.

"I don't know," Hecubah shrugged.

"Yes, you do," Ceci insisted.

"Then, I ain't saying," she replied stubbornly. "It's a surprise. Christmas is all about surprises."

As if to confirm her statement, the first one arrived only minutes later, heralded by a knock at the front door. A group of men were ushered in, as Ceci's father came out of his day room to meet them.

"I recognise some of them men," Ceci remarked ominously, as they peaked out into the hall.

"They've done it," the leader of the group announced solemnly. "On this day, December 20, 1860, South Carolina has seceded from the Union," he paused, as if to savour the moment. "It's begun."

Her father invited them into his day room and closed the door, as another heated debate got under way.

"What's begun?" Ceci asked anxiously. "What's going to happen?"

"Pay it no mind," Hecubah counselled, "it's just one state."

"A mighty important one," Ceci was wise enough to know.

"This is just political wrangling," Hecubah advised her. "One half of the country trying to get leverage on the other. South Carolina's left the Union. As soon as they agree on terms, with Congress, they'll come back."

"And if they don't?" Ceci asked flatly.

"Now, don't you go worrying all over again," Hecubah told her. "It's just a lot of old men, full of hot air," she finished dismissively. "Now, help me put up this mistletoe."

"What's the point of that?" Ceci frowned. "Ain't going to be no one here but family."

"Well, I'm sure your daddy would like a kiss," Hecubah suggested. "I know I would."

Ceci rolled her eyes. "You know, as well as I do," she told her. "It ain't for that kind of kissing."

"Oh, now I remember," Hecubah recalled. "You prefer the French manner."

"Not so loud," Ceci glanced furtively around. "Someone might hear you."

"Let's put it up anyway," Hecubah persisted. "It's traditional, and while you're at it," she added, "you can hang your stocking over the fireplace and put out some sugar plums for Saint Nicholas."

"That's just for children," Ceci sighed in exasperation.

"Oh, I forgot, you is all grown up now," Hecubah observed. "I guess the only thing you wants in your stocking these days is Trent's hand, but I doubt he'd stop there."

"Hecubah, please," Ceci blushed, uncharacteristically prudish, "that's hardly in keeping with the Christmas spirit."

"I guess not," Hecubah shrugged, aware that Ceci was no longer worrying about the state of the nation.

★★★

As soon as Celeste arrived, Ceci realised that in all her nineteen years, she'd never actually seen a pregnant woman, at least, not this close. Celeste was huge. The spectacle both alarmed and fascinated her, at one and the same time. It evoked in her a host of new and unfamiliar emotions. Thoughts she'd never entertained before.

"My condition ain't contagious," Celeste remarked, holding out her arms.

Ceci couldn't even hug her sister in the usual way. She had to stand to one side. "Does that hurt?" she wondered.

"Of course, not," Celeste smiled. "Plays havoc with my back though." She took Ceci's hands and placed them on her bulge. "It's the most natural thing in the world," she assured her. "You'll find out, soon enough."

The way Ceci felt now, the prospect held a certain appeal. She glanced at Clay. He looked just the same. Tall, square jawed, with dark hair and brown eyes. In Celeste's day, he'd been the pick of the crop. He was still a handsome man. Not that she was attracted to him, she never had been, but now fatherhood had endowed him with a new quality, a potency that excited her. It was something that Trent had yet to acquire. Something she knew she could provide, given the chance.

"Clay ain't contagious either," Celeste broke into her trance. "Now give your brother-in-law a kiss and say hello."

"I'm sorry," Ceci blinked. "My mind must have been wandering. I don't know what came over me."

Celeste smiled, patting her stomach. "I think I do," she told her.

Once Celeste and Clay had retired to their room to rest and refresh themselves from the rigours of their journey, Ceci drew Hecubah to one side. "Did you see the size of her?" she shivered. She pressed her hands against her waist, looking down at her figure. "Do you think I'll be that big if I get pregnant?"

"Possibly," Hecubah guessed, "but I don't reckon it's a question of if, just when."

"That was uncalled for," Ceci objected.

"I saw the way you were looking at your sister," Hecubah told her. "Now don't you go getting all broody on me. Things is complicated enough."

"You were looking at her too," Ceci retorted.

"I was just being polite," she sniffed.

"No you weren't," Ceci scowled. "You couldn't take your eyes off her, and now you're blushing. You feel just the same way I do."

"That's enough," Hecubah held up a warning finger.

"Don't matter anyway." Ceci hung her head sullenly. "As things stand, we don't have a man between us."

"Oh, don't start that again," Hecubah sighed. "Trent'll be back. As far as I'm concerned, you can do anything you like with him. Just so long as you remember, that what Miss Celeste is doing, is for a married woman, not a single girl."

Ceci glanced up at her, her eyes full of mischief. "Anything I like?" she asked.

"God almighty," Hecubah swore in frustration. "Child, you is incorrigible."

"That's what Trent said," Ceci grinned.

★★★

Having rested, Celeste and her husband returned downstairs. They all gathered in the parlour, as Hecubah brought in a tray of fresh eggnog.

Mr Prejean raised his glass. "To my new grandchild," he announced proudly. "A long and happy life."

"I doubt if it'll be the only one, Daddy," Celeste told him. "And I'm sure Ceci will eventually add to the pile."

"She don't know how close you already come, to doing just that," Hecubah whispered in Ceci's ear, stepping nimbly aside, just before Ceci jerked her elbow at her.

★★★

90

"You been feeling these, as usual?" Celeste asked, as she helped Ceci place the presents under the tree.

"Of course, not," Ceci contested. "I grew past that, years ago."

"I take it from that," her sister divined. "You mean Hecubah wouldn't let you get your hands on them until Christmas Eve and even then, only when I'm here."

"You'd think she'd trust me by now," Ceci sighed, seeing no point in denying the truth.

"Can she?" Celeste pressed her.

"I guess not," Ceci felt bound to admit.

"Oh, Ceci," Celeste laughed. "You're incorrigible."

"So, I've been told," Ceci sighed again.

They stood back, satisfied with the arrangement.

"You put Mama's star up," Celeste noticed.

"I thought it only right," Ceci told her. "This is the first time, since you got married, that we've all been together for Christmas." She neglected to mention, that having everyone she loved around her only made her feel Trent's absence more acutely.

"You miss him very much, don't you?" It was the tone of Ceci's voice that prompted her sister's question.

"I feel like I got a big hole, right in the middle of my chest," she admitted dejectedly. "There's nothing I can do to fill it up. At least you fell in love with a man who lived nearby. Months pass before I see Trent, and then it's only for a few weeks at a time."

"I don't think we really choose who we fall in love with," Celeste suggested. "It just happens."

"It's that devil," Ceci scowled. "Ol' Magic."

"Now, that's Hecubah talking," Celeste recognised the reference.

"She's right though, ain't she?" Ceci insisted.

"I guess so," Celeste humoured her. "There's just no

accounting for who we fall for. You and Trent will be married soon," she reminded her. "Then, you can be with him all the time."

In her present state of mind, Ceci gained little consolation from the thought.

"I need a breath of air," Celeste decided. "Will you accompany me while I walk in the garden?"

"Now?" Ceci stared. "It'll be dark soon."

"Please," Celeste urged, taking her arm. "It'll do us both good. Take me on a tour of my old hunting grounds."

Celeste seemed bent on revisiting every foot of the garden. They were out there for almost an hour. Ceci didn't mind, too much. She was aware that women in Celeste's condition were often prone to strange fancies, and she was happy to indulge her.

"My my." Celeste paused halfway across the lawn. "I've broken so many hearts in this garden, there ought to be a monument erected."

Ceci stared into the twilight. All she could see, were the places she and Trent had frequented. It made her heart ache all the more.

"Do you feel it?" Celeste touched Ceci's arm. "He's still out here."

Ceci glanced around. "Who?"

"Why, Ol' Magic, of course," Celeste laughed. "He's still prowling around. He's already stung us both, but he don't want to go away."

"I can't think why he's still hanging around," Ceci remarked sullenly. "Not much I can do on my own."

"You ol' sourpuss," Celeste chided. "Perhaps, he knows something you don't."

"Then I hope he's wise enough to know," Ceci responded indignantly. "If I catch him. I'm going to kick his behind right out of this state."

"You can't blame him, for making you fall in love with

Trent," Celeste told her. "He just works with what you give him."

"Now, you're the one who sounds like Hecubah," Ceci pointed out. "She's right though, ain't she?" she nodded. "I guess we must have made it easy for him," she admitted. "Me and Trent together, and them blue eyes of his."

"I'm feeling a little fatigued," Celeste remarked. "Let's go back to the house."

They came in across the veranda, past the Christmas tree, pausing for one last look.

"I think I'll lay down for an hour, before supper," Celeste excused herself.

"You go on ahead," Ceci waved. "I think I'll stay here for a while." She stood, staring at the star on the tree, wondering if she dare wish for the thing she wanted most, but, even to her, the idea seemed futile.

"You messing with them presents again?" Hecubah asked, making her jump.

"No," she snapped. "And don't creep up on me, like that. It's disconcerting."

"I didn't think anyone was in here." Hecubah began to turn down the lamps. "What you doing, then? Wishing on that old wooden star?" she guessed. "It's probably wore out by now. Why not step onto the veranda, there's a big shiny new one rising, right over the bayou. That'll work much better."

"It's just a piece of nonsense," Ceci dismissed the idea.

"You saying I don't know what I'm talking about?" Hecubah challenged.

"No," Ceci faltered, startled by her attitude. "I ain't saying that."

"Wasn't I right about Ol' Magic?" Hecubah was unappeased.

"Yes, you were," Ceci blushed to admit it.

"Did you listen to me then?"

"No."

"Then, try listening to me now," she wagged a finger at her.

"All right, all right," Ceci gave in. "If it makes you happy."

She walked out onto the veranda and looked up into the twilight. A single star had begun to rise in the darkening sky. It shone so brightly, with such energy, she almost believed that Hecubah might be right. "This better not be one of Ol' Magic's tricks," she muttered, staring at the intense point of light.

She pulled herself up straight. Took a deep breath. Closed her eyes and wished with all her heart for what she wanted most. When she opened them again, nothing had changed. She rebuked herself for having been taken in. "There," she demanded, "are you happy now?"

"I am, if you are." A man's voice answered from behind her.

Startled, she turned. Trent was standing there.

She cast an incredulous glance, back across her shoulder, at the star and into the garden. She fancied, she could feel a presence lurking out there. In the distance, she thought she could hear Ol' Magic, laughing.

Chapter Eleven

Ceci's knees turned to jelly. She didn't dare put one foot in front of the other. Afraid, that if she tried to approach him, Trent would dissolve, like a soap bubble, and she'd wake up.

"Am I dreaming?" she asked eventually.

"Not unless I am," he told her. He crossed the room and put his arms around her.

Ceci laid her head on his chest. "How is this possible?" she asked, still unable to believe what was happening.

"I think it's what you call a conspiracy," he was happy to divulge. "Hecubah spoke to your father. He wrote to mine. As chivalrous men, they agreed there was a lady in distress. Then my father packed up his entire family and came to spend Christmas here. We arrived half an hour ago."

"So, that's why Celeste kept me in the garden for so long," Ceci realised.

"So you wouldn't hear the carriage drive up," Trent continued. All part of the conspiracy. Everyone knew about it, except you."

"I hate you all," Ceci sobbed.

"I know," Trent accepted casually. "By the way, Hecubah asked me to remind you. Christmas is all about surprises. Oh, and you're going to get that dress you asked for."

Ceci looked up at him. "Ain't you going to kiss me?" she asked.

"Not until you stop crying," he told her. "And I'm prepared to wait all night."

He only had to wait a few minutes. Finally, reluctantly, he unwrapped Ceci's arms from around his neck. "Everyone's in the salon," he told her. "My parents would like to see you. We shouldn't keep them waiting much longer."

Ceci took a moment to compose herself, as best she could, before allowing Trent to escort her into the salon, where everyone was enjoying a glass of eggnog.

"Ah, here they are at last," Colonel Sinclaire rose, inclining his head in a slight bow.

Ceci released Trent's arm and returned an elegant curtsey.

"Why, child, you look as though you've been crying," he observed. "Is anything the matter?"

"She's just been reunited with her betrothed," Mrs Sinclaire intervened. "That's enough to make any girl cry."

"You're right, of course," he nodded. "I understand".

"My, you're even more beautiful, than I remember," Mrs Sinclaire crossed the room and kissed her. "Don't they make a handsome couple, Colonel?"

"They certainly do," he agreed.

"Thank you all," Ceci addressed the entire gathering. "Thank you all so much for this wonderful surprise." She intended to say more but the lump in her throat silenced her.

"You see," Mrs Sinclaire observed. "We ladies always cry when we're happy."

Their guests had travelled a long way to be there and, after a light supper, everyone decided to retire early. Ceci was only just getting used to having Trent back again. Her mind was buzzing. She was too excited to sleep.

"Let's go into the garden," she suggested to Trent. "Just for a little while."

"I forgot how hot it is down here," he admitted, as they stepped out onto the veranda. "It's already started to snow in Boston, but it's still sixty degrees down here."

"That's why we southern girls are so hot blooded," Ceci smiled.

Trent took her in his arms. "Now, what's this I hear about all the fuss you've been making?"

"No, I ain't," Ceci attempted to deny it.

"Hecubah says different," he told her. "She says you've become impossible. Is it all this talk of secession that's worrying you?"

"I can't help it," she confessed, "it frightens me. It'll split us up. I'll never see you again."

He cupped her face in his hands. "No, it won't," he told her forcefully. "I don't care if there's a war between the states. I don't care if we end up on different sides. I don't care if this country goes up in flames, or the moon falls out of the sky. I will never stop loving you. If you love me as much as I think you do, then you'll believe me."

"What if there is a war?" she trembled. "What if you get killed?"

"So, that's what this is all about," he realised. "My life is in God's hands, same as yours, but for your sake, I swear I won't take any unnecessary risks, and you must believe that too." He sealed his pledge with a long kiss.

For once, Hecubah decided a discreet cough was in order. "Mr Trent, I put your folks in the east wing, along with Miss Celeste and her husband. That only leaves the room next to Ceci's, so I put you in there."

"That'd be the most practical solution," Ceci confirmed eagerly, compounding Hecubah's failure to mention that there were at least twelve other bed rooms in the house.

"Are you sure that's appropriate?" Trent felt that at least one of them should pay lip service to discretion.

"Why, that's mighty chivalrous of you," Hecubah commended. "But don't you think it's a little late to defend her honour?" She spared Ceci a thin smile. "I guess we all know, that ship's done sailed already."

"It's all right," Ceci assured him. "She does this to me all the time. She thinks it's funny."

"At least, this way, I'll always know where the pair of you are, come nightfall," Hecubah pointed out. "Instead of having to send a search party into the garden."

"There, you see?" Ceci reaffirmed. "I told you."

"I got plans of my own," Hecubah informed them. "So, I'll wish you both a Merry Christmas and a very good night," she emphasised, before leaving.

"I can show you your room now, if you'd like," Ceci offered, taking his hand. "I think I may have a surprise for you this time."

★★★

"This is my room and that's yours," Ceci pointed.

"Where's the surprise?" Trent wanted to know.

"It's coming," she assured him.

"Don't I even get a goodnight kiss?" he asked.

"Not yet," she teased. "Not until you go into your room."

"How's that going to work?" he frowned.

"You'll see," Ceci smiled. "Now go on."

She waited until he was inside, then dashed across her room, unlocked the connecting door and threw it open. "Surprise," she cried.

"I like it," he approved. "But they haven't even bothered to make the bed up in here," he gestured at the bare mattress.

"I guess Hecubah thought it'd be a waste of time," she shrugged.

"I mean, just for the look of the thing," he explained. "What if my parents come by?"

"Why, Mr Sinclaire," she purred seductively. "Are you going shy on me?"

"You know better than that," he reminded her. "But I dread to think what would happen to us if your father, or mine, discovered this arrangement."

Ceci didn't care. She hadn't seen Trent in months. She

loitered in the doorway, slowly unfastening her blouse, one button at a time. "My bed's made up," she breathed, her eyes large and enticing. "It's real comfortable. Unless, of course, you're too tired." She began to do up her blouse.

His eyes blazed. "Do I look tired to you?" he began to advance on her.

Ceci backed away, leading him on. "I guess I'll find out soon enough."

★★★

Christmas Day began early with breakfast on the veranda and continued with party games on the lawn. In the afternoon, they took jugs of cider and Christmas fancies to the slave quarters. Afterwards, they exchanged gifts and sang carols. The day flowed seamlessly by, lubricated with liberal quantities of fresh eggnog, heavily laced with brandy. In the evening, they sat down to a festive dinner of oysters and salmon, baked ham, roast beef and turkey, before returning to the parlour where they lit the candles on the tree. Celeste and Mrs Sinclaire took turns at the piano and everyone danced, in their fashion, until exhausted and mellow they paired off, or sat around in small groups and talked the night away.

"Is it my imagination, or is there something different about Hecubah today?" Trent asked, as they sat together in a window seat.

"She's wearing her hair down, is all," Ceci shrugged. "And she got a new dress too. Didn't say who from, just came down wearing it."

"That's not what I meant," he explained. "She kissed me this morning, on the lips, after I caught her singing to herself, and she hasn't scolded me once all day." He looked down at Ceci. "What happened to her?"

Ceci pressed herself closer to him. "Same thing that happened to me," she replied meaningfully.

His eyes widened. "You mean…"

Ceci nodded. "I think she and her mystery man shared a very special present last night."

"Which one?" he recalled that Ceci suspected that there were possibly two of them.

"It has to be the one who gave her the dress," she guessed.

Trent glanced over to where Hecubah, looking more radiant than he'd ever seen her, laughed and gossiped with Clay and Celeste. She caught him looking at her and gave a little wave. "No wonder she was so anxious to get away last night," he realised. "Are you sure?"

Ceci nodded again, returning the wave for him. "Same cologne. I almost gagged on it this morning. It was so familiar," she frowned. "I just couldn't put my finger on it. Whoever he is, he's somewhere close by."

"She still won't tell you his name?" Trent asked.

Ceci shook her head. "Tight as a clam."

"Does it still bother you?"

"No," Ceci smiled, "not any more. I'm just so happy for her."

Trent glanced across the room again. "She certainly does look happy," he agreed. "I hope her mood lasts through Christmas."

It was well after midnight before anyone thought of sleep. Ceci couldn't wait to get Trent into bed, but he had other ideas.

"There, I hope you're satisfied at last," she finished smoothing the sheets on his bed. "I've made up the bed and you've unpacked." She looked around. "Good, now it looks as though the room's fully occupied. It don't matter if your parents do come in."

"The bed doesn't look as though it's been slept in," he pointed out.

Ceci sighed, jumped on top of it and wriggled around. "Now it does," she told him, getting up.

He put his hand on her shoulder and pushed her back. "Seems a pity to waste it," he grinned rakishly.

Ceci narrowed her eyes at him. "Don't you dare crease my new dress," she warned.

He leaned closer. "Then take it off."

"What you going to do, if I don't?" she goaded.

He sat down on the bed, thrust his arm beneath her waist and dragged her across his lap, pinning her arms behind her back. "There, now your dress is out of the way," he told her, pulling it up over her hips. "Maybe I'll just slap your bottom for a while, until you change your mind."

"You wouldn't dare." Ceci struggled.

It was a full ten minutes, before he let her go.

"You didn't have to do it so hard," Ceci pouted, letting her dress fall to the floor and rubbing her behind with both hands. "I'll be sore right into tomorrow."

Trent was unrepentant. "Next time, do what I tell you," he remarked assertively. He picked her up and dropped her back onto the bed. "You got what you asked for."

"Oh, is that what you think?" she fumed.

"Certainly," he replied with conviction. "I didn't crease your dress, did I?"

★★★

Ceci's sore behind only lasted a few hours, but she was already painfully aware that Trent's visits were few and far between and that the days she spent with him were fleeting. Christmas was no exception. Despite all the assurances she received to the contrary, she still couldn't rid herself of the feeling that this time would be the last time. The thought of it tormented her constantly, giving rise to a mood that compelled her to cram him into every minute she had left. Having Celeste and her unborn baby so close, only served to exacerbate the situation. She ached to be married.

"Trent and Clay are becoming good friends," Celeste observed, as Ceci sat beside her on the veranda the next day.

The two men strolled across the lawn, deep in conversation.

Ceci laid her hand on Celeste's swollen stomach. "What's it like?" she asked. "Knowing you're going to have a baby?"

"It's the most wonderful thing in the world," she assured her.

Ceci glanced away for a moment. "Do you remember Mama?"

"I was only four when she passed away," Celeste reminded her.

"What was she like?" Ceci asked anyway.

"You've seen the painting in Daddy's study."

"I know, but that's just a picture," Ceci persisted. "What was she really like?"

"Oh, she was beautiful and spirited," Celeste searched her memory. "I favour Daddy, but you look a lot like her."

"She died the night I was born," Ceci recalled.

Celeste put her hand under Ceci's chin, turning her face towards her. "That was God's will," she advised her gently. "He wanted you in the world and Mama's time had come."

"Don't it make you afraid?" Ceci wondered. "About having babies, I mean?"

"No," Celeste was adamant, "it's what God made us to do. I love Clay with all my heart. This is his child and I'm proud to be its mother. When my time comes to bring a new life into the world, I will put my faith in the doctor and God's mercy." Celeste allowed Ceci a moment of quiet contemplation, before she spoke again. "I'm wondering why you ain't asked me the obvious question."

"What question?"

Celeste raised an eyebrow. "What you do to make a baby."

Ceci's eyes widened. "I couldn't possibly ask questions like that," she blustered.

"Not the least bit curious?" Celeste persisted. "Now why would that be?"

"Stop it," Ceci buried her face in her hands.

"Why, Cecile Prejean," Celeste tapped her arm. "I see it all now. I believe you are a fallen woman."

"You can talk," Ceci retorted, trusting her hands into her lap, her cheeks scarlet. "What about all them boys you used to run around with. Don't tell me you never dipped your toe in the water before you finally decided to take the plunge."

"Only with Clay," she didn't bother to deny it. "After I decided he was the one. Did Hecubah make you drink that awful potion?"

Ceci nodded, "Vile, ain't it? Worth it though."

"Saved my reputation more than once," Celeste admitted.

"Dear Lord," Ceci pressed the back of her hand to her face. "I swear you could fry bacon on my cheeks. I wouldn't be surprised if the men could see me glowing from all the way over there."

They looked out to where Trent and Clay stood talking in the distance. They glanced up and waved.

"You see," Celeste leaned into Ceci, indicating Clay. "A real southern gentleman. Looks like butter wouldn't melt in his mouth, but once he's in the bedroom..." she paused suggestively.

"Then what?" Ceci prompted, all agog.

"Like a wild animal," she mouthed at her.

"I'd never have imagined," Ceci gasped, clasping a hand to her breast, staring at the hapless man whose character they took such delight in assassinating.

"What about Trent?" Celeste was eager to know.

Ceci gazed across the lawn at him, sighing heavily.

"I know that feeling," Celeste sounded impressed. "I'll tell you another thing," she whispered in Ceci's ear. "When you're pregnant, it just keeps getting better and better."

Ceci's mouth fell open. "You don't say," she shivered.

Celeste flicked open her fan and fluttered it in front of her face. "All this talk is heating my blood," she confessed.

"I'm going back into the house and find myself a cool glass of lemonade."

Ceci chewed her lip, unable to take her eyes off Trent. "I guess I'd better go down to the bayou," she muttered to herself. "And throw myself in."

Chapter Twelve

Ceci didn't throw herself in the bayou, but perhaps she should have done. The nature of her conversation with Celeste stayed with her all day. It obsessed her every thought, further enflaming her mood. That night Trent took the brunt of it.

"Let's do it again," she panted insatiably, crouching over him and pinning him to the bed.

"Straight away?" he stared in astonishment. "There's only so much flesh and blood can stand. What's got into you?"

"Only you," she tightened her grip on him.

"Oh, now I remember," he recalled. "I saw you talking to Celeste this morning. What's she been telling you?"

"Nothing I didn't know already," she flashed her eyes at him.

"Did you two compare my performance to Clay's," he guessed.

"What if we did?" she dug her nails into his shoulders.

"Are you trying to kill me?" he winced.

Ceci wasn't about to take no for an answer. "At least you'll die happy," she told him.

When they came down to breakfast, in the morning, Celeste and Mrs Sinclaire were already at the table. Ceci bounced in, full of the joys of life, whilst Trent seemed tired and somewhat out of sorts.

"What's the matter, son?" his mother enquired, with concern. "You look a little peaked. Did you have a hard night?"

Ceci and Celeste began to snigger.

"Did I say something funny?" Mrs Sinclaire asked.

"No, Mother," Trent did his best to ignore them. "I think I'm missing the army."

Celeste looked at Ceci, raising an inquisitive eyebrow.

Ceci held up three fingers.

Celeste's eyes widened. "Careful honey," she whispered. "You don't want to kill him before the wedding."

The passage of time was relentless, steadily eroding the days she had left with Trent. She raged against it, as if it were an unjust penalty, an exorbitantly high price she was constantly forced to pay for just a few moments happiness. What made it worse was all the uncertainty that surrounded her. She thought she might feel better, if she could only find out what was truly going on.

There were two influential men in the house, her father and Colonel Sinclaire, as well as Trent and Clay. They had discussed everything under the sun, but none of them had ever touched upon what was happening in the country. Doubtless, it was a matter of courtesy, not to raise a contentious subject, but their reticence only served to frustrate and infuriate her. Finally, she decided to take matters into her own hands and, that night at dinner, she put the question directly to Colonel Sinclaire.

"Is there going to be a war between the states?" she blurted across the table.

The room fell silent.

"Cecile," her father cautioned, "now is not the time."

"No, no," Colonel Sinclaire disagreed, ever indulgent where Ceci was concerned. "She has a right to be concerned about her future." He looked directly at her. "I can tell you that there are a great many men arguing for division, but there are also other men, like myself and your father, who are constantly seeking a peaceful settlement. More than that is impossible to say now. However, I give you my word, as an officer and a gentleman, that no matter what happens, you will always be welcome as a member of my family." He looked away, addressing the entire gathering. "At times, like this," he suggested, "we must rely on courage and faith. Courage in the face of adversity, and faith in the belief that this situation will resolve itself in time."

That night it was a rather subdued Ceci that lay in Trent's arms. "Did I make a fool of myself tonight?" she asked.

"Of course not," he reassured her. "But you're asking for answers no one has now."

"We've only two days left," she reminded him.

"We've discussed this already," he told her firmly. "You always knew I'd have to leave again. We all will. My father has his business and I have my duties. It'll only be a few months before we're together again. Try and be patient for just a little longer."

Patience was a virtue Ceci seldom aspired to. "Take me with you," she pleaded.

"Oh, Ceci, I only wish I could," he sighed. "But I think your father would shoot me, and if he didn't, I know mine certainly would."

"I found some more books in the library," she thought it worth mentioning. "Even Hecubah don't know about them." She pressed herself closer against him. "You'd shoot yourself, if you knew what you were missing."

★★★

Another day fell off the calendar. The old year was dying. After dinner, they all gathered in the parlour once more to welcome the new year in. As Ceci considered each and every smiling face, that awful feeling, that this time was the last time, reasserted itself. There was no accounting for it. It was just an impression she had.

It hung, like a pall over the gathering. She hated it. She hated herself for thinking it. The premonitions might have plagued her all night, if Trent hadn't come to the rescue.

At a quarter to the hour, he rose, took Ceci by the hand and drew her into the centre of the room. As everyone watched, he drew a small black box from his pocket. "Ceci, I have something else for you," he told her. "I didn't give it to you at Christmas, because it's not that kind of a gift." He opened the box and took out a gold ring, encrusted with diamonds. He lifted Ceci's hand and slipped it onto her finger. "With this engagement ring," he continued earnestly. "I pledge you my life and my love. As the new year dawns, it will be our year. The year we will be married."

Ceci stared at the ring, speechless.

"I hope you like it," he continued hesitantly, a little concerned over her silence. "Mother helped me choose it, after she kicked me in the behind for not thinking of it in the first place."

Ceci promptly broke down in a flood of tears. Hecubah came over and drew her aside, while the rest of the women clustered around her, all wanting to see the ring.

Trent looked at his mother, a puzzled frown creasing his brow. "I thought it would make her happy," he told her.

She put her hand on his arm. "It has, Son," she smiled. "Can't you see? It has."

Trent looked at Ceci. She was still crying. So was Celeste now and Hecubah had just started. He turned to his father. "Do you understand women?" he asked.

Colonel Sinclaire shook his head. "No," he shrugged philosophically. "There's no understanding them, Son. You just love them, that's all."

Ceci recovered just in time to toast the new year in. Trent raised his glass to her. "To us," he smiled, his blue eyes washing over her, like ocean waves.

Ceci couldn't bear to share such a special moment with anyone but him. "Take me into the garden," she entreated.

As more champagne corks began to pop, they excused

themselves from the party and stepped outside.

"Look," Ceci pointed, "it's a crescent moon, just like the one we first made love under."

"How could I ever forget," he replied, taking her hand.

Ceci turned and looked at him. "Let's go to our secret place," she suggested.

"There's an awful lot of people back there," he nodded at the house. "Some of them might come out."

"I don't mean for that," she clarified her intention. "I just want to be alone with you there, one more time, before we're married."

Happy to indulge her, he followed her through the shadows, across the garden and down to their secret place. They sat on the bank of the bayou, arms around each other, gazing up at the moon. All around them crickets hummed and bullfrogs called from the reed beds, as the emerald waters of the Atchafalaya flowed gently by.

"I think this is what Heaven must be like," Ceci sighed.

"I can't imagine Heaven with bullfrogs," Trent replied.

"I'm sure they have souls to," she decided. "They have to go somewhere when they die."

"I thought they just sank to the bottom of the river," he teased.

"Stop that," she admonished him.

He pulled her closer to him, kissing her lips, drawing her gently down onto the grass.

She pressed her hands against his chest, holding him back. "There's an awful lot of people up there," she reminded him of his own words. "Some of them might come out."

This time it was Trent who wouldn't take no for an answer. "If Hecubah can't find this place," he persisted. "I doubt anyone else will."

"You're forgetting," she continued to resist him, waving the engagement ring in front of his face. "I'm an engaged woman now."

He brushed her hand aside, pushing her down to the ground. "Never stopped you before," he recalled.

★★★

They had celebrated Christmas together and toasted the new year in. Now the time had come for them to go their separate ways. The fact that everyone was leaving at the same time as Trent, softened the blow for Ceci, but it was a blow nonetheless. They assembled in the salon to say their farewells, exchanging hugs and kisses, each pair discreetly withdrawing from the room, until Ceci and Trent were left conveniently alone.

Ceci suspected it was another, albeit, minor, conspiracy contrived by her family, but there was nothing she could do about it now. There were only a few things that could put her into an obstinate frame of mind, not getting her own way was one of them. She desperately wanted Trent to stay, or take her with him. Neither of which were going to happen, at least, not this time.

Without a word, Trent took her hand and walked over to an armchair. He sat down, perching her on his knee.

"I ain't a baby," she objected moodily.

He put his arms around her waist, settling her on his lap. "Of course, you are," he dismissed her meagre protest.

Ceci hadn't the will to argue.

"Now, what did we agree?" he asked.

Ceci remained silent, hands clenched in her lap, refusing to look at him.

He put his hand under her chin and turned her head round. "Well?" he persisted quietly.

Ceci heaved a huge sigh. "I ain't going to worry. I aint going to panic," she recited tonelessly. "I'll eat properly and sleep well."

"And?" he prompted gently.

Ceci sighed again. "And I ain't going to drive Hecubah crazy."

"She particularly asked me to remind you of that," he told her. He leaned forward, his cheek brushing hers. "Now, we both know none of that's going to happen," he deduced correctly, "but I have an idea that might help."

His remark peaked Ceci's interest. She began to pay attention.

He took the picture she'd had made for him from his breast pocket. "From now on," he explained, "no matter where I am or what I'm doing, I shall look at your picture each evening at nine o'clock, and think only of you. If you do the same, it won't feel as if we're so far apart."

Ceci nodded. It was little enough, but better than nothing.

"What are we going to do now?" he asked softly.

Ceci's face lit up. "We could sneak out the back door, find the nearest minister, and get married," she deviated wildly from the plan they'd discussed.

Trent was determined to be patient with her. He waited.

Ceci's shoulders slumped. "I'm going to say goodbye to you," she sighed again, reluctantly returning to the plan. "I'm going to behave like a lady, conducting myself with dignity and composure, as befits the future wife of an officer. I'm going to make you proud."

"I'm sure you will," he encouraged her.

They shared a kiss that was the sweetest Ceci had ever tasted. She clung to him, wanting it to go on forever, but, in the end, she had to let him go.

★★★

"Imagine," Celeste smiled, as she prepared to leave. "The next time I say goodbye to you on these steps, you'll be a married woman."

Ceci caught her breath, a pang of anxiety clutching at her

heart, afraid that her sister's words might tempt providence, but she made light of it. "Next time," she placed her hand on Celeste's bulge. "You'll be carrying that in your arms."

"I never had a daughter before," Mrs Sinclaire told her. "I'm so glad it's going to be you."

"Remember, child," Colonel Sinclaire took her hand and touched his lips against it, the soft strands of his moustache brushing her fingers. "Courage and faith. Trent's a good man. He won't let you down."

She put her hands on his shoulders, reached up and kissed his cheek. Then she turned to face Trent.

For a moment, she just stood there, drinking him in, wondering if she could, by some superhuman effort of will, hold him there. Transfix this moment in time, so that they might remain together forever, realising, even as she considered it, that if time stood still, what would be the point.

She ran over to him, threw her arms around his waist, crushing him to her, until he gasped. "Come back to me," she sobbed. "Whatever happens, please come back to me."

He cupped her face in his hands, looking down at her. "You know I will," he promised. "Even if the moon falls from the sky."

The blue of his eyes matched Heaven's vault. Her soul took flight, tumbling through eternity, until the touch of his lips brought her back to earth. He eased himself away from her and, after a last lingering look, climbed into the carriage.

As they started down the drive, Ceci clenched her left hand into a fist, digging her fingernails into the palm and continued to wave with her right. She even managed to smile, but as soon as they had driven out of sight, she dashed up to her room, locked the door, and cried all day. She would have cried all night, if Hecubah hadn't threatened to call Joshua and break the door down.

★★★

To her surprise, Ceci discovered that Trent's idea worked better than she'd imagined. Each evening at nine o'clock, she looked at his picture, knowing that he was looking at hers, and for a few moments each day, it didn't feel as if they were far apart at all. Sometimes, she'd count the months off on her fingers. There was some of January, all of February and March, and most of April. She drew solace from the fact that it was only four fingers.

Courage and faith, Colonel Sinclaire had said. She took his words to heart. They strengthened her. Every day that passed was one less day to wait. Gradually, the pain of separation eased. Her impatience was replaced by optimism and she began to look to the future with a renewed sense of excitement.

★★★

Trent had only been gone a week, before Mississippi followed South Carolina and seceded from the Union. It continued right through the month with Florida, Alabama and Georgia. The southern states shedding from the Union, like autumn leaves falling from a great tree. January was almost spent, before Louisiana, her home state, joined the others in secession.

She didn't share the elation her compatriots displayed. All she felt was an overwhelming sense of isolation and foreboding. The unthinkable had happened. The Union had torn itself apart. She began to wonder if courage and faith would be enough to sustain her now.

Chapter Thirteen

"The southern states are in rebellion," Ceci read aloud. "Does that make me a rebel?" she asked, looking up from the newspaper.

"Honey, you was that long before anyone thought of secession," Hecubah told her.

"I'm serious," Ceci insisted. "I want to know what's going on. All these papers are saying different things. Mostly they contradict each other."

"That's the trouble with opinion," Hecubah advised her. "Depends on who you talk to."

"I had hoped Trent would mention something about it in his letters," Ceci continued, a hint of disappointment in her voice.

"What does he say?" Hecubah asked.

"Only that he loves and misses me."

"Nothing else?"

"No," Ceci blushed.

"Ah huh, so he's still writing them kind of letters," she divined. "That boy should have been an author. I'd like to see one of them on the front page of the newspaper. That'd sure as hell, start a war."

"My point is," Ceci pressed on, anxious to change the subject. "He's a soldier, he must know something. Maybe he don't want to give that kind of information to a southerner."

Hecubah stared at her. "Girl, when you stood in line for beauty, didn't you notice there was a queue for brains?"

"What'd you mean?" Ceci stiffened at the effrontery.

"I mean," Hecubah continued pointedly. "Of course, he ain't gonna tell you anything, because he knows it makes you crazy. Do you imagine he sees you as some kind of threat now? You is a young woman, barely twenty, head full of love and marriage. What you gonna do, attack Washington singlehanded?"

"I just wondered, is all," Ceci blustered indignantly.

Hecubah shook her head. "Sometimes I'm tempted to drop you in ol' Abe's lap. That'd sure put an end to this nonsense. That man'd break his arm trying to resign."

"I ain't that bad," Ceci protested.

"Like I told you before," Hecubah reminded her. "That's the trouble with opinion."

★★★

"Ain't you ready yet?" Hecubah called. "The buggy's bin waiting half an hour. We got an appointment in town with Armenia Ewing and her daughters for the first fitting of your wedding dress. They may be the best seamstresses in Louisiana, but they sure do take their time. So, if you don't want to walk down the aisle in your drawers, you'd best get a move on."

"I'm coming, I'm coming," Ceci dashed down the stairs, waving a newspaper. "Have you seen this?" she asked breathlessly, shoving it under Hecubah's nose. "Texas seceded from the Union last week. That makes seven states now."

Hecubah snatched the paper from her hand and threw it on the hall table. "If I hears one more word about secession outa you," she glared. "I swear you aint gonna live long enough to get married."

"Ain't you worried?" Ceci frowned.

115

"What good would it do, if I was," Hecubah told her. "Wouldn't change nothing. Unless you imagine all them senators and congressmen are gonna get together and say. Oh my, Hecubah is worried, let's put a stop to all this."

"There's no need to be sarcastic," Ceci glowered.

Hecubah drew a deep breath. "Have you got your gloves?"

"Yes." Ceci showed her.

"And your parasol?"

"It's right here."

"What about your hat?"

Ceci chewed her lip. "I left it upstairs."

"Remembered the newspaper though, didn't you?" Hecubah pointed out. "I've a good mind to make you wear that into town."

***

Secession seemed to be the only topic on anyone's mind, judging from what they saw and heard, as they drove down the main street. Every store window had a banner in it, proclaiming Louisiana's independence from the Union.

"What's that?" Ceci pointed, as they entered the town square.

A new flag flew from the mast outside the telegraph office. It had a red square in the top left-hand corner, with a yellow star in the centre of it, the rest was red white and blue horizontal stripes.

"Where's our old Pelican flag?" she wondered.

"I don't know," Hecubah admitted, "but I bet Armenia does. She lives right here in town. She knows everything that's going on."

Hecubah was right. Armenia and her daughters were full of the news.

"It's our new state flag," she told them, through a mouth full of pins. "Since we declared our independence from the

Union, it's the only one we're going to fly. Don't fidget, honey."

Ceci did her best to stand still. It was difficult perched on a foot stool, with yards of silk and lace wrapped around her. "Have all the states done that?" she asked.

"I reckon they have," Elizabeth, Armenia's eldest daughter, confirmed, holding up the hem of the dress so that her mother could pin it. "Just yesterday, representatives from all the seceded states met in Montgomery, Alabama and created the Confederate States of America."

"The Confederate States of America," Ceci repeated in amazement.

"That's right," Sara, Armenia's second daughter, confirmed, as she busied herself with a sleeve. "Now we got our own government, even named Jefferson Davis to be President."

"They said they would," Ceci recalled what she'd overheard her father discussing. "I met him once. My daddy said he was a hero of the Mexican war."

Armenia leaned back on her knees. Satisfied that the hem was straight, she took the last of the pins out of her mouth. "We'll need a strong leader," she told them. "Lincoln and Congress don't recognise our right to leave the Union. There'll be trouble over that, mark my words. Step down, honey. Let's see how it hangs."

Ceci stepped off the stool. Even only half finished, the dress looked magnificent.

"Turn around, honey," Armenia directed. "That's coming along just fine," she seemed happy with her efforts so far. "You know," she turned to Hecubah. "Since Victoria, the Queen of England, got married in white, all the girls want it now."

"Ain't it supposed to represent chastity?" Hecubah asked.

"I guess so," Armenia shrugged, "virgin white."

"In that case, perhaps you should sew some little blue flowers onto it," Hecubah suggested, glancing at Ceci.

Ceci narrowed her eyes at her, itching to reply, knowing she had to hold her tongue in company.

Gasps of dismay came from the Ewing's. "Now why on earth would you want us to do that?" Armenia asked in surprise. "It looks beautiful the way it is. Just like the girl who's going to wear it," she smiled at Ceci.

Ceci did her best to look innocent, despite her blushes.

"One more fitting, or two, Mama?" Elizabeth asked, helping Ceci out of the dress.

"Two, I think," Armenia judged. "I believe Ceci is beginning to lose a little weight. There's bound to be more adjustments."

"You must be so excited," Sara helped Ceci back into her own dress. "Have you set a date for the wedding yet?"

"April 30th," Ceci told her. "I intend to invite you all. You will come, won't you?"

Cries of elation echoed round the room.

"I love weddings," Elizabeth sighed dreamily. "I like them better than dancing."

★★★

"Did you hear that Elizabeth Ewing?" Hecubah remarked, as they drove back to the plantation. "I love weddings. I like them better than dancing." She shook her head. "That girl should stick to dancing. The closest she's ever gonna get to a wedding is yours. God almighty, I never seen a plainer pair of girls than Armenia Ewing's daughters."

"That's cruel," Ceci chided. "So was suggesting they sew blue flowers on my dress."

"You heard them," Hecubah reminded her. "White's supposed to be for chastity. Don't reckon Queen Victoria was chasing Albert round the garden before she got married."

"You don't know that," Ceci pouted. "Besides, it's the thought that counts. Don't you ever get tired of making fun of me?"

"Not hardly," Hecubah was happy to admit. "Let's face it, when you're married, I'll have to think of some other way to amuse myself."

★★★

"All the invitations have been sent out," Hecubah drew a line through another item on her list. "The dress is almost ready," she paused, glancing at Ceci. "You sure you don't want them blue flowers on it?"

"That wasn't funny when you said it a month ago," Ceci complained.

"Just checking," Hecubah continued casually. "Your daddy's spoken to the minister, and in a couple of weeks, we'll begin to decorate the ballroom." She set the list aside. "I guess I don't have to give you the bride talk, do I?"

"The bride talk?" Ceci stared. "What's that?"

"It's what a mother would pass on to her daughter," Hecubah explained. "About what's expected of a new wife on her wedding night, and her duties to her husband. A lot of young girls get mighty nervous about it, as the time gets close, but I guess you done jumped that hurdle already."

"Oh," Ceci sighed. "You just had to say it, didn't you?"

"Is there anything you wanna know?" Hecubah enquired soberly.

"Well," Ceci began hesitantly. "How will I know, if I'm going to have a baby?"

"You planning to get off to an early start?" Hecubah wondered.

"I just want to know, is all," Ceci persisted.

"You'll miss your flow, and you'll start getting sick in the morning. Then you'll know," Hecubah told her. "It's not happening already, is it?"

"Of course, not," Ceci cried indignantly. "You saw to that." She calmed down. "But it will, one day," she promised herself.

Hecubah reached out and stroked Ceci's cheek. "To think," she murmured, "that in a few weeks' time, you'll be Mrs Trent Sinclaire. Then you'll be off to start your new life with him, in Boston. Lord, girl," she sighed heavily, "I'm gonna miss you so much."

"I thought I made you crazy," Ceci reminded her.

"Not that crazy, child," Hecubah admitted, on the verge of tears.

"There's so much I want to say to you," Ceci hugged her. "But I can't find the words."

"You don't have to, honey," Hecubah assured her. "I already know."

"Are you sure you won't reconsider?" Ceci asked. "About coming to live with us, I mean."

"I done told you," Hecubah sighed. "My place is here. Besides, you won't want me under foot. You'll be the lady of the house, with your own home to run, just like I showed you."

"It's him, ain't it?" Ceci deduced. "The reason you're staying. It's him. Your gentleman. The mystery man. The one who gave you that dress for Christmas. I'm right. I know it. That's only the second time I've ever seen you blush."

"What if it is?" Hecubah shrugged dismissively.

"You going to tell me his name now?"

"No."

"Can I try and guess then?"

"No."

"I'll find out one day. You know that, don't you?"

"Maybe," Hecubah agreed. "But it ain't gonna be today."

★★★

Evening was Ceci's favourite time to be in the garden. The scents, the sounds and the soft colours had always enchanted her, even as a child. She stood on the edge of the veranda, gazing out across the acres of immaculate lawn. At the magnolias, lilac, and clumps of jasmine and honeysuckle, winding sinuously along paved walks which crossed the lawns, that stretched all the way down to the bayou. To the banks of the Atchafalaya. She'd wanted to be with Trent so much, she'd never considered what she'd be giving up.

Everything she'd hoped for was only weeks away. She knew she should be happy, but now she felt a twinge of panic, a hint of last minute nerves. This was her home. She'd spent her whole life here. Everything she knew was here. The garden, the plantation, her father, and Hecubah. Hecubah, mother, sister, friend, she was all of those. Ceci vaguely recalled a succession of nursemaids and nannies. Indifferent women, who had told her to eat up her dinner, or go to bed on time, paying her little more attention than that. Then Hecubah had come, and everything had changed. Whenever she acted unwisely, or behaved poorly, Hecubah was always there to set her straight. She wondered, desperately, how she would ever cope without her guidance and her humour.

Even as she thought it, she sensed a familiar presence in the garden. The night breeze blew towards her, caressing her cheek, like a soft hand. It reminded her of what the future held, assuring her that this would always be here, and that she would never forget it.

She thought of Trent, his arms around her, his gentle smile and those blue eyes. Suddenly, she felt strong and confident again. She stared into the twilight, but there was nothing to see, except the shifting shadows in the garden and the silhouettes of the cypress trees in the bayou. At last, she realised that Ol' Magic wasn't out there. He wasn't in the garden, and he never had been. He came from within, and that she, like every other man and woman who had loved before her, had invoked him with their heart. No matter where she went with Trent, he would always be there. Nevertheless, she pressed her palm to her lips and blew a kiss into the empty air. "Thanks for everything," she smiled.

★★★

"I declare, Ceci," Armenia Ewing stared at the tape measure. "You've lost a full inch off your waist since the last fitting." She looked at Hecubah. "Don't you feed this child?"

"It's wedding nerves, that's all." Hecubah told her.

"C'mon girls," Armenia clapped her hands at her daughters. "We got some work to do."

Ceci found herself perched on the foot stool again, as the three women toiled at the fabric of the wedding dress, unpicking and restitching with such vigour, she feared she'd end up with the dress sewn to her skin. "What's been happening between the states?" she asked, if only to take her mind off the darting needles.

Armenia looked up in surprise, needle poised. "Don't you read the papers, honey?"

"Hecubah keeps hiding them from me," Ceci told her. "She says reading them only worries me."

"Well, I can see the sense in that," Armenia agreed, as she sewed a line of thread. "Not much to tell though."

"Lincoln was inaugurated on Tuesday," Sara reminded her, squinting as she threaded another needle.

"There's more than that," Elizabeth joined in, deftly snipping at a piece of lace. "The Confederacy has been seizing Union property on Confederate land. Now they've issued an ultimatum to Congress to evacuate all Union troops from Fort Sumter."

"That's nothing new," Armenia grunted with concentration. "Ever since South Carolina seceded, they been itching to get their hands on Charleston Harbour."

"What if they don't want to go?" Ceci asked.

"Who, honey?" Armenia remarked distractedly.

"The Union troops," Ceci elaborated. "What if they

refuse to leave Fort Sumter. What happens then?"

As one, Armenia and her daughters stopped sewing, and just stared at each other. This time they had no answers. It was anyone's guess…

Chapter Fourteen

"You still playing with that wedding dress?" Hecubah sighed, as she came in.

Ceci stood in front of the mirror, holding the dress against herself. "I can't help it," she admitted. "I can hardly believe, that in a few weeks, I'll be wearing this, as I walk down the aisle on my daddy's arm, with Trent waiting for me. I'm so excited, I could burst."

"Your daddy would like to talk to you," Hecubah revealed the reason for her being there.

"About the wedding?" Ceci wondered.

"Yes, child. It's about the wedding." For once, Hecubah didn't seem to share her enthusiasm. "It's important," she urged, "let's not keep him waiting."

Ceci followed her down to her father's day room, still happily preoccupied with the coming events. "Morning Daddy," she ran around his desk, put her hand on his shoulder and kissed him. "You wanted to see me?" Her smile faded. He seemed so serious and contemplative. "Is something wrong?" she asked nervously.

He patted her hand, returning a humourless smile. "Sit down, Cecile," he gestured at the chairs in front of his desk.

She did as he asked. Hecubah sat next to her. Ceci began to sense an atmosphere in the room, cold and austere. It filled her with trepidation. "What's happened?" she asked. "Is it

Trent?" she began to panic.

"No, honey," Hecubah was quick to reassure her. "Trent's fine. Just listen to your daddy."

For a moment, her father sat rubbing his chin, deep in thought, then he drew a deep breath. "A week ago, our troops attacked and captured Fort Sumter," he began gravely. "Abraham Lincoln has responded by citing it as an act of insurrection. He has raised 75,000 volunteers to supress the rebellion." He paused, shaking his head. "I never thought I'd see the day when an American President assembled an army to attack his own country."

"Does that mean we're at war?" Ceci began to tremble.

"Yes," her father replied flatly, "I'm afraid it does." He picked up a letter. "I received this from Colonel Sinclaire, today," he continued. "Trent has been called to active service. He will not be able to return here for the foreseeable future."

It was as if one of Armenia Ewing's needles had been thrust through her heart. Ceci felt her whole body go numb. The information slid off her mind. She didn't want to believe it. "No," she began to sob, "It can't be true. It's a mistake. I've been getting letters from Trent every day. He didn't say anything about this."

"I told you before," Hecubah reminded her. "He didn't want to worry you. Now things have changed."

"He ain't coming back," Ceci stared down into her lap, hands clenched together. "There ain't going to be a wedding."

Her father rose from behind his desk, hands raised in a calming gesture. "Take it easy, Cecile," he advised. "Flying into a panic won't help anything." He reached for the decanter at the corner of his desk, and poured a large glass of amber liquid, which he passed to Hecubah.

"Drink this, honey," she offered the glass to Ceci.

"What is it?" Ceci pulled her head away.

"It's brandy," Hecubah told her. "It'll settle your nerves."

"I don't want it," Ceci leaned further back.

"Drink it," Hecubah insisted forcefully, pulling her head round and pressing the glass to her lips.

Ceci opened her mouth to raise a further objection, only to have it filled with brandy. Instinctively, she swallowed. It burned her throat. The fumes went up her nose, making her eyes water. "You trying to drown me?" she spluttered.

"Colonel Sinclaire goes on to say," her father consulted the letter again. "That, despite what has happened, he still welcomes you as a member of his family, and that Trent will honour his pledge to marry you, subject to the cessation of hostilities."

"What does that mean?" Ceci was distraught, confused and just a little tipsy.

"After the war, honey," Hecubah clarified. "There's still gonna be a wedding. It's just postponed."

"Trent put a note in with Colonel Sinclaire's letter," her father went on, offering a folded page across the desk. "He didn't want you to read it before I'd had a chance to prepare you."

Hecubah took it from him and passed it into Ceci's trembling hands. Hardly daring to breath, she opened and began to read.

"My own sweet Ceci," it began. "I cannot express to you what is in my heart, because it is broken, as I know yours has just been. I would give anything to be there with you now, but fate has decreed otherwise and we must wait again. Remember, we are still young and time is on our side. Believe me when I tell you that the moon has not fallen from the sky, and we will be together again someday. I pray to God that it is soon."

Tears dripped from Ceci's eyes, splashing the page, smudging the ink, sending it into little black rivulets.

"I think of you constantly," the letter continued. "I will write as often as I can, although the war may stop the mail. If you don't hear from me, don't worry. I have no concerns for my own safety. My only fears are for you. I beg you to stay safe at home with your father and Hecubah until I can return to you. I live for that day, as I know you do. Forever, Trent."

As she finished reading, Ceci felt her whole world crumble. All her hopes and dreams faded away, to be replaced by her worst imaginings. The letter slipped from her fingers. She put her face in her hands and wept.

"I'm so sorry," her father came over and put his arm around her. "I wish it could have been different."

"We were so close," Ceci sniffed. "Just another few weeks."

"I know," he kissed her forehead. "Just remember, it isn't over, only postponed. Try and hang onto that."

Ceci felt limp and drained. All she could do was nod.

"Let me take you back to your room," Hecubah offered, putting a hand under her arm. "You need to lay down."

Ceci collapsed onto the bed, oceans of tears pouring down her cheeks. "I don't want to live anymore," she cried, pressing her face into Hecubah's breast.

"I know, honey," Hecubah did her best to console her. "But you will. Not just for yourself, but for Trent as well."

"He didn't say much," Ceci recalled tearfully. "It might be his last letter to me and that's all he said."

"I believe he said as much as he could manage," Hecubah told her. "Just imagine how he feels."

"You're right," Ceci pressed a hand to her eyes. "I'm being selfish. He has to be as devastated as I am."

"I don't doubt it, honey," Hecubah agreed. "You gotta be strong for both of you now. Write to him. Tell him you understand and you'll wait for him. That'll give him courage."

"If the war stops the mail, he won't get my letter," Ceci fretted.

"You just keep writing," Hecubah advised calmly. "One of them will get through."

Ceci rallied a little, managing a weak smile. "Still got the wedding dress," she remembered.

"And a groom," Hecubah added. "Even if he has been

delayed. All the invitations have been sent out. All we gotta do now, is tell the guests to wait, just like we is doing. Let's hope it ain't for too long."

Ceci managed another brave smile, but the seeds of doubt had already been planted in her. Seeds that found themselves in fertile ground.

★★★

The attack on Fort Sumter signalled an escalation of intent, which could not go unanswered. Virginia seceded to the Confederacy, followed by Arkansas, Tennessee and North Carolina, until eleven southern states stood in defiance of the Union. One side fought for its independence, the other for the preservation of the Union. They agreed on only one thing. The outcome was in God's hands.

★★★

All but oblivious to what was going on around her, Ceci tried to make the best of things since the postponement of her wedding. It was, after all, she realised, merely an event, which could be rescheduled. It was the thought of losing Trent. The possibility of his being killed in the war. The thought that she might never see him again, that constantly tormented her mind. She couldn't live with it. She couldn't rid herself of it. Finally, she isolated it in her heart, like a pearl in an oyster, and carried on despite it.

She resigned herself to waiting. For months, for years, if need be. She made a truce between her mind and her heart, after that, she knew a kind of peace, but, occasionally, the truce was broken.

"It's almost noon," Hecubah addressed the heap of blankets in the middle of Ceci's bed. "Ain't you ever gonna get up?"

"No." A shapeless form twitched slightly, pulling the blankets closer around it.

"Why not?" Hecubah asked, with the utmost restraint.

"You know what day it is today?" a disembodied voice asked.

"Ah huh," Hecubah knew. "It's the day you would have been married."

"I don't want to see it." The blankets pulled in closer.

"That's plain foolish," Hecubah argued. "Get outa bed, or I'm gonna get a bucket of ice water and throw it over you."

"I don't care."

Hecubah's patience was wearing thin. "Child, if you make me do that, I'm gonna take a switch to you at the same time."

"I still don't care."

Hecubah exhaled sharply. "This country ain't the only body with a war on its hands," she muttered to herself. "All right then," she conceded, "you stay there. I guess I'll just have to take this letter from Trent and throw it away."

The pile of blankets instantly erupted, as Ceci rose, phoenix-like, from the middle of her bed, to snatch the letter from Hecubah's hand.

"It's been opened."

"Don't look at me," Hecubah remarked. "You know as well as I do they got censorship now. That letter come from the North to the South. Naturally, they is gonna check it for information. I bet they got more than they bargained for," she added ruefully.

"It ain't that kind of letter." Ceci quickly scanned the pages, carrying out her own version of censorship, before settling down to read it properly. "This was written two weeks ago," she pointed at the date.

"Just be grateful it got here at all," Hecubah advised.

"He got one of my letters," Ceci sighed with relief. "You know," she confided, "I've been putting colour on my lips and

129

pressing them to the bottom of the page. Trent says, he kissed that spot."

"You mean, he walks around the camp, with colour on his lips? That should make him popular with the rest of the men."

"No, silly. It's dry by then. I do it as a token of my love for him."

"I hate to think of what he's doing, as a token of his love for you."

"Hecubah, please." Ceci showed her the bottom of the last page. "All these little crosses are his kisses to me."

"What's that sign mean?" Hecubah interrupted.

Ceci faltered. "That's private," she dismissed the question.

Hecubah pursed her lips and let out a low whistle. "If those northern boys knew what these letters contained, they'd be changing hands for cash money."

"Stop it," Ceci scolded, folding the pages and returning them to the envelope. "Whatever it means, it ain't going to happen any time soon."

"At least you know he's alive and well, and that he's thinking of you," Hecubah pointed out.

Ceci nodded. "I'm going to start writing twice a day," she decided. "I'm going to cover the North with my letters."

"Sure, honey," Hecubah approved. "You do that, but don't you think you ought to put some clothes on first?"

***

"I'll drown myself in the bayou, if you don't."

"No, you won't."

"I'll throw myself out of a window then."

"No. You won't."

"All right," Ceci went to even greater extremes. "I'll go down to the slave quarters and get myself pregnant by a field hand."

Now she had Hecubah's attention. "You want me to go and tell your daddy what you just said?" she threatened.

Ceci dropped to her knees, hands clasped together. "Oh, please," she begged, "let me look at a newspaper. The war's almost a year old. I just have to know what's going on."

"Trust me, honey," Hecubah remarked solemnly. "You don't wanna know."

"That makes it worse," Ceci complained. "Not knowing, just makes it worse."

Hecubah studied her for a moment. "All right," she agreed reluctantly. Not because Ceci had made a good point, but only because she knew, if she didn't give her what she wanted, she'd never have a moment's peace again. "It'll serve you right, if you have nightmares."

Once she'd got her hands on a newspaper, one thing soon became abundantly clear to her. She wasn't alone in the misery of separation. There were thousands of other women, all over the country, who were experiencing the same thing. Many of them now knew that they would never see their loved ones again. It was a chilling prospect. One which, Ceci realised, she had escaped so far, only by the grace of God.

The war was being waged across the states, from Bull Run Virginia, to Lexington Missouri. The death toll was staggering. She'd never imagined that so many people could be killed at one time.

These days, Trent's letters were few and far between, but, at least, some still got through. If it hadn't been for that, Ceci was certain she'd have gone mad with worry by now. Trent wasn't the only one in danger. All that stood between the plantation and the Union army was Confederate troops. They weren't invincible. Sometimes they won a battle, sometimes they didn't. The threat of invasion terrified her. It haunted her every waking thought.

★★★

"After the attack on Fort Sumter. Thousands of coloured men tried to enlist in the Union army. They were refused, this time. Lincoln's no fool. Eventually, he'll emancipate the slaves and raise a coloured army, putting thousands of fresh troops into the field. We'll find ourselves outnumbered and outgunned."

Ceci paused by the hall table, the fruits of her morning's letter writing still clutched in her hand. She hadn't heard anyone arrive, but clearly there was another meeting in her father's day room. She put the letters on the table and tip-toed up to the door. Eavesdropping was an old habit she'd never reformed.

"What about the British?" a voice suggested. "The mills of England rely on our exports. Cotton's a powerful persuader."

"Hell," another man swore, "we'll appeal to the world against northern oppression."

"The British government," she heard her father tell them. "Like every other government in the world, will not ally itself with any faction that supports the institution of slavery. They don't even see us as a country, just a group of belligerent states. As far as the rest of the world is concerned, we're on our own."

Ceci had heard enough. She crept back along the hall, through the parlour and out onto the veranda. She breathed deeply, trying to clear her mind of all its troubled thoughts. She looked out across the garden. It comforted her. Everything there was safe and familiar. She began to wonder how much longer it would remain that way. She had hoped, with all her heart, for a brief war, a swift reunion with Trent, and marriage. Now only two things seemed certain to her. This war would not end quickly, and no one was safe.

Chapter Fifteen

"Still nothing from Trent?" Hecubah asked, as Ceci entered the morning room.

"Just my own letters returned," Ceci held up a pack of envelopes. "Most of them anyway. No telling if any of the others reached Trent." Ceci flopped onto the couch beside her. "I ain't giving up though," she remarked with determination. "Why, I've a mind to address my next letter to Abraham Lincoln and ask him to pass it on."

"I doubt it'd get any further than Richmond," Hecubah told her. "And you'd probably be arrested for fraternizing with the enemy. Don't you think it's time you found something else to occupy your mind?"

"You mean knitting socks for soldiers?" Ceci sneered disdainfully. "Or sewing battle flags, like Armenia and her daughters are doing. I can't think of anything I want to do less."

"You can't spend all your time fretting after Trent," Hecubah warned. "It ain't healthy."

"It's been so long since I seen or heard from him," Ceci sighed heavily. "Is this war never going to end? It's already in its second year. It ruined Christmas. No one wanted to travel because of the fighting. Stores in town are running out of provisions."

"Only some things," Hecubah corrected her. "We grow most of what we need, right here on the plantation."

"Yes, but for how much longer?" Ceci shuddered. "All the fighting's in the South. Hancock, Maryland. Middle Creek, Kentucky," she counted off the battles on her fingers, "Fort Henry, Tennessee and Rowen Oak in North Carolina. Why, I read they even had a battle in the New Mexico territory. That's behind us. We're surrounded."

"I told you, time and again," Hecubah repeated her warning. "No good comes of reading the newspapers."

Ceci wouldn't be stopped. "I read reports of towns and plantations being looted and burned, women raped, civilians murdered."

"That's enough," Hecubah snapped. "Sometimes the papers exaggerate, just to make our boys fight harder."

"Can't all be lies," Ceci remained sceptical. "How long will it be, before the Union army gets here? You'd have your freedom, I'm glad for that, but what would happen to me?"

"God almighty," Hecubah exhaled. "You is just a girl. These men ain't fighting so they can beat up on girls."

"If they don't burn the plantation, they'll surely free the slaves. I'm glad for that to, but how would my daddy run it after that?"

"Most of them would stay, if he paid them," Hecubah pointed out. "Most of them would stay in any case. This is the only home they know."

"Sometimes, I wonder what Trent's doing out there," Ceci confided. "What's he being ordered to do to southern folks, like me?"

"Honey, you really do need something else to occupy your mind," Hecubah decided. "I bin telling you about men since you was a little girl. You know as well as I do by now, most of them are good people, but there's always a few you can never trust. You know exactly what kind of man Trent is. All these crazy thoughts come from reading the newspapers, and sitting around all day with nothing to do. Well, not anymore." Hecubah stood up, grabbing Ceci by the hand.

"Where are we going?"

"Into the parlour. There's a whole stack of yarn in there, and needles."

Ceci pulled back. "I already told you. I don't want to knit socks."

"Honey, you is gonna knit socks," Hecubah informed her assertively. "Until your eyes ache, your fingers are raw and your mind is empty. Then maybe you'll stop worrying about this war and doubting Trent's character."

Ceci stiffened. "I won't do it," she remarked obstinately. "And you can't make me."

★★★

"If I see another pair of socks," Ceci sighed, "I'm going to kill myself."

"Ah huh," Hecubah inspected her latest effort. "I reckon that's what our boys are gonna be doing when they get these socks." She held up the shapeless woollen bag. "You make this for a man with no heels?"

"You made me knit socks," Ceci glowered. "You didn't ask if I was good at it."

"Ain't that the truth."

"Anyway, that's five pairs," Ceci pointed out. "It took me all week to do that. You promised I could write a letter to Trent for every five pairs. Now give me back my stationery."

"All right," Hecubah was willing to honour the condition. "But after that, it's back to socks."

"Oh, no, please," Ceci begged, "no more socks. I haven't been outside in a month. I can't bare the sight of another sock."

"If I let it go," Hecubah replied firmly. "I don't want to hear any more crazy talk about plantations burning, rape and murder. You start that again and you'll be knitting socks until the war ends or you dies of old age, whichever comes first."

135

"I swear, on a stack of bibles," Ceci crossed her heart.

"All right then," Hecubah relented. "I'll take your word on that. No more socks. It'll be something for our boys to celebrate."

★★★

Ceci was woken early by the sound of someone running past her room. She rose, pulled a robe over her nightdress and went to see what was happening. By the time she stepped out onto the landing, it was empty. She followed it all the way down to the west wing, before she noticed the door to her father's bedroom was open. She looked in.

His bed was strewn with clothes, whilst Hecubah hurriedly helped him pack a large valise. On the bed, beside it, was a holstered pistol.

"What's happening?" she asked, with a frown of concern.

Her father glanced up. "Not now, Cecile. Go back to bed," he dismissed her abruptly.

"Please," she insisted. "What's going on?"

"I've just been informed that federal troops are moving up the Mississippi," he continued to pack the choices Hecubah made into the valise, whilst he talked. "They're about to attack Fort Jackson and Fort St Philip. If they break through, they'll be in New Orleans."

"Celeste and the baby," Ceci gasped.

"Clay's off fighting somewhere," Hecubah added, handing a bundle of shirts to Ceci's father. "She's all on her own."

"I'm going for her now," her father informed her. "I'm going to bring her back here, where's she's safe."

"Give me a minute," Ceci responded recklessly. "I'm coming with you."

"No, Cecile," her father shook his head, "it's too dangerous." He drew the pistol, checked that it was loaded and threw it into the bag. "I'm taking Joshua and no one else."

"But Daddy," Ceci argued.

"No," he barked. "And that's final. Go back to your room."

"Go on, honey," Hecubah waved her away. "There ain't nothing you can do here."

Ceci returned to her room, threw on some clothes and re-emerged just in time to see her father going downstairs. She finally managed to catch up with him in the hall where Joshua was waiting by the open front door.

"Please, be careful, Daddy," she cried clutching his arm.

He turned, looking dishevelled and unshaven. "Simon Robicheaux, the overseer, is in charge of the plantation," he told her. "You be a good girl, and help Hecubah run the house. Don't worry," he smiled. "I expect to be back in five days. A week at the most" He paused distractedly, then stooped and kissed her. She felt his whiskers scrape her cheek, smelt a trace of yesterday's cologne, before he turned and left.

"He's forgot his watch," Hecubah had it in her hand. She followed him out, closing the door behind her.

"Take care, Daddy," Ceci breathed, raising her hand in a pointless wave.

★★★

"He said five days," Ceci recalled, as she and Hecubah picked at their breakfast. "A week at the most. It's been ten days now and still no word."

Hecubah was about to answer, when they heard the front door open, then close.

They jumped up, ran down the passage and into the hall, but it was only Joshua. He was alone. His head was bandaged and his left arm was in a sling. He grasped his battered old straw hat in his good hand.

Ceci came to an abrupt halt. A chill swept through her. The spectacle suggested something too terrible to contemplate. She shrank against Hecubah, clutching her hand. For what seemed like an eternity, no one spoke. Then Ceci drew a deep breath and let it slowly out, into the thunderous silence. "Have they been hurt?" she asked. It was the best she could hope for.

Joshua hung his head.

Ceci winced, as Hecubah's hand crushed hers. "All of them?" she heard herself say. "Dead. The baby too?"

Joshua nodded.

The very core of her being shuddered under the hammer blow. She felt her soul tear loose, crashing around inside her, like a bird frantically beating its wings against the bars of a cage. Until, all that remained was a void inhabited by some formless, nameless thing. A dark creature, born of pain and anguish, that assaulted the shattered bastions of her heart, seeking to dominate and enslave her. The moment she knew her family were dead, a part of her died with them.

"What happened?" she asked, abandoning herself to despair.

Joshua looked up. "New Orleans fell, without hardly a shot being fired," he recounted. "The mayor surrendered the city a few days after the Yankee men arrived. It was a freak accident. A stray cannon shell. I was coming back to the buggy, when it was hit."

Hecubah's hand went limp. She sagged against Ceci, slipping down to the floor. Ceci caught her, cradling her head in her lap. "Get help," she shouted.

Moments later, Joshua returned with two kitchen hands. Ceci had them carry Hecubah up to her room and lay her on her bed. Then she dismissed them, allowing Joshua to stay.

"She's always been so strong," she confided, stroking Hecubah's brow. "I've never seen her like this before."

"She loved your family," Joshua told her. "It was her whole world."

Ceci glanced up across Hecubah's prone figure. "Where are they now?" she asked flatly. "What happened to the bodies?"

Joshua's face creased in anguish. "As God is my witness,

I couldn't bring them home. The rail lines was cut. No boats running. Your daddy had friends in New Orleans. They took care of it. They're buried in the cemetery there. It was a descent Christian funeral," he assured her.

"And Clay?" Ceci pressed him.

Joshua shook his head. "They sent word out, but they ain't bin able to find him. Some folks reckon he might have died in battle, but no one knows for sure."

Ceci's jaw tensed. She reached over and put her hand on his shoulder. "You've done all you can," she told him. "Thank you for that. Now get some rest, let those wounds heal."

Joshua rose, then paused. "I believe in the Lord God," he told her, with profound sincerity. "I know your people are with him now, and that they are in a better place. Try to believe that, Miss Cecile, and maybe your wounds will heal too."

Ceci sat with Hecubah until she regained consciousness. They smiled at one another, until Hecubah's smile faded. She reached up and laid a hand against Ceci's cheek. "Don't do It, child," she murmured.

Ceci flinched back. "I don't know what you mean."

"I can see it in your eyes," Hecubah sighed. "All the light's gone out of them. Don't put a rock where your heart should be. Don't go looking for vengeance. It ain't gonna bring no one back. You'll only destroy yourself."

"You're delirious," Ceci dismissed her remarks. She lifted the hand from her cheek and lay it back on the bed. "You don't know what you're saying."

"You know that I do," Hecubah insisted. "Come back to me, honey. I can't bear to lose you too."

Ceci was in no mood to listen. "You need to rest," she ignored her, rising to leave. "Try and sleep a little. Call me if you need anything."

Ceci returned downstairs, gripped by an insatiable restlessness. She prowled the house all day and into the night, staring endlessly into empty rooms, remembering the faces she would never see again. Drop by drop, the void within her began to fill with poison, nourishing the dark creature, that drove her tirelessly on, clouding her mind with anger and hatred.

She had prayed so hard for one man's safety, she'd never considered that fate could strike from another direction. Fate, be damned. It was the Union, Lincoln and this God forsaken war, that had destroyed her life and robbed her of her family. If she could have transformed herself into a weapon, there and then, she would have done so. She would have hurled herself into the heart of the North and destroyed it all, in an instant. She wanted to act now. Strike a blow now. It was her total inability to do so that frustrated and enraged her. It was a cold rage, and yet it warmed her, because her heart was colder. It kept the creature alive within her, giving it the strength to control her actions.

Eventually, she retired to her room, for the sake of the sleeping household, if nothing else. She didn't undress, but lay down on top of the bed, staring listlessly into the shadows. At length, her eyes alighted on the picture of Trent, she kept by her bedside. She caught her breath and shivered. For a moment, all she could see was a Union soldier. The dark creature cried out from the utter depths of her despair, urging her to level all her anger at him. In that very instant, Ol' Magic rose and cast it effortlessly down. Even her burning hatred of the Union could not destroy her love for him. She picked up the picture, touched it to her trembling lips and pressed it to her breast. Then she turned down the lamp and lay in the silent darkness, knowing, that somewhere out there, in the endless night, a tiny ember glowed, and nothing on earth would extinguish it.

From that moment on, Ceci existed in a state of perpetual conflict. Torn between what she wanted most, and what she felt she had to do. From day to day, God alone knew which mood would prevail.

Ceci was unaware of the passage of time. She didn't know how long she'd lain there. Gradually, she became aware of a sound, a soft sobbing sound, that permeated the darkness. She turned her head to listen. It seemed to be coming down the hall, from Hecubah's room.

She rose, turned up the lamp and took it with her. She didn't knock, but just walked in. As the lamplight banished the darkness from the room, she saw Hecubah sitting on the floor, at the foot of her bed. Her nightdress half on, half off, her hair hanging loose about her shoulders. She was a vision of desolation, of reddened eyes and tear stained cheeks. She shuddered and sobbed uncontrollably, as if nothing in the world would ever console her.

Even though she couldn't fathom the depth of Hecubah's emotion, Ceci didn't question it. She set the lamp down, knelt, and put her arms around her. She held her close, held her tight, until the sun rose over the bayou, but for her own grief, she shed not one tear.

Chapter Sixteen

Hecubah carried the tray into the morning room. She took a plate of food and a cup of coffee from it and placed them on the desk, in front of Ceci. She barely glanced up. Reaching forward, she pushed the plate aside with the back of her hand.

Hecubah thrust her hands onto her hips. "How long you gonna go on, like this?" She demanded.

"The plantation won't run itself," Ceci continued to write.

"Simon Robicheaux can do that," Hecubah informed her. "It's his job, and you know it."

"There are accounts to balance," Ceci gestured at the stack of papers in front of her. "Bills to pay."

"They can wait," Hecubah would have none of it. "How long's it bin since you wrote to Trent? A month, more?"

Ceci paused to glance at his picture, perched on the corner of the desk, next to the one of her father and Celeste. "What's the point?" she shrugged dismissively. "He don't get my letters and I haven't heard from him in ages. Besides," she added tonelessly. "He don't need my encouragement to kill southerners."

"There it is," Hecubah slammed her fist onto the desk. The coffee cup danced in its saucer, making Ceci flinch. "Right there. That's what I'm talking about," she barked. "What have you become? What are you allowing yourself to be?" she demanded. "You know, as well as I do, Trent ain't that kind of man. He'd have died, before he let harm come to your

folks. Why, if he knew anything about it, he'd be here."
She jabbed her finger on the desk top. "He'd have deserted,
on pain of death, and he'd be here, right now."

Ceci folded her hands in front of her. "I'm busy," she
sighed dispassionately. "I've no time for this."

"Ah huh," Hecubah fumed. "No time. Is that right? You
think you is the only one with a broken heart? You think you
is the only one whose suffering?" She grabbed the picture
of Ceci's father. "You think throwing your life after theirs is
gonna make a difference?"

Ceci put her palms flat on the desk and stared balefully at
her. "Someone has to pay."

Hecubah stood back, her eyes narrowed. "Oh yeah,
that's it. Now we're getting there," she grinned mirthlessly.
"Someone's gotta pay. Who's that gonna be?" she goaded. "The
Union? Lincoln? God? The only one I see paying is you. You
keep eating into yourself this way, you gonna die. You gonna
die bitter and alone."

Ceci refused to rise to the taunts. She merely lowered her
eyes, without deigning to answer.

Hecubah lunged forwards, thrusting a finger into her face.
"You think you lost a lot," she flared. "One day, you is gonna
wake up and realise you got a whole lot more to lose, unless
you get off that ugly road you're on." With that, she turned
and stormed out.

For a while, Hecubah saw fit to leave Ceci to her own
devices, to let her stew, hoping she would come to her senses
in time. Ceci hardly noticed her absence, preoccupied with
the running of her late father's estate, obsessed by dark and
reckless thoughts.

That morning, a maid came in, bearing a small silver tray.
On it was a single calling card. Ceci picked it up and read
it aloud. "Mr Henry Doucet." The name seemed vaguely
familiar.

She instructed the maid to show him into the morning

room. She rose from behind the desk, pausing only to glance at herself in the mirror. She saw the pale face, the gaunt features, the haggard expression and the black dress. She hadn't yet been a bride and already she looked like a widow. She sighed indifferently. Tomorrow, she would have the mirror removed.

Doucet was waiting, hat in hand. He bowed his head in greeting, as she entered the room. Now she remembered him, from the night of the ball. Tall, lean, sallow complexion. Ordinary to look at. She'd have passed him in the street without a second glance.

"To what do I owe the pleasure of this visit?" she enquired, inviting him to sit.

"I read about your family, in the paper, recently," he explained. "I was passing. I thought I would stop by and offer you my sincerest sympathies for your tragic loss."

Ceci wasn't as gullible as she'd once been. Recent events had honed her mind and sharpened her wits. "While I appreciate your condolences," she replied. "I doubt that it's the only reason for your visit."

A thin smile parted his lips. "Very astute," he approved. "I did right in coming here." He paused and glanced around, to be certain they were alone. Then he leaned forward in his chair, speaking in a low voice. "As things stand now," he advised her. "The outcome of the war is far from certain. I can offer you an opportunity to strike a blow for the South, and at the same time avenge the death of your family."

His words dripped, like venom, into her ears. The creature inside her stirred, howling for release. "How so?"

He allowed himself another thin smile, noting her interest. "You recall, when we first met," he continued. "I told you that my speciality was gathering intelligence."

"By that, you mean espionage," Ceci interrupted. "You want me to be a spy."

Doucet sat back, clearly impressed by her insight.

"Do you honestly expect me to open a salon in the North?" she continued. "Fraternise with inebriated young officers, and listen to their pillow talk?"

"Such places do exist in the North," he acknowledged. "As I know they do in the South. Those ladies perform a vital service to the cause, but I have something far more radical in mind."

"Which is?"

He leaned forward again. "I intend to train an elite force of women, who will penetrate deep behind enemy lines. For any purpose," he emphasised.

His answer failed to impress her. "What is it that this elite force of women can do that men can't?" she enquired.

"There still exists, in this country, despite the war, a code of conduct towards women," he advised her. "A woman can go where a man can't. She poses no threat. A man will confide in her, in ways he would never dream of doing with another man. No man, not even in his wildest imaginings, would ever believe her capable of doing, what I will train her to do." He paused, studying her for a moment, assessing her potential. "I intend to exploit this advantage, for the good of our cause."

This was the chance she'd been waiting for. The chance to hit back. To avenge her dead father and her dead sister, but she remained cautious. "And if I choose to decline your offer?"

He gestured vaguely. "Certainly, you are at liberty to do so. I have given you no sensitive information. I will merely take my leave of you and we will never meet again," he finished, reaching for his hat.

The creature inside her howled once more, and this time, she listened. "What'd I have to do?"

Again, the thin smile. "Two weeks from today, at four o'clock in the afternoon, a launch will arrive at Jenson's Warf. It will fly a blue flag with a white star."

"The Bonnie Blue flag," Ceci recognised it.

"Precisely," Doucet nodded. "It will wait five minutes and then depart for a secret location. A hidden training camp. You will be gone for three months. Tell anyone you need to satisfy that you have volunteered to be a nurse in the field hospital at Opelousas. They are overwhelmed with casualties since the battle of Baton Rouge. You will say nothing else, to anyone, ever, especially when you return." He slipped his hand into his coat pocket and withdrew an envelope, which he placed on the table between them. "In here are directions to Jenson's Warf, train times, money, details of the plan, and what you may bring with you."

As Ceci reached for the envelope, he placed his hand over it. "Once you have read the contents of this envelope," he warned. "You will not be permitted to change your mind. You will be committed for the duration of the war. Once you have completed your training, you will return home. However, you will be expected to accept any assignment offered you thereafter. Which means, you may not see your home again, until the end of the war. That is, if you survive. Any change of heart. A failure in any one of these areas, will make you a liability to my operation."

"You mean, you'd have to have me killed?" Ceci interpreted.

He lifted his hand off the envelope. "The choice is still yours," he replied.

Ceci had heard all she wanted to hear. Briefly, she recalled Hecubah's warning, about the ugly road she was on, but, for now, it was the only road she could see. It was the only road she wanted to see. She leaned forward and picked up the envelope.

★★★

"I thought they didn't allow women in them places," Hecubah stared in alarm.

"They do now," Ceci informed her. "Since Baton Rouge fell, they're overwhelmed with casualties."

"Nursing in a field hospital in Opelousas," Hecubah was far from happy. "Honey, that's almost a hundred miles away. You ain't never bin anywhere on your own before."

"I already told you," Ceci repeated her cover story. "Other women will be joining the train along the way. I won't be alone for long."

Hecubah wrung her hands, frowning. "There's battles going on, all over the South. It ain't a good time to travel. I don't like it. Where'd you hear about this?"

"I told you," Ceci continued to coerce. "There was a notice in the newspaper, calling for volunteers."

"Honey, do you realise what kind of things you're gonna see when you get there?" Hecubah warned.

"I know it won't be pretty," Ceci agreed. "But I'll manage. Besides, you said it yourself," She reminded her. "I can't sit around the house moping forever. You can't coddle me for the rest of my life. I got to stand on my own two feet one day. This way, I'll be helping others at the same time."

"It might be good for you, at that," Hecubah conceded grudgingly. "But I'm coming with you."

"No," Ceci was adamant. She'd expected Hecubah to say something like that, and she was ready. "If you come. I won't be standing on my own two feet, will I? Besides, I need you here, to look after the house. You're the only one I trust to do it. It's only for three months. Please, I have to do this."

"If anything happens to you, I'll never forgive myself," Hecubah sighed heavily.

Ceci took her hands in hers. "You'd have nothing to blame yourself for," she reassured her. "I'm a grown woman, free to make my own choices. I'm not asking for your permission to go. I'm asking for your blessing on my endeavour."

"I know," Hecubah sighed again. "I can't stop you, if your minds made up, but I ain't gonna get a wink of sleep until you come back."

★★★

"Is this all you're taking?" Hecubah gestured at the contents of the carpet bag. "No change of clothes, no extra linen. You ain't gonna last a day on that."

"Everything I need will be provided, once I reach Opelousas," Ceci told her. "You can imagine the conditions I'll be working in. If I took my own clothes, they'd be ruined in no time."

"Blood and disease," Hecubah shook her head. "The more I hear about this, the less I like it. Tell me again why I can't write to you?"

"It's a field hospital," Ceci pointed out. "They don't exactly have addresses. Besides, I'll be moving around. I've already promised, I'll write to you every week, just to let you know I'm safe."

"Make sure you do," Hecubah insisted. "Or Opelousas is gonna have a war on its hands. Meanwhile, take this with you." She offered Ceci a small vile. It looked like a scent bottle.

"What's this?" Ceci made to open it.

"Good Lord, don't pull the cork out, "Hecubah cried. "That's skunk oil. The kind the critter squirts when it's riled."

"Skunk oil?" Ceci stared incredulously. "Now, why would I want that?"

"Some man tries to force his attention on you. You throw it in his face," Hecubah instructed. "It'll blind him."

"I swear, you're more nervous than I am," Ceci laughed. "I'm sure there'll be plenty of chivalrous men on the train, who'll be happy to see I travel safely. Now will you quit worrying."

"I ain't never gonna quit worrying, as far as you is concerned," she glowered. "You put that hundred dollars emergency money in the pocket I sewed in your drawers?"

Ceci rolled her eyes. "Yes."

"Show me."

Ceci raised her skirt. "Happy now?"

"I ain't gonna be happy till you get back." She grabbed Ceci, hugging her until she gasped. "I'm worried outa my mind," she confided. "But I'm proud to. I'm so proud you found this strength."

Lying this way to Hecubah was the hardest thing Ceci had ever had to do in her life. It was a necessary evil, but that didn't make it any easier. She knew the day would come, after she took her first assignment, when Hecubah would discover her deceit. Then there'd be hell to pay. For now, whenever she felt a twinge of conscience, or a pang of remorse, she thought of her dead father and sister, then the dark creature within her would rise up and smother it.

★★★

"You got your ticket?" Hecubah fussed.

"Here," Ceci showed her.

"And your smelling salts?"

"In my bag."

"What about that hundred dollars?"

"I ain't pulling up my skirt, right here, in front of the train," Ceci objected.

"I guess you is ready then," Hecubah glanced up and down the busy platform. "You can still change your mind, you know," she suggested hopefully.

"I ain't going to change my mind. Stop worrying. I'll be fine," she assured her. "Now, I have to go. The train's leaving any minute."

Hecubah caught Ceci's face in her hands and kissed her on the lips. "You be careful, child," she began to cry. "You hear me? You keep yourself safe."

"I will," Ceci nodded. She picked up her bag and boarded the train. Moments later, it began to move.

"Don't forget to write," Hecubah shouted up at the open

window of Ceci's car. She kept pace with the train, for as long as she could, waving all the time.

Ceci waved back, as Hecubah dwindled into the distance. Now she was truly alone, for the first time in her life. She felt a stab of terror surge through her, a brief moment of doubt, but it was quickly replaced by a strengthening resolve to avenge her family.

Ceci travelled twenty minutes down the line, got off at the next station and boarded the train for Jenson's Warf. Now, even Hecubah didn't know where she was. It was a long, slow journey. At every station, every depot, she had to wait for freight trains to pass, loaded with war supplies and munitions. Everywhere she looked, thousands of Confederate troops waited to embark. Sometimes she saw men returning from battle. The wounded and the dead, shipped back in the same cars. It was a harrowing sight. One which the printed newspaper accounts, no matter how lurid, had not prepared her for. It was her first glimpse of what war was really like. So much had changed so quickly. She'd met Trent. Fallen madly in love with him. All she'd wanted was to be married and spend the rest of her life with him. Now, there was only war and confusion, death and tears.

Ceci checked her watch as the train pulled into Jenson's Warf. It was three thirty in the afternoon. She alighted from the car, pausing only to ask the conductor for directions. Then she hurried down the street, through the town, and onto the dock, just in time to see the launch arrive.

Chapter Seventeen

Without a moment's hesitation, Ceci stepped into the launch. Three young women were already on board. They regarded each other with obvious curiosity. Doucet had told her not to speak to anyone. Clearly, he had said the same to them. They all looked, but no one spoke.

The launch continued up-river, leaving a long trail of acrid black smoke drifting out across the bayou. Ceci attempted to memorise the route, but there were so many tributaries, twists and turns, that she very soon realised she would never be able to navigate her way back without a map. Doucet had chosen his position well.

After an hour, they arrived at a small island nestled among a vast tract of cypress trees, shielding it from prying eyes. Doucet was waiting on the jetty.

Once they had alighted, he motioned them to follow him. Silently, he led them to a small cabin in a clearing in the woods, ushered them inside and closed the door.

"You will never tell anyone your real names," he addressed them, without the curtesy of a greeting. "Or disclose where you come from. From now on, you will be known only by your operating name." He produced a small wooden box. "In here are the names of four common native birds. You will all choose at random and thereafter, be known by that name."

He moved among them, offering the box to each one in turn. "You will familiarise yourself with your bird," he told them. "Know it's habits and its habitat. You will be taught to mimic its song. This will be your call sign. It will identify you to our agents, no matter what alias you are travelling under."

A tall, athletic looking, brunette chose first. Doucet took the folded slip of paper from her, and opened it. "Oriole," he announced, crushing the slip in his fist.

A petite redhead, one mass of freckles, chose next. "Bunting," Doucet moved on.

The third young woman took a slip of paper. She was clearly a mountain girl. She wore her blonde hair in long braids underneath a frayed straw hat. Everything she wore had seen better days. "Cardinal."

Doucet turned to Ceci, offering her the last slip. She dipped her fingers into the box. It felt as if she were passing through a door, into another world. Doucet took the paper from her, and read it aloud. "Whippoorwill."

He set the empty box aside. "You may ask questions," he invited.

"Why are there so few of us?" Bunting was first to speak.

"Because you are the first," Doucet replied simply. "If this enterprise succeeds, more will be recruited. No page of history will ever record your existence," he addressed them all. "From now on, you will be completely anonymous. You will never disclose to anyone what you are about to do here. The Union has its spies, as do we. The slightest breach of security, would have the direst consequences. Your friends and families believe that you have volunteered as nurses in Opelousas, and that is all they will ever know. You will be permitted to write one letter a week, to maintain the illusion. Keep it short, keep it simple."

The mountain girl, Cardinal, raised a tentative hand. "Why weren't we allowed to bring a change of clothes?"

Doucet pointed to a heap of rough garments, shirts, trousers and leather sandals, piled on top of a small table in the corner of the cabin. "These are what you will train in, live in and sleep in," he explained. "The clothes you are wearing now, are the ones you will return home in."

"What happens after that?" Ceci asked.

"You will resume a normal life," Doucet replied. "Until a suitable assignment is found. Then you'll be contacted again."

"Where do we wash and sleep?" Oriole asked, gesturing at the spartan interior of the cabin.

"Conditions here reflect those you can expect to find in the field," Doucet informed them. "You will all live in this shack. If you want to wash, the bayou's that way," he pointed. "If you need to do anything else, the woods are out there. You will all be issued with one blanket," he continued briskly. "If you don't want to sleep on the floor, you must make your own bed out of moss and bracken. You will be provided with minimum rations. If you want more, you'll have to hunt for it."

"Why do we have to endure these conditions, when our purpose is to gather and pass on information?" Ceci interrupted, voicing a question that had doubtless crossed all their minds.

"That's only part of it," Doucet replied, abandoning his martial attitude for a moment. "I told you all at the beginning that you would be trained to penetrate deep behind enemy lines, for any purpose. That may include sabotage, assassination, and anything else that's deemed necessary to win this war." He paused, allowing them time to digest the information. "You may have to cross open country in hostile territory," he continued. "You will need to know, how to live off the land, defend and disguise yourselves, whilst enduring extreme privation. You'll require all these skills, and more, if you intend to survive."

Ceci began to realise, as no doubt the others had, that there was a lot more to this than she'd first thought.

Noticing their change of attitude, Doucet distanced himself from the group. "You must understand," he advised them, with some gravity. "This was never about merely gathering information. It's about winning a war, by all available means. Because of who you are, and what you do, the enemy will show you no mercy. You must be tough, resourceful and alert if you are to stand any chance at all. That is what you will become in the next three months."

"All that, in three months?" Cardinal remarked doubtfully.

"The time allotted, is sufficient," he responded brusquely. "It's up to you how quickly and how well you learn. The more you know, the better your chances of survival. However," he continued darkly, "anyone who does not achieve the required standard by the end of the training period will not be sent on active service."

"What happens to them?" Ceci enquired nervously.

"Your only concern for now, is what lays ahead of you," he evaded the question.

"When do we begin?" Cardinal asked.

"Now," Doucet answered succinctly. "Each of you take a set of clothes and come with me."

They followed him for about half a mile until he stopped in a grove where some burlap sacks were hanging from the branch of a tree. He pulled them down and threw them on the ground. "Pick up the sack with your name on it," he ordered. "Remove the clothes you have on and put them inside. Then put on the clothes you brought from the cabin."

As one, they hesitated, glancing suspiciously at him.

"You're asking us to take off our clothes, in front of you?" Bunting frowned.

The tone of Doucet's voice never varied. "You may have to adopt a disguise at a moment's notice, anywhere, anytime. Modesty is a luxury you cannot afford. If you can't do this, you can't continue here."

One by one, they began to undress, until the entire group huddled together, naked, their arms wrapped about them, in a vain attempt to preserve what little was left of their dignity.

"Put your clothes in the sacks," Doucet reminded them. "And put on the things you brought from the cabin." When they'd done that, he produced two pairs of shears. "Now, cut your hair."

A howl of dismay went up from the group. Doucet remained unmoved. "This country is swarming with troops," he informed them. "In order to reach your target, it may be necessary to disguise yourself as one of them. No woman can successfully pass as a man wearing girl's hair. I'm not asking you to shave your heads, just cut it shorter. When you return home, tell your people that is was necessary, to prevent lice and disease," with that, he made to leave.

"Where are you going?" Ceci asked.

"My headquarters are a mile yonder," he replied. "You have the rest of the day to gather bedding, firewood, and acclimatise yourself to the area. Today's rations have been left at the shack. Tomorrow, at first light, we begin in earnest."

Ceci stared after the receding figure, as her golden curls began to shower down around her. She began to wonder if she'd done the right thing in coming here, but like it or not, there was no going back now.

"It's such a pity," Oriole sighed, as she snipped at Ceci's tresses. "You have such lovely hair. I'll try and leave as much as I can. Make sure you do the same for me."

★★★

"Any man would have been aroused, by the sight of us standing there naked," Bunting remarked, as they piled heaps of moss and bracken onto the cabin floor. "Ol' Doucet wasn't excited at all. That ain't natural. He must be made of stone."

"He's a seasoned professional," Ceci told her. "A cold, hardened, professional, but he'll train us well."

"He better had," Oriole joined in. "I didn't come here, just to play games."

155

"Why did you come?" Bunting asked, despite Doucet's rule of silence.

Oriole's face clouded. "I had a husband and a baby once," she growled. "The Yanks killed them both. Now I'm going to kill some of them. What about you?"

"Union deserters robbed my house," Bunting replied. "Burned it down, raped me and my two sisters. Only two of us got out alive. What's your story, Cardinal?"

The mountain girl shrugged. "My daddy died years ago. Lost my three brothers at Georgia Landing, all in the same day. When Ma found out, she hung herself in the barn. Now, there's only me and Grandma left."

They all looked at Ceci. "My daddy, my sister and her baby. When New Orleans surrendered," she responded, realising, for the first time, that she wasn't alone in her grief, or her desire for vengeance. Another thought occurred to her. Doucet had only chosen women who'd had family killed in the war. She wondered if he thought that would make them more dedicated, or if he hoped they were just too bitter to consider the consequences of what they'd embarked upon.

"Ol' Doucet's got himself quite a pack of hellcats, don't he?" Bunting grinned. "Heck, I reckon we could win this war by ourselves."

"If we're going to do that, we'd better get our heads down," Oriole advised. "I've a feeling, tomorrow's going to be a long day."

Far from home, in a strange place, Ceci lay her head down on the rough bracken, pulled the coarse blanket up around her shoulders, and shivered. She'd never felt so alone before.

It was barely light, before the door crashed open and Doucet marched in. "You must be ready to move in an instant," he shouted, as they stared blearily up at him.

"The enemy can come upon you at any time. A sleeping target, is an invitation to attack. Everyone outside."

"I think I got some varmint living in my bed," Cardinal

muttered, as they filed out. "I been scratching all night."

Doucet was waiting for them, accompanied by a huge man. He had hands like hams, a thick bushy black beard and an ugly white scar creasing his left cheek.

"This is Bear," Doucet introduced him. "He's spent his entire life living off the land. There's nothing he don't know about survival. So pay attention to him."

He began to distribute canteens and leather satchels. "This is one day's rations," he informed them. "That's breakfast, lunch, dinner and supper. That goes for the water too, so don't use it all at once. Take one swallow of water, then I want you to run around the perimeter of the camp," he indicated the route, with a sweep of his arm. "Don't stop until I tell you."

An hour passed, before Doucet appeared in front of them. Hand raised.

"I can't feel my feet anymore," Bunting panted.

"See this tree?" Doucet laid his hand on the tall cottonwood next to him. "Climb it."

"There must be thirty feet of clear trunk," Oriole observed. "How we are going to climb that?"

"Is that what you're going to say, when it's a telegraph pole, with a wire at the top, you need to tap into?" Doucet asked, nodding at Bear.

The man drew a large knife from his belt and proceeded to cut some nearby saplings. Stripping the bark from them, he quickly platted a crude rope, which he threw around the trunk, enclosing himself in the loop. With this makeshift harness, he quickly began to ascend. For a big man, he was remarkably nimble.

"You try," Doucet pointed at Oriole.

After a good deal of effort, grunting and cuss words, she managed to get about half way, before she slipped, crashing heavily to the ground.

"Try again, later," Doucet dismissed the attempt. "Now you," he waved the harness in Ceci's direction.

She stepped forward, declining the support, as all her years of running wild on the plantation, came flooding back. Placing her hands and feet on each side of the trunk, she shinned up it in no time, straddling the first branch she came to.

"How in the hell did she do that?" Cardinal stared in amazement.

"Very good." Doucet observed, mildly impressed.

At length, with Bear's harness and Ceci's technique, they all mastered the tree.

"See that log?" Doucet pointed, before they'd even had time to catch their breath.

"Pick it up. Two on each side. Stand six feet apart and throw it to each other, until I tell you to stop."

The log was about fifteen feet long and as broad as a railroad tie. As they struggled to pick it up, Doucet sauntered over to a boulder, sat down and lit a cigar.

"I wish he'd chosen a shorter cigar," Bunting grunted, as the weight of the log crashed into her chest.

Doucet took his time with his smoke. Eventually, to their relief, he tossed the stub away. However, their joy was short lived. "Drop that," he ordered "And follow me."

For the rest of the day, he took them over a wide variety of obstacles, including rope swings, pit falls, and a twenty-foot tunnel they had to crawl through blind. Allowing them only thirty minutes to rest, eat and relieve themselves.

"I damn near lynched myself on that blamed rope," Cardinal grumbled, as they sat on the ground, eating.

"I saw that," Oriole acknowledged. "Weren't nearly as funny as Bunting hanging by her leg."

"Thanks for your sympathy," she spluttered through a mouthful of bread.

"Whippoorwill," Cardinal turned to Ceci. "When you stepped on that boat, with your fine hair and soft skin, I took you for a soft living lady. So why is it all this comes so easy to you?"

"I weren't always a lady," Ceci smiled. "What it took to

make me one was a lot harder than anything here."

"That's enough jabbering," Doucet cut in. "On your feet and start running. Don't stop until sundown. Then you can go back to the cabin."

As dusk fell, they limped and crawled back to the shack.

"I ain't going live long enough to be a spy," Oriole groaned, staggering inside and lighting the lamp, before collapsing, like the others, onto her bed.

"I don't see how my having to shit in the woods, is going to help the South win the war?" Cardinal complained.

"Where else do you think you're going to go when you're in the field?" Oriole asked. "Besides, an experienced hillbilly girl like you should be used to that."

"At least you learned something new," Bunting told her. "Now, you know you're supposed to wipe your behind when you're finished."

Howls of laughter echoed round the cabin.

"Oh, you're all so full of humour," she narrowed her eyes at them. "I don't know where you find the strength for it."

"Just make sure you don't use any poison ivy leaves," Oriole warned. "Or you'll be sorry you took a shit in the first place."

Over the next few weeks Doucet concentrated on improving their physical fitness. He had them running, climbing, hauling rocks and wading through swamps. The relentless pace and meagre rations began to tell on them all.

"What the hell died in that swamp?" Cardinal lay on her bed, too tired to move. "I smell like a privy."

"We all smell pretty bad now," Ceci pointed out. "I think Doucet knew we couldn't wash in the bayou, when he suggested it. The water's so full of mud and silt, you go in there, and you come out worse than you went in."

"Are we supposed to wear these clothes all month?" Bunting fidgeted. "I've been sweating in mine for weeks. They're going stiff."

"I think they're the only clothes we're likely to get whilst we're here," Ceci deduced. "I think Doucet's trying to make a point. After all, we ain't likely to get a change of clothes in the field."

"Darn," Cardinal threw down her canteen. "I gone and drunk up all my water and I'm as dry as a mule's ear."

"Here," Ceci offered her canteen. "It's still a quarter full."

"Thanks, Whippoorwill," she smiled. "I dreamed of you, last night, Oriole," she went on after quenching her thirst.

"Oh yeah! What was I doing?"

"Roasting over an open fire. You looked mighty tasty."

"That's horrible," Oriole scowled. "I can't believe you're that hungry."

"I don't think I can stomach any more of this stale cornbread," Cardinal grimaced. "It tastes like it's made outa birch bark and horse sweat."

"Probably taste better, if it was," Ceci joined in.

"Think ol' Doucet will find any more excuses to make us take off our clothes in front of him?" Bunting asked. "I'm beginning to wonder if he's training us to be spies, or saloon girls."

"At least they eat good," Cardinal sighed.

"To hell with Doucet," Ceci spat. She gathered up all the canteens, and poured one into the other, until they all contained roughly the same amount. She passed them out. "Here's to us," she toasted. "The Bird spies, the South and victory."

"Amen to that," they all cheered.

Doucet had warned them against fraternisation and the dangers of becoming too close, but, after all, they were still young women, united by a growing bond of camaraderie. Friendships were bound to be made.

Chapter Eighteen

"The woods are full of the sound of bird song," Cardinal announced dramatically. "And some of it's coming from actual birds." She tilted her head back and repeated her well-practised call. A beautiful sequence of notes, soft and lilting, that drifted away on the still air.

Suddenly, there was a flash of scarlet, as a small red bird alighted on a branch above them, looking inquisitively down. Seeing none of its own kind it took flight in another flash of scarlet and was gone, leaving them all staring in amazement.

"God almighty," Oriole spoke at last. "You called one in. That was incredible. I've never seen anything like it."

"I'm going to keep practising, 'til I can do that," Bunting remarked with determination.

"Don't you think it remarkable, that Doucet was able to find a college professor?" Cardinal asked. "An orni, ornery. Whatever the hell they call him?"

"Ornithologist," Ceci came to her assistance. "It's someone who studies birds."

"That's right," Cardinal recalled. "An ornithologist, no less, who was able to teach us these bird calls?"

"Then there's the weapons expert," Oriole added. "And the cypher expert."

"There was that man who showed us how to disguise our southern accents," Bunting reminded them. "Where'd he find all those people? How'd he manage all that?"

"All I know," Ceci told them, "is, that he fought in the Mexican war with Jeff Davis. I guess he has the entire resources of the South at his disposal. His organisation must be bigger than we can possibly imagine."

"That's what bothers me," Bunting confided. "If he has all these experts, why's he need us?"

"He told me that a woman can go where a man can't," Ceci recalled. "She arouses no suspicion and offers no threat."

"That's what he told us," Oriole confirmed. "But, what if he's lying? What if he has something entirely different in mind for us?"

"All I can tell you," Ceci sighed, "is that my family were killed, during the capture of a city, where hardly a shot was fired. Pointless, unnecessary deaths that tore away part of my life I'll never get back. I loved – love," she corrected herself. "A northern man. Ain't heard from him, since the beginning of the war. That's another part of my life. I had a choice. I could do nothing, and watch the North sweep over the South, destroying what is left of my world. Or, I could accept Doucet's offer and learn to fight back, make a difference and help win the war. If I live through this, I will build a new life, on the ashes of the old. If Doucet can help me do that, I will follow his instructions, no matter what they are."

As she spoke of her former life, she remembered Ceci, the wild girl, running free in the Louisiana summer, and Ceci, the lovesick young woman. Since then, a new Ceci had been added. A dark creature, full of anger, hatred and vengeance, that lurked in the shadows of her mind, awaiting any opportunity to gain the upper hand. She knew that, no matter what she faced in the future, it was her greatest enemy and that, for now, she had no power to resist it.

In the month that followed, Doucet put them through an intensive training programme, honing their skills with weapons and self-defence. At night, they practised their codes and cyphers by the light of an oil lamp until they became so proficient they could converse with one another in this secret language. In all that time, none of them ever questioned Doucet's motives again.

★★★

"The art of camouflage," Doucet told them. "The ability to conceal yourself in plain sight."

He had gathered them in a broad clearing, arranging them in a large square, one at each corner. There were no trees, bushes or rocks anywhere within it, only a thick carpet of dead leaves underfoot. They glanced around, perplexed. Suddenly, the leaves in the centre of the square erupted and Bear appeared out of a shallow scrape in the ground, making them all scream.

"That's one method," Doucet remarked. "This is another." He opened the saddlebag he had with him and produced a square of cloth, no bigger than a napkin. He unfolded it, to reveal a complete Confederate uniform. "This is a new kind of material," he told them. "Looks exactly like the standard army issue, but it's only a fraction of the weight. Put it on over what you're wearing," he offered it to Oriole.

She did as he asked.

"Now you can see why you had to cut your hair," he pointed out.

He was right. Oriole made a convincing soldier, almost.

"What do we do about these?" she asked, cupping her breast over the fabric.

"Bind them down, with strips of linen," he responded casually, taking another square of cloth from the saddlebag. This time it was a Union uniform. "Put it on over the first," he told Oriole. "The advantage of passing from one army to the other," he continued, once she'd done so, "must be obvious, even to you."

That wasn't the only thing that was obvious. Only now

did they truly understand, the kind of risks they were expected to take.

"If we're caught, wearing both uniforms," Ceci began to say.

"That's what this three months is all about," Doucet interrupted, preventing them from dwelling on the possibilities. "To ensure that you're not." He withdrew a third and final square from the saddlebag. With a flick of his hand, it opened into a complete dress. "Not very stylish," he admitted, once Oriole had put it on. "But, with this, you're just another woman in the crowd. Use it in the field, and most men, even battle-hardened veterans, will hesitate to attack a woman, and therein lies your chance to neutralise him."

"In case you hadn't noticed," Bunting pointed out. "We're all different sizes."

"That was obvious in the clearing," he remarked, making them all blush. "You will all be issued with a set of these clothes, tailored to your measurements," he assured her. "Altogether, these three items do not constitute the weight of one regular uniform," he began to summarise. "They can be worn one over the other and packed into a small space. If you're forced to abandon any of this equipment, try and retain the dress. You can always scavenge uniforms from fallen soldiers, along the way."

"You mean, pull them off dead bodies?" Cardinal asked dubiously.

"I doubt that any living soldier, will agree to give you his uniform," Doucet stated the obvious.

★★★

Bunting was tiny compared to Bear. He towered over her diminutive figure like a giant over a midget.

"Hit him," Doucet ordered.

"Hit him?" Bunting stared in alarm. "He's liable to kill me."

"Nothing will happen," he assured her calmly. "Now, hit him."

Bunting drew back her arm and drove her clenched fist into Bear's stomach, with all the strength she could muster. He didn't so much as blink, whilst she reeled away, clutching her fist in her other hand. "That hurt," she yelped.

"Does anyone here not believe that Bunting can bring Bear down?" Doucet asked.

All their hands went up together.

Doucet nodded. Clearly, he'd expected no less. "Watch carefully," he demonstrated, placing his foot behind Bear's right knee. "Bunting, come around here and do as I have done, only quickly."

She did as she was told, taking a run at Bear, and he went down, like a felled oak.

"Self-defence," Doucet explained. "It's about using your opponent's weight against him. You will be shown all the vulnerable areas on a man, where you can disable him with little or no effort."

"That could come in handy," Oriole remarked suggestively, making them all grin.

Doucet wasn't amused. "To finish here," he continued, straddling Bear's prone form. He drew a knife from his belt. "At this point," he knelt, pressing the blade against Bear's throat. "You fall upon your enemy's back and thrust your knife into his neck. This will sever the jugular vein. Your enemy will die quickly and quietly." He rose, noting with some satisfaction the change in their expressions. "This isn't a game," he warned. "Always remember. If he is not the one who dies, it will be you."

★★★

Very occasionally, Doucet allowed them an hour to forage for themselves, to supplement their meagre diet and gain experience in living off the land.

"It works something like this," Cardinal demonstrated.

She lay flat on her stomach, at the edge of the bayou, arm in the water, up to her shoulder. "My daddy showed me when I was a little girl. You stay real quiet," she explained, in a hushed voice. "Find a fish under the bank and begin to stroke it, real gentle, with your fingers."

Ceci and the others watched with interest as she edged forward, her brow creased in concentration.

"Fish gets real calm," she continued to whisper. "Then you put your hand under its belly, and throw it up on the bank."

Oriole had other ideas. Winking at the others, she grabbed Cardinal by the ankles and tipped her deftly into the water.

She rose spluttering to the surface, to be greeted by a storm of laughter.

"That's the first bath you've had in weeks," Oriole jeered. "Stay in there and wash your clothes at the same time."

"Real funny," Cardinal coughed, thrashing at the murky water with her arms. "I hope you find it as amusing when you're still hungry tonight."

That evening, they had to admit that she was right. A joke, no matter how good, was no substitute for a square meal.

Fortunately for them, Bear was at hand. They didn't know if it was his real name, and they never asked. He didn't talk much, didn't smell too good either, but he was a consummate backwoodsman, and the most patient man Ceci had ever met.

He taught them how to survive in the wild. How to read signs and animal tracks. He showed them how to fish and hunt. Lay traps and snares. What berries and roots to eat, which fungus to avoid, endlessly repeating the lesson until they understood, with never a hint of temperament.

One particularly hot day, he stripped off his shirt to cool himself, revealing a tableau of ragged scars, his torso a monument to the life he'd led. Ceci and the others, eaten up with morbid curiosity, gathered around to look.

"What did that?" Bunting asked.

"Bar," he grunted.

"A bear? And that one?" she persisted.

"Another bar."

"And this?" Cardinal ran her fingers along five regular grooves in his back.

"Bobcat."

"What about that?" Ceci pointed at his cheek.

"Gal, I used to run with," he grinned for the first time they'd ever seen. "Part injun, part gator. Handsome woman. Mighty fierce temper."

They never fully appreciated the isolation of his existence, until one day Oriole asked him. "How's the war going?"

Doucet had denied them this news, as well as any indication of the passage of time. Citing such information as a distraction to their training.

Bear merely shrugged. "What war?"

There was a guileless innocence about him, a natural integrity which Ceci had seldom found in other men. She imagined that if the North did conquer the South, Bear would quietly slip away, back to the mountains and never be seen again.

★★★

By now they were all a lot fitter than they had been when they'd arrived. Stronger, leaner and less prone to the exhaustion associated with their arduous training. They had energy to spare, and that presented its own particular set of problems.

"How long do you suppose we've been here?" Cardinal asked, as they sat outside the shack one evening, eating the last of the day's rations.

"I truly couldn't say," Oriole responded thoughtfully, "couple of months, maybe more. How many letters have we written?"

No one could remember. All the days had bled into a single routine.

"Do you ever think about Bear?" Cardinal muttered

167

restlessly.

"Every time I eat something more than these awful rations," Ceci replied.

"No," Cardinal snapped irritably. "I mean, as a man."

"Good Lord," Oriole cried, throwing down a half-eaten chunk of cornbread. "Do you mean, what I think you mean?"

"Bear's the only man living, full-time on the island," Cardinal pointed out. "Unless you count Doucet."

The thought of making love to him, made them all shudder.

"God, no," Bunting scowled. "He probably does everything by numbers. You will be issued with one kiss," she began, adopting a ludicrously gruff voice. "Make it last all day. If you want anymore, you'll have to find it yourself."

"What in the hell has gotten into you, Cardinal?" Oriole demanded. "Ain't you got enough to think about?"

"It's been a while," she insisted defensively.

"If you're that desperate," Oriole suggested. "Why don't you just do it yourself?"

"Ain't nothing like the real thing," Cardinal objected.

"Sure ain't," Bunting murmured wistfully. "Bear's a fine big man, and he won't care how we smell."

"Oh, no," Ceci groaned, "not you too. You, of all people."

"Just because it was stole off me one time," she retorted indignantly. "Don't stop me getting the urge to give it away every now and then."

"I have a friend," Ceci smiled in recollection. "A very wise woman. She talks about Ol' Magic. He's what's afflicting you now. He mighty powerful," she recited from memory. "Comes when you least expect him."

"What about you?" Cardinal asked. "Ain't you feeling Ol' Magic."

"Of course," Ceci admitted. "I'm just as human as the rest of you."

"I guess you're saving it for that northern man, you spoke

of," Bunting assumed. "No telling when you'll see him again."

Ceci surged to her feet, driven by a sudden emptiness that clutched at her heart. Without another word, she walked away.

"You damn fool," Oriole snapped. "Now see what you gone and done."

"I'm sorry," Bunting was full of remorse. "I didn't think."

Ceci roamed the woods alone for hours, desperately trying to come to terms with her emotions. For the first time, since her family had been killed, she began to doubt the course of action she'd chosen to take. All she could think of now, was Trent. The way he looked, the way he spoke, the way he smiled. She hugged herself, imagining, it was his touch she felt. That she was in his arms again. That nothing had ever come between them. That he was there, beside her. The thought that she might never see him again ate into her mind, almost robbing her of her sanity. She wondered how she had come to this, raging against the hopelessness of her situation. Presently, she noticed a light in the distance, and made her way towards it. It was Bear, sitting on a log, by a small camp fire, whittling a piece of wood. He said nothing, not even looking up, as she sat on the log opposite him. She remained silent for some time, watching him carve the wood, trying to make sense of her feelings, but no answers came to her.

"You're likely to get a visitor, or two, shortly," she spoke at last.

"I figured," Bear kept whittling. "Saw it in their faces." He stopped carving and looked at her. "Not you though," he remarked astutely.

Ceci looked away.

"Got a man, somewhere out there?" he pointed the stick into the shadows.

"Once," Ceci gave a disconsolate shake of her head. "Maybe," she sighed.

"Seems like you still have," he observed intuitively. He jabbed the wood into the air, making her look up, just in time to see a large bird glide overhead, silhouetted against the evening sky. "Hawk flies far," he told her. "Very far, but he always comes back to the same tree. If you be that tree, your hawk'll come back. Just make sure you don't fall afore that happens."

Ceci stared through the fire-light, the dancing flames illuminating a gentle smile, that framed Bear's battered features. She began to smile as well. She rose and walked round to him, bent and kissed his weathered brow, as he began to whittle again. "Don't let them be too rough with you," she warned, in a motherly fashion. "That little one's a wild cat."

Chapter Nineteen

It was the last day of the third month. Doucet had instructed them to assemble in the cabin, and put on the lightweight dresses they'd been issued with.

"At least he didn't stay and watch us this time," Bunting remarked. "I wonder what this is all about?"

They stood there another half hour, before Doucet returned. He strode into the cabin and pointed at Oriole. "Come with me," he ordered abruptly.

"Where are you taking her?" Cardinal demanded anxiously.

Doucet paused in thought. "You have learned everything we can teach you," he answered eventually. "There is one final test which each of you must face alone. It is a test of readiness. A test of nerve." With that, he motioned to Oriole, and the pair left the cabin.

"I don't like the sound of that," Cardinal fretted.

"Yeah, sounds mighty final," Bunting agreed. "Remember what he said about those who don't reach the required standard."

"He didn't say anything," Ceci recalled. "He avoided the question."

"I know," Bunting nodded. "That's what bothers me."

"Did you think you were going to get a medal at the end of all this?" Ceci asked. "I know Doucet. He's ruthless. He has to know we're ready before he sends us out."

"Never mind," Cardinal realised. "We'll soon find out what's going on, when Oriole gets back."

★★★

Oriole didn't come back. Doucet was alone.

"What's happened to Oriole," they chorused in alarm. "Where is she?"

"That's no concern of yours," he remarked curtly, crooking his finger at Cardinal. "Let's go."

Cardinal hesitated, glancing anxiously at the others. None of them knew what to do.

"Now," Doucet barked, making them flinch.

Reluctantly, Cardinal followed him outside.

"I don't like this," Bunting clutched Ceci's arm. "What do you thinks happened to Oriole?"

Ceci shook her head. "I've no idea." She licked her dry lips. "I know he's ruthless. I just hope he's not crazy."

The time seemed to drag by. It was another hour before Doucet returned, alone again. "You next," he told Bunting.

She shrank against Ceci, terror in her eyes.

"This is the final, ultimate test," Doucet snapped, reaching forward, and grabbing the girl's arm. "No one is exempt." He moved off, dragging Bunting with him.

Ceci waited alone, a growing sense of apprehension weighing down on her. Perhaps, after all, she had made a poor choice in coming here. She began to pace in an attempt to alleviate her anxiety. Doubts crowded into her mind, clouding her perception. She found it difficult to think clearly, allowing her imagination to run riot.

Suddenly, the door banged open making her jump. "Where are the others?" she was beside herself. "Why haven't any of them come back?"

"You don't need to know," Doucet responded coldly. "Now, are you coming? Or do I have to carry you?"

Ceci hesitated, wondering if her newly acquired skills in self-defence would prevail against Doucet. Somehow, she doubted it. After all, he was the teacher. Doubtless, he'd forgotten more than she'd ever know. She took a deep breath and nodded, following him out of the cabin.

He guided her through the clearing, along a hidden track she'd never taken before. "Where are we going?" she asked in a tremulous voice.

"My headquarters," he replied, without looking back. "Don't lag behind."

After about a mile, they came to a huge log cabin, surrounded by several out buildings. Doucet pushed the door open and Ceci followed him inside. It was a veritable palace compared to the stark confines of the shack she'd spent the last three months in. There were thick carpets under foot, fine furniture, draperies on the walls, all illuminated by a crystal chandelier.

"You do pretty well for yourself," she observed.

"I know what I'm doing," he told her, taking a Colt revolver from his desk and strapping it on. "You're the one who still has to pass the test."

"Did the others?" she demanded.

He regarded her dispassionately. "You need only concern yourself with what is about to happen," he remarked ambiguously.

She followed him out of the cabin to a small isolated shack. Inside was a narrow open space and beyond that, a cell, with a tiny window cut in the heavy door. Doucet dropped the flap, revealing a set of iron bars, and peered cautiously through them.

Apparently satisfied with what he saw, he withdrew a large key from his pocket, fitted it into the door lock, and turned it once. He slipped the pistol from its holster, cocking the hammer. Then, placing the flat of his hand against the door, he began to push it open, indicating that Ceci should follow him. With a growing sense of trepidation, she stepped inside.

The cell stank of urine. She gagged, her eyes adjusting slowly to the dim glow of a single oil lamp. A man sat behind a crude wooden table, glaring balefully at them. His aspect was like that of an animal to which a few human features had been added. His long hair and beard were matted and greasy, his skin covered in some unrecognisable filth. His feral eyes lit up as he saw her enter, his face splitting into an awful grin. Saliva dripped from the corner of his mouth, down his beard and onto the table top, where his hands, fingers like claws, dug into the splintered wood.

"Who is he?" Ceci cringed against Doucet.

"His name doesn't matter," Doucet replied calmly. "This man has raped and killed nine young women in the last year. He's been sentenced to hang."

"What's he doing here?" Ceci stared.

"The sheriff is a friend of mine," he told her. "I borrowed him, you might say."

Ceci's eyes had become accustomed to the gloom. She looked around the cell, horrified. Besides the urine stains, the floor was spattered with fresh blood and shreds of torn clothing. "What in the hell have you done?" she demanded, beginning to panic.

"There's no law here," he remarked ominously. "I told you, this is a test of readiness. It will test your nerve. If you cannot come through this, you are useless to me." He placed his hand under her arm, raising it up, transferring the pistol into her trembling fingers. "All you have to do, is keep the gun on him," he instructed softly, stepping back.

"What am I supposed to do now?" Ceci's pulse began to race.

"Just keep it on him," Doucet repeated, his voice growing distant.

"And then what?" Ceci gripped the gun with both hands, trying to steady it, aiming directly at the man's chest. "Doucet," she repeated urgently. "Then what? Doucet."

The door slammed shut behind her. She heard the key turn in the lock.

"If he moves; kill him," Doucet answered through the bars.

Ceci's mouth dried. Her heart began to pound, her breath coming in ragged gasps. Suddenly, the man rose. She took a step back. "Stay where you are," she faltered. "Don't move, or I'll shoot," her voice lacked conviction. The man grinned, fresh saliva drooling down his beard, as he edged slowly around the table. "Stay away," Ceci warned in a shrill voice, taking another step back. "Stay away, or I'll fire."

Suddenly, she realised that she'd never harmed a single living thing in her life, let alone kill another human being. It was as if she'd crashed into a stone wall. The gun wavered. It went against everything she knew, everything she believed in.

The man moved closer, as if sensing her conflict, an inch at a time, stalking her. She glanced down at the bloodstains and torn clothing, evidence of a frenzied attack, that almost paralysed her with terror. Suddenly the man surged forward. She reeled back, closed her eyes, and pulled the trigger.

The hammer fell with a dull click. Her eyes flew open, as her heart missed a beat. She yanked on the trigger again. Once more, the hammer clicked uselessly. She held the weapon at arm's length, pumping the trigger to no avail. The gun was empty. She flung herself at the cell door, screaming through the bars. "Doucet. You bastard."

★★★

Ceci felt the man's presence closing behind her. She turned, grabbing the pistol by its barrel holding it like a club, and lunged forwards, arm raised.

Suddenly, a hand came from behind her, catching her wrist. She spun round, as Doucet wrested the gun from her. She staggered back, panting, confused, glancing at each of them in turn.

"I told you," Doucet reminded her calmly. "This was a test of nerve, to prove your readiness. In the field, you must kill, or be killed. Not everyone is capable of that. You've just proved that you are."

She looked at the condemned man. He'd just pulled off his wig, and was wiping the greasepaint from his face with a cloth.

"Booth," she gasped.

He bowed theatrically. "We meet again, Miss Prejean. Or should I say, Whippoorwill?"

Ceci stared, speechless.

"You may recall I once told you," he continued lightly, "that I hoped to have the opportunity of performing for you."

Ceci glanced down at the floor, her senses reeling, at the blood and torn clothing.

"My idea," Booth informed her, with an idle gesture. "Animal blood and scraps of clothing. A nice touch, don't you think. Very authentic."

Ceci began to shudder violently, tears streaming down her cheeks. She closed her eyes in humiliation as she felt warm liquid begin to trickle down the inside of her thigh. Then her bladder relaxed completely. She shuddered again, letting out a faint choking sob, as a large puddle began to form on the floor.

"It's only shock," Doucet told her. "No need to feel ashamed. Most of the others reacted in the same way."

Ceci began to calm down. She breathed deeply, summoning what little remained of her strength. Then she lashed out, slapping Doucet across the face. "You ever pull anything, like that, on me again," she flared. "You'll find out just how ready I am to kill a man." With that, she stormed outside.

"She's ready," Booth continued to wipe the paint from his

face. "They're all ready." He paused, the rag hanging limp in his hand. "You disagree?" he questioned Doucet's silence.

"None of them fell back on their self-defence training, once they discovered the pistol was empty," Doucet gave voice to his doubts. "Any one of them could have dropped you, without a weapon."

"You designed the test to prove if they could kill under stress," Booth reminded him. "They all pulled the trigger. If you wanted a different reaction. You should have sent them in unarmed, and not intervened so soon."

"In that case, you might have been killed," Doucet told him.

"Then the fault lies with the test, and not with them," Booth pointed out.

"All right then," Doucet conceded. "We'll send them home tomorrow. Let them rest before assigning them. We'll soon find out how many of them are strong enough to survive in the field."

Booth threw the cloth onto the table. "When do we send them after Lincoln?" he asked.

"I told you before," Doucet growled. "That won't happen. Not unless we lose the war."

★★★

As he emerged from the shack, Doucet found Ceci standing right out in the middle of the clearing, making sure she had as much open ground around her as possible. He made no attempt to approach her. "Come on."

"I ain't going anywhere with you," she shouted back.

He studied her for a moment. "The others are waiting."

"Others?"

"Come on."

Ceci followed him at a distance, back to the main cabin, lingering at the threshold as he traversed the room and opened the door to a small annex, allowing the rest of the Bird spies to swarm out.

"I thought you were all dead," Ceci cried, rushing forward.

It was an emotional reunion, until they remembered why they were all in this state in the first place. As one, they turned, glaring at Doucet.

He remained unperturbed. "Contrary to your imaginings. I derived no perverted pleasure from your ordeal," he told them. "A day will come, in the field, when your life is threatened. You will not hesitate, but react on instinct, and survive, only because of what you have endured here today."

Without waiting for a response, he walked over to the double doors at the back of the cabin and thrust them aside. The room beyond blazed with lamplight. At its centre was a huge wooden tub, as big as a wine vat, clouds of vapour hanging over it, brimming with hot water. Beyond that, their own clothes, freshly laundered, were laid out next to a sideboard laden with plates of beef and venison, fresh bread, cheese and wine.

"You have earned this," he pointed into the room. "Next door are four soft beds with clean sheets. Enjoy." He paused, taking a bundle of bank notes from his waistcoat pocket and offered them to Ceci. "That's a good trick," he told her. "A pocket in your underwear. The organisation will adopt it for future use."

"I pity the next batch of recruits coming through here," she didn't mind admitting.

"No one else is coming here," Doucet replied. "After tomorrow, the island will be abandoned, and all traces of our activities will be erased."

"But you said you were recruiting other women," Oriole recalled.

"And so we shall," he assured her. "But we won't train them here. Another lesson for you," he told them. "Keep moving. Keep the enemy guessing. That's how you stay alive." With that, he strode out of the cabin, closing the door behind him.

The four of them clustered around the entrance to the room, staring cautiously inside.

"Do you think it's another test?" Oriole wondered.

"I'm willing to risk it," Cardinal remarked, the aroma of roast beef teasing her nostrils.

"Doucet said that the cell was the final test," Ceci recalled. "I think it's safe for us to go in."

The mention of the cell made Oriole shudder. "In that room," she confided. "I've never been so terrified in all my life." She broke off, her cheeks reddening. "I couldn't control myself. It was awful."

"I haven't peed my drawers since I was a little girl," Cardinal admitted, with her usual candour. "But I sure cut loose in there."

Ceci touched a finger to her lips, gesturing at Bunting. "The man was supposed to be a rapist," she reminded them of her history.

The diminutive redhead looked up at them. "What?" she shrugged, pushing past, pulling off her dress, as she headed for the tub. "I tried to shoot the bastard, as soon as Doucet put the gun in my hand. I guess I passed straightaway."

★★★

"I'd forgotten what it feels like to be clean," Cardinal sighed, as she joined the others in the tub. "Who volunteers to scrub my back?"

Ceci began to soap her down realising that although she'd known the passionate love of a man, once she would have considered it entirely inappropriate to bathe with other women, but a lot had changed since then.

"Do you think ol' Doucet is out there, peeking in?" Bunting wondered. She raised her arms, flaunting her breasts at the window.

In a moment, out of sheer exuberance and bravado, after months of privation, they were all doing it, until, finally, they collapsed back in the tub, afflicted by a fit of laughter.

"I don't think he's that kind of a man," Ceci suggested, in hindsight.

"Honey, they're all that kind of man," Cardinal disagreed vehemently.

"No, really," Ceci insisted. "He's a seasoned professional. There's good reason behind everything he does. Although it may not be apparent at the time."

"When it comes to men," Cardinal told her. "There's always a good reason, and it usually becomes apparent, once their hand is in your drawers."

Gusts of laughter rose into the room. They began to splash each other, starting a boisterous free-for-all that nearly drowned Bunting.

As the layers of ingrained dirt began to wash off, they noticed that they were all covered in huge bruises. Colourful souvenirs of their rigorous training. Ceci's whole left side was black and blue. The relentless pace and hard living had allowed them no time to consider these superficial injuries.

"I don't know about the rest of you," Oriole winced, "but mine are beginning to hurt."

"It's the hot water," Ceci realised. "It's relaxed us. Now we're going to suffer."

"I'd suffer a little less, if you didn't poke your fingers into mine," Cardinal complained to Bunting.

"Well, I'm sorry. I thought it was dirt."

Eventually the water began to cool, forcing them out of the tub.

"I'm starving. Let's eat." Cardinal wrapped a towel around herself, advancing on the sideboard.

"Don't eat too much," Ceci cautioned. "You're not used to it."

Her warning fell on deaf ears. The banquet was just too

tempting, and they had been hungry for too long. All of them, including Ceci, despite her initial prudence, gorged themselves until their stomachs groaned.

Exhausted by the day's events, they moved into the dormitory and donned the plain cotton nightdresses that had been left for them.

"It's a pity, after all we've bin through together," Bunting mused, as she climbed into bed. "That we can't tell each other our real names, or where we come from. It means we'll never see each other again."

"I know," Oriole agreed. "But we mustn't be tempted to break Doucet's rule of silence. If we do, and one of us is captured and forced to talk, they'll betray the rest, and that'll be the end of us all."

Her statement caused a profound silence to descend on the room, as each one of them considered their future. At the camp, all their mistakes had been forgiven. Where they were going, there would be no second chances.

Chapter Twenty

When Ceci returned home, Hecubah was overjoyed. Her face lit up, when she saw her, but the smile quickly faded.

"What happened to your hair?" she stared in dismay.

Ceci repeated Doucet's cover story. "It'll grow back," she assured her. "But I'm keeping it short for the duration of the war. It's my protest." It was a small lie, but she needed to give Hecubah a reason for keeping it short.

"Suit yourself," Hecubah shrugged. "Lord, child. You look so thin," she continued to fuss. "Didn't they feed you?"

"I'm fine," Ceci assured her. "Nothing a little home cooking won't put right."

"It's so good to have you back." Hecubah threw her arms around her and hugged her.

Ceci gasped in pain.

"What's the matter, child?" Hecubah frowned with concern.

"It's nothing," Ceci made light of it. "I fell while I was moving some beds. I hurt my back."

"I'm gonna get you to your room," Hecubah remarked purposefully. "Give you a good meal and tend to your hurt. Then you can tell me all about it."

★★★

"God almighty," Hecubah swore, when she saw the huge purple bruise spreading over Ceci's side. "I'm gonna fix a poultice for that."

"It's all right," Ceci declined. "It don't hurt that much now."

"Was it very bad, out there?" Hecubah enquired tentatively. "You didn't say much in your letters."

"Bad enough," Ceci told her. "If you don't mind, I won't talk about it."

"I understand," Hecubah accepted her decision without complaint. "I bin so worried whilst you was away," she confessed. "But now you're safe home again."

"It's good to be back," Ceci agreed, but in truth, she felt no joy in her homecoming because she knew she wasn't here to stay. This was merely a pause, before she continued the journey she had committed herself to. Where it would take her, she didn't know. There was only one thing she was certain of. In the near future, she was going to break Hecubah's heart.

★★★

Thanksgiving came and went, although there seemed little to be thankful for. Christmas was a quiet subdued affair, haunted by the ghosts of lost loved ones. She and Hecubah together, could find no cheer in it.

As the new year dawned, Ceci took the engagement ring from her jewellery box, where she'd left it for safe keeping before going to the island, and slipped it on again. It was 1863, and still the war continued, with no clear end in sight. No more letters from Trent had reached her, and she saw little point in writing to him. She looked at his picture, twisting the ring around her finger, and sighed. The dark creature within her heard her sighs and began to whisper. By now, she could have been a wife, a mother, with a loving husband at her side, but all of that had been denied her. Lincoln, and the accursed Union, had robbed her of it. A whole new year stood before her. It could have meant so much, but now, there was nothing to look forward to. She took off the ring and put it away. She hoped, with all her heart, that it would not be too long before she put it on again. That is, if she ever did.

★★★

"That damn bird was out in the garden again, last night," Hecubah complained, as they finished breakfast. "Calling all hours of the night. I've a mind to take a gun and shoot it."

"What bird?" Ceci asked.

"You mean, you ain't heard it?" she stared in surprise. "Blamed whippoorwill turned up, just after you come back. Gone and made its home out there."

"It ain't doing any harm," Ceci smiled to herself. "Leave it be."

"I don't like it," Hecubah admitted. "The way it arrived when you come home. It's an omen. Has to be."

"Don't start that," Ceci objected. "You'll have us both jumping at our own shadows."

"I guess so," she agreed. "It ain't as if you're not skittish enough already."

"What's that supposed to mean?" Ceci demanded.

"You bin kinda restless, since you got back," Hecubah told her. "It's like you is waiting for something, or someone."

Ceci hadn't realised she'd been so obvious.

"You flinch every time there's a knock at the door," Hecubah continued. "Is you expecting someone to call?"

"Of course, not," Ceci dismissed her concerns. "It's just nerves, is all."

"Ah huh," Hecubah nodded, "you know, child, there's nothing you can't tell me. There ain't nothing we can't fix. All you gotta do is confide in me."

"All I want to tell you is that I love you," Ceci replied earnestly. "I always will. You know that, don't you?"

"Of course, honey," Hecubah shot her a quizzical glance.

"Remember, I told you once. No matter what happens, I'll always be your Hecubah."

★★★

Ceci never heard the knock at the door, she'd anticipated for so long. It wasn't until a maid came into the day room holding a silver tray with Doucet's calling card on it that she knew the time had come.

She sent the maid away and went and fetched Doucet herself, locking the door behind them.

"I'm glad to see you looking so well," he greeted her pleasantly.

"No thanks to you," she responded coldly.

"Everything I did was necessary," he defended his actions. "As you'll soon find out." He placed a large, thick envelope on the desk between them. "The position of housemaid awaits you in the home of Mr Josiah Douglas of Washington."

"I endured three months of misery just to become a housemaid?" Ceci scoffed.

"Don't underestimate this assignment," he warned her. "You'll be right in the heart of enemy territory. If they discover what you're doing, they will execute you."

"What's the plan?" Ceci asked soberly.

"Our friend Douglas is a minor official at the White House," Doucet explained. "One of several secretaries assisting President Lincoln, which gives him access to a lot of confidential information. He has three qualities we find attractive. He has an over inflated opinion of his own importance, a very loose tongue, and he loves to entertain, especially military men and politicians. You will travel to Alexandria, Virginia, cross the Potomac into Washington via the Long Bridge, near Fort Jackson, and take up the position."

"You make it all sound so simple," Ceci remarked.

"Oh, it is," he assured her. "Just so long as you use your

185

head and keep your nerve. Your alias is Mariah Johnson of Akron, Ohio. Your identity has already been established. You're expected. No one will question your arrival."

There was no doubting Doucet's ability, or the far-reaching influence of his organisation. "Who's my contact in Washington?" she asked.

"You remembered your training, that's good," he approved. "It's Mrs Enola Sykes, a southern sympathiser. She runs the General Store on the corner of Maple Street. You will identify yourself to her by asking for Indian Gold Thread. Thereafter you will pass all the information you gather onto her in the form of coded grocery lists. If any of our other agents are ordered to contact you, they will use the phrase, 'Shake the Pillars of Heaven', in conversation. When you hear this, wait until it's safe to meet with them, and then give your call sign. They will find you."

"When do I leave?" she asked.

"In three days' time," Doucet tapped the envelope. "Everything you need, is in here. Details of the route, train tickets, travel passes and expenses, in gold, and both Confederate and Federal dollars."

Ceci leaned back in her chair, gazing around the room. "How long am I likely to be there?" she wondered.

"For as long as is necessary," Doucet replied, noticing her expression. "I did warn you, that you might not see your home for some time. In case you're having some second thoughts on this, let me assure you that what you do in Washington could turn the tide of the war in our favour, possibly even end it." He paused, adding with emphasis. "Your father would be proud."

Doucet was ruthless, with years of experience in manipulating others. Ceci was vulnerable. His words stirred her dark creature. It howled from the depths of the void within her, cancelling any misgivings she might have had.

"I have every intention of seeing this through," she

assured him resolutely. "I will not allow the death of my family to go unavenged."

"I'm glad to hear it," he seemed satisfied with her answer. "Then it only remains for me to wish you good luck and Godspeed."

★★★

That evening, Ceci went to her room and began to pack a bag. She couldn't afford to be hampered by a large trunk, which limited what she could take. Some dresses, linen, spare shoes. She could replace what she'd left behind when she got to Washington. Doucet had given her ample funds for that, and if she needed more, Enola Sykes would provide it. As she stood there, pondering what to take and what to leave, the door burst open and Hecubah stormed in.

"You lied to me," she shouted. "You bin lying all along. What you got yourself into?"

"I don't know what you mean?" Ceci prevaricated.

"Doucet was here," Hecubah fumed. "And not for the first time. How'd you meet him?"

"I made his acquaintance on the night of my ball," Ceci answered calmly. "Then he turned up a few months ago, to offer his condolences for the loss of my family."

"Ah huh," Hecubah interrupted angrily. "I bet that ain't all he offered. What's he persuaded you to do?"

"Nothing, I wouldn't have done by myself, had I been able," Ceci remarked defiantly.

Hecubah couldn't believe what she was hearing. "Do you have any idea of what kind of a man he is?"

"He's a patriot," Ceci replied with conviction.

"A fanatic, more like," Hecubah raged. "I heard your daddy speak of him. He didn't trust him, and neither should you."

"He'll help me avenge the death of my family," Ceci responded recklessly.

"He don't care about your family," Hecubah sneered. "He can't help you. All he can do is drag you down to hell."

"My mind's made up," Ceci told her stubbornly.

"Putting your life in danger ain't gonna bring no one back," Hecubah attempted to reason with her. "Don't do this, honey. You got so much to live for."

"If I have so much to live for," Ceci countered, "then I should be prepared to defend it."

"That's Doucet talking," Hecubah scowled. "Can't you see, he's using you? Trent begged you to stay safe at home. Why don't you listen to him?"

"Trent's out there, fighting my people," she reminded her.

"He's only doing what he has to do," Hecubah flared.

"So am I," Ceci yelled back.

"God almighty," Hecubah wrung her hands in frustration. "If I had that hickory switch now. I'd whip your bottom raw." At her wits end she lunged forward, grabbing Ceci roughly by the arm. "You ain't going," she told her. "I ain't gonna let you go."

Acting out of blind instinct, Ceci broke free, the palm of her hand cracking down across the woman's face. "I won't tolerate that kind of behaviour from a slave," she spat tersely.

Hecubah staggered back, eyes wide, lips trembling, astounded by the blatant insult. In the next instant she surged forward, pushing her face into Ceci's. "When I stepped into that room, all them years ago," she told her, her eyes misty with tears. "And saw that unhappy, angry little girl, my heart went out to you. All I can see now, is that same unhappy, angry little girl." She began to cry in earnest. "I'm so sorry your family was killed, but that don't give you no call to do what you're gonna do. All that's out there is death and tears, and it breaks my heart to know that you're gonna be right in the middle of it." She grasped Ceci by the shoulders, tears flooding uncontrollably down her amber cheeks. "I raised you, just like you was my own baby," she sobbed. "But I don't

188

know who you is now." She stepped back, pushing Ceci away, tore the silver dollar from her throat and threw it on the bed. "I don't wanna know who you is now." She spared Ceci a last, withering, glance, then marched out of the room.

Drained and exhausted, Ceci sank onto a chair, put her face in her hands and breathed deeply. She couldn't believe she'd been capable of such cruelty. It was, she told herself, like the lies, a necessary evil. After all they'd meant to one another, it grieved her to part company with Hecubah in such an acrimonious fashion, but it was the only way. All she could hope for was, that one day, Hecubah would understand why she'd acted as she did and find it in her heart to forgive her.

★★★

Ceci had little time to dwell on the incident. She had only a day to put her affairs in order, before she left for Washington.

The rap of knuckles on wood, sharp and brief, made her glance up. Simon Robicheaux stood in the doorway of the day room. He was a tall, powerfully built man, with greying hair and a face burned brown by the sun. He wore a dark jacket and waistcoat, tan breeches and tall leather boots. In his hand, he held a white, wide brimmed felt hat. A shrewd man of few words and even temper, he knew the plantation better than anyone.

"Thank you for coming, Mr Robicheaux," Ceci invited him in, indicating the chair on the other side of the desk at which she sat.

He crossed the room in a few strides, and sat down.

"You have been overseer on this plantation for more than thirty years," she recalled, pouring two glasses of Sazerac and offering him one. "My father trusted you implicitly, and so shall I."

He accepted the glass, taking a large swig, the merest nod acknowledging her statement.

189

"I must leave tomorrow," she informed him solemnly. The very idea of what she was embarking upon, chilled the marrow in her bones. She took a sip from her glass. It didn't help. "I may be gone for quite some time," she continued tonelessly. "I want you to run this plantation in my absence, not only for the benefit of the people here, but also in the cause of the South."

Robicheaux drank again, offering her another stoic nod. There was nothing in her request that was beyond his ability.

Ceci opened a drawer in the desk, and produced a slim leather wallet. "In here are some documents that will empower you to act in my name." She laid the wallet on the desk in front of him. "I wonder if you would do some personal things for me," she added.

"You have only to ask," he told her.

"These are Hecubah's papers." She placed a large white envelope on top of the wallet. "The death of my father means, that I can set her free." Her heart sank. She averted her eyes, biting at her lip. She knew, that having uttered these words, she might never see her again. "If she chooses to stay here," she forced herself to go on. "I want her to have the position of housekeeper, with a salary of fifty dollars a month, in gold," she emphasised, "not Confederate currency."

Robicheaux listened, a puzzled frown beginning to crease his brow.

"If she chooses to leave," Ceci paused, running her tongue over her dry lips. "There's a bank draught for a thousand dollars, in gold. Will you see that she gets it?"

Robicheaux glanced down, his fingers pinching nervously at the brim of his hat.

"Is something the matter?" she asked, noticing the man's agitation.

"There's been some mighty wild rumours circulating," he prevaricated.

Ceci leaned back in her chair. "Rumours?"

"You and Ms Hecubah was like kin," he finally came to

the point. "Now…" he broke off with a shrug.

"Mr Robicheaux. I have a very dangerous journey to make," she explained as best she could. "Hecubah has been like a mother to me. I know that she would try to follow me, and likely get herself killed doing it. I would rather she remained here, with a broken heart, alive, than out there, dead beside me." She paused, her heart aching as she recalled the terrible exchange between her and her beloved Hecubah. "It will take a very great deal to stop her. I can only pray, that I have done enough."

The light of understanding, banished the frown from Robicheaux's face.

Ceci produced a second envelope and placed it on top of the first. "You know the girl, Tilly?"

"I know her," he confirmed.

"I have freed her also," Ceci told him. "I want you to ask Hecubah to find her an education, and then an occupation on which she can live comfortably for the rest of her life. I would have freed them all," she confided. "Despite Mr Lincoln's proclamation, but that would have aroused too much suspicion."

She fell silent, staring at the desktop, preoccupied with what lay ahead of her. Robicheaux took it as a sign that the meeting was over. He rose, tossed back the remainder of his drink, returned the glass to the table, and gathered up the documents with a single sweep of his hand. He made to leave, then turned back. "God go with you, Miss Cecile," he remarked vehemently. "We'll all be looking for you every day."

"If," Ceci began. "If I," she almost choked on the thought. "If I should fail to return…"

"I shall run this plantation," he anticipated her, "to the best of my ability. To the day, I die."

"Thank you, sir," she sighed with relief. "You are very gallant."

He inclined his head to her, and began to withdraw.

"Oh, Mr Robicheaux," she stopped him half-way between

the desk and the door. Leaving her chair, she crossed the room to face him, stretching out her clenched fist.

Instinctively, he opened his hand beneath it. Ceci dropped a drilled silver dollar into his palm, the gold chain, that had newly been threaded through it, dangling between his fingers.

"Would you please give this back to Hecubah for me?" she asked. "Tell her. Tell her, she won it fair and square."

★★★

That night, Ceci checked that she had packed everything she needed. Then waited, sleepless, for the sun to rise. She felt strangely calm, at peace for the first time in months. She couldn't account for it, but she was glad of it.

As the first light of dawn began to suffuse the night sky, she rose, picked up her bag and made her way softly down the back stairs. The house was still, deathly quiet, as if it mourned her departure. All the life seemed to have fled out of it.

She passed through the empty kitchen and on to the side door she had chosen to leave by. She unlocked it and stepped outside. There, she paused, gazing out across the garden, the cypresses and cottonwoods, to the bayou beyond. This was all she'd ever known. All her hopes and dreams had been born here. All her joys, her sorrows, her love and her heartache. Although she knew a part of her would never leave here. She wondered if she would ever see it again.

She closed the door. It clicked shut with an aire of finality. She realised that all the world stood before her, and that she had little understanding of it. All she could rely on now were her wits and her training. She hoped that it would be enough.

Hecubah had been right. She'd warned her that one day she'd wake up to discover that she'd a whole lot more to lose. This was that day.

Chapter Twenty One

For the time being, Ceci had no option but to put the past behind her so that she could concentrate on what lay ahead. She began her journey in Louisiana and continued through Mississippi, Tennessee, and on to Richmond, Virginia, the capital city of the Confederacy. The further north she went, the more evidence she saw of the terrible devastation the war had wrought on southern towns and cities. Burned houses, ruined crops and deserted plantations. While thousands of dispossessed people, black and white, clogged the roads in search of safety and shelter. There were even times when the train had to be diverted to avoid sections of rail that had been destroyed.

It was many days of arduous and exhausting travel. She had brought some food with her. Not enough for the entire journey, but she was able to buy more whenever they came to a station, which she ate on the train. Every so often it would stop for an hour to take on wood and water, allowing the passengers to alight, stretch their legs, find something to eat and relieve themselves. Most towns had hotels where a traveller could rent a comfortable room for the night before resuming their journey. Ceci had something of a schedule to keep, and preferred to remain on the train. Sometimes travelling all night, snatching a few hours of sleep, whenever she could.

The railroad cars were packed with both civilians and soldiers, all of whom were required to carry travel passes. These had to be shown to the conductor whenever they crossed a border, or to the commanding officer of any picket line they had to pass through. Doucet had supplied her with both Confederate and Union passes. The federal documents had been forged by experts, and her passage was never questioned. Which amused her somewhat, considering the passes had been intended to deter spies and saboteurs. She kept herself to herself, rarely engaging in conversation with other passengers. Never saying anything that would give them cause to remember her.

Delays were inevitable. Since conscription had come into force, thousands of new recruits had swelled the ranks of the Confederate army. From the windows of her railroad car, she saw whole regiments waiting to embark for the front line at every depot she passed through. She'd read that, at the beginning of the war, there had been a good deal of confusion over the colour of uniforms, making it difficult to tell which side a man was on. Finally, the Confederacy had settled on grey, and that's what she saw now, oceans of grey uniforms. Although on some occasions, she noticed that many men had no uniforms, some didn't even possess shoes. Since the Union had gained control of the Mississippi, it had become increasingly difficult to ship supplies to the troops. It was a worrying sign.

After more than a week of continuous travel, she arrived in Richmond, Virginia. According to the plan Doucet had given her, she stopped for the day, rented a hotel room, bathed, changed her clothes and got a good night's sleep. In the morning, she boarded the train to Alexandria, and Fort Jackson.

The city was of enormous strategic importance to both factions, being on the southern side of the Potomac, only a few miles from Washington, the capital of the United States.

It had fallen to the North, early in the war, and was guarded by a strong federal garrison, which controlled all the traffic on the river, as well as all the bridges across it.

It was like entering a foreign country. The language and the customs were the same, but now the uniforms were blue. She noticed, in sharp contrast to what she witnessed further south, that all the men here were well equipped. It was here that she saw her first negro soldier. She recalled the concerns of the man in her father's day room, some years before. Lincoln had emancipated the slaves and was now recruiting thousands of black troops to throw against the Confederacy. The sight of a black man was nothing new to her, but to see one in uniform was quite a different matter. In the South, many viewed coloured people as simple, childlike creatures, without the intelligence to make useful decisions. Here, as soldiers, they represented a formidable fighting force, motivated, no doubt, by the grudge they bore towards the South. They had left as slaves. They intended to return as conquerors.

Ceci left the train and walked the rest of the way, reaching the Long Bridge in the early afternoon. As a key crossing into Washington, it was heavily defended against a rebel assault. For miles around, all the land had been torn up, buildings demolished, fences pulled down and trees felled to provide space for artillery emplacements and trench works. Besides several large forts in the area, there was also a detachment of cavalry, which guarded the bridge twenty-four hours a day. Security was tight.

Ceci knew something that Doucet could never have taught her. By the time she'd turned sixteen, she was already well aware that a pretty girl, especially around older men, usually had no trouble in getting her own way. She considered battle weary soldiers, far from home, to be even easier prey, and she was right. A coy smile and the flutter of her eyelashes, proved to be more effective than the forged travel pass. Ultimately, the officer of the guard escorted her personally across the bridge, carrying her bag for her. She considered it her first victory over the Union.

At last, she stood on the outskirts of Washington city. Only now did she deviate from the plan. Following the directions the officer had given her, she trudged the extra miles to the White House. It was a personal pilgrimage. Something she had promised herself she would do as soon as she got here.

As she looked across the grounds at the imposing edifice, she felt the dark creature stir within her. This was the home of Abraham Lincoln, the seat of government in the United States, and the object of all her hatred. She ground her teeth and clenched her fists. If she could have torn it down with her bare hands she would have done so, there and then. For now, she contented herself with the thought that if she played her part well, one day, the only flag flying from the mast outside would be the Southern Cross.

It was getting late, and the Douglas house was still some miles away. Turning her back on the impressive building, she set off across town ready to initiate the first part of her plan.

The size of the city didn't impress her. She'd been to Lafayette, New Orleans and Baton Rouge. One big city was much like another, crowded, noisy and dirty. She continued walking, until she found the address she was looking for. The Douglas residence was a fine town house, standing in its own grounds. Somewhat grand for a minor official, but Ceci already knew that Josiah was living precariously beyond his means.

She paused for a moment, a sense of trepidation stealing over her. The success of her assignment relied on her being able to gain access to this house. If anything went wrong now, the plan would fail, which could cost her her life. It was her first real test of nerve. She drew a deep breath, her hand tightening on the handle of her bag.

Then, as instructed, she made her way around to the back door and knocked. She waited for a tense moment, before the door was opened by the housekeeper, Florina Winthrop, an aging spinster with little or no idea how to do her job.

The information Doucet had supplied, informed her that Florina was a distant relative of Josiah's who had fallen on hard times. He'd taken her in, more as a favour than practical help. She seemed pleased to see Ceci, even more so when she'd offered her cover story. She told her that she was experienced in running a house, which wasn't all lies. Hecubah had taught her the basic skills required of a married woman to run her own household. It wasn't much, but it was a lot more than Florina knew.

In the weeks that followed she seemed happy to leave Ceci mostly to her own devices, gradually relying on her meagre ability to cover what she lacked. Absent minded and prone to vacillation, Ceci found it easy to manipulate her to her own ends.

The cook occupied a room adjacent to the kitchen, in the basement. The two other maids that worked in the house, had to share a room in the servant's quarters on the ground floor. Ceci got a small box room all to herself. Doucet had seen to that. Privacy was of paramount importance.

She soon discovered that although the hours were long, her duties were relatively light, allowing her plenty of time to eavesdrop. Despite any misgivings she might have had about Doucet, she couldn't help but admire his ability. His meticulous groundwork and attention to detail had allowed her to enter the Douglas household, unchallenged and virtually unnoticed. As time passed, they paid little more attention to her than they did the furniture, allowing her considerable freedom of movement.

The Douglas's were a small family. There was Josiah and his wife, Lydia, and their two daughters. Constance, sixteen, bright and inquisitive, full of energy and questions, and Amelia, twenty-two. Like Ceci, she had succumbed to the caresses of her young man, but without someone like Hecubah to help her she now bore the evidence of her encounter. Her father had banished her to the upper floors of the house, to hide her shame from the neighbours, where she now lived in virtual isolation. They reminded Ceci a little, of how her family had once been. She both envied and hated them for having what she'd lost.

As part of her duties, Ceci was required to run errands. Again, Doucet had made it easy for her to move around. At her earliest opportunity, she made her way to the General Store on the corner of Maple Street, barely a mile from the house.

She paused, glancing apprehensively through the window. Several customers were roaming around inside. This was her second test of nerve. She had to remain calm and act normally. She entered, loitering furtively at the back of the premises, as if perusing the merchandise. It wasn't until the last of the clientele had left that she felt it was safe to approach the counter.

A tall woman of about forty, stood behind it. Clearly she had been attractive once, but her looks were fading now. Judging from the description, she'd been given, she assumed it was Enola Sykes. She smiled as Ceci came up to her.

Ceci drew a deep breath. "I wonder," she began. "Do you have any Indian Gold Thread?"

The smile wavered a little. "Why, of course, my dear," she replied, the smile returning. "I think I have just what you need." She produced a small carpet bag from behind the counter and set it down in front of her, placing her hand on top of it. "Don't open it in here," she advised, in hushed tones.

Ceci thanked her, then introduced herself as Mariah Johnson of Akron Ohio, learning in return that it was, indeed, Enola Sykes, to whom she was speaking.

"You have a fine store, Mrs Sykes," she complimented her. "I think I shall do all my errands here from now on."

"I'm so very glad to hear that," Enola's smile broadened. "I shall look forward to seeing you again, very soon."

Carrying the bag through the street made Ceci feel nervous and self-conscious. It was like having a stick of dynamite in her hand. She rebuked herself for her paranoia. She'd been trained better than this. She forced herself to calm down, her footsteps becoming easy and measured. No matter what happened, she must not attract attention to herself.

As soon as she reached the house, she went straight to her room, locked the door and opened the bag. It contained, amongst other things, the two lightweight uniforms and the dress. There was also a compass, maps, codebooks, and a Colt revolver with ammunition. The contents of this bag would not have passed inspection at the Long Bridge in Alexandria. Again, Doucet had done his job well. Ceci hid the bag in her bedside cabinet and locked it, keeping the key with her at all times. Now she possessed the means to carry out her espionage. On the other hand, it also represented irrefutable evidence of her being a spy.

★★★

Everything Doucet had told her came to pass. Josiah Douglas did indeed love to entertain, almost every night. His many guests included soldiers from the rank of Lieutenant up, congressmen, town dignitaries, anyone in fact that could boost his ego, and what he felt was his position in the community. He was a creature of outstanding imprudence, openly discussing sensitive issues right in front of anyone who happened to be there. More often than not it was Ceci, in her guise as a maid, serving drinks or coffee. What she missed she could usually catch up on when he repeated the information to his wife once his guests had left. The rest she gathered by listening at doors. If anyone chanced to find her there, which didn't happen often, quite naturally she was just about to enter, to serve or clear away. It was incredible the amount of information that flowed out of that house. It was just like taking candy from a baby.

The winters in Washington were cold. It was the first time Ceci had ever seen snow. The damp air seeped into the marrow of her bones. She missed the Louisiana sunshine. She missed her home on the plantation, and most of all, she missed Hecubah. She hoped that, one day, she might be able to make a reconciliation with her, if such a thing were even possible. She hoped that, one day, she might go home again, but above all, she longed to see Trent.

There were some nights, when she would sit alone in her room sobbing quietly to herself out of sheer loneliness. When she got very low, she'd force herself to remember her dead father, her sister, and the niece she had never seen. Purposely evoking the dark creature within her to remind her of why she was here. It gave her strength and purpose, driving her endlessly on, regardless of hope or desire, without conscience or emotion, towards–what? She wasn't sure she knew. She wasn't sure if she'd ever known.

★★★

The upstairs maid had twisted her ankle and been confined to her room for a few days. Florina asked Ceci if she would take Amelia's dinner up to her on a tray.

As she entered the room, Ceci saw a pale young woman, in an advanced state of pregnancy, sitting at her dressing table. She'd let her hair down, and was attempting to brush it, in long listless strokes.

"Please put it on the table," she requested, without turning.

Ceci did as she asked, pausing to look at her, as she struggled with her wayward tresses.

"Let me do that," she offered, advancing.

Amelia glanced round. "Oh, I'm sorry," she gasped, "you're the new girl. I hadn't realised."

"I've been here three months now," Ceci replied, taking the brush from her.

"That long," Amelia sighed, glancing down at her swollen stomach. "How the time has flown."

Ceci could see, from the reflection in the mirror, that Amelia didn't have much longer to wait.

"As you can see," she gestured, noticing her interest. "I am a fallen woman. Do I disgust you?"

"No," Ceci answered truthfully. "Of course, not." She continued to brush the girl's hair for a moment, before asking. "Do you still love him?"

Amelia reached out and picked up a picture, much like the one Ceci kept of Trent. "With all my heart," she sighed, touching it to her lips.

"Where is he now?" Ceci kept brushing.

"Frank is away, fighting in the war," Amelia sighed again. "He left before he knew of my condition. Otherwise, he would have married me." She paused. "I pray every day for his safe return."

Ceci couldn't fail to see the similarities between them. "What will you do, if he doesn't come back?" she felt bound to ask.

Amelia tensed. "If that is God's will," she declared resolutely. "I will be proud to raise Frank's child, in his name, on my own. I don't care what people think, or say, about me."

Ceci stopped brushing, and placed her hand gently on the girl's shoulder. "You're very brave."

Amelia looked into the mirror, at Ceci's reflection. "I see it in your eyes," she observed. "You have a young man fighting in the war as well."

Ceci couldn't help but smile. Not only did she have a young man fighting in the war, he was on the same side as Frank. "Yes, I do," she admitted.

"What's his name?" Amelia seemed eager to know.

There were no real names in the world Ceci inhabited now. "James," she plucked it out of the air.

Amelia placed her hand over Ceci's. "I will pray for him too."

"I'd best be getting back to my duties," Ceci put the brush back on the dressing table.

"Please, come again, whenever you can," Amelia pleaded. "I am starved of company."

"I'll see what I can do," Ceci assured her.

She closed the door behind her, and leaned back against it. For the first time, since she'd crossed the border, she'd met a northerner she didn't view with malice. The dark creature within her stirred, growling a warning but this time she ignored it. No matter what had happened to her in the past, she couldn't find it in her heart to hate this young woman.

★★★

"I'm afraid it's quite a long list today, Mrs Sykes," Ceci informed her, as she passed the coded message across the counter.

"Not to worry, honey," Enola smiled, as the customers around them looked on. "I'm always so grateful for your custom, but you'll have to pick them up tomorrow."

"That's all right," Ceci assured her, continuing to play her part. "In the meantime, I'll take this with me." She always made a point of buying something whenever she visited the store, to add authenticity to the transaction.

Enola wrapped her purchase and gave it to her. "Don't forget your receipt," she remarked, as Ceci made to leave.

She faltered a little, glancing at the other customers. In all the time she'd passed information, she'd never got a message back. As she reached for the slip of paper, she knew something had changed.

Chapter Twenty Two

As soon as she was able, Ceci decoded the message to discover that Mrs Sykes had a new customer. A young soldier, a telegraph operator, with a taste for hard rock candy. Apparently, he came into the store at the same time, on the same day, every week. That was all the message contained, but the opportunity it presented, was obvious.

When the day came around again, Ceci put on the best dress she'd brought with her, made a special effort with her hair, applied some lip colour and a dab of perfume, arriving at the store fifteen minutes before her target was due. As she entered, Enola produced a pile of bogus packages and placed them on the counter. Then they both waited. Presently, the young soldier came in. "Good morning, Ma'am," he smiled broadly. "A bag of hard rock candy, if you please."

He was square jawed, with a shock of black hair, and long sideburns that swept down his cheeks. He appeared friendly, and somewhat naive.

Ceci waited until he'd paid and begun to move away from the counter. Then she picked up the packages and stepped forwards, allowing him to collide with her, knocking the packages onto the floor.

"Oh, Lord. I'm so clumsy," he apologised. "That was entirely my fault."

She made as if to pick them up.

"No," he insisted. "Please, allow me." He knelt, hastily

gathering up the packages. After a moment, he rose, placing the pile on the counter.

She put her head on one side, and smiled sweetly. "Thank you, sir," she breathed softly. "You are so very kind."

He seemed momentarily taken aback, lost for words. Then, suddenly, he came to his senses. Tearing his cap from his head, he thrust out his hand. "Charles Zephron Munroe," he introduced himself. "At your service, ma'am." His face creased into a boyish grin. "Everyone calls me Charlie."

Ceci took his hand, holding it just a little longer than was necessary. "It's very nice to meet you, Charlie," she responded, still smiling, before releasing him and reaching for the packages.

"Allow me," he intervened. "I'd be proud to carry them home for you. It's the least I can do."

"I just knew you were a gentleman," she fluttered her eyelashes at him.

His chest swelled. He scooped up the packages in one arm, offering her the other.

She took it, pressing herself shamelessly close to him. As he began to escort her from the store, she managed a glance at Mrs Sykes. Enola nodded approvingly. At that moment, Ceci recalled the time she'd sat on the bank of the bayou with Hecubah, and watched a heron swallow a fish whole.

★★★

"I see you're in the army," Ceci observed casually, as they sauntered along the street.

"Yes, Ma'am," he nodded.

She stopped, regarding him with large eyes. "Please," she invited. "Call me Mariah."

He gulped. "Yes, Ma'am – I mean, Mariah."

"What do you do in the army, Charlie?" she asked innocently.

"I'm a telegraph operator," he told her.

"What does that mean?"

"I send and receive messages," he explained. "Mighty important ones," he rattled on. "Sometimes, top secret, to Generals, even the President."

"My, that sounds so exciting," she gasped, pressing a hand to her breast.

His chest swelled again. Then, suddenly, his face fell. He hesitated. "I guess I really shouldn't talk about it," he began to reconsider.

"Oh, I see," she remarked bluntly, making her disappointment obvious. "Oh, well," she sighed dismissively. "If you'd rather not."

He faltered, impaled on the horns of a dilemma. Confronted with the agony of decision. Reluctant to lose an opportunity to impress her. Finally, he shrugged. "Oh, I guess it can't hurt," he grinned again. "You being a girl an' all."

"That's right," she encouraged him, "I doubt if I'll understand a single word of it."

When they reached the Douglas house, he returned her packages to her. She made a point of giving him a peck on the cheek, ostensibly in gratitude for his service to her, but her motives were entirely different.

He touched his fingers to the spot, emboldened by her display. "May I see you again?" he asked tentatively.

"I'd like that," she smiled. "My employer doesn't allow followers at the house," she told him, just to make sure he never turned up unannounced and cause a lot of awkward questions. "But I'd be happy to meet you outside the store tomorrow, at the same time."

"Tomorrow, then," he nodded his agreement, before walking away, a spring in his step.

Ceci watched him leave. So, she pondered, was that the face of the enemy? The object of all her hatred? Those she'd sworn vengeance on? Or was it merely a lonely young man, far from home, who thought he'd found himself a sweetheart?

Again, the dark creature within her growled a warning, and again, she ignored it.

★★★

"What are you doing?" Ceci jerked her head back, as Charlie leaned forward.

"I was just trying to kiss you," he seemed surprised by her reaction.

"Well, don't," she told him flatly.

For a moment, he seemed at a loss for what to say. "We've been going together for three weeks," he pointed out. "You'd think I could kiss you by now."

Ceci narrowed her eyes at him. "What kind of a girl do you think I am?" she remarked primly.

"I didn't mean it like that," he attempted a clumsy apology. "It's just that I thought we had an understanding."

"We do," she kept him dangling. "It's just that I don't like to be rushed."

"It's just a kiss," he coaxed. "Where's the harm in that?"

"Kissing leads to other things," she was beginning to sound like a schoolmarm. "A young woman at the house where I work, has ruined herself. That all started with kissing."

"I'd never do that to you," he assured her vehemently. "I was raised to behave like a gentleman."

"That's what you say now," she replied prudishly. "What happens if I give in?"

He thought about what she'd said, for a moment. "Are you thinking of giving in?" he asked hopefully.

She let him dangle a little longer. "I might," she shrugged casually. "It all depends."

"On what?" he couldn't wait to know.

"I'm bored," she suddenly seemed to lose interest in the conversation. "You haven't told me any exciting stories in days. You still operate the telegraph, don't you?"

"You know I do," he frowned.

"Well then?" she urged.

He clicked his tongue in frustration. "I told you before. I shouldn't. It's confidential."

"How'd you expect me to trust you, if you don't confide in me?" She turned her back on him.

"All right," he conceded desperately. "If I do, will I get a kiss?"

She turned around, smiling. "Maybe," she teased, knowing full well that the best he could expect was a peck on the cheek. He still seemed undecided. She upped the ante a little. "I'll let you put your arm around my waist," she offered. "As long as you don't squeeze."

"Well, that's more like it," he grinned appreciatively, all thoughts of national security fleeing from his mind. He reached out, pulling her towards him. "I've heard some things that'll take your breath away."

★★★

The room was rank with the pungent odour of cigar smoke, mingled with the aroma of freshly brewed coffee. It hung in the air in pale blue clouds, drifting around the room like vagrant ghosts.

"I can't understand what happened at Chancellorsville," a Union Major bit down on the end of his cigar. "We should have prevailed there. It was as if the Confederate troops knew exactly what we were thinking."

"Spies, sir. Spies." Josiah Douglas exhaled another cloud of smoke. "Insidious people, all around us." He didn't know, how right he was. "We must be constantly on our guard. More brandy?" he motioned to Ceci.

She brought the decanter over, as the Major held out his glass, without giving her a second glance. She smiled, as if at the Major. Chancellorsville, that was one of Charlie's little indiscretions. She'd helped the South gain a victory. She was feeling good about herself, but it didn't last long.

"You have no idea, sir, how low these rebels will stoop," the Major went on to confirm Josiah's suspicions. "Only the other day, an entire ammunition train was lost to a Confederate saboteur dressed as a Union soldier." He took another swig of brandy. "Fifteen box cars, each one guarded by a dozen men, just blown to smithereens. The whole depot was destroyed. Hundreds of yards of track torn up. Only a few high-ranking officers knew it would be passing through there. God alone, knows how they found out about it." He paused, to empty his glass. "Biggest explosion north of the Potomac. The fire ran out of control, cutting off the perpetrator's escape."

Josiah plucked the cigar from his mouth. "Are you saying, just one of them did all that?" he stared in amazement.

"That's only the half of it," the Major interrupted, waving his glass at Ceci. "This rebel fought like the very devil, killed five of our men before a Gatlin gun put an end to it."

Ceci refilled his glass, and was on her way back to the sideboard as the Major continued.

He leaned over his chair, prodding Josiah's arm with his finger. "When they examined the body, they discovered it was a young woman."

Ceci stiffened, her fingers tightening around the decanter. Then she set it purposefully down on the sideboard, turned to face the two men, and listened.

A large chunk of ash fell into Josiah's lap, as he started forward. "God damn. You don't say?"

"I do indeed, sir," the Major reaffirmed. "I ask you, have these southerners no honour? No courage, that they have to send their women against us?"

One of the Bird spies had made the ultimate sacrifice. Ceci hung her head, remembering the little band of eager volunteers, she'd trained with. She recalled all their faces, wondering which one of them had fallen. It brought home to her, the precarious nature of the business they were in. She found herself glancing around the room. These congenial surroundings, this comfortable family home, could become a death trap, if she wasn't careful.

★★★

The war was already in its third year. It had gone on far longer than anyone had imagined. The death toll was staggering. Most of the battles were being fought in the South. From what Ceci read in the newspapers, it seemed that the Union was gaining ground, tightening its stranglehold on the Confederacy.

Every day, they seemed to edge closer to the vicinity of the plantation. She knew Simon Robicheaux was a resourceful man, but what he could do against a Federal invasion? She couldn't guess. What would it profit her, she wondered, to strike a blow in the North, if her home in the South was destroyed? The recent death of one of the Bird spies preyed on her mind. Doucet had warned her, many times. The chances were she would never see Louisiana again.

★★★

"Charlie was in yesterday, buying candy," Enola mentioned, as Ceci passed her latest batch of information across the counter. For once, the store was empty and she spoke openly, a hard edge to the tone of her voice. "He doesn't seem too sure of your affections."

Ceci was taken aback by the criticism. "I've given him no reason to doubt me," she defended her position. "I play my part. I do enough to keep him interested. After all, we both know why I associate with him."

"The point is," Enola told her, "he mustn't know. He's a valuable source of information. We can't afford to lose him."

"What am I supposed to do about it?" Ceci shrugged.

Enola looked her up and down, like a fox eyeing a chicken. "Give him what he wants," she replied. "Give him what all men want."

Ceci found the suggestion both repugnant and offensive. She had already given herself to Trent. There was nothing she wouldn't do for him. The thought of another man, touching her in that way, disgusted her. "That's not what I came here to do," she snapped.

Enola reached across the counter and caught her by the wrist. "You were trained to penetrate deep behind enemy lines – for any purpose," she reminded her.

Ceci yanked her hand away. "If it's that important, you offer it to him," she retorted angrily.

Enola exhaled softly. "Honey," she replied, offering her a thin smile, illustrating the stark difference in their degree of commitment. "If I thought he'd take it, I would."

★★★

"Don't you think he's handsome, Mariah?" Constance Douglas lingered in the hall, hands behind her back, leaning against the wall, sighing after the man who'd just left.

"Who?" Ceci teased, as she closed the door.

"You know who," Constance clicked her tongue in annoyance. She was young and fresh faced, with long blonde hair and blue eyes, and still innocent enough to wear her heart on her sleeve.

"Oh," Ceci mused. "You mean Lieutenant Wade Anders," she recalled the latest member to join Josiah's guest list, watching the girl shiver at the mention of his name. "He's all right, I suppose."

Constance jerked upright. "All right," she cried, eyes wide in disbelief. "Just all right? He's only the most handsome man in the world."

Ceci couldn't resist a smile. These sentiments sounded awfully familiar. She'd heard it all somewhere before. "Don't go throwing your heart after a soldier," she advised her. "Take a lesson from your sister."

The girl's chin tilted up. "That's never going to happen to me. The love I have for Wade, is a pure love."

Ceci smiled again. Yes, she had heard all this before. She'd said much the same herself. She wasn't that much older than Constance, and hardly any wiser, concerning affairs of the heart. She'd have loved to loiter there, trading sighs with her, but here, she was only a housemaid, and, on top of that, a Confederate spy. It was at times like this she wished she wasn't.

★★★

It was almost April, and still Ceci couldn't shake the northern chill from her bones. She'd taken to wearing a thick cloak that Enola Sykes had given to her, whenever she went out.

She'd grown accustomed to seeing Union soldiers on the street and paid them little attention, other than to avoid them. Especially on a day like today, when she had a long, coded message in her purse.

A detachment of cavalry came to a halt adjacent to the street she was on. It was just a little too close for comfort. Pulling the hood of the cloak up to shield her face, she began to hurry past, sparing them the merest glance. It was then that she saw it, faded and frayed, tied to the bridle of the lead horse. A white ribbon.

Chapter Twenty Three

Ceci came to an abrupt halt. She felt herself sway, on the point of fainting. She caught her breath, clasping a hand to her breast, her heart pounding uncontrollably. She forced herself to turn away, facing a store window. The grimy glass acted like a mirror, reflecting everything behind her.

She could hardly believe her eyes. After all this time, it was him. It was Trent. She pressed her hand against the glass, as if to touch him, tears streaming down her cheeks. "Oh, God," she sobbed, "Trent." Ceci, the love sick young woman, rose up, returning with a vengeance, reminding her of all the times she'd spent with him. She ached to hold him, to feel his touch, to taste his lips. She burned with the agony of despair. He was only a few feet away. What could she do?

Ceci hovered, transfixed by a moment of indecision. It was what she had become that held her. She felt herself cursed to stare, helplessly, into this glass and witness the reflections of her past, knowing that if she turned, to embrace them... If she turned, and was discovered here. It could cost her her life.

All at once a strange calm settled on her. All she had to do was turn and go up to him. One look at her and he would pull her into his saddle, smother her in kisses, and ride off with her.

The dark creature within her screamed a warning, as she felt an invisible force grip her legs, edging her away from the window. In a moment, she could be free of Doucet, and the war. She could remain with Trent for the rest of her life. She continued to turn. Images of her dead father and dead sister flashed through her mind, hovering around Trent's reflection. The screams of the dark creature echoed in her ears. She glanced into the glass again. Trent turned. She could see his face clearly, her eyes drinking him in.

In that instant, all her anger and her hatred drained away. The dark creature fell silent, subdued, laid low. She forgot everything, moving as if in a dream. She could feel herself turning, reaching for the hood of her cloak, ready to pull it back. She could feel his name, swelling in her throat. She opened her mouth to call it out.

"Are you all right, Miss?" A hand caught her arm.

Ceci flinched back. "What?" she blinked.

It was the proprietor of the store. "I saw you from inside," he remarked, with concern. "Are you all right?" he repeated.

She put her hand on her brow, dazed and confused. Then, the thud of hooves made her glance up. Trent was galloping away. "Oh, no," she cried, stretching out her hand in a vain effort to stop him. But it was too late.

"You don't look well," the proprietor insisted. "Come inside. I'll call a doctor."

Gradually, she came to her senses. A crowd had begun to gather, attracted by the commotion.

"No. I'm all right," she shrugged the man's hand away, suddenly aware of the danger she was in. "I felt a little faint, that's all." She pulled the cloak tightly around her. "Thank you," she nodded briefly, before hurrying away from the curious stares of the bystanders.

She still had the coded information in her purse, but she couldn't stand the thought of Enola Sykes interrogating her over the way she looked. She'd deliver it tomorrow, or not at all. It wasn't important now. She felt confused and disorientated. She had to get back to the house. She was in no fit state to be out on the street. A mistake now could be fatal.

As Ceci opened the door, Florina was coming down the hall. "Good Lord, Mariah," she stared. "What happened? You look as if you've seen a ghost."

"I nearly fainted in the street," she answered truthfully. "I think I must be coming down with something."

"You certainly don't look well," Florina observed. "You'd best go and lay down. I'll tell Mrs Douglas that you're indisposed."

Ceci went to her room and tore off the cloak, letting it fall to the floor. Then she threw herself on the bed, buried her face in the pillow, and just cried and cried. Seeing Trent again, and losing him in the same instant, was a cruel blow. She felt so alone and miserable. All she wanted to do was die. She thought about the pistol in her bedside cabinet. All she had to do was take it out, put it to her head, and pull the trigger. That'd be the end of it.

Before she had time to consider it any further, she heard a gentle tapping at her door. She jerked upright, hastily brushing the tears from her face. "Who is it?" she challenged.

The door opened slowly, Amelia put her head round, touching a finger to her lips. Then she let herself in and came over to sit on the bed next to Ceci. "I heard you come in," she explained her reason for being there. "Something didn't sound right. So, I crept downstairs to see how you were. Mrs Winthrop says you're indisposed, but I know it's not that."

The muscles in Ceci's jaw tightened. She wondered if Amelia suspected anything. "I'm all right," she tried to dissuade her from any further inquiry.

"No, you're not," Amelia contradicted softly, "you've been crying. The only time a woman cries like that, is over a man. Trust me, I know."

Ceci relaxed, letting out a sigh of relief, which Amelia accepted as confirmation.

"You've seen him, haven't you?" she surmised.

Ceci was immediately back on the defensive. "Who?"

"James," Amelia continued, in hushed tones. "You saw him today, but he didn't see you."

Ceci was astounded. "How'd you know that?"

"It happened to me once," Amelia recalled. "I heard Frank's regiment was passing through the outskirts of Washington. So, I slipped out of the house and went clear across town."

"Did you see him?" Ceci asked with interest.

"Yes," she sighed, "but he didn't see me. It broke my heart to watch him ride away. That's what happened to you, isn't it?"

Ceci nodded. "He was so close," she confided. "I haven't seen him for so long, and then he was gone."

Amelia took Ceci's hand in hers. "Why don't you find out where he is, and go to him?" she suggested.

"I can't do that," Ceci was adamant. It was out of the question. "I don't even know if he's staying in Washington, or just passing through."

"I understand," Amelia sighed again. "The army doesn't permit followers. It distracts the men. It doesn't matter to them how we feel." She glanced up at the door. "I'd better get back," she excused herself. "If my father catches me down here, he'll kill me."

"Thank you for coming," Ceci smiled. "It was very thoughtful."

"When you're feeling better, come up to my room," she invited. "We can console each other."

★★★

For the first time, since she'd left Louisiana, Ceci felt she needed a friend. She didn't care to sit in her room with nothing but a loaded pistol for company. As the evening drew in, she climbed the stairs to Amelia's room, knocked and went in. She was sitting on a couch, reading.

"I'm so glad you came," she smiled, glancing up from her book, as Ceci entered. "Sit here, beside me."

They chatted for over an hour. Ceci was careful to keep the war out of conversation. They spoke of love, the men they were missing and of broken hearts. By the end of the evening, they'd both become quite tearful.

Amelia put her arm around Ceci. "Good Lord," she laughed. "What fools we women are." Suddenly, she flinched, pressing a hand to her stomach. "Oh, my," she gasped.

Ceci jumped to her feet. "What's the matter?"

Amelia shot her a pained expression. "I think my water just broke."

"Are you sure?"

"Oh, yes," she winced, "quite sure."

"Come and lay down." Ceci assisted her to the bed. "I'll fetch help."

She ran downstairs and roused the household. A maid was sent to fetch the doctor, and by the end of the night, Ceci was watching Amelia give birth to a son. The sight of that new life, coming into the world, assuaged all the sorrows of the day. She felt reborn herself.

When it was all over, Josiah Douglas was admitted to view his new grandson. "Let's hope Frank comes back to claim him," he remarked, somewhat coldly.

Lydia Douglas slapped his arm, with the back of her hand. "Your daughter has been through quite an ordeal," she berated him. "This is your first grandchild. Show a little compassion, sir."

He softened visibly. "He's a fine looking boy," he admitted, with just a hint of pride in his voice. He bent over the bed and kissed his daughter's cheek. "I'm sure he'll make us proud. You get some rest now."

"Mariah has consented to watch over them today," Lydia told him. "So, don't expect to see her tomorrow evening."

He acknowledged the arrangement without argument, allowing his wife to lead him away.

"Would you like to hold him?" Amelia asked, once they were alone.

Ceci came over to the bed and picked up the baby, cradling it in her arms. As she stood there, holding the tiny, helpless creature, she vowed to herself, that she would survive this war, be married and have children of her own. That day, the dark creature within her was diminished. She knew it would never be as strong again.

★★★

Ceci was immediately suspicious. Charlie was waiting in their usual spot, but the familiar grin was missing. He hung his head, appearing ill at ease and sullen. She looked up and down the street, paying particular attention to alleys and doorways. Searching for anomalous groups of soldiers, or Federal agents, who might be waiting to ambush her. If her identity had been discovered, they'd take great pains to capture her alive.

Seeing nothing amiss, she continued, keeping a watchful eye on her surroundings.

"What's wrong, Charlie?" she asked, as she came up to him.

He looked at her, ashen faced. "My brother, Ned," he let out a gasping sob. "I heard, today. He was killed at Lake Providence."

"I'm so sorry," she put her hand on his arm.

Charlie was inconsolable. "When our folks died he raised me, like I was his son," he sniffed. "He was all I had in the world, besides you," he added.

Again, Ceci found herself seeing things from a different perspective. Learning that heartbreak, sorrow and pain were not exclusively her province. As the war went on, the ranks of those who mourned, and swore vengeance, swelled daily.

"He was shot down by some God damn rebel scum," Charlie ground his teeth, tears trickling down his sallow cheeks. "I'm going to kill them all."

Ceci was all too familiar with these sentiments. She knew she shouldn't care. It might have been Ned, at New Orleans, who fired the shot that killed her family. Who and why no longer held the same significance for her now. Suddenly, all life seemed precious. It didn't matter if wore blue, or grey.

Charlie took a deep breath, dragging a hand across his face. "I doubt any woman wants to be seen with a man who cries," he began to turn away.

She pulled him back, cupped his face in her hands, and kissed him. She didn't know why. She just felt she had to.

"I got my first kiss," he stared in surprise, his face brightening a little.

"I'm proud to be your sweetheart." She told him what she thought he wanted to hear.

He was clearly pleased and just a little bemused by her sudden display of affection, after all her months of reticence. "Just my luck," he grimaced. "I came here today to tell you I won't be able to see you again for a while."

"Why not?" she frowned.

He shrugged. "Something big's going on. The whole army's preparing to move out. I'm moving out with them."

"I'm sorry to hear that." She did her best to sound disappointed. "Do you know where you're going?"

He shook his head. "There are no details. I only know it's soon. Will you wait for me?" he asked uncertainly.

"Of course, I will." Again, she told him what he wanted to hear.

"I have to go," he sighed again. He paused, looking at her, as if trying to fix her image in his mind.

She knew she should be flattered. Her training had taught her to remain indifferent. Nevertheless, it didn't stop her from feeling tawdry.

He bent forward, took her by the shoulders and pressed his lips against hers. She allowed it. After all, she'd debased herself thus far, what did another notch matter?

"I'll say goodbye then," he released her.

"Take care, Charlie," she replied sincerely.

***

"He's in there, isn't he?" Constance bobbed about in front of Ceci as she made her way down the hall.

"Careful," she warned, "you'll have this tray out of my hand."

"Oh, please. Just one look," she begged, unable to keep still. "That's all I ask."

"I can't," Ceci insisted. "I'll lose my job."

"No, you won't," Constance pouted. "They'll never even know I'm there. All you have to do, is leave the door ajar, so I can look in."

"Your father told you not to come down here while he's entertaining," Ceci reminded her.

"I'll only be a minute," Constance persisted. "Just one peek. Oh, please."

"All right," Ceci relented. "When I go in, I'll hold the door for a minute, then I'm closing it."

Ceci kept her word, lingering by the open door, as Constance gazed longingly in at the object of her desire, Wade Anders. She began to close the door slowly, aware that the girl was craning her neck for one last look, in danger of getting her nose pinched.

***

"This could be the most decisive engagement of the war, since Antietam," Josiah Douglas was saying. "If we pull it off."

"If we pull it off," Anders replied. "It would shake the pillars of heaven."

Ceci was just about to set the tray down, when she heard

her contact phrase. It dropped from her hands, a quarter inch above the sideboard, making the cups and saucers, on it, rattle conspicuously.

Josiah looked up. "Careful, girl," he snapped. "That's the good china."

"I'm sorry, sir," she mumbled an apology.

As she poured the coffee, she had to steady the jug with both hands to stop herself from spilling it. When all the cups were full, she paused to compose herself, then passed the tray around. As usual, none of Josiah's guests spared her the merest glance, all except Anders. He raised his eyes, without moving his head.

When everyone had been served, Ceci left the room. Returning the tray to the kitchen, she went out of the back door and round to the side of the house.

"I'll be damned," Josiah broke off in mid-sentence. "Did you hear that?"

The room fell silent, as everyone listened.

"There it is again," he raised a hand to his ear. "It's a whippoorwill calling. Well I'm blessed," he laughed. "It's the first one I've ever heard in Washington. Must be pretty desperate to hang around here."

A ripple of amusement penetrated the cigar smoke.

"Where's Mariah with the brandy?" Josiah glanced around.

"No matter," an artillery captain pointed. "It's over there, on the sideboard. I guess we'll just have to serve ourselves."

"You'll have to excuse me for a moment, Gentlemen," Anders rose from his chair. "Call of nature."

★★★

Ceci waited pensively in the shadows, shuffling her feet on the stone path, wondering if anyone had heard her. Then Anders came around the corner.

"You almost gave yourself away, in there," he whispered.

"I didn't expect my contact to be a Union lieutenant," she hissed at him.

"My people are from Georgia," he confided. "My heart is with the South."

"Yet you wear that uniform," she pointed suspiciously, backing away, as he approached her.

"Doucet placed agents within the Union army, even before Fort Sumter," he advised her. "More than one southern sympathiser wears a blue uniform."

"Then why'd he send me here, when he already had you?" she demanded.

"Different people, different jobs," he replied simply. "I'm a tactician, not a spy. In this case, I'm merely a messenger, a go between."

The mere fact that he knew Doucet's name were credentials enough. "Very well," she accepted his explanation. "What's happening. I've been hearing all kinds of rumours."

"Stand close," he instructed, "I don't want to be overheard. If anyone comes out, I'll kiss you. They'll just think I've taken the opportunity to dally with the maid."

She nodded her understanding, narrowing the gap between them.

"Lee's on the move," he informed her. "He's taken the entire army of Northern Virginia, along the Shenandoah valley, heading north. In response to this threat, the army of the Potomac has mobilised to pursue him," he continued, without a pause. "Lee's plan is to lure it out onto open ground, and destroy it, in one decisive battle. Once this has been achieved, a letter, which has already been drafted, will be placed on Lincoln's desk, offering peace. This could end the war in a week."

"I sense, you're not telling me everything," Ceci deduced from the tone of his voice.

Anders leaned closer, drawing her in, until she could

smell the cigar smoke on his breath. "The movements of the Union army are constantly relayed back to the White House," he continued quickly. "My position in Doucet's organisation, allows me to know where the Confederate forces are. New information arrived, just over an hour ago, that enabled me to calculate that a large section, at least three corps of the Union army, is much closer to Lee than he realises. He must have scouts out everywhere but, obviously, they have failed to recognise the situation. A premature engagement could be disastrous."

"Does Doucet know?" she asked anxiously.

Anders nodded. "I telegraphed him straight away. As there is no other form of communication between here and Lee's position your orders are to ride out and warn him of the impending danger."

"Why me?" she wanted to know.

Her response clearly surprised him. "I was under the impression that Doucet trained you specifically for this kind of operation." He glanced back at the house. "I'd say your talents are wasted here."

"I meant," she elaborated, "I'm not the only one Doucet trained."

He took a step back. "You mean, you don't know?"

"Know what?" she asked.

"Doucet hasn't told you?" he continued to prevaricate.

"Perhaps you'd be good enough to correct his oversight," she remarked impatiently, "before the sun comes up."

"All the Bird spies are dead," he replied bluntly. "You're the only one left. You're the only one with the training to do this job."

The sudden, overwhelming sense of isolation Ceci experienced on hearing the news would have been the same had she just found herself standing on the moon. "That can't be right," she started to say.

Suddenly, Anders grabbed her, forcing his mouth against

hers. Over his shoulder she saw Constance standing at the corner. The girl's smile quickly faded, to be replaced by a look of dismay, before she clamped a hand over her mouth and ran back into the house.

Anders let Ceci go. "Who was that?" he demanded.

"Constance," she identified her, "The youngest daughter of the house. She must have followed you out. She has a crush on you."

"Not any longer," he grunted. "We must hurry."

"What do I have to do?" she asked, realising she would have to mourn her comrades later.

"You leave tonight," he informed her. "There's a fast horse tethered beyond that gate," he pointed. "Follow the Union army until you're outside of Washington. Then strike out alone. When you reach the Confederate lines, give your call sign. Doucet anticipated such an eventuality. We have men in every regiment, with orders to respond to any of the Bird spies. They'll take you directly to General Lee. Once you've delivered your information, remain with the army. Doucet will contact you with further instructions."

"Where's Lee, now?" she asked.

"He crossed the border into Pennsylvania, two days ago," Anders pulled a folded map from inside his jacket. "His men are foraging for supplies in a small town, barely eighty miles from here. The positions of both armies, as well as the route you will take, are marked on the map."

"It's too dark to see," she squinted. What's the name of the town?"

Judging by his reaction, it couldn't have been of much strategic importance. He had to think for a moment, before it came to him. "Gettysburg."

Chapter Twenty Four

"I'll need a few minutes to prepare," she told him. "Will you wait here and keep watch?"

Anders nodded his consent. "Hurry," he urged.

Ceci returned to her room, her mind racing, filled with a mixture of trepidation and excitement. This was what she'd been waiting for. A chance to strike a blow, to avenge her dead family but, after all she'd seen and heard, her motives had changed. If she could warn Lee in time, and help end this war in a week, it was well worth any risk she had to face. She was only sorry that the rest of the Bird spies wouldn't be there to see it. Then again, if things didn't go according to plan, she might very soon be joining them.

Unlocking the cabinet, she pulled out the carpet bag and threw it on the bed. Tearing off her clothes, she bound her breasts with strips of linen and dressed in the Union uniform. Lastly, she strapped on the pistol, took the satchel containing the compass, maps and code books from the carpet bag and looped it over her shoulder. Everything else she packed in the bag she'd brought from Louisiana. No matter what happened, she wouldn't be coming back.

Her final act was to scribble a brief note to Florina. She'd been treated kindly here. She felt she owed her that much. She wrote that her mother had been taken seriously ill, and that she'd had to leave immediately. It didn't matter whether she believed her or not. Thanks to Constance's testimony, they'd probably think she'd run off with Anders. Either way, her duty was clear. To put an end to this war. So that Frank and Trent, and all the other men, could go home to their wives and sweethearts.

Anders started in surprise when she returned. "Very impressive," he approved. "I'd take you for a soldier, any day."

"In here are all the things I have to leave behind," she offered him the bag. "Will you see that Enola Sykes disposes of it."

"I've been ordered to stay here with the garrison," Anders volunteered, as they started towards the gate. "So, I doubt that we will meet again." He offered her his hand. "Good luck."

Ceci shook it, then mounted the horse. Anders stood back and saluted. All her training, that had lain dormant these many months, took over. She reacted instinctively and returned it.

★★★

Ceci rode all night, following in the wake of the departing regiments. Being surrounded by enemy soldiers, with a Confederate uniform and code books in her satchel, made her feel like she was sitting on a powder keg. She could always fall back on the dress. If she found herself threatened, she had the advantage of transforming herself back into a woman, and throw any would-be pursuer off her scent. She hoped it wouldn't come to that. She recalled Doucet's words, 'Use your head and keep your nerve.' They endowed her with a confidence she'd never known before. In a perverse way, she actually found the danger exhilarating.

As the sun began to rise, she slipped away from the Federal column and set out across country. Riding hard, she made good time until the horse went lame. She unsaddled it and turned it loose, taking her canteen and saddlebags with her. It was an infernal piece of bad luck, leaving her with no choice but to continue on foot.

She pressed on through the day, traversing woods, fording rivers, rarely pausing to rest or eat. She desperately had to make up the time the lost horse had cost her. By mid-afternoon, she began to hear distant cannon fire. It sounded like thunder, far away. Both armies were strung out for miles, on either side of her, with pockets of men milling about everywhere. She hoped that what she heard was only a minor skirmish.

She hurried on, through the night, without food or sleep. There had been times, on the island, when she'd wondered why Doucet's training had been so rigorous. Now, she understood. Here, everything she'd learned, came into its own. She carried on, pushing herself to the limits of her endurance, the fate of the Confederacy in her hands.

By the morning of the second day, she just had to stop. Too exhausted to go on, she found some high ground, with plenty of cover, and crawled into it. Taking the binoculars from her saddlebag, she began to scan the terrain. To the north, she could see vast numbers of Confederate troops, marching in columns, batteries of artillery and supply wagons, all moving in roughly the same direction. The cannon fire had fallen silent during the night, now it resumed. It was much closer. By the sound of it, a major battle was in progress. The thought that she might be too late, spurred her on. She clambered to her feet, every muscle complaining, changed uniforms, and set off in the direction the Confederate troops were taking, following the sound of the gunfire.

As dusk began to fall, she found herself in a thicket on the edge of open fields and farmland. The stench of spent gunpowder and rifle smoke stung her nostrils, making her eyes water. She stepped out of the thicket and stood, staring open mouthed, tears trickling down her travel-stained cheeks, at thousands of bodies that littered the ground, for as far as the eye could see. In the half-light it was impossible to tell if they wore blue or grey. She could hear the moans of wounded men all around her. Some begged for life, others prayed for death. All thought that God had abandoned them on that day. Ceci pulled off her cap and bowed her head. It wasn't only the flower of the South, she saw dying here. It was the soul of a nation, torn and bleeding, that lay at her feet.

She was just about to move on, when she heard the sound of hooves approaching.

Retreating to the cover of the thicket, she crouched down and waited. A troop of Union cavalry began to ride past, the lead horse well in front of the main body, a white ribbon fluttering from its bridle. Ceci stared aghast, wondering if her eyes were playing tricks on her. She hadn't slept for three days. Was the fatigue she suffered making her mind see what it wanted to see? Even as she looked, a musket shot rang out. The horse reared, throwing its rider to the ground. "No," she screamed, surging to her feet. Careless of her own safety, she broke cover and dashed towards the motionless body.

★★★

Trent was lucky. The Confederate musket ball that was intended to kill him merely grazed his brow. He lurched violently back in his saddle. His horse reared wildly, throwing him, unconscious to the ground, directly into the path of his own cavalry advancing only yards behind him.

At the far end of the field, Sergeant Nathanial Pike and his men, engaged in the hasty formation of a skirmish line, watched helplessly as the scene unfolded. As Trent hit the ground, a Confederate soldier appeared out of the shadows. Small and slight, little more than a boy, he lunged forwards, grabbed the officer by the lapels of his coat and dragged him out of the path of the galloping horses. Throwing himself across the man's prone body, he shielded him from the pounding hooves. The cavalry thundered past oblivious, in the half-light, to the fate of their captain.

As the danger passed, the rebel rose to his knees and appeared to search the unconscious man.

"God damn thieving rebs," Pike snatched his pistol from its holster, his thumb wrenching back the hammer. Before he could take aim, the rebel stopped searching. He leaned forwards and, cradling the officer's face in his hands, bent down and kissed him, full on the lips, long and hard. Pike's pistol, arm and jaw dropped simultaneously.

Something, some noise, some movement, made the rebel look up and glance furtively around. He jumped to his feet and, with a final backwards glance at the fallen man, melted into the shadows, like a wraith.

It was some moments before Pike's jaw snapped shut, his teeth meeting with an audible click. He rounded on his men. "Did you see what I just saw?" he demanded.

His question was answered with shrugs and scowls. Not one man there could swear he hadn't dreamed it. Then suddenly, they heard it, far off, plaintive and eerie, the cry of a whippoorwill.

★★★

Apart from a thin gash on his brow, Trent didn't appear to be badly hurt. He was already regaining consciousness. Ceci might have risked everything to stay there with him, but she'd noticed some stretcher bearers moving up the field towards them. Trent would soon be in good hands, and it would profit neither of them if she were captured here. Reluctantly, and with a last backwards glance, she left him, to seek the relative safety of the Confederate lines.

She moved softly through the shadows, the taste of his lips lingering on hers, haunted by the sight of him lying there, pausing now and then to utter her call sign. Eventually, she heard a horse moving slowly through the undergrowth. She hid behind a tree and watched. A Confederate cavalry lieutenant rode out of the woods, pistol at the ready. He appeared to be looking for something, or someone. They were both wearing the same uniform. Ceci took a chance and stepped out into the open. He reined his horse to a standstill and studied her for a moment. "I thought I heard a whippoorwill," he spoke at last.

Ceci simply repeated her call sign.

"So, it's you." He holstered his pistol and climbed down. "I've orders to take you directly to General Lee."

"It looks like it's a little late for that," Ceci observed, coming up to him. "What happened?"

"Battle lasted three days," he told her. "We almost had them surrounded once, until we lost the advantage. Then General Lee ordered General Longstreet to send fifteen thousand men across a mile and a half of open ground, straight at the Union centre. Pickett's division was all but annihilated. It was a massacre. Lee's turning back."

"No," Ceci gasped. "He can't do that. We must remain on the offensive. The Mississippi is closed. We can't win this war from a defensive position."

"Nevertheless, those are his intentions," he shrugged.

With her hopes of ending the war dashed, Ceci had no option but to follow her orders. "I've been told to stay with the army," she advised him. "Until I receive further instructions."

"I'd best take you to the General, then," he concluded.

The Lieutenant led her away from the front line, a mile through the woods and out into a clearing where the main Confederate camp was situated. They advanced on a large tent at the edge of the clearing. Leaving Ceci outside, he went in. Moments later he emerged, holding the flap back for her. "General Lee will see you now," he invited her in.

Ceci stepped inside, to find an elderly man, his face care-worn, with white hair and a white beard, sitting by a table littered with maps. She came to attention and saluted.

"I am aware I am to ask you no questions," he remarked, returning her salute.

"Nevertheless, I fear the message you carry, has come too late."

"Yes, sir. I'm afraid it has," Ceci admitted. "I'm sorry."

"No. Pray, don't apologise," he sat forward, raising a hand. "I'm sure you did everything you could. Every man here has and, by the grace of God, we will yet prevail."

This was the man, Ceci knew, to whom Abraham Lincoln had offered control of the Union army. He had refused the president of the United States, declaring that his duty was to his home and his people, in Richmond, Virginia. There was something about him, a presence, that made her heart glow. In his company, anything seemed possible. She felt that it was, indeed, only the will of God that could defeat him.

"You look weary, sir," he observed. "Doubtless you have travelled very far in the service of the Confederacy. I'll have the Lieutenant find you food and shelter. Stay with us for as long as you need to."

As she thanked him, his smile reminded him of her father. She knew she would never forget this moment for as long as she lived.

★★★

As Trent lay on his bed, nursing his sore head, he overheard two orderlies talking outside the field hospital.

"Hell of a battle," the first one remarked. "Every one of those Sesesh fought like he had a personal grudge."

"Not all of them," his companion reminded him, a trace of humour in his voice.

"That's right," the first man recalled. "They sure love Captain Sinclaire."

"Yeah," his companion agreed, "they're real fond of him."

Trent felt a tremor run through the ground as they snapped

230

to attention, before recognising the voice of his old friend and comrade, Captain Howard Pierce.

"A lot of strange rumours circulate, after a battle," he told them. "Men think they see all sorts of things. If I hear you two, passing any of them on you'll be digging privies for the duration." He paused. "Do I make myself clear?"

"Yes, sir," they chorused.

"How you feeling?" Pierce asked, as he came into the tent.

"Hell of a headache," Trent smiled. "Apart from that, I'm fine."

"Lucky for you you've got a thick skull," Pierce grinned. "Another quarter of an inch, and we'd be digging a grave."

"I'm not sure whether to thank God, or the poor marksmanship of that Confederate sniper," Trent confided.

"I guess, one goes with the other," Pierce shrugged.

"Is it true, the things I'm hearing?" Trent frowned. "A rebel soldier saved my life, and then tried to rob me?"

"So I'm told," Pierce replied casually.

"What about the other thing?" Trent pointed to his mouth.

"Pay no attention to it," Pierce waved his concerns aside. "Just an incident that was badly observed. Mind you," he recalled. "I've heard of some old Indian tribes that used to sneak up on their enemies whilst they slept, and leave some token. It was a sign of their courage, and an insult to the other."

"Doesn't sound like any rebel I've ever come across," Trent declined the idea. "Why take the trouble to save my life, when all he wanted to do was rob me?"

"Perhaps he didn't," Pierce suggested. "Like I said, perhaps he left something on you, like one of those red savages. Have you checked your pockets?"

"There's nothing that shouldn't be there," Trent assured him.

"What about your coat?" Pierce handed it to him.

Trent began to go through the pockets, pausing, when his fingers touched something that hadn't been there before.

"Found something?" Pierce enquired, noticing his expression.

"No." Trent withdrew his hand, he had no intention of adding credence to the rumours. "Nothing's out of place."

"As I said before," Pierce reminded him. "In the heat of battle, a man can imagine all kinds of things. Get some rest. In a couple of days we'll have you back in the saddle."

Alone once more, Trent pushed his hand into his coat pocket and pulled out a crumpled piece of paper. He smoothed it out. It was a fragment, torn from a map. All that was left on it, was the state of Louisiana. Perhaps his rescuer wanted him to know where he came from, but that didn't account for the kiss. Maybe he was part Indian, after all. He stared at the fragment. It didn't make any sense.

Then, the thought struck him, harder than the musket ball. He looked round at the picture by his bedside. A beautiful young woman stood, gazing demurely over her shoulder at him. His vision blurred. Suddenly, all he could see, was that wild girl, on that hot Louisiana afternoon, facing him defiantly, as he held her and tried to kiss her. "Ceci?" His lips, silently, framed her name, as he stared in disbelief. "No." He shook his head, wincing as he did so. It was impossible. The idea soared beyond all reason.

Chapter Twenty Five

Ceci hadn't washed for three days. Even though she'd been trained to tolerate it, didn't mean she preferred it. She'd selected a towel from amongst the items the Lieutenant had given her and set out in search of water.

It was comforting to hear so many southern accents again. She'd missed that in Washington. Now, she heard them all around her, as men scurried back and forth, occupied with the duties of the day. Nevertheless, she remained cautious. Doucet had taught her never to let her guard down, under any circumstances.

She hadn't gone very far before she came across a group of men sitting around a campfire, drinking coffee. She could see, from the insignia they wore, that they were from an Irish regiment. Before the war, thousands of Irish immigrants had come to America looking for a new home. Even the Union had Irish soldiers.

"Coffee smells good," she remarked.

One of the men looked up. "Help yourself," he nodded towards the pot.

Ceci knelt and poured herself a mug. It was the best thing she'd tasted in days.

"I left the old country and travelled to the new world, in search of a better place." The man who'd invited her in, continued his conversation. His accent was thick, the brogue difficult to understand. "Me, and the rest of the lads from my village," he went on. "When we arrived here, some of us went this way, some of us went that. I'm barely off the ship, when this fella comes up to me and says, sign here, fight for your country. I thought I had to sign. The next thing I know, I'm standing behind a stone wall, shooting at the same boys I come across with. He tossed the dregs of his mug into the fire. "Three thousand miles, I come, in search of a new life, only to end up killing my own kind." He dragged his hand across his chin. "Jesus, Joseph, and Mary," he swore. "I thought the English was bad enough, but this is something else."

Ceci drained her mug, and left them to their thoughts. Her country was at war with itself. Brother against brother. Father against son. She had always considered it a tragedy. The predicament of the Irish troops was not so very different. She carried on through the camp, still in search of a place to bathe.

Presently, she noticed a flight of ducks descending, behind a grove of trees, indicating that there was a river, or a lake beyond. She made her way towards it. Eventually, she discovered a broad lake, surrounded by reeds and clumps of tall trees. She began to skirt its perimeter, looking for a secluded spot.

She saw what looked like a good place, just ahead of her. She walked softly. Bear had taught them all how to move without making a sound. With the stealth of a cat, she approached a patch of willow scrub, that concealed the bank beyond. She moved silently through it, and peered out. She drew her head back sharply. This section of bank was already occupied. A soldier, stripped to the waist, crouched over the water, splashing it over himself, oblivious to her presence. Ceci waited, hoping he'd soon finish and depart. After a moment, he stood up, sweeping his hair back with both hands. As he did so, he turned. Ceci caught her breath, as feminine breasts bobbed into view.

The soldier heard her gasp and whirled round, folding her

arms over her chest. Ceci reacted quickly. Stepping out from behind the screen of willows, she yanked up her shirt, pulling away the linen bindings.

The girl paused, staring in astonishment. "I thought I was the only one left," she remarked, after a moment.

"You mean, there's more of you?" Ceci stared back. "Women soldiers?"

The girl dropped her arms, reaching for her shirt. "Lots of us," she replied, "on both sides, I hear."

"I had no idea," Ceci admitted. "Why'd you do it?"

The girl seemed puzzled by her remark. "Same reason as you," she gestured at Ceci's uniform. "Ain't only men that can fight."

"Does anyone know?" Ceci asked.

The girl shook her head. "As far as anyone's concerned, we're men, like the rest."

"How'd you pass inspection?" Ceci wondered.

"Do you think they bother to check?" the girl snorted. "All they want is fighters, and that's as far as it goes."

"If they did, it would shake the pillars of heaven," Ceci tested a theory that had just occurred to her.

The girl merely cast her a quizzical frown. Clearly Doucet had nothing to do with this.

"You say, there are more of you?" Ceci continued quickly.

"In different regiments," the girl told her. "There were three of us here, until yesterday. Now there's only me." She looked Ceci up and down. "I ain't seen you before."

"I arrived last night," she told the truth. "I haven't washed in three days."

"Go ahead," the girl nodded towards the water. "I'll keep watch for you. These may be our boys, but they're boys, just the same, and you know what they're like when they see a naked girl, especially after a battle."

"How long have you been here?" Ceci asked, as she began to strip.

"Since the beginning," she gestured casually.

"How'd you manage for so long?" Ceci was keen to know.

"I keep my wits, and this, about me," she held up a formidable looking knife. "Even a boy bent on having you will think twice if it means losing his manhood."

Ceci stepped off the bank and lowered herself into the water. It felt good.

"My real name's Natty Taylor," the girl confided. "Here, they call me Jack. If you're gonna be around for a while, we could help each other out."

It was the first piece of good luck Ceci had had, since she left Washington. "Mariah Johnson," she answered, retaining her alias. "I call myself Frank," she borrowed the name from Amelia's lover.

"All right then, Frank," Natty acknowledged. "How about we look out for each other? Sure would make life a whole lot simpler."

Natty had got this far on her own. With no training and no equipment. She'd make a useful ally. It was a proposition Ceci couldn't afford to pass up. "That's a deal," she confirmed.

★★★

As Lee's army of Northern Virginia retreated along the Shenandoah Valley, towards Richmond, it was constantly harried by Union forces trying to cut off its escape. Almost every day, the Confederate troops were rallied to defend its flanks, or fight a rear-guard action. Due to Doucet's influence, Ceci was spared from the fighting, but Natty wasn't. Indeed, she insisted upon it.

While she waited for Doucet to contact her, Ceci occupied herself with menial tasks around the camp, or helped with the wounded. In fact, anything she could do to be useful. She could have spent the entire time sitting on her behind, but she had no intention of doing that, not when others were dying in the cause of the South. Besides, such blatant inactivity would have drawn attention to herself. She very soon became a familiar face around the camp. Many called her by name. She had blended in.

It always came as a great relief when Natty returned unharmed. Ceci had already lost, or abandoned, too many people she cared for. She didn't want it to happen again. Trent was always in her thoughts. At Gettysburg, she'd held him in her arms, briefly. She wanted him so badly that there were occasions when she thought she saw him standing in front of her. A lone Union officer, in the midst of a Confederate camp. At night, he came to her in her dreams. Sometimes, they were so vivid, she'd wake up sweating. At other times, she'd cry out. Even the sentries didn't take much notice. Many dreamed and cried out in the night, but for different reasons.

"I ain't been with a man, for nigh on three years," Natty remarked one morning, as they sat by the lake shore. "For all that time, I've been surrounded by them." The paradox was obvious.

"Have you never been tempted?" Ceci asked.

Natty's round face creased, wrinkling her button nose, making the freckles on it dance. "Hell, yes."

"You mean you'd risk them finding out you're a woman?" Ceci stared in astonishment.

"I thought about knocking one of them out, one time. So, they wouldn't know it was me, but what would be the point of that?" she concluded, with a shrug.

"That would defeat the purpose," Ceci agreed.

"What about you?" Natty was equally curious. "How long's it been?"

"About the same," Ceci sighed.

"You never been tempted?" Natty returned her question to her.

"No," Ceci was adamant. "I've given my heart to just one man."

Natty's mouth fell open. "He has to be one hell of a man,"

237

she sounded impressed.

"He is," Ceci assured her wistfully.

"I get it," Natty pointed. "He's rich, ain't he? What is he, a plantation owner, a banker?" She broke off, staring contemplatively at the water. "Last boy I laid with, was a store clerk, didn't have a cent to his name. Well-endowed, in other ways, though."

"No. He's not any of those," Ceci sighed again, Trent's face swimming before her eyes.

Natty looked up from the water. "Have you ever tried it with another girl?"

Ceci shook her head. "I've read about such things," she admitted. "I can't say it ever appealed to me."

"I did, once," Natty volunteered casually. "The kissing was nice, but let me tell you, it ain't nothing like having a man."

"Natty Taylor, you are a living scandal," Ceci chided. "What on earth's going to happen to you after the war?"

"I already know," Natty declared. "I'm gonna get married, have a dozen brats, and get fat."

★★★

Ceci quickly discovered that, in her line of work, there were often long periods of total calm, followed by two or three incidents all arriving at once. As she moved through the camp that morning, she noticed two old timers watching her. Obviously veterans of many campaigns, they lounged against the side of a wagon, each of them chewing a thick wad of tobacco, their chins stained brown by the liquid.

She nodded an acknowledgement as she passed by, heading for a water butt, where she paused to take a drink. They began to discuss her, unaware that she was still in earshot.

"That's the one, I was talking about," the first man said to his companion. "Voice is kinda shrill. I was wondering if he's old enough to fight."

His companion pursed his lips, squirting a jet of oily brown liquid onto the ground, letting the remainder dribble down his chin. "If he's here, he's old enough."

"I'm told, he don't like to wash with the other men." The first man, shifted his wad of tobacco to the other side of his mouth, with a flick of his tongue. "Some fella reckoned he caught a glimpse of him, through a tear in his tent flap. Looked like he was holding a dress."

His companion spat a second time, his eyes following the stream as it arced through the air. "How in the hell could he hide something as big as that? Must have been a blanket."

The first man remained unconvinced. "You suppose he's one of them strange boys you hear tell of?" he wondered. "Likes to wear girl's clothes?"

"As long as he's killing Yanks," his companion replied, indifferently. "I don't care what he wears."

Their interest was merely idle curiosity, but it warned Ceci that her cover was wearing thin. She'd stayed with the army too long. It moved so slowly. She could have made better time on her own, but without a direction, or a destination, she was stuck here. There was still no word from Doucet. She chaffed on the delay. Something had to happen soon.

As she raised the ladle for a second sip of water, she saw an infantryman carrying an empty ammunition box. He set it on the ground and stood on top of it, as other soldiers gathered around.

"A newspaper man has just arrived, all the way from Richmond," he announced, holding his arms out. "He wants to talk to the ordinary soldier," he touched a hand to his chest, "about his experiences in the war. I'm gonna be famous."

His audience cheered. "What's he look like?" one of them called out.

"You'll see, soon enough," the infantryman quietened them. "Big fella, tall hat, grey hair, moustache. Kinda religious. Keeps talking about the pillars of heaven."

Every muscle in Ceci's body went ridged, as she heard her contact phrase. Somewhere, in this camp, there was a reporter, looking for her.

She pushed her way through the crowd, and shouted up at the infantryman.

"Where is he now?"

He bent his head, putting his hand behind his ear and stared at her.

"I said." She repeated, raising her voice above the din of the crowd. "Where is he now?"

He pointed down the camp. "Somewhere, yonder," he yelled back, "way over there."

Ceci went in the direction he'd indicated until she noticed another crowd of soldiers ahead of her. There, in the middle of them, a sheaf of paper in one hand and a pen in the other, stood the object of her search. A large, grey haired man in a tall hat laughed and joked with the men. Ceci lingered on the edge of the gathering, and listened.

"My name's Clarence Peabody." The soldier watched intently, as the reporter wrote it down. "I got this scar on my face at Antietam, when a cannonball exploded right beside me."

The reporter continued to write. "Why, sir," he exclaimed. "That would shake the pillars of heaven."

"Sure, as hell, shook me," Clarence assured him, much to the amusement of his audience.

This was her man all right. He was trying the phrase on just about everyone he met. Ceci waited half a day, while he took the testimony of scores of soldiers, before he finally called a halt to the proceedings and retired to his tent. Now she knew where he was, Ceci slipped away.

At the earliest opportunity she found Natty and took her to her tent.

"I think I'm going to be transferred, very soon," she told her. "I just wanted this chance to say goodbye."

Natty hung her head. "That's a shame," she sighed. "We

was getting along so well together."

"I know," Ceci agreed. "But winning the war comes first."

"Do you know where you're going?" Natty asked.

"No," Ceci shook her head. "Not yet." She put her hand on the girl's arm. "When this war's over, you find that man," she urged. "Have those brats and get fat, in peace."

Natty nodded. "What about that man of yours?" she asked. "When'd you reckon you'll settle down?"

Ceci exhaled sharply. The prospect seemed so distant. "I've no idea!" she exclaimed. "I've a long way to go yet."

Natty hastily unbuckled the belt at her waist. Holding up a leather sheath, she pulled a foot long knife from it, and offered it to Ceci. "Be careful," she warned. "It's got an edge like a razor. Wherever you're going, this'll help make sure you get there in one piece."

As evening fell, Ceci made her way down through the camp. Hiding behind a bush, a few feet from the reporter's tent, she gave her call sign.

The men of the army of Northern Virginia, glanced up, as they warmed themselves at their camp fires. Momentarily distracted from the rigours of war, their thoughts fled back to hearth and home and the loved ones they'd left behind. Their hearts aglow, touched by the sound of birdsong, the cry of a whippoorwill.

Chapter Twenty Six

The canvas of the reporter's tent rippled briefly as he threw back the flap and stepped out in time to see Ceci emerge from behind the bush. "I've been looking for you, all day," he whispered, glancing around.

"I've been waiting for you for three weeks," she countered.

"Why, sir," he remarked, in a loud voice, for the benefit of onlookers. "I'd be glad to take your testimony. Step into my tent. We'll get on with it right away."

"You're not really a reporter," she guessed, once they were inside.

"You're not really a man," he retorted. "That makes us both liars."

There was no denying, he had a point there.

"Earl Hamilton. I'm a Colonel in the Confederate intelligence service," he identified himself. "Attached to Doucet. You've been reassigned," he told her, spreading a map on the table between them.

In the yellow lamplight, Ceci could see that it was the state of Tennessee, on which several positions had been marked.

Hamilton touched a finger to one of them. "We hold Chattanooga, and the vital rail hub there," he began. "That is to say, the Army of Tennessee, under the command of Major General Braxton Bragg." He paused, allowing her time to absorb the information. "Opposing him," he continued, his finger moving across the map as he spoke. "Is the Union

Army of the Cumberland, commanded by Major General William.S. Rosecrans. Bragg expects an attack to come from the north-east. We have recently intercepted information that Rosecrans intends to exploit this, and out manoeuvre him." He paused again, to make sure she was still following him.

"I can read a map," she assured him.

"As a diversionary tactic," Hamilton went on, "Rosecrans will send artillery to the north-east, and position his guns where Bragg can see them, confirming his suspicion that the attack is coming from that direction. He will begin a bombardment of the city, forcing Bragg to concentrate his forces in the north-east. Meanwhile, the bulk of Rosecrans' army will cross the Tennessee river, far to the south and west, coming up on Bragg's flank." He waited for her to assess the situation.

Ceci studied the map intently, before finally looking up. "That would be the end of it," she concluded.

"Exactly," he concurred, "if we lose Chattanooga. If Bragg is forced out of Tennessee, it will open a door for a Union invasion of the Deep South."

As far as Ceci was concerned, that meant, Mississippi, Alabama, Arkansas, Georgia, and, most importantly, Louisiana.

"I take it that the telegraph's been cut," she assumed.

"Even if it wasn't," Hamilton advised her, "we wouldn't send this over the wire. If it were intercepted, and the code broken, they'd know we were aware of their plans and change them. You must take this information, personally, to Bragg."

"What are my orders?" she asked.

Hamilton's finger began to move again. "You leave here in the morning. A horse will be provided. Go to this address in Richmond," he dropped a slip of paper on top of the map. "There, you will be furnished with a new identity. The train will take you the first four hundred miles, as far as Tullahoma. The Union has closed the line from there. Nothing gets in or out of Chattanooga. You'll have to travel the rest of the way on horseback. That's only seventy-five miles or so. You have three weeks to get there, before the assault begins."

"Where am I going?" Ceci wanted to know.

"Your destination is the Moss Creek plantation," Hamilton indicated its position on the map. "It's the closest point at which you can cross over to the Confederate lines."

"What's this?" she pointed to a curious looking symbol.

"That's the problem," Hamilton glowered. "It's a narrow strip of woodland, which divides the two armies in that section. Unfortunately, because of the direction in which you must travel, you will arrive on this side," he indicated the Union emplacements. "Moss Creek is on the other side."

"Is this a road?" she noticed a thin line, dissecting the woods.

"More like a narrow track," Hamilton elaborated. "It's patrolled day and night. Normally, it would be impossible for anyone to get through unnoticed. However," he continued quickly, "every month, the unit guarding the road, is relieved. It takes approximately three hours to make the change, leaving the road vulnerable. Which means," he summarised, "that you must be within sight of that road, on August 21, between the hours of nine and midnight. If you miss your chance, you will be trapped on the Union side of the woods."

It was at times like this that Ceci truly appreciated Doucet's conscientious approach to her training. This assignment would require every skill she'd learned. The risks were enormous, but so were the stakes.

★★★

The ride back to Richmond was child's play compared to what lay in front of her. She went to the address she'd been given. It was the home of a widow, Alma Birchwood. To a person of Ceci's age, Alma looked to be about a hundred years old. Her body was shrunken, her shoulders hunched, and she walked with the help of anebony cane. Her face was as wrinkled as a dry potato, her hair was pure white, and so thin that Ceci could see her head through it. However, as she was soon to learn, her great age had in no way dulled Alma's wits, which were as sharp as they'd ever been.

"I've been expecting you, honey," she greeted her.

Ceci hesitated on the threshold. "You can see I'm a woman?" she asked suspiciously.

"Don't fret, honey," Alma's eyes twinkled, like dew soaked berries. "Your disguise is most convincing but seeing as how I got a dress waiting in the back for you I figured you weren't no man." She looked Ceci up and down. "You must be one of Doucet's girls. Oh, don't look at me like that. I've known him since he was a boy. Sly little bastard. Born to be hung, that's what I say. You coming in or what?"

"You don't seem to be too concerned about security," Ceci mentioned, as Alma closed the door behind her.

"Oh, really," she grunted disdainfully. "What they going to do if they catch me? Cut short my young life?" she laughed hoarsely. "Let's see about fixing you a bath. That uniform you're wearing, smells like a she bear littered in it."

It was the first hot bath, with real soap, Ceci had enjoyed in a month. If she'd had her way, she'd have stayed there forever.

"I got this nightdress for you," Alma laid it over a chair, next to the tub. "No sense in getting all dressed up tonight. When you're finished here, I got pork and beans on the stove. After that, you'd best get your head down. I guess you've got a long way to go."

In the morning, it felt good to dress as a woman again. Soft, comfortable clothes, petticoats and clean linen. Vain as ever, Ceci admired herself in the mirror.

"You're a real pretty girl," Alma hobbled into the room behind her. "I guess, if it wasn't for this war you'd be married with young un's by now," she remarked astutely.

245

"It almost happened," Ceci sighed. "But that seems like a long time ago now."

"You're still young," Alma observed. "You still got plenty of time." She placed an envelope on top of the dresser. "Here's all your papers," she told her. "Travel passes and whatnot. Your new identity is Ellen Franklin of Maine. Doucet sent down a new set of uniforms, and a dress. Leave the old ones. I'll burn them."

"How do I look?" Ceci asked, holding out her skirts.

"As pretty as a picture," Alma approved. "Going to get them Yankee boys all hot and bothered. Here," she offered Ceci a lace garter. "Try this on for size."

"I'm already wearing garters," Ceci told her.

"This ain't the kind of garter for holding up your stockings," Alma turned it over, to reveal a small holster, from which she took a Derringer. "See," she showed Ceci, "fits right into the palm of your hand. Two forty-four calibre bullets. Mighty effective at close range. I used to wear this when I was in the territories. Killed my first injun with it when I was just sixteen."

Ceci accepted it, put her foot up on the chair, raised her skirt and slipped it on up to her thigh.

"A perfect fit." Alma seemed satisfied. "It looks good on you."

"I must remember, never to underestimate you again." Ceci lowered her foot to the floor, adjusting her dress.

"Honey," Alma gave her familiar wheezing laugh. "Here's all there is to know about me. I've had three husbands and fifteen children. I killed eight injuns, four Mexican bandits, and one black horse thief. Apart from that, my life's been quite ordinary. If I was your age again, I'd be doing just what you're doing."

★★★

Ceci bought a ticket to Tullahoma and rode the train into Tennessee. The view from the window of her railroad car was much the same as it had been on her journey from Louisiana to Richmond. Only here, the devastation was greater. Whole plantations had been burned to the ground. Fields and crops left in ashes. Entire towns destroyed. The Union presence seemed stronger, more concentrated, the further south she went. Their strangle hold on the Confederacy seemed to be tightening.

For the first time since the war began she saw Confederate prisoners, hundreds of them. Forced to march at the end of a Union bayonet, they moved dejectedly along the roads towards hastily constructed prison camps. They were disarmed, defeated and downcast, without flags or drums. It made her heart bleed.

Travel passes were checked more rigorously than before. The Union ever watchful for saboteurs and infiltrators. Ceci no longer experienced the exhilaration she'd once felt in the midst of danger. Now, there was only a cold desire to survive, and a constant need for caution.

Even though it was of considerable strategic importance, Tullahoma was still little more than an outpost. The recent heavy rains had turned its unpaved streets into a quagmire that had been churned up by the constant passage of artillery and supply wagons.

Ceci lifted her skirts and picked her way through the cloying mud, her feet sinking into it up to her ankles. There were no hotels or boarding houses here, little to suggest the presence of civilian life.

Ceci noticed that she was beginning to get glances from the passing troops. She doubted, that they suspected her of being anything other than a woman, but some of the attention didn't seem too friendly. Occasionally, a man would look at her in that certain way, a hunger in his eyes. She pressed her hand to her thigh, reassured by the presence of Alma's

Derringer. Nevertheless, she couldn't afford to have her mission jeopardised by something as trivial as mere lust.

Leaving, what passed for the main street, she retreated down an alleyway and out towards the edge of town, until she came to a corral and a ramshackle storehouse. She went inside and changed into the Union uniform, exchanging Alma's Derringer for her Colt revolver. She spattered some mud from her shoes onto her uniform, to make it appear travel stained. The rest of her clothes, and everything else, she had to leave behind, she hid under some old grain sacks and settled down to wait for nightfall.

There was only one sentry guarding the corral. He propped his musket in the crook of his arm and began to roll a cigarette. He was unaware that anyone else was there until the butt of Ceci's pistol cracked down on the back of his skull.

Everything she needed was here, compliments of the Union army. A horse, a saddle, saddlebags and canteens. Packing the saddlebags with the equipment, and the beef jerky she'd brought with her from Richmond, she filled two canteens from a nearby water cask, mounted the horse and trotted quietly into the darkness. After she'd put some distance between her and Tullahoma, she dug her heels into the horse's flanks and began to gallop.

The route she took avoided the vast majority of military positions, and after two days of uneventful travel she found herself deep in the heart of Tennessee. It was the farthest south she'd been in well over a year, even the ground felt familiar. It was a fine warm night. She pitched camp on a low ridge and ate her rations cold, a fire was too risky. As she chewed the beef jerky, she gazed up into the night sky. It was full of stars, with the moon waxing half full. Then she realised that this moon and those stars shone over Louisiana and the plantation. Suddenly she felt old and tired, beyond her years, wondering what it was that drove her endlessly on. She thought of her home, Hecubah, her father and Celeste, and of Trent, and all the things that had once been. Would anything ever be the same again? She doubted it, but this much she was sure of, if she didn't continue with her mission there would be nothing at all to go back to.

The jerky was dry. She reached for her canteen and shook it. It was empty. Taking the second one from her saddle, she slaked her thirst in one long draught. After a moment, she paused, licking her lips. There was a strange after taste. She took another sip. Now she couldn't taste anything. She shrugged dismissively. Doubtless, it was just the flavour of the jerky mixing with the water. Thinking no more of it, she lay down, rested her head against her saddle and slept.

Dawn was barely a streak of colour on the horizon when she started from her sleep, hands clutching at her stomach, a gnawing pain eating into her. She tried to rise, sinking to her knees she bent forward and vomited uncontrollably. She felt chilled to the bone, sweat oozing from every pore. When the last of the jerky was gone, she wiped her mouth on her sleeve and reached for her saddlebags. Taking out the parcel of dried meat, she sniffed it. It was sound. She opened her canteen and inhaled. It was the water. It was tainted. It was the same water, she'd been drinking for the last two days. It had to be something in the second canteen that had fouled it.

There was nothing she could do about it now. Emptying it onto the ground, she hoped the worst was past. She looked at her watch, consulted her maps and compass. Her destination was only a day away. If she started now, she'd arrive in plenty of time.

Even under the glare of the hot Tennessee sun, she felt cold. She'd begun to tremble and sweat, her muscles aching. Her throat burned with a raging thirst, but she had no water.

As the sun began to set, she was grateful for the cover of night. Now, only a mile from the Moss Creek plantation, she slithered out of the saddle, took it off the horse, turned it lose and continued on foot. Patches of cloud scudded across the sky passing over the face of the rising moon, bathing the land with shifting patches of light and shade. She crept to the top of a ridge and found herself at the edge of the woods, looking down on the narrow road.

Lifting the binoculars to her eyes, she could see that the guard had already begun to change. Union troops were withdrawing along the track, back to camp. She slipped back a few yards, pulled off the federal uniform and dressed as a Confederate soldier. When she came out of those woods she'd be right on top of the rebel lines and she had no intention of being shot as one of the enemy.

The road had remained clear for at least ten minutes as Ceci lowered herself over the edge of the ridge and down the bank. It was only a matter of thirty feet or so, but she felt weak and numb, her faculties impaired, making it difficult to concentrate. Finally, she dropped silently to the ground. The road right in front of her was swathed in shadow.

This was her chance. She looked up; the cloud appeared solid against the face of the moon. She left the cover of the bank and stepped out into the middle of the track. Unexpectedly, the cloud lifted, trapping her in a pool of milky light.

She froze, glancing down the road. About a hundred feet away stood a Union soldier, a straggler. From the way he was fastening his trousers, it looked as if he'd been delayed on some personal business, behind a nearby bush. For a moment they just stared at each other, then she saw him go for his gun.

Ceci didn't want to risk alerting the entire Union army with an exchange of gun fire, not when she was this close to her goal. She turned and plunged into the woods. The shadowy undergrowth was full of briars, making it all but impenetrable. The thorns plucked at her clothes and tore at her skin. Long, sinuous vines wrapped themselves around her legs, holding her back, causing her to expend more energy than she could spare in her weakened state.

She struggled blindly on, hardly aware of which direction

she was going, forcing her aching muscles to respond. She was burning up, her body wracked by cramps and chills. Sweat poured down her face and into her eyes, blurring her vision. At last, she stumbled into a small clearing. Convinced that she'd gained a few minutes on her pursuer, she paused, gasping for breath.

Seconds later, a twig cracked behind her. She whirled, drawing her pistol, but the fever slowed her down, making her reactions sluggish. A gunshot exploded against her ears. Her pistol flew from her hand as a burning pain tore through her left side. She gasped, staggered back against the trunk of a tree, sliding down it, sitting heavily on the ground.

Pressing her hand to her side, she could feel warm blood trickling through her cold fingers. The Union soldier advanced towards her, out of the gloom. She glanced to where her weapon had fallen. It was just out of reach. The soldier loomed over her. She watched him raise his pistol, beads of sweat burning her eyes, making everything hazy. She glanced at her weapon again, trying to calculate the distance, wondering how many seconds it would take her to roll out and grab it, before her assailant could fire. She pressed her back against the tree, her breath hissing between her teeth, every movement was agony.

She began to feel light-headed as the fever reasserted itself, making her vulnerable. She tried to move, but couldn't. She slumped back against the tree, realising she was helpless under his murderous scrutiny. She could see nothing but cold unremitting hatred in his dark eyes as he raised his weapon, cocked the hammer, and took careful aim.

Ceci had always known the risks, was well aware that this could happen but, somehow, she'd never believed it would. She was the last of the Bird spies. Now, it looked as if their time was over.

"Trent," she murmured. Her last thoughts were of him.

A second gunshot rang out.

Chapter Twenty Seven

Ceci flinched, squeezing her eyes shut. After a second, she opened them again. She ran her hands hurriedly over her chest, but there was no second wound, no coup de grace, only the throbbing pain in her side.

The Union soldier still towered above her. He hadn't discharged his weapon. A puzzled frown began to cloud his expression. His arm dropped to his side, the gun falling from his limp fingers. He began to sway as his legs buckled, sinking to his knees, before crashing onto his face, a crimson flower blossoming on his back.

Ceci glanced nervously along the tree line, trying desperately to focus, then at her pistol, then back to the trees again. Finally, she saw it, a figure, cloaked and hooded, standing in the shadows, a smoking pistol in their hand.

Before she could react, the figure surged forward, stood over her, then knelt. The cloak fell open and a silver dollar on a gold chain swung out, glittering in the moonlight.

"Hecubah," she gasped, overwhelmed by a sense of astonishment and relief.

Hecubah pulled the hood from her head and laid her pistol aside, cradling Ceci in her arms. "Oh, God, honey," she cried. "I hope I ain't too late."

Ceci tried to push herself away. "I have to get a message to Bragg," she struggled weakly.

"Let's just concentrate on getting you outa here," Hecubah advised. "Those gunshots have stirred up a hornet's nest. These woods are crawling with troops, and now they'll all be heading in this direction." She began to remove her cloak. "This is all I have to cover that uniform," she clicked her tongue at the inadequacy of it.

"Wait," Ceci pointed to the satchel she had, slung over her shoulder. "In the pouch, there's a dress."

Hecubah looked doubtful but, nevertheless, opened the bag and emptied its contents onto the ground. As Ceci had told her, a complete dress fell out, amongst other contentious items, followed by a Union uniform. She looked back at Ceci. "What, in God's name, have you gotten yourself into?" she demanded. "If they catch us with all this, they's liable to hang us both."

She took the pouch, and what remained of its contents, and stuffed it under the roots of a tree, covering it with dead leaves. Then she helped Ceci out of the Confederate uniform, gasping at the ugly wound in her side. "I have to try and stop the bleeding," she told her, pulling up her skirt and tearing two ragged strips from her petticoat. She made a pad of one, tying it in place with the other. "I'm sorry if I'm hurting you, honey," she sighed, prompted by Ceci's groans, "but we gotta hurry." She helped Ceci to her feet, got her into the dress and finished it off with her cloak. "There's a horse tethered yonder," she pointed. "It ain't far. You just lean on me."

In the shifting patches of light and shadow they glimpsed armed men moving all around them. Often only a few feet away. They picked their way cautiously through the woods, dodging both Union and Confederate soldiers. Under the circumstances, one could be as lethal as the other. It was hard going. Ceci often had to stop to rest. Sometimes she collapsed altogether or began to mumble feverishly, forcing Hecubah to put her hand over her mouth until she'd quietened down.

It felt like an age had passed before they reached the thicket where Hecubah had left the horse. She helped Ceci mount, then climbed up behind her. Leaving the cover of the trees, they began to move slowly along an empty stretch of road, shadows and moonlight dancing around them, the darkened woods full of sound and movement.

They'd gone less than a hundred yards before a small detachment of Union cavalry appeared in front of them, cutting them off from the Confederate lines.

"Stay quiet, child," Hecubah whispered. "These ain't our boys."

"Who goes there?" the officer challenged, pistol at the ready. Then he noticed that they were women. "What the hell are you doing out here?" he barked. "Don't you know there's a battle going on?"

"We was trying to get away," Hecubah told him the truth. "But we got lost. My friend was hit by a stray bullet."

The officer approached, drawing his horse up beside them. Then he reached out, lifting Ceci's cloak aside. She held her breath, swaying slightly in the saddle, barely able to stay conscious. If he became suspicious now, nothing would save them.

"That looks bad," he muttered, seeing the large bloodstain spreading out on the side of Ceci's dress. "All our surgeons are fully occupied with our own casualties," he told them. "But there's a small town nearby with a civilian doctor. Better have him look at it." He beckoned to a cavalry corporal. "I'll have one of my men escort you in," he offered. "Don't want you getting lost again."

The Corporal led them through the Union lines and into town. In the distance, they could hear the thunder of cannon fire, as powder flashes flickered across the night sky, an eerie glow lighting up the horizon.

"Count yourselves lucky you aren't there tonight," he remarked casually. "Chattanooga's taking a pounding."

He helped Hecubah get Ceci down from the horse and

254

carry her into the doctor's office, where they laid her on his examination table. By now, the pain and blood loss had rendered her unconscious. Hecubah counted it as a blessing. Now, at least, she couldn't blurt out anything incriminating under the influence of the fever. His task completed, the Corporal saluted and left, taking Hecubah's thanks with him.

The doctor was a southerner, born and raised in Tennessee. A man of advancing years and considerable medical experience. Too old for war, yet a man who had lately seen more death than was good for anyone.

"What happened?" he asked, recognising Ceci's injury as a gunshot wound.

"We was trying to escape from Chattanooga," Hecubah was careful to tell him the same story. He may have been a southerner, but that was no reason to take unnecessary risks. "But we got lost, and my friend was shot by mistake."

"War," he shook his head disparagingly. "It's always the young and the innocent that take the brunt of it. Let's see what the damage is."

Hecubah assisted him, as he cut away the bloodstained dress. "That's it?" he looked up puzzled. "That's all she's wearing, just a dress?"

"She's just a poor, simple, farmgirl," Hecubah explained forlornly. "Farm ain't bin doing too good since the war. She's destitute."

The doctor shook his head again, sighing. "There are some Christian people in the town," he told her. "Methodists mainly, who are putting together parcels of food and clothes for refugees, like yourselves, fleeing from Chattanooga. I'll have them send something over for her."

Hecubah thanked him profusely, drifting into an anxious silence, as he proceeded to clean and dress the wound. When he'd finished, he covered Ceci with a blanket, then filled a bowl with hot water and began to wash his hands, turning back to her as he towelled them dry.

"She was lucky," he told her. "The bullet went right through, missed all the vital organs. The wound itself is not that serious, but she's lost a lot of blood. I'm detecting borderline malnutrition, but she seems strong." He paused, placing his hand on Ceci's forehead. "It's this fever that bothers me," he admitted. "Has she been drinking polluted water?"

"It's possible," Hecubah guessed. "What are her chances, Doctor?"

He exhaled sharply. "The wound's not infected. It should heal quickly. As for the rest," he shrugged. "I'd say fifty fifty, but," he added gravely, "if she develops pneumonia, that'll be the end of it."

Hecubah stooped and kissed Ceci's fevered brow. "Hold on, child," she whispered.

"She's too weak to travel yet," he advised. "There's a boarding house down the street that's opened its doors to refugees. You can stay there, at no cost," he reassured her, remembering her claim to poverty.

Whilst Hecubah waited anxiously beside Ceci, he went into the street and called a boy to fetch help. Twenty minutes later, two men and a woman arrived, Methodists, who had volunteered to help the displaced people from Chattanooga. The woman had brought a parcel of clothes with her, mainly nightwear, as she'd been told that the recipient would be bedridden. She helped Hecubah get Ceci into a nightgown. Then the men laid her on a crude litter and carried her to the boarding house, accompanied by the doctor. They were given a small attic room and, once Ceci was safely in bed, the three of them withdrew leaving Hecubah and Ceci alone with the doctor.

He took his watch from his waistcoat pocket, holding Ceci's wrist between his fingers. "Pulse is steady." He seemed satisfied. "I'll leave fresh dressings and a bottle of antiseptic for the wound," he continued. "As for the fever, make sure she drinks plenty of liquids. See if you can get a little food into her, where feasible. Will you be nursing her yourself?"

"Me and no one else," Hecubah was adamant, afraid of what Ceci might say, in her delirium.

"Then be prepared for the long haul," he warned. "I've known these fevers to last for months. At times she will be completely lucid, but she will also be prone to vivid hallucinations. Are you sure you can cope?"

"Yes, sir," Hecubah confirmed. "I bin taking care of this little girl most of her life. I ain't about to give up on her now."

The doctor consulted his watch again. "I have other patients to attend to," he informed her.

"We've a deal to thank you for," Hecubah told him sincerely. "I don't know what we would have done without you."

"Let's hope it's not all in vain," he responded. "Send for me, if her condition changes."

Alone, at last, Hecubah heaved a huge sigh of relief, wondering how they'd managed to come through it all. Luck had played a part, but there was no denying that the common decency of the Union officer who had found them on the road had a good deal to do with it.

"Mercy, child," she addressed Ceci's prone figure. "The Lord was sure watching over us today." She patted her limp hand. "I'm gonna make you strong and well," she promised. "Then I'm gonna take you home. And when we get there, I'm gonna whip your behind, so's you never sits down again." She knew, as she said it, she probably wouldn't, but after all she'd been through, it made her feel better.

Fortune had smiled on them, this time. The boarding house was a relatively safe hiding place. Every room was occupied by refugees, escaping the depredations of war. Hecubah knew that they'd be too preoccupied with their own problems to take any notice of a sick girl. However, that didn't alter the fact that she and Ceci were now in the middle of an enemy occupied town.

"Where am I?" It was almost dawn, before Ceci regained consciousness. "Where am I?" she asked again, trying to sit up.

"Hush, child," Hecubah eased her back against the pillow. "You is safe. That's all you needs to know for now."

"Hecubah," Ceci smiled weakly, beginning to remember the events of the previous day. "How, on earth, did you find me?"

Hecubah dipped a cloth into a bowl of cold water, wrung it out, and began to mop Ceci's brow. "When Simon Robicheaux told me what you'd said, returned this silver dollar to me and handed me my freedom, I realised what you were trying to do. So I decided to bring you home." She refreshed the cloth and laid it on Ceci's forehead. "I knew that devil, Doucet, was behind it all," she continued, sitting down beside the bed. "I began to search through the plantation records. Took me almost a year, but in the end, I found what I was looking for. The guest list for the night of your ball. There was an address for Doucet in Lafayette."

"You went to see Doucet?" Ceci stared incredulously

"Men like him, don't frighten me," Hecubah scowled. "He ain't as smart as he thinks he is. Otherwise, he'd have remembered to tie up that loose end before he started spying again." She took a glass from the table beside the bed, and helped Ceci take a few sips of water. "I found his house," she went on. "I knocked on the door, pushed past his hired man and barged into his office. I shoved the barrel of a pistol into his ear and told him if he didn't tell me where he expected you to be next month, I'd ventilate his skull. Adding, that if he lied, he could count his life in weeks. I guess the man knew I was sincere."

"How'd you get all the way out here?" Ceci wondered. "That's a journey of more than four hundred miles, with a war going on."

"It weren't easy," Hecubah admitted. "I guess Doucet figured I'd never make it, but a thousand dollars, in gold, buys a lot of friends and a lot of leeway." She paused, raising the glass to Ceci's lips again. "I knew the date, the place and the time. I arrived half a day before you. I saw those battle lines, that strip of woods and the narrow road. I hid and waited. I knew you had to come down that road sooner or later. So, you did, followed by that ugly Yank."

"I was wearing a Confederate uniform," Ceci recalled. "How'd you know it was me?"

"Honey, I bin watching over you the best part of your life," Hecubah reminded her. "I could pick you outa a crowd of a thousand. Don't matter to me, if you was wearing a mule skin and a sack over your head. I'd still know it was you."

"Lucky for me," Ceci realised, wincing from the pain in her side.

"Luck?" Hecubah raised a sceptical eyebrow. "Honey, you come that close to dying. It must have bin your guardian angel watching over you that day."

"You're my guardian angel," Ceci smiled.

"No. I ain't, child," she responded vehemently. "But, whoever that is, he is white haired and worn out by now. Don't ever get yourself into a fix like that again. He may not be there, next time."

Ceci stretched out a trembling hand, her fingers brushing Hecubah's cheek. "I'm so sorry for what happened," she began to sob. "I was so cruel to you. Can you ever forgive me?"

"I already have." Hecubah caught Ceci's hand in hers, pressing it to her lips. "Didn't I tell you, one time. No matter what happens, I'll always be your Hecubah."

Ceci's hand went limp as she lost consciousness again. Hecubah tucked it back under the covers, pulling the blanket up under her chin. "That's right, child," she crooned, "you sleep. Ain't nothing gonna hurt you, while I is here."

Chapter Twenty Eight

As the days wore on, Ceci continued to slip in and out of consciousness. There were occasions, rare moments, when she was entirely herself, but mostly she remained in the grip of the fever. Sometimes, her delirium would make her rave incoherently. There were other times, when she would say things so terrible, that they soared beyond Hecubah's understanding.

"Cecile Huguette Prejean," her father loomed over her, hickory switch raised to strike. "Look at yourself," he roared. "Just look at yourself."

Ceci glanced down at the Confederate uniform, she was wearing. "It weren't my fault," she sobbed. "He started it." She pointed to where Trent stood, in his West Point uniform, nose dripping with blood.

Henry Doucet appeared. "Take off your clothes," he ordered, "and put them into this bag."

Ceci did as she was told, only to discover that she was heavily pregnant.

Then Celeste came in. "No, Ceci," she demonstrated a perfect curtsey. "Like this."

"It weren't my fault," Ceci cried. "It weren't my fault."

She surged up in the bed. "It weren't my fault," she screamed.

"It's all right, honey." Hecubah put her arms around her. "Easy now. You is only dreaming."

Ceci was trembling violently. Hecubah held onto her

until she'd calmed down. "How long have I been like this?" she panted.

"Almost three weeks," Hecubah told her.

"Three weeks?" Ceci scowled. "Are we still in the boarding house?"

"Yes, honey," Hecubah confirmed. "You is still too sick to travel. We has to stay here."

"What's been happening?" Ceci asked, as Hecubah poured a glass of water and held it to her lips.

"Chattanooga has fallen," Hecubah informed her grimly. "Battle went on for about two weeks. Then our boys retreated. The Army of Tennessee has moved down to Georgia. The Union holds the city, and everything around it."

"Do you think they'll find us?" Ceci asked, after draining the glass.

"I doubt it," Hecubah reassured her. "Hundreds of people have bin flooding into this town. Union soldiers are trying their best to keep order. They ain't got no time for us."

"We're losing the war, aren't we?" Ceci guessed.

"I don't know what's going on," Hecubah admitted, with a dismal shake of her head. "I ain't bin outside in weeks. Don't you go worrying about it either," she chided. "You just concentrate on getting well. Here, try and take a little of this hot broth."

Ceci managed to eat a small bowl of broth before she passed out again.

A full moon rose high above the cottonwoods in the Louisiana bayou, flooding the garden with soft silvery hues. The warm night was rich with the fragrance of jasmine and lilac, and filled with the song of cicadas.

Ceci found herself in Trent's tender embrace, tasting the sweetness of his lips. She looked up at him. "What do you think of Hecubah?" she asked. "As a woman, I mean."

He glanced aside. "She's very attractive," he breathed heavily.

Ceci followed his gaze, to where Hecubah was standing,

wearing the nightdress she'd bought for her. Her long black hair cascaded over her shoulders and down onto her bare breasts. "It's just like wearing spider's web," she murmured seductively, moving her hands sensuously over her body. "I can't hardly bring myself to take it off. Seems only right, a man should do it."

Trent let Ceci go and went over to her. In one swift action, he stripped the diaphanous garment away, before dragging her roughly to him, kissing her fiercely.

"Kissing in the French manner," Hecubah gasped. "Where'd you learn that?"

"From some books in the library," he replied, before scooping her into his arms.

"Is she prettier than me?" Ceci asked, as he carried Hecubah into the darkness.

A dull orange light began to permeate the shadows. Ceci went towards it. The patch of colour grew larger and brighter, until finally, she opened her eyes and stared blearily around the attic room. An oil lamp flickered erratically in the corner, then Hecubah's face swam into view.

"Was Trent here?" she asked feebly.

"No, child," Hecubah responded softly. "It was just your imagination playing tricks on you."

"It all seemed so real," Ceci recalled. "We were together again, in the garden."

"You can't believe everything you see, honey," Hecubah soothed her. "It's the fever that makes you think that way."

Ceci felt unhappy and confused. To have been in his arms once more, only to discover that it was just a dream, was a bitter pill to swallow. "How long have I been here?" she asked.

"Almost seven weeks," Hecubah told her.

"Seven weeks," Ceci sighed. "Is this the first time I've woken up?"

"No, child," Hecubah sighed, "you bin awake lots of times. We talked. Don't you remember?"

Ceci shook her head. She felt as if she were living in a twilight world, where reality and imagination bled into each other. She couldn't trust her own senses. She was as helpless as a baby and prey to any fantasy the fever chose to inflict on her mind. The thought of it terrified her. "Am I going to die?" she asked.

"You stop that, now," Hecubah scolded. "I won't hear that kind of talk. No one's gonna die. Not while I'm here." She stopped short. Ceci had already drifted back into that twilight world.

As summer turned into fall, the Union garrison finally managed to establish some semblance of order in the town. Now, there were patrols every day and a curfew every night. Hecubah couldn't have cared less, her only concern was for Ceci. She seemed to be making no progress at all. Her wound had almost healed, but the fever was unabating. It was all she could do to get her to eat a little soup and drink a sip of water.

One night, things got so bad, she had to tear up a sheet and tie Ceci down so that she could keep her hand over her mouth, always afraid she might smother her. After that, Ceci fell silent. She hadn't come round in days. She just lay there, limp as a rag doll, thin and pale, the shallow rise and fall of her chest, barely discernible.

Hecubah had continued her vigil, strengthened by the fervent hope of Ceci's recovery. Now, she was forced to admit to herself that she was wasting away before her eyes. Finally, she could stand it no longer and summoned the doctor.

"There's nothing more I can do for her," he gave Hecubah the news she least wanted to hear. "There's nothing anyone can do." He put his hand on Hecubah's shoulder. "It's all in God's hands now. Let me know, if anything changes."

Hecubah knew, as he closed the door behind him, that he expected Ceci to die. She went and knelt beside the bed, clasped her hands together, and bowed her head. "Dear Lord," she prayed.

"Here is a poor lost child. Please help her find her way back to me."

Ceci stood on the edge of a battlefield, strewn with hundreds of bodies, just as dusk fell. She heard a whippoorwill call. Instinctively, she answered it. The bird rose from a thicket and soared high into the sky. Suddenly, a hawk appeared and plunged down on it. She heard it scream, as it died. She looked back at the field. The dead men rose and beckoned to her. She stepped back, shaking her head. Then, she felt a presence behind her. She turned. It was the rest of the Bird spies.

"Come with us," Oriole invited.

"It's peaceful, where we are," Cardinal told her.

"Ain't you had enough?" Bunting sighed.

They crowded in on her, cold hands plucking at her clothes, hollow eyes beseeching her to follow them.

To her relief, Trent rode past. She could see the ribbon he had taken from her, fluttering from his horse's bridle.

"Trent," she screamed, but her cries were drowned by the crack of a musket shot.

Trent's horse reared, throwing him from the saddle. He crashed to the ground and lay still.

Now, the field was empty, save for the two of them. Ceci lunged forwards, but her feet sank into the ground, anchoring her to the spot. She reached out to him, straining every sinew, screaming at the top of her lungs. "Trent."

"It's all right, child," Hecubah held her tightly. "I got you, honey." She pushed her gently back down onto the bed. "I'm here. You're safe."

Ceci's head flopped against the pillow. She sweated from every pore. Her nightdress and bedclothes were soaked. Her head ached and her vision was blurred, but she could hear Hecubah's voice.

"The Lord be praised. I think the fever's broken."

The doctor confirmed her diagnosis. "Her recovery was one in a thousand," he remarked with astonishment.

"Something must have been holding her here."

"Or, someone," Hecubah was closer to the truth.

"The battle's not over," he warned. "She'll need time to recuperate. That means plenty of bed-rest. A light diet, to start with, and a little exercise every day." He paused, studying Hecubah. "You could use some rest, as well," he observed solicitously. "You look exhausted. Why not accept the offer those Methodist women have been making all these months and get some help. Be my pleasure to give them the good news."

Hecubah nodded wearily. "That would be a blessing," she agreed, no longer afraid that Ceci might, inadvertently, give herself away during some delirious episode.

The doctor looked at his watch. "It's nearly time for the Yankee curfew," he scowled. "I'll send them over in the morning."

Once the doctor had left, Hecubah stripped the bed and remade it with fresh linen. She changed Ceci's nightgown and bathed her. As the evening drew in, Ceci felt better than she had for a long time. She was still weak and very tired, prone to dozing off at any given moment, but at least she was free of the fever.

"How long have we been here?" she asked.

Hecubah sat beside her, holding her hand. "You bin sick for more than three months."

"It doesn't feel that long," Ceci admitted.

"That's because you was outa your head most of the time," Hecubah pointed out.

"Did I say anything?" Ceci enquired tentatively. "I mean, anything strange?"

In her present condition, Hecubah wasn't about to burden her with the truth. "No, child," she lied. "Nothing that made any sense."

"Did you tell anyone our names?" Ceci persisted. "Or where we come from?"

Hecubah mulled it over. "I told them we was escaping

265

from the bombardment at Chattanooga when you got shot. I don't recall any names being exchanged. Now I think about it. I don't even know what the doctor's called."

"That's good," Ceci relaxed visibly. "Keep it that way. We must choose new names for ourselves while we're here."

"What's going on, honey?" Hecubah's brow creased with concern. She leaned forwards, lightly brushing a vagrant curl from Ceci's cheek. "Won't you tell me what it is you've bin doing? What have you got yourself into?"

Ceci glanced away. "It's better," she paused. "It's safer," she corrected herself. "If you don't know." She looked back at Hecubah. "One day, I'll explain."

"All right," she conceded grudgingly. "My only reason for coming out here was to find you and bring you home. If I must change my name to do that, then that's what I'll do. I won't ask no questions."

"Home," Ceci warmed to the thought. "Tell me about home."

"It's just as you left it," Hecubah was happy to reassure her. "The plantation, the house and the garden. Even Ol' Magic," she laughed. "You get any time to think about him?"

"Now and then," Ceci smiled.

"What about Trent?" Hecubah asked.

"I think about him all the time," Ceci sighed wistfully. "You know, I've seen him twice. Once in Washington and then again at Gettysburg, but he didn't know I was there."

A hint of doubt crossed Hecubah's face. She couldn't be sure if Ceci was telling the truth, no matter how fantastic it sounded, or if it was just something her fevered imagination had conjured up. In any event, she thought it best to humour her.

"At Gettysburg Trent was injured," Ceci went on. "I had to leave him." She chewed her lip in anguish. "I don't even know if he's dead or alive. Maybe I'll never see him again."

"Nonsense," Hecubah objected, "that boy's indestructible. When this war's over, he's gonna come looking for you."

"What if he does," the thought didn't cheer her. "When he finds me, and discovers what I've been doing, will he still want me then?"

Hecubah wasn't about to let her give up hope now. "I done told you already," she reminded her. "Never underestimate Ol' Magic, but most of all, don't underestimate Trent Sinclaire."

Ceci brightened a little. She yawned, gazing into the shadows. Her mind wandering off to happier times. "Hecubah?"

"Yes, child?"

"Talking of Ol' Magic. You never did say who that mystery man was. The one who saved you from the auction block."

"Mercy, child. Ain't you never gonna give up on that?" she clicked her tongue, feigning annoyance, inwardly glad that Ceci was becoming more like her old self.

"Please, won't you tell me?" Ceci begged, clutching at her hand.

"All right," Hecubah relented indulgently. "If you must know, it was Simon Robicheaux."

"The overseer?" Ceci sounded disappointed. "But he's old."

"He weren't so old then," Hecubah pointed out. "He was thirty-two, strong and handsome. I was eighteen. He took a shine to me right off, risked everything to save me and he was an easy man to love."

"Did he ever ask you to marry him?" Ceci wondered.

"Lots of times," Hecubah smiled.

"Then, why didn't you?"

Hecubah's smile faded. She'd always dreaded this moment. Hoped that it would never come, but now that it had, there was nothing she wouldn't do, or say, to keep Ceci on the road to recovery.

"There was another man," she confessed, tears beginning to well up in her eyes.

"I knew it," Ceci proclaimed weakly. "I was right all along. I did smell two different colognes. Who was he?"

"He was a widower," Hecubah pressed her free hand to her breast, finding it hard to speak. "Oh, Lord," she gasped. "Ol' Magic certainly had his way with us. I fell for him, so hard, and he loved me the same." She sniffed, brushing the tears from her cheek. "We had our time together, even though we knew it couldn't go nowhere. He was an influential man, a plantation owner, and I was just a creole girl. Don't matter anyway," she sniffed. "He's dead now." She fell silent, waiting for Ceci to make the connection, if she could.

Some moments passed. "Hecubah?"

"Yes, child?"

"Are you talking about my daddy?"

"You asked me, so I told you," she responded defensively. "You chew on it. If it makes you angry, makes you strong, then so much the better." She paused, waiting nervously for the condemnation she felt sure would come. Instead, she felt Ceci's hand gently squeeze hers.

"I'm glad you made him happy," she murmured drowsily. "I'm glad he made you happy."

Hecubah gazed down at her, fresh tears spilling down her cheeks.

"Hecubah?" Ceci's eyelids began to droop.

"Yes, child?"

"Is that why he asked you to take care of me?" Ceci's eyelids fluttered, then closed, as she began to breathe deeply.

Hecubah bent down, and kissed the brow of the sleeping figure. "No, honey," she answered anyway, "I asked him."

Chapter Twenty Nine

As promised, a group of Methodist ladies arrived early in the morning, all anxious to be of assistance. From the very first, they made a great fuss of Ceci. She seemed to represent to them a symbol of life over death, of resistance against federal oppression.

Foremost among them was Twyla-Fae Fuller and her daughter Savannah. Savannah was like a breath of fresh air, wafting into the stale atmosphere of the attic room. She was about the same age as Ceci, auburn haired, with green eyes and skin as pale as buttermilk. She was inquisitive, naive and clearly addicted to romantic novels, which she brought with her every day to read to Ceci, whether she wanted her to or not.

Endlessly swooning over some fictitious hero, like most young women, she was always curious about the physical side of love, whilst, at the same time, displaying a complete and obvious lack of experience. Whenever Hecubah wasn't around, Ceci would drop her the odd juicy titbit. She felt it was the least she could do in return for all the girls attention. Savannah would listen in breathless silence, eyes wide, mouth open, hand clasped to her bosom, until Ceci had finished. "My Lord, that's shocking," she always said the same thing. "Then what happened?"

"What you bin telling that girl, when I ain't here?" Hecubah would ask. "Sometimes, she leaves here pink as a boiled shrimp."

"Nothing she don't want to know," was all Ceci would say.

As Ceci grew stronger, Savannah would arrive with ribbons and lace, lip colour and rouge, all of which they'd try out on each other and then on Hecubah, for as long as she'd put up with it. By now, Ceci's hair had begun to grow long again. Savannah took great delight in combing it for her, whilst they gossiped and giggled for hours. Even though it made Hecubah's head spin sometimes, she tolerated it. It was good to hear Ceci laugh again. She was like a sapling that had been cut down, only to grow back even stronger.

Once Ceci was back on her feet, Savannah came in with some dresses, donated by the Methodist women.

"Why, you look just divine, Ellen," she admired her. "Tomorrow, I'm going to take you out on your first walk. If that's all right, Tallulah?" she deferred to Hecubah.

"I don't mind," Hecubah agreed. "As long as it ain't too far."

"It's nearly time for curfew," Savannah noticed. "So, I'll say goodnight. I'll show you what I told you about," she whispered to Ceci, before leaving.

"What's she so all fired up about?" Hecubah wanted to know, once she'd left.

"She's going to show me some black soldiers," Ceci replied indifferently. They seem to fascinate her. I can't make out if they frighten or excite her. Probably some of both."

"You be careful out there tomorrow," Hecubah advised. "Don't go getting into anymore mischief."

"I'll be glad to get out of here," Ceci admitted, glancing around the attic room. "It's like living in a coffin."

"It very nearly came to that," Hecubah reminded her soberly. "Besides, you ain't the only one who'll be glad to leave. I gets no great joy from wearing hand-me-down clothes and sleeping on that mattress, they put on the floor. I thinks it's stuffed with rocks. I can't wait to get back to my own bed."

The subject of which bed Hecubah slept in, prompted

Ceci to raise a question that had been preying on her mind for some time. An incident, which had, ultimately, brought them both here.

"Sit by me, on the bed," she asked, patting the covers.

Hecubah sat down beside her, holding her hand.

Ceci remained silent for a moment. "That day," she began quietly. "When we learned my daddy was dead. I couldn't understand why you cried so hard. Now I know, I wish you'd said something to me then. I could have done more."

"You did all you could," Hecubah sighed. "I couldn't bring myself to tell you at the time, you had your own sorrows to contend with. Besides, I weren't sure if you'd understand. I was afraid you'd feel betrayed."

"You were already like a mother to me," Ceci told her. "What difference would it have made?"

"That's the trouble with life," Hecubah advised her. "The not knowing. If we could see the future, we'd do things a whole lot differently. Then again," she reconsidered. "If we already knew what was gonna happen, what would be the point of doing anything at all. We'd never learn, never grow. If the South knew it was gonna lose the war, would it have happened in the first place?"

Ceci didn't say anything, but somehow, she thought it probably would.

★★★

"Quit fussing, Hecubah," Ceci took a step back. "I look fine. Besides, Savannah will be here in a minute."

"Ain't you supposed to call me Tallulah," Hecubah pointed out.

"Yes. Damn, I forgot" Ceci reproached herself. "Why'd you have to pick an awful name, like that?"

"You said change my name," Hecubah reminded her. "It's the first one that come to me. That, and Jezebel. Anyway,

271

what kind of name is Ellen Franklin? It makes you sound like some dried up old virgin spinster and we both know, you ain't that."

Ceci narrowed her eyes at her. "Perhaps I should call you Jezebel, after all."

"Ah huh."

Savannah couldn't wait to get Ceci into the street.

"See," she nodded, "didn't I tell you," she gripped Ceci's arm, her breath quickening. "Just look at the size of that one. Imagine what he could do."

"It sounds like you're imagining it already," Ceci remarked. "Don't stare." Her concern wasn't out of mere politeness. She was well aware that racial inequality wasn't confined to the Confederacy. The fact that the Union paid coloured troops three dollars a month less than white, made this abundantly clear. Besides, she'd noticed a group of white soldiers who'd seen the black man saluting two white women, and they didn't look too pleased about it. "This is Tennessee," she recalled. "You must have seen black men before."

"Of course," Savannah couldn't take her eyes off them. "But they were slaves, not like this."

"They're just men, like any other." Ceci forced her to move on.

The strong sunlight made her eyes ache. She'd spent so long in the attic, she'd grown unaccustomed to it. As her vision adjusted, she began to notice her surroundings. Most of the stores had been boarded up. Those, still in business had little to offer. The blockades of Confederate ports by the Union navy, made sure that little in the way of supplies got through. Apparently, local produce was hard to come by. Often as not, it was requisitioned by the army of occupation. If the war didn't end soon, the South would starve to death.

Ceci bitterly regretted her failure to warn Braxton Bragg. Chattanooga had fallen. The gateway to the Deep South was open. She'd been ill for so long, she wondered if Doucet counted her as dead. She had no way to contact him and no further instructions. She certainly couldn't stay here forever. It seemed her only option was to go home, back to Louisiana. She didn't mind admitting the idea appealed to her.

"Oh, look, look," Savannah grabbed Ceci by the wrist. "You can see his muscles, right through his shirt."

"Will you calm down," she pulled her arm free. "You'll get us both arrested. Is there anywhere around here where I can get a drink of clean water?"

Savannah seemed disappointed by her reaction. "Why, sure," she pouted. "My house ain't far from here. Mama'll be glad to see you."

"My goodness, honey. You look so much better than when I last saw you," Twyla-Fae beamed. She looked like an older version of Savannah. "And what have you two been doing on this fine day?"

Savannah glanced at Ceci, eyes wide, her pale cheeks suffused with colour.

"Just walking," Ceci replied casually. "Getting my strength back."

"That's good, honey," Twyla-Fae approved, failing to notice her daughter's sigh of relief. "I still have some tea, if you'd like it," she offered.

"Thanks for not giving me away to my mama," Savannah remarked, somewhat shame faced, as they returned to the boarding house.

"It's not as if I don't think about the same thing you do," Ceci confided. "Well, more or less, but you mustn't be so obvious about it. If a boy takes a fancy to you, you have to make him work for your attention, or he'll just take you for granted. Life isn't like the books you read."

"I suppose so," Savannah agreed grudgingly.

★★★

273

Only a few days of October remained. Ceci was now fully recovered. Both she and Hecubah knew that they couldn't rely on Methodist charity for much longer. Even though Hecubah had a purse full of gold, they couldn't spend it openly without attracting unwanted attention. It was time to think about leaving. Meanwhile, it was necessary to keep up the pretence of being refugees.

Hecubah had left Ceci alone in the attic room and gone out to see what the chances were of finding a passage home. When Savannah arrived, on one of her regular visits, she appeared flushed and breathless, as if she'd been running.

"I've some real important news to tell you," she announced dramatically.

Ceci was in no mood for anymore tales about black soldiers, or muscular heroes from the pages of a novel. "Has the Union surrendered?" she guessed wildly.

"Why, no, silly," Savannah replied, taken aback. "That would shake the pillars of heaven."

Ceci froze, the smile draining from her face. "I thought you were my friend," she remarked stonily.

"I am," Savannah faltered, noticing the change in Ceci's expression.

"Where did you hear that phrase?" Ceci continued coldly.

Savannah began to look worried. "A man," she told her, obviously surprised by her behaviour. "He's waiting on you now, back at the mission house in that little room I showed you. He said to be sure to tell you, that if you come, he guarantees Tallulah a safe passage home."

Ceci sprang across the room, grabbed Savannah by her hair and yanked her head back. "You little witch," she spat. "Don't you ever threaten her."

"I wasn't," Savannah screamed. "I just said what he told me to say. Stop it, you're hurting me."

"You don't know what pain is yet," Ceci warned. "How long has he known I was here?"

"I can't say," Savannah winced, struggling against Ceci's hold on her. "I was told I had to keep it a secret, even from my mama."

Ceci yanked her head further back. "If you don't tell me what I want to know," she threatened. "I'll strip you naked, tie you to that bed, call up half a dozen of those black soldiers you're so fond of, and feed you to them whole."

"No. Don't," Savannah began to cry. "You're frightening me."

"Tell me," Ceci shouted into her face.

Savannah was clearly terrified. "A couple of weeks after you arrived, some men come by the mission house," she blurted out. "They knew your name and what you looked like. They said, if I watched over you and let them know as soon as you was well, I'd be doing a service for the South."

Ceci released her, pushing her away. "The man at the mission house. Is he one of the men you saw before?"

"No, he's new," Savannah sniffed tearfully.

"Did he tell you his name?" Ceci demanded.

"No," Savannah sniffed again. "He just gave me that phrase to tell you. He said you'd know who he was." She looked distraught and confused. "Why'd you have to be so mean to me?" she sobbed. "We're on the same side. I thought you'd be pleased."

"Go home, Savannah," Ceci sighed. "Go home and stay home. Have nothing more to do with these people."

Savannah hesitated, looking miserable and afraid.

"Get out," Ceci screamed.

Savannah flinched, then burst into tears and fled the room.

So, Doucet hadn't forgotten her after all. He was here, in person, and he'd threatened Hecubah. Ceci's blood was boiling. Lifting the corner of her mattress, she picked up the small hand gun, Hecubah had left there for protection. Putting it in her purse, she went out into the street and on towards the mission house.

She wasn't surprised to find that the building was deserted. Crossing the main hall to a small annex room at the back, she took the gun from her purse and kicked the door open. It flew back, crashing against the wall. Doucet was sitting behind a small wooden table, smoking a cigar. Ceci didn't hesitate for a moment. She flew across the room, jamming the barrel of the pistol into Doucet's cheek.

"Take it easy," he advised, raising his hands, letting the cigar fall to the floor.

"You don't threaten Hecubah," she jabbed the pistol deeper, making him catch his breath. "If any harm comes to her, I'll kill you," she jerked the hammer back. "You, of all people, know I will pull this trigger."

"Calm down," Doucet spoke softly, "it wasn't a threat. It was a guarantee. I don't know how she managed to get out here, but things have changed now. She'll never get back alive without my help. As I said, a guarantee. It's my gift to you."

Ceci kept the pistol in his face a moment longer, then relaxed and stepped back.

Doucet slowly lowered his hand, touching his fingers against his bruised cheek. "Glad to see you're feeling better," he remarked dispassionately.

Ceci sat down opposite him, the gun still in her hand. "How'd you find me?"

Doucet put his foot on the fallen cigar and crushed it out. Then proceeded to light another. "It wasn't difficult," he shrugged, through a cloud of smoke. "You're still using the same alias, and travelling with Hecubah, you stuck out like a burr on a saddle blanket."

"Hecubah saved my life," Ceci snapped.

"Then we both owe her a debt of gratitude," he pointed out. "Let her go home. I've other work for you."

"What kind of work?" Ceci asked suspiciously.

"I'm sending you back to Washington," he told her casually.

"Are you insane?" Ceci stared. "I'm known in Washington."

Doucet interrupted, with a raised hand. "Josiah Douglas has fallen from grace," he informed her. "He was removed from office, as a security risk. He's since moved his family to New York. Charles Munroe is currently serving with Sherman, on his advance towards Atlanta. You've nothing to worry about."

"Oh, really?" Ceci's finger twitched on the trigger of the gun. "Is that what you told the rest of the Bird spies? Is it true, what I've heard? They're all dead?"

Doucet registered her reaction, with the mere blink of an eye. "I never once lied to any of you about the risks," he reminded her calmly. "You all accepted them of your own free will. What else do you want me to say?"

It galled her to admit it, but he was speaking the truth. "What am I supposed to do this time?" she snapped curtly. "Another maid?"

"Just so," Doucet nodded. "Only this time, you'll be in the White House."

Ceci's jaw dropped. "You're making fun of me."

"I never joke," he responded drily. "Your application has already been accepted."

Ceci couldn't see the point in it. "It's not going to be like the Douglas home," she guessed. "I doubt if they'll be giving away many secrets there."

"It doesn't matter," Doucet gave a dismissive wave of his hand. "I'm putting you in as a sleeper. You won't be required to do anything except your duties as a maid," he explained. "If the opportunity arises for you to act, you'll be contacted. You may yet get your chance to strike a vital blow for the South."

By agreeing to work for Doucet, Ceci felt as if she'd sold her soul to the devil. There was no escaping him. No going home. This wouldn't end until the war was over, or she was dead. It wasn't that she'd resigned herself to that fact, she still harboured the vain hope that she could help turn the tide of the war, free the South from Union tyranny and protect her home state of Louisiana. "When do I leave?" she asked.

"Today," Doucet pushed a valise from under the table with his foot. "Everything you need is in here. Retain your alias as Ellen Franklin."

"I have your word that Hecubah will get home safely," she insisted.

Doucet pulled an envelope from inside his coat and tossed it onto the table. "As long as she follows these instructions, my people will watch over her every step of the way."

Ceci picked it up. "She won't be back yet," she sighed. "I'll leave this at the boarding house and go."

"Be quick about it," Doucet advised. "Your train leaves in forty-five minutes."

★★★

As soon as Hecubah entered the attic room, she sensed something had changed. She saw the note and the envelope, laying on the bed. Her heart sank. She sat down, picked it up and read it.

'Your safe passage home is guaranteed.' it said. 'Please follow the instructions in the envelope and trust me. I am so sorry to do this to you. One day I will explain. Forgive me. I love you, Ceci.'

Hecubah's shoulders slumped as she let out a great sigh. "I should'a chained that girl down," she muttered to herself. She crushed the note in her fist. "I should'a killed Doucet, when I had the chance."

Chapter Thirty

God had a sense of humour. Ceci was sure of it. Once she'd stood outside this building and sworn vengeance on it, now she was a member of the household. A Confederate spy, right at the centre of Union power.

Life at the White House was entirely different to what she'd experienced in the Douglas home. Security was tight, troops were posted in every corridor and there was a strict regime to follow. Mary Todd Lincoln was ultimately responsible for all domestic issues. Beneath her was a loyal housekeeper, Abigail Bowen. Unlike Florina Winthrop, she knew exactly what she was doing. Ceci was only one of a score of maids, two of which she shared a room with, Catherine Meadows and Susan Langtree. Being able to mix freely with other young women came as something of a relief and often reminded her of her time on the island with the Bird spies.

Apart from her false identity, Doucet had asked nothing of her. She didn't have to risk herself in any way. She began to relax a little, adapting to the world around her. For now, she was free of hardship, hunger and sickness. She was no longer called upon to cut her hair and dress as a man. Now she could be loyal to her sex. Just a young woman in the company of other young women.

"I got another letter from Eli today," Cathy gloated, as the three of them prepared for bed. She was dark haired, vivacious and forthright. "He says he's coming home on leave next month and you all know what that means."

"You shouldn't let him," Susan, thin, prim and serious, sat on her bed, plating her hair. "Not before marriage, anyway." She was nearsighted and wore spectacles to correct the condition.

Cathy ignored her. "How'd you manage to snag a Captain, Ellen?" she asked Ceci, glancing at the picture of Trent she kept on her bedside table.

For once, Ceci could display it openly. He was, after all, a Union soldier, although she still called him Frank.

"Isn't it obvious?" Susan stopped plating and pointed. "She's beautiful. Just the kind of girl officers want to be seen with. Not like me." She lifted her specs off her nose and peered over her shoulder. "Do you think my behind's too big?"

"I don't know about that," Cathy glanced back at her. "But if you showed it to Jed occasionally, he might write more often."

"I'm not that kind of girl," Susan's nose wrinkled in disgust.

"Well, I know Jed's that sort of man," Cathy informed her, with conviction.

"How'd you know?" Susan asked suspiciously.

"Because he's a man," she stated the obvious. "Have you never had a letter from Frank?" she asked, returning her attention to Ceci.

"Not whilst I've been here. He's not one for picking up a pen," Ceci lied. "He's got better things to do than write to me."

"I bet he's a quiet one," Cathy guessed. "Does all his talking with his hands." She grabbed Ceci round the waist to illustrate her point, making her shriek. "I never noticed that before," she remarked, stepping back. "You have a little scar there and another at the front," she pointed at the bare space between Ceci's drawers and her camisole. "It looks new. Is that a bullet wound?"

Cathy's curiosity came as a sharp reminder of her vulnerable position here. She could never allow herself to slip into complacency. "Just an accident," she made light of it. The last thing she needed was awkward questions. "Why, does it spoil me?"

"No, honey." Fortunately, Cathy was easily distracted. "It's not as if anyone else is going to see it, except Frank, and I'm sure there'll be plenty of other things on display to keep him occupied."

"You're awful," Susan complained. "Don't you ever think of anything else?"

"If you come across something better than men," she replied disdainfully. "You let me know and I'll think about that."

Even though she wasn't expected to gather information, Ceci kept her eyes and ears open and remembered what she saw and heard. The war raged on, with both Confederate and Union victories, but no clear end in sight. As winter gave way to spring and spring to summer, the northern chill, she found so disagreeable, dissipated. She'd been in the north and suppressed her southern accent for so long, she doubted if she could ever call it back, but her intentions remained unchanged. She felt marooned in Washington, forgotten, abandoned, isolated from the theatre of war, where she could make a difference. Why did Doucet insist on keeping her here? There seemed no purpose in it.

Her position as maid in the White House had become a way of life. She was used to the routine. She'd actually begun to enjoy it. Initially, she'd been provided with funds to tide her over. Now, she existed on her wages, like any other employee. She was allowed one day off a week. Invariably, she went shopping. Unlike the stores in the south, Washington was packed with things to buy. There were no shortages here. Sometimes, it made her angry. She'd think of her hometown, in Louisiana, doubting that it fared so well. At times like these, the dark creature within her would howl impatiently, making her isolation seem all the more profound. It strengthened her resolve to strike against the Union, with or without Doucet's orders. Alone, if necessary.

Preoccupied with these dark thoughts she continued with her errands, until, from the corner of her eye, she saw she was being watched. Glancing up, she noticed a young woman, accompanied by a Union soldier, standing across the street. She held a small child in her arms and, as their eyes met, she smiled and began to wave. Ceci recognised her at once. It was Amelia Douglas. She must have married Frank and remained in the capital after her family had left.

Without thinking, Ceci waved back, then stopped abruptly, realising she'd given herself away. Amelia faltered. The soldier spoke to her, looking in Ceci's direction. She saw Amelia shake her head, believing herself to be mistaken, before moving on.

Doucet's instructions were clear on this point. 'If you are recognised, at your earliest opportunity, draw that person in and eliminate them.' He had trained her well, but he hadn't eradicated her humanity. She wasn't about to murder a young mother merely to protect her identity. She let it pass, and in doing so, broke the first rule of survival.

Ceci hurried back to the relative safety of the White House, showed her pass to the sentry and went inside. Pass still in hand, she headed for her room. Her position had been compromised and that's all she could think about. When she finally bothered to look up, she realised she was in the wrong part of the house. This was a restricted area, where only senior members of staff were permitted. Obviously, the guards had assumed she was one of them. Seeing the pass in her hand, they'd let her through. She clicked her tongue in annoyance and turned to retrace her steps, only to find herself confronted by a tall thin man.

He wore a beard but no moustache and there was a

distinctive mole on his cheek. She gasped, her eyes widening. It was him. The author of all her misery. Abraham Lincoln. The dark creature within her bared its teeth and growled. She could kill him now, it whispered. She could become that weapon she'd thought of on the day she learned of her family's death. She could throw herself into the heart of the Union and destroy it. That was the reason for everything. That was what she'd lived for.

"Are you lost?" he enquired, his voice soft and mellow.

It completely disarmed her. "Yes," she stammered, "I believe I am."

"In that case, young woman," he smiled wryly. "You find yourself in good company."

She was transfixed by the sight of him, unable to act. She had expected to find a monster, but it was only a man. He looked so old. Old before his time. Worn thin and threadbare, bowed and haggard. There was an overwhelming aire of melancholy about him that was almost tangible. It was as if he bore the weight of the world on his shoulders. Despite herself, her heart went out to him.

"Allow me," he gestured towards a door at the end of the passage. She followed him, pausing as he opened it for her. "As one American to another," he remarked, with the same wry smile. "Let us hope that we can exit this war as swiftly as you have left this corridor." He took her hand in his and shook it.

Ceci couldn't help herself. She continued to stare up into his face. There was something in his expression, the look of destiny. She had seen it once before, on General Lee at Gettysburg. In that moment, she felt herself to be in the presence of true greatness. These were men whom only the will of God could destroy and she knew, full well, that she was not his chosen instrument. She blinked, waking from her trance, nodded dumbly, retrieved her hand and returned the way she'd come.

Her chance meeting with Lincoln had initiated a change

within her. She could feel it happening, even as she stumbled blindly along, his words echoing in her ears. 'As one American to another'. Reaching her room, she staggered inside. Falling against a table, she gripped its edges for support until her knuckles whitened, her breath rasping over her teeth. She thought of her father and her sister, of the Bird spies, and of her home in Louisiana. The images crowded into her mind until she thought it would explode. She had failed them all. She had been tested and found wanting, but, under the circumstances, how could she have acted otherwise?

In her frustration, she turned all her anger and hatred in upon herself. She began to tremble, the dark creature thrashed in the void, the table rattling under her hands. She felt as if a higher force was at work, negating her fury, stripping the pain from her soul. She wanted to keep it. It made her angry. The anger gave her strength. She struggled against it, but to no avail. She could see her father's face and that of Celeste. The vision touched her heart. How could she ever have believed that she could honour their memory with murder? How could the death of one man atone for their lose, after so many had died? She had been driven by the utter futility of revenge. The dark creature within her howled a final time and fell silent. The void closed, the poison flowing from her eyes as tears, long overdue.

She collapsed onto her bed, feeling dazed and confused, drained and exhausted, with no clear idea of what to do next. She had no intention of abandoning the Confederate cause, although vengeance no longer played a part in it, but without the violent emotions that had driven her thus far, she felt powerless. She considered what so many others, who'd found themselves in this position, had said. What happened next would be the will of God, but, as she already knew, God had a sense of humour.

★★★

Christmas at the White House was a lavish affair, not that Ceci saw much of it. The Lincolns' had been generous enough to distribute presents amongst the staff. The maids received silk handkerchiefs with a tiny Union flag embroidered in the corner. For Cathy and Susan, they were treasured keepsakes. Ceci merely wiped her nose on it.

There was a modest celebration in the servant's hall. Defiant as ever, Ceci sat in on it, determined to be the only speck of southern soil in the heart of Union territory. Mistletoe had been hung and Cathy appeared to be kissing anything in trousers that passed under it, much to Susan's dismay.

Ceci remained indifferent to the festivities. The sound of laughter and the chink of glasses only served to remind her of the last Christmas she'd spent, with all her family on the plantation in Louisiana. Finally, she could stand it no longer.

"Where are you going?" Susan asked in surprise. "You're not on duty yet. The party's just getting started."

"I have a headache," she responded, touching a hand to her brow. "I need some air."

She made her way through the busy kitchen and out into the White House grounds. Wrapping her arms around herself, she shivered in the cold night air, gazing out across the frosted lawns. Again, she was reminded of her home in Louisiana and the garden there. She exhaled, watching her breath drift off in vaporous clouds. She missed the warmth of the South. If only Trent were here, she could bare it. The heat of his body would drive the chill from her bones. She wondered how many northern winters she would have to endure before she went home.

More than a year had passed and still Doucet hadn't contacted her. She began to think he'd left her here on purpose, to punish her for her failures. Bottled her up in a place she couldn't escape from, just to keep her out of the way.

If that was the case, she was surprised he'd spared himself the expense of a bullet. Then another thought occurred to her. What if he'd been killed. It was likely that he was the only one who knew she was here. She could spend the rest of the war working as a maid at the White House. The irony wasn't lost on her. God's sense of humour was becoming irksome.

★★★

Easter was fast approaching. Ceci had been in the employ of the White House for sixteen months. She felt as if she'd done more service, albeit cleaning grates and polishing silver, to the Union, than she had to the Confederacy. It was her day off and she was getting ready to go out when suddenly the door burst open, making her jump. Susan stood there, red faced and breathless.

"It's just come over the telegraph," she panted. "It's all over the house. Robert. E. Lee has surrendered. Today at Appomattox."

The news hit Ceci like a thunderbolt. She tottered back, slumping into a chair, tears beginning to trickle down her cheeks.

"I know. It's wonderful news. Isn't it?" Susan misinterpreted her reaction. "You've dropped your gloves and purse." She bent forwards, picked them up and placed them on Ceci's lap. "I'd better get back to work. I just had to come and tell you."

The room seemed to shrink around her. The world shrank around her. How could this be, she wondered, recalling her meeting with General Lee and the words he'd spoken at Gettysburg. 'By the grace of God, we shall yet prevail.' Perhaps it was the issue of slavery that had caused God to favour the Union. The Pharaoh's had enslaved the Israelites and he'd sent plagues on them. Perhaps servitude to the North was his punishment on the Confederacy? Then again, what if God had nothing to do with it? Maybe it was all about iron and steel, factories and northern industry, against southern cotton. Whatever it was, she couldn't stay in this house a moment longer.

The streets of Washington thronged with people. Union flags flew from every mast, draped every balcony. Bands marched along the roads playing 'The Union Forever.' The crowds joined in, singing the words, laughing and cheering. All Ceci could do was stand there and cry. The champion of the Southern cause had fallen. His battle flags lay in the dust, crushed under the feet of the Union, along with the hopes of the Confederacy. She had nothing to celebrate.

Blinded by her tears, she pushed through the milling crowds that surged around her, hardly aware of where she was going. She was pushed and jostled, like a leaf in a windstorm, until finally, one man barged right into her, knocking her purse from her hand. She stood there, dazed, as he mumbled an apology and stooped to pick it up. As he rose, she recognised him. "Booth."

"In the purse," he whispered, before tipping his hat and vanishing into the sea of bodies.

Her meeting with Booth imbued Ceci with a renewed sense of hope. If he was here, Doucet couldn't be far behind. Perhaps there was still something that could be done. Something that could be salvaged from this disaster. When she decoded the message, Booth had slipped into her purse, she discovered it was a room number at the National Hotel in Washington. He told her to meet him there, on Good Friday at five o'clock. It would be difficult to absent herself from the White House, but this was one appointment Ceci was determined to keep.

Chapter Thirty One

The National Hotel wasn't hard to find. Ceci went to the room and tapped lightly on the door. It opened ajar and Booth peered cautiously out. Pulling the door wide, he caught her by the arm and dragged her inside.

"I thought Doucet would be here," she told him, noticing they were alone.

"No," Booth shook his head. "This is my operation."

Before she could say anything else, he spoke again.

"I want you to go into the next room. There you'll find one of Doucet's satchels. Put on the Union uniform, then the Confederate and the dress, in that order. Be quick."

Ceci complied, pinning her hair back, until she thought she could wedge a soldier's cap over it. It felt good to be going into action again. After all her months of isolation, she was eager to be of service.

"Good," Booth nodded his approval, as she emerged. "I belong to a group of southern patriots," he explained. "We have a plan that will revive the fortunes of the Confederacy."

"How's that possible?" she asked doubtfully. "General Lee has surrendered the Army of Northern Virginia."

"That's not the only army at the disposal of the Confederacy," Booth informed her. "We still have Johnston's Army of Tennessee. The Army of the Trans-Mississippi, as well as Arkansas and New Mexico. There are still thousands of men, ready and able to fight."

"Surely, they'll surrender as well," she guessed. "Once they discover what's happened at Appomattox."

"That's the point of our plan," Booth replied. "We intend to cut off the head of the Union snake. This will throw the Union government into chaos and allow the Confederacy time to regroup and reorganise. There'll be no more surrenders, after that. The South will rise again."

"How'd you intend to do that?" she asked. "Cut off the head of the snake, I mean."

"Tonight, Abraham Lincoln will attend a play at Ford's Theatre," he told her. *"Our American Cousin*. It's a fine play. I've acted in it. You are, by now, a familiar face at the White House," he continued. "Arrangements have been made for you to accompany Mrs Lincoln, as her personal maid." He took a Derringer from his pocket, much like the one Alma had given her, and laid it on the table. "At the appointed hour, the policeman guarding Lincoln's box, will be distracted. You will take this gun, put it against the back of the President's head and kill him. This is the chance you've been waiting for," he smiled confidently. "You will have the honour of executing the President of the United States."

Once again, Ceci felt as if a higher force was at work, compelling her towards a course of action she had already decided not to take. Before she'd met Lincoln face-to-face, she might have considered it, but now it was out of the question. She was a southern patriot, not a rabid fanatic.

"You're out of your mind," she told him bluntly. "What good would that do?"

"Hear it all," Booth cautioned. "At the same time, my associates will eliminate Vice President Andrew Johnson and Secretary of State William Seward. Thus, cutting off the head of the Union snake. This is what Doucet trained you for. This was his ultimate plan, if we began to lose the war."

Ceci was astounded. "You mean to tell me he sacrificed the lives of three brave young women, in the name of this mad idea?" she reminded him of the other Bird spies.

"Fortunes of war," Booth shrugged dismissively. "Only the lucky or the strong survive. They were neither. Remember what you agreed to do. To penetrate deep behind enemy lines, for any purpose."

That phrase took on a new and more insidious meaning, every time it was repeated to her. Ceci couldn't believe what she was hearing. The whole plan sounded insane. It smacked of desperation. She didn't like the way Booth had casually dismissed the deaths of the other Bird spies. She didn't trust his judgement now.

"If anything goes wrong," she warned him. "Northern reprisals against the South will be unimaginably severe."

"Nothing can go wrong, as long as you do your job," he responded brusquely. "There's a warehouse, a few blocks from the theatre. In it are some Confederate prisoners awaiting parole," he continued to outline the plan. "They will be allowed to escape. When you leave the theatre, remove the dress and join them. You can cover your tracks in the ensuing mayhem. Once you're far enough across town, discard the Confederate uniform. As a Union soldier, you can make good your escape. Return to Richmond. Doucet will contact you there."

The more Ceci heard, the less she liked it. It sounded like a suicide mission. She had always been ready to give her life in the service of the Confederacy, but she didn't intend to put a rope around her own neck. She'd been in the White House long enough to realise that the Union wouldn't collapse from the loss of these men. Others would replace them. She and Lincoln would die for nothing.

"I won't do it," she told him flatly. "This isn't an act of patriotism. It's nothing but revenge."

Booth's expression hardened. "I guess Doucet was right," he remarked disdainfully. "He said none of you were ready. Happily, I have a contingency plan. Lincoln admires my talent. He has often asked to meet me. Tonight, he will."

Ceci darted forward and snatched the Derringer from the table. "You're not going anywhere," she hissed, levelling it at him. "I won't let you drag the Confederacy down with you."

He smiled in the face of her threat. "Doucet was right, after all," he sneered. "You're just not good enough." He pointed at the Derringer. "You forgot your basic training. Did you check to see if there were any bullets in it?"

Ceci glanced at the gun. Suddenly, the flat of Booth's hand cracked against her cheek, knocking her to the floor.

He picked up the Derringer and loaded it. "I'd kill you right now," he aimed the gun at her, "but that would only raise the alarm. Instead, I'll lock you in this room. By the time, they find you, I'll be long gone." He raised his arm, in a sweeping gesture. "Surrounded by all this incriminating evidence, they'll probably hang you straight away." He began to smile. "Of course, you could always try climbing out of the window, we're only four floors up. Or, you could scream for help," he suggested, toying with her. "Then they'd find you all the sooner. One way or the other, I guess you're going to die. So, I'll say goodbye," he bowed flamboyantly. Let himself out and closed the door.

Ceci waited until she heard the key turn in the lock and his footsteps recede down the hall. In his desire to pour scorn on her, Booth had underestimated Doucet's methods and Ceci's abilities. As soon as he left, she pulled a long pin from her hair and set to work on the lock. It was old and stiff. Several hours passed before it yielded to her. Once she was free, she dashed out into the street and on towards Ford's Theatre. If she hurried, there might still be time to forestall Booth's insane plan.

By the time she arrived, the audience was already spilling out into the street. The same sentence was on every tongue. The President had been shot.

"I know that woman," someone shouted.

Ceci froze, searching the faces of the crowd, until she found Amelia Douglas and her husband. Constance was with them, doubtless on a visit to her sister, the theatre a special treat.

"I know her," Constance spat venomously. All she could see was the woman who'd stolen the man she loved. "Something's not right about her."

In the grip of hysteria, it was all the crowd needed. Some of them began to advance towards her. Ceci backed away, then turned on her heel and ran. She dodged down an alley, then another, until she heard the mob pass by. Keeping to the narrow thoroughfares, she worked her way back across town, until her path was blocked by a Union soldier.

"Sorry miss, you can't go down there," he warned her. "Some Reb prisoners have broken out of the warehouse. They're all over the place. It's not safe out here. You'd best go back the way you came."

Even as he spoke, a group of Confederate soldiers appeared behind him. They retreated, scattering, with him in hot pursuit.

Ceci tugged off the dress, just as another group of escapees ran past. She joined their number, as they scurried through the warren of shadowy back streets. It was sheer chaos. Booth's escape plan was working perfectly. She was able to disappear in the melee, but as more and more Confederate prisoners were rounded up, their numbers in the darkened alleys began to dwindle. Finally, she left them altogether and struck out on her own.

She'd left the mob far behind, but now she was surrounded by Union soldiers. She could hear them moving around in the shadows, calling from one passage to another, closing in on her. Left with only one direction to go, she turned a corner, to find herself facing a brick wall. It was a dead end. She was trapped.

She was just about to tear off the Confederate uniform and

reveal the federal blue, when she heard footsteps approaching behind her. She turned and looked back towards the mouth of the alley to see the ragged light of a torch dancing on the walls that hemmed her in. There was no time to change. She glanced around. In the corner was a pile of discarded packing cases. Wrenching a length of wood from one of them, she pressed her back against the wall, prepared to fight her way out.

Seconds later, a Union officer turned the corner, torch in one hand, pistol in the other, and froze. "Put it down, son," he spoke softly. "I don't want to have to kill you."

From the shadows, Ceci could see his face illuminated by the light of the torch he was holding. She stood in the middle of Washington, the heart of federal territory, on the night the President had been shot. She was wearing a Confederate uniform, with a Union one underneath. She faced a man with a gun and all she had was a piece of wood. At best, her situation appeared dire. Nevertheless, she still managed to smile. Dropping the wood, she put up her hands. There was no doubt about it. Now she was quite sure. God certainly did have a sense of humour.

In that moment, Ceci recalled something Hecubah had said about her guardian angel, on the night she lay wounded and feverish in the attic room, outside Chattanooga. 'Whoever that is, he is white haired and worn out by now. Don't ever get yourself into another fix, like this. He may not be there next time.' She was right. He wasn't. But he'd sent someone else, in his place.

The officer approached cautiously, holding the torch out in front of him, its flames guttering in the slight breeze. All Trent could see, was a fresh-faced boy, half obscured in shadows. He was relieved that the lad had capitulated so easily. He would have regretted harming one so young. As he drew closer, he noticed that there was something oddly familiar about this one. The way he stood, the way he smiled, those yellow curls poking out from under his cap. He lowered the torch a little, the flames hissing in the draught. "God almighty," the vision tore the words from his throat. Suddenly, all he could see was the wild girl. "Ceci," he stared incredulously. "What the…"

"Are you all right, Captain?" A squad of his men were moving down the alley in support.

He couldn't risk her being questioned by his men. In one swift action, he dropped the torch, balled his fist and clipped Ceci across the chin. Catching her as she collapsed, he threw her over his shoulder, just as his men turned the corner.

"Are you all right, Captain?" his sergeant repeated, as the rest of his squad clustered around him.

"I'm fine," he assured them. "I've taken care of this one. It's just a boy. You men spread out and find the others. They went off that way," he misdirected them.

They saluted and left to carry out his instructions.

Trent had to think quickly. Without pausing to wonder what Ceci was doing here in the first place, he pushed the packing cases away from the wall and laid her down in the space between. After a couple of light slaps, she began to come around.

"Oh, I think you broke my nose," she groaned.

"Damn your nose," he snapped, "I ought to break your neck." Impulsively, he grabbed her face in both hands and kissed her, making her yelp. "Ceci, what in the hell are you doing here wearing that uniform?" He pulled at her jacket and saw the blue beneath. "Jesus Christ," he swore loudly. "What have you done?"

Ceci gazed blearily up at him. "Can I have another kiss?" she asked. "That first one was a mite rushed."

Trent was beside himself. There were a thousand things he wanted to say, but now was not the time to say them. He couldn't decide if he wanted to kiss her again, or kill her. "I should put my boot in your behind," he barked. "Don't move," he ordered, pushing the cases in around her. "Don't make a sound. Stay where you are until I come back."

For once, Ceci did as she was told. In the distance, she could hear voices, people running, the occasional gunshot, but she made no attempt to move until Trent returned.

He pulled the packing cases aside and knelt in front of her. "Get rid of those uniforms." He pulled a dress from the sack he was carrying.

Ceci was still groggy from his blow. "Did that come off some woman's washing line?" she asked.

"Never mind," he dismissed her question. "Get out of those uniforms and put it on." Seeing that Ceci was slow to respond, he began to undress her himself.

"This is just like old times," she giggled. "I've missed you so much."

"Stop it," Trent would have none of it. "Do you have any idea of the danger you're in?

"Not now I'm with you," she answered truthfully.

Trent sighed heavily. Yanking her to her feet, he pulled the dress over her head and fastened it up.

"It's too big and I don't like the colour," Ceci complained mildly.

"Be quiet." Trent pushed the packing cases back against the wall, concealing the uniforms. Then he linked arms with her and began to walk. They left the maze of alleys and emerged onto the street. "Don't say anything," he cautioned her. "That soldier approaching is my commanding officer, Colonel Shaw."

Trent let Ceci go and snapped to attention, as Colonel Shaw came up to them.

"Well done, Captain Sinclaire," he returned the salute. "Your men have recaptured all the escaped prisoners." He looked at Ceci. "Who is this?"

"My wife, sir," Trent replied. "She arrived this evening from Boston. Even though I forbade her to follow me."

"It's a poor thing when a man can't make his wife obey him," Shaw commented. "She appears to be injured," he observed.

"That was me, sir," Trent had no need to lie. "I felt it necessary to chastise her."

"Nevertheless, the streets tonight are no place for a woman," Shaw advised. "I suggest you find her a room and report to me in the morning."

Trent took Ceci to the first hotel he could find, paid for a room, marched her upstairs and shoved her inside.

"What possessed you to come here?" he rounded on her. "What were you doing wearing those uniforms?"

"My daddy, Celeste and her baby were killed when New Orleans fell," she snapped back. "I wasn't going to let that pass."

"Oh, I see," his temper abated for a moment. "I'm so sorry to hear that. They were fine people. I'd have come back, if I'd known."

"I know you would," she agreed soberly.

"Even so, what did you think you could achieve by joining this God forsaken war?"

Ceci raised her bruised chin. "I wanted to liberate my country from federal oppression."

"Your country?" Trent wasn't sure he understood.

"The Confederate States of America," she replied haughtily.

Trent clutched at his brow. "God in heaven, Ceci," he sighed. "When your letters stopped coming, the only thing that kept me sane through this whole bloody mess, was the thought that you were safe at home. I begged you to stay there. I begged you."

"You promised me you wouldn't take any unnecessary risks," she retorted hotly. "But there you were at Gettysburg, riding right out in front of your men. Why, if it hadn't been for me, you'd have been trampled to death."

Trent's jaw sagged. "So it was you," he stared in astonishment. "Jesus Christ, Ceci," he dragged both hands through his hair, in frustration. "What in the hell were you doing at Gettysburg?"

"Saving your life," Ceci faced him, stiff with indignation, clenching and unclenching her fists.

Trent was angry about one thing. Ceci was angry about another. In the end, it was all the same thing and there, right in the middle, was Ol' Magic, whipping up a storm. It could only end one way.

Chapter Thirty Two

This was the moment Ceci had dreamed about, every day, for the past four years. She was back in Trent's arms again. She hadn't felt this safe, or been this content, since she'd left home. She recalled the first time they'd made love, in the garden at the plantation. Then, she'd thought that she would never experience anything as profoundly beautiful again. Now she had. She'd exorcised all her demons and laid the dead to rest. If only she were back in Louisiana, it would be perfect.

"Oh, no," she draped her arms around Trent's neck as he tried to leave the bed. "Stay with me."

"I can't," he disentangled himself from her embrace. "I have to report to headquarters."

"Wouldn't you rather stay here, with me?" she asked drowsily.

"Of course," he assured her, "but I'm still an officer in the Union army. I must report for duty. Promise me you'll stay in the room," he asked, as he began to dress. "Don't go wandering around."

"Where am I going to go?" Ceci pouted. "I left everything I had at the White House. All I own is that threadbare old dress you found for me. I don't even have any underwear." She curled up in the bed, eyeing him coquettishly. "But I guess that's the way you like me."

"Please, Ceci," he insisted. "I'm serious. It's too dangerous for you out there. Stay in the room. If you want anything to eat, have it sent up. I'll see what I can find for you before I get back."

Trent returned in the evening, carrying a large paper parcel which he gave to Ceci. "I had to guess the size," he told her.

Ceci opened it to discover the badly needed underwear.

"I felt pretty foolish having to buy those," he didn't mind admitting.

"Why?" Ceci asked innocently, examining his purchases. "Did the store clerk think they were for you?"

Trent was in no mood for flippant remarks. He sat down on the bed beside her, wresting the garment she was preoccupied with from her hand. "There's a hue and cry going on out there," he informed her gravely. "They're still looking for Booth and his co-conspirators. They'll stop at nothing to find them. Now they think he had another accomplice. They found a dress in his room. They're saying it's a woman. A Confederate spy. A maid from the White House, no less." He grasped her by her shoulders and looked into her eyes. "Please tell me you had nothing to do with the assassination of the President of the United States."

"No, I didn't," Ceci made a stringent denial. "It was Booth. I tried to prevent it."

Trent was clearly relieved. "Thank God," he sighed. "Anyway, all hell's breaking loose out there. They've been searching buildings all day."

"No one's come this way," Ceci shrugged.

"That's because I told them you're my wife," Trent reminded her.

"Well, after what we've been doing," she remarked indignantly. "I should say I am. In all but name, anyway."

★★★

The death of Abraham Lincoln sent the whole of the North into a state of mourning. Booth was eventually traced to a farm in rural northern Virginia, where he was hiding in a barn. The barn was set on fire by his pursuers and as he tried to escape he was shot dead. The hunt for the rest of the conspirators continued. Anyone, who'd ever known Booth, fell under suspicion. Trent insisted Ceci stayed in the hotel room. Fearing for her life, he brought everything she needed into her. Despite the danger, Ceci soon began to chaff on her confinement.

"I've been cooped up in this room for three weeks," she complained, the instant he came in, pacing restlessly up and down. "It wouldn't be so bad if you'd stay with me."

Trent was used to her impatience by now. "You know very well, I have my duties to attend to," he reminded her. "Besides, we can't make love all day and all night."

Ceci stopped pacing and thrust her hands onto her hips. "Why not?" she demanded. "Don't you love me no more?"

Trent was aware that the claustrophobic conditions left her prone to making irrational remarks. At least, that's what he told himself. It wasn't as if she needed much of an excuse. "Good Lord, Ceci," he sighed. "I'm only human. I can't make up for four years in three weeks."

"Got to admit, you had a good try at it though," she smirked.

Trent sighed again. "Ceci, you're incorrigible."

"That's what people keep telling me," she began to pace again.

Trent had foreseen that this situation might occur and had taken steps to alleviate it. He let her pace a moment longer. "I've an old friend waiting to see you," he told her.

Ceci stopped pacing and cast him a puzzled frown.

He went to the door and opened it.

"Hecubah," Ceci flew across the room, threw her arms around her and smothered her with kisses. Then they both started crying.

When they'd recovered a little, Hecubah stood back and

looked at Ceci. "By rights, I should be whipping your behind about now," she chided. "But I'm too tired from the journey."

"Oh, Trent. How could you drag her all the way out here?" Ceci began to admonish him.

"Hey," Hecubah put a stop to it. "Before you go barking at him. I want you to know, he only told me where you were. When I got the telegram, it was my decision to come here, and to do that I had to leave a husband and a baby behind."

Ceci was staggered by the news. "A husband? Simon Robicheaux," she guessed. "So, you finally married him."

"There'll always be a place in my heart for your daddy," Hecubah confided. "I'll never forget that man. Ain't a day goes by, I don't think about him." She paused in a moments reflection, before continuing. "When I got back from Chattanooga, Simon sat me down and gave me a real good talking to. He said I should quit hankering after ghosts and look to the future. I brought that message with me, all the way from Louisiana, to give it to you."

"A baby," Ceci recalled.

"Ah huh," Hecubah nodded. "A little girl. "I named her Celeste, after your sister. I hope you don't mind. I would have called her Cecile, but I already got a baby by that name."

Ceci slumped into a chair, fresh tears trickling down her cheeks. It seemed as if the whole world had passed her by. "What about the plantation?" she asked, recalling the scenes of devastation she'd witnessed on her travels.

"My husband is a very clever man," Hecubah informed her. "When he heard the Yanks was coming..." She broke off, glancing at Trent.

He merely smiled and gestured indulgently.

"As I was saying," she continued. "When he found out the Union was on its way, he freed all the slaves and gave them parcels of land on the east side. When those boys turned up, I answered the door and told them it was my house. All they found was a bunch of free black folks working their own land.

301

They had no choice but to let us be. After all, that's why they fought the war."

"I can't believe it was all for nothing," Ceci hung her head at the mention of the war. "Surely there's still something we can do?"

Hecubah came over to her, put her hand under her chin and lifted her face up. "I was afraid you'd be thinking that way," she admitted. "That's why I come. Honey, General Lee has surrendered. The Confederate armies are defeated. You got the whole world coming down on your head, and still you won't quit." She spoke softly, looking deep into Ceci's eyes. "Don't you understand, child? It's over. Let it go."

"We have to think of a way to get Ceci out of here," Trent cut in. "I'll resign my commission as soon as possible and then we can make a plan."

"I can't allow you to give up the only life you've known, just to be with me," Ceci objected.

"The only life I want to know, is with you," he told her vehemently. "Remember, we agreed not to let anything come between us."

"I swore I'd die, before I let that happen," Ceci recalled. "But other people died instead."

"I know a lot has changed," Trent agreed. "But we still have each other." He bent forward and kissed her. "I have to report back to headquarters tomorrow," he told them. "Some big-wig's arriving on an inspection. After that, we can start making our preparations."

★★★

What Trent thought would be a routine military briefing, turned out to be a personal interview with none other than General Ulysses S. Grant himself. It didn't bode well for his future plans.

Grant appeared casual in his manner, almost genial, as he

302

lounged at his desk, lighting a cigar. Trent sat opposite him, stiff with apprehension.

"We have won the war against the Confederacy," Grant began. "And now we are faced with the unenviable task of reconciliation. To create a whole nation under God. A task made more difficult to achieve by the resentment born by our people, towards the South, over the assassination of President Lincoln by the traitor Booth." He paused, drawing on his cigar. "This man's name has been linked with the Confederate spy master, Henry Doucet," he continued with slow deliberation. "And the Bird spies, including the only one of those still unaccounted for, Whippoorwill. Can you shed any light on that, Captain?"

"I'm afraid not, sir," Trent lied without compunction. "All I've heard is rumours."

"I see," Grant didn't seem particularly surprised by his answer. "The people are calling for the execution of Jefferson Davis, but there's no need for that. So much blood has been shed already," he went on. "I, personally, have no stomach to spill anymore. No matter how great the crime." He studied Trent for a moment. "I am reliably informed that your family owns property in Canada," he seemed to digress from the main topic.

"That is correct, sir," Trent replied, wondering where this conversation was going.

"You have served your country, with a full measure of devotion," Grant came to the point. "And distinguished yourself in battle. For that reason, and those previously stated, I shall be happy to grant you a full and honourable discharge, in the morning. This will leave you free to take your wife to Canada and live there with her, in peace and safety," he emphasised. "Do I make myself clear?"

There was no mistaking his meaning. "You are clear, sir," Trent assured him.

★★★

"Canada?" Ceci glowered. "I hear the winters are cold there."

"Very cold," Trent confirmed. "Also, very safe. Be reasonable, Ceci. Your life could depend on this."

"I don't see why," she objected. "They don't have any proof and virtually no evidence. It's all rumours and speculation. Only four people know who I am and two of them are in this room. Booth is dead and they'll never find Doucet. So, why do I have to go into exile?"

His recent conversation with General Grant had left Trent with a different point of view. He could see the danger of remaining in America, even if Ceci couldn't. "I'm not going to argue with you, Ceci," he told her assertively. "You're going to Canada with me, even if I have to tie you in a sack and carry you there."

Ceci could see that there was no point in trying to change his mind. "Very well, Trent," she lowered her eyes submissively. "I'll do anything you say."

"I'll arrange passage in the morning," he told Hecubah, as she prepared to leave the room. "You see," he confided, in a low voice. "All you have to do is be firm and she falls right in line."

Returning to her own room, Hecubah rolled her eyes and sighed. "Sweet Jesus. That boy's got a lot to learn."

She wasn't in the least surprised when Trent returned to the hotel room the next morning, alone. "You couldn't find her then?"

"No," Trent shook his head wearily. "No sign of her. Washington's a big place. She could be anywhere. Under the circumstances, I couldn't ask too many questions."

"All you have to do, is be firm and she'll fall right in line," Hecubah recalled what he'd said the night before. "Oh, yeah, that was a real good idea."

304

Trent was in no mood to listen to criticism. He marched up to her, gripped her by the shoulders and thrust her against the wall.

"Oh, my," she murmured appreciatively. "Ain't you a big strong boy."

"Enough," he snapped, "I'm tired of your nonsense. No more games. No more riddles. I think you know where she's gone."

"And so do you," she put her hand against his chest and eased him away. "Just stop. Get your head outa your behind and think for a moment."

Reluctantly, he did as she suggested. Then it came to him. "Oh, no," He clapped his hands over his face. "No, no, no. She hasn't. Not after all that's happened. She hasn't gone back. Not back to Louisiana and the plantation?"

"It's her home," Hecubah pointed out. "That's where she was born. That's where she wants her baby to be born."

Trent dragged his hands from his face and stared at her. Hecubah was just full of insight today. "Are you saying she's pregnant?"

Hecubah rolled her eyes at him. "Well, unless you two spent the last month holding hands and discussing the weather," she stated the obvious. "I guess something's gonna happen. I weren't here with my potion. Too late now anyway."

"I'm going to the railroad depot, right now." Trent made for the door.

"Hold on." Hecubah caught him by the arm. "If they ever takes the trouble to find out who she is, they's liable to execute her," she warned him. "They's liable to execute anyone they find with her. If that happens to be an ex Union cavalry captain, they's liable to execute him twice."

Trent pulled his arm free. "Do I buy one ticket or two?"

"That ain't even a question," Hecubah snorted.

★★★

305

The journey from Washington to Richmond was relatively easy. However, the southern railroad system had never been equal to that of the north. What hadn't been destroyed during the war was now virtually derelict. Gangs worked around the clock just to keep it patched up. The shortage of locomotives and railroad cars only served to exacerbate the situation.

Eventually Trent abandoned the idea of continuing by train. Accepting Hecubah's advice to return the way she'd come, he purchased them passage on a riverboat. It would take them down the Mississippi all the way back to Louisiana. It was a comfortable way to travel, although extremely slow, but as Hecubah had rightly pointed out, there would be no unforeseen delays.

The further south they travelled, the warmer the climate became. Hecubah was used to it, but Trent wasn't. He spent much of his time on deck, where it was cooler. Often Hecubah would join him there.

"I blame myself for Ceci leaving," he confided one night, as they leaned on the rail watching the river flow past. "I pressed her too hard."

"I doubt it made much of a difference," Hecubah told him. "She'd have gone anyway, no matter what anyone said."

"When I think of her out there, on her own," he sighed. "My blood runs cold. Anything could happen and I'm stuck on this damn boat. I could move faster if I swam."

"Calm down," she advised him. "Unless I'm mistaken, she's survived worse journeys than the one she's on now."

"Nevertheless, when I find her, I'm never letting her out of my sight again," Trent remarked.

"I reckon that's what she had in mind, when she left." Hecubah was sure of it.

They lapsed into silence for a moment, listening to the sound of the paddlewheel as it churned the water.

"Do you ever find yourself getting the urge to beat her with a stick?" Hecubah asked casually.

"I'm warming to the idea," Trent admitted.

"That's what we'll do then," Hecubah decided. "When we get home, we'll chain her in the cellar and beat her every day."

Trent just looked at her, without saying anything.

"All right," Hecubah conceded, "every other day. I ain't cruel."

They left the riverboat well before Baton Rouge, where the Mississippi joined the Atchafalaya, and continued in a smaller craft until they were only a few miles from the plantation. Trent bought a horse and buggy and drove the rest of the way. At the gates of the mansion, he pulled the horse up, hesitating to go further.

"What if she's not here?" he fretted. "What if she didn't make it?"

"Oh, she's here all right," Hecubah remarked confidently, pointing up at the overhanging branch of a tree, to where a small mottled, brown bird hugged the bark.

"What is that?" Trent squinted, shielding his eyes from the sun with his hand.

"It's a whippoorwill," she identified it for him. "Ceci's bin calling them in. I'm gonna put a stop to that. Noisy little devils keep you up till all hours."

They left the horse and buggy at the steps of the mansion and let themselves in. Alerted by the sound of the door opening, Simon Robicheaux came out to see who it was. Instantly he caught Hecubah in his arms, kissing her passionately. "I've been out of my mind with worry," he confided. "I haven't had a good night's sleep since you left." He wasn't referring to whippoorwills.

"And you won't be getting any tonight," she promised him. "How's little Celeste?"

"She's fine," he put her mind at rest. "Misses her mama though. She's back at our house, with Tilly."

"When did she get back?" Hecubah asked.

"Miss Cecile." He knew exactly who she was talking about. "She turned up almost a week ago. We couldn't believe our eyes when we saw her walking up the drive. She was acting mighty curious," he began to frown. "She went and lay, face down, on the front lawn, just like she was kissing the ground. We thought she was ailing, so we went out and she told us to go away." He scratched his head at the recollection. "She stayed there for an hour. Then she came inside and sat in the tub until nightfall. She came down, ate enough for two men, then went to bed." He paused, smiling broadly. "The place seems just like its old self, now she's back. Every day, since then, she's been dressing in all her finery and going out into the garden. It's as if she's waiting for someone to arrive. I guess he's here now. Welcome back Captain Sinclaire."

Leaving Simon, they went through the house and out onto the veranda. As they looked across the lawn, they saw, in the distance, the figure of a young woman in a white dress with a silk fan and a lace parasol, strolling serenely along the banks of the bayou.

"To look at her, you'd think nothing had ever happened," Hecubah stared in amazement. "You want me to cut that switch now?"

Trent wasn't listening. He gazed, entranced, at the vision before him. By now, the figure had stopped walking, folded the parasol and stood watching them.

Hecubah put her hand on his arm. "What you thinking?" she asked.

He flinched at her touch, as if waking from a dream. "Oh," he sighed, eyes still fixed on the distant figure. "My mind goes back, to where it all began. That hot Louisiana summer when I was a boy. I saw this wild girl. I sneaked up on her, pinned her to a tree and kissed her."

"Ah huh. Got your nose broke that time," she reminded him.

Trent took off his jacket and cast it aside as he prepared to cross the lawn. Then he glanced at Hecubah and winked. "Let's see what happens this time."